Await Not In Silence

Book 4 of the Elektros Saga

Marcellus Durrell

Await Not in Silence
Book 4 of The Elektros Saga

©2018 by Marcellus Durrell

CreateSpace Publishing
Seattle, Washington, U.S.A.

Cover illustration: Leeanne D'Alesio

Cover design: Marcellivision

TABLE OF CONTENTS

1. MILTIADES 5
2. ASSEMBLY 21
3. LANIKE 33
4. EKPHORA 45
5. LAURION 61
6. PARNASSOS 79
7. AEGINETES 103
8. MELI 113
9. PHAEDRA 133
10. NOBILITY 143
11. ATHANATOS 157
12. OSTRAKOPHORIA ... 173
13. SLINGER 185
14. KORINTHOS 205
15. ALLIANCES 225
16. WALLS 241
17. TEMPE 251
18. TRICKSTER 265
19. ARTEMISIUM 281
20. INTELLIGENCE 299
21. SALAMIS 317
22. REGRET 335
23. ANTIO 353
24. ANIMPOROS 361

NAMES & TERMINOLOGY ... 367

1—MILTIADES

"I wake up slowly. Don't know where I am. Can't remember anything. Can't move. Something crushes my chest. Can't breathe. Can't see. Am I blind? Am I dead? No, not dead, a dead man's head wouldn't hurt this much. Feels like someone is jabbing a dagger into the side of my skull. Can't feel my arms and legs, although my right hand is stuck in something cold and wet. I smell shit. Blood. Festering fear, probably my own.

"I can see a little now. My head starts to clear. Still hurts, though. The thing on my chest is a dead man. I push him off. I can almost breathe again. There are dead men beneath me, beside me. The cold wet thing against my hand is another man's face, or what used to be his face. The front has been sheared off, probably by a sword, and is now cold mush. How did I end up here?"

Our storyteller Simeon fought at Paros, the disaster that resulted from the overconfidence Marathon had given Athenians. We'd all heard parts of Simeon's story before, but none of us had heard it all. The survivors, and there weren't many, rarely spoke of it.

"Slowly, it comes back to me," Simeon continued. "Miltiades led us so brilliantly at Marathon, when we sent the fucking Persians scurrying back to their ships like scared rats. It went to Miltiades' head. I wasn't at Marathon, but my buddy Elektros was"—he nodded to me as he said this—"and he told me that Miltiades was a *great* commander who didn't panic in the middle of a battle and always had a plan, a backup plan, and a backup plan to his backup plan. Everyone else said so, too.

"So when the old man needed soldiers, for a punitive expedition against Paros and some other dinky islands who'd sided with the Persians, I jumped at the chance."

Almost everyone here would have done the same. I would have, if I'd been here. Krios would have, if he didn't have a broken arm at the time, from a riding accident, although I'd seen Krios ride before and the accident was him getting on the horse. Diodoros would have gone but he needed to stay home and run the family business because his father had taken ill. Philostratos was at sea, on his way to Korinthos on business with his father. Only Hyperion, who was here in Athens when Miltiades raised his army, and whose hospitality we enjoyed this evening, refused to join, on principle. Fair-minded to a fault, Hyperion empathized with the Parians. They'd sided with the Persians, he said, because they had no choice. When the Persians came, no other Hellene polis, including Athens, raised a spear in their defense, so the Parians had to submit to the Great King or get massacred.

"I missed out on Marathon," Simeon continued, "so I craved action, adventure, and maybe some plunder. In the army of our most successful general, how could we fail? The Parians didn't have a chance against the might of Athens.

"Yet I ended up in a pile of dead bodies. Whoever put me there assumed I was dead too, or would be soon.

"The expedition went wrong from the start. A few hours away from Paros, a storm wrecked our supply ships, although our troop ships landed on Paros intact. Our expensive Thracian cavalry also disappeared. Whether they were lost in the storm, or the fuckers just deserted us, no one knew. So Miltiades ended up with three thousand drenched hoplites shivering on a beach at Paros without cavalry support or food. None of us could sleep. The smart thing would have been to get back on our ships and sail back home.

"But by sunrise, the skies had cleared. Miltiades was there to fight. We all were. Miltiades knew we were tired from a tough journey and a sleepless night, so the plan was to start and end the battle quickly, before true fatigue set in. We had no problem with this. Most of us were young, we could handle a sleepless night and a missed breakfast. The Parians would be lucky to have four hundred men against our three thousand. Their precious Persians had left them to their fate. So we formed up, two hundred and fifty men across and twelve deep, and marched on the town.

"The Parians had formed up a few hundred yards ahead of us. We advanced at a walk. The enemy held their line until we were a hundred paces away, then they broke and ran. Encouraged by the thought of an easy victory, we chased them. Our officers screamed at us to slow down. Running men tire quickly and lose formation. So we slowed to a fast walk. The Parians stopped and faced us once more. Again, when we were a hundred paces away, they broke and ran.

"'It's a trick,'" I muttered to Hermanos on my left. "'They're leading us somewhere.'

"'If they are,' said Hermanos, 'then they're fools. The only thing behind them is their piddly little town.'

"Hermanos was right. The town walls were straight ahead and were wood, not stone, and old wood at that. The Parian soldiers were hoplites, like us, but they were ragged. Their lines were sloppy. Undisciplined. Half of them had leather caps instead of proper helmets, and not all of them had shields. Miltiades had insisted that we all have matching helmets, shields and breastplates. We had to pay for them ourselves, before we left Athens, and some of us grumbled about it, but Miltiades swore that we'd all take enough plunder to buy ten panoplies, and no one could deny that our burnished steel and bronze looked impressively intimidating.

"The Parians stood and faced us a third time. This time they didn't run, but just before we engaged, I heard the *rat-a-tat-tat, rat-a-tat* of small stones hitting bronze, and some of our men fell.

"'Slingers!' somebody shouted. 'Rhodian mercenaries!'

"Slingers from Rhodes are legendary. They start slinging as toddlers, and by the time they're ten years old they can make headshots on birds in flight. On the battlefield, they're devastating when properly deployed. Which they were here: they were on both sides of us. We had no cavalry to run them down, and no slingers or archers of our own. Miltiades quickly ordered a column of our men on each flank to turn towards the slingers and advance on them. These men held their shields up as they advanced and were well armoured, so the slingers no longer killed them, but our heavily armoured hoplites had no hope of catching the unarmoured slingers, who simply ran away. Miltiades ordered our men back into formation.

"We refocused on the enemy in front of us. The Parians stood their ground. They were well rested and well fed, and had the extra motivation of defending their homes, but we still held the advantage. We were well trained and awash in confidence as the men who'd defeated the Great King. Both sides took casualties. Hermanos took a javelin to the shoulder and dropped his shield. He howled and cursed in agony, but managed to fall back without breaking up our line. After that, I never saw him again.

"We pushed the Parians back. Despite our tiredness and hunger, and without cavalry and missile troops, we backed them up against their shoddy walls. The slingers returned and killed a few more of us, but once again Miltiades sent our outside columns to chase them away.

This time, the columns would stand and guard against the slingers if they returned.

"Victory would soon be ours. Some of us, in our heads, were already picturing all the Parian wine we'd drink and all the Parian gold we'd get. Paros would be the first of many victories.

"Then there was a sudden crash into our rear. A cavalry charge. How did the Parians possibly get cavalry without us knowing about it? The men at the rear of our phalanx were skewered by lances before they even knew the horsemen were there. Many of us turned around to see what was happening, and the now emboldened Parians rushed at our front again.

"The horsemen, we now saw, were Thracians. *Our* Thracians. We never found out if it happened before or after the storm wrecked our supply ships, but the Parians had paid the Thracians to change sides. With mercenaries, that's always a risk.

"Of the battle afterwards, I remember little, and none of it glorious. A thousand more hoplites, also mercenaries, poured out the Parian gates and charged us. We were surrounded, cavalry behind us, hoplites in front, slingers on both sides. We panicked. Our lines collapsed, the slingers returned and killed us at will, and the fucking Thracians skewered us with smiles on their faces. We had become the easy prey that we thought the Parians would be. I got hit in the side of the head with a sling-stone, and the next thing I remembered was waking up in a pile of dead bodies.

"Miltiades managed to escape on one of our ships—that asshole left us to die, I never forgave him for that—but the gods did not let him get away with it. He took a leg wound during the battle and it was gangrenous by the time he got back to Athens. It killed him. He was on trial for treason at the time, so death was a blessing for him.

Turned out he was broke, too."

We'd all heard about Miltiades' money woes. A couple of years before Marathon, he'd returned from Thrace with all of his family and a shipload of treasure, mostly Persian gold, enough money to live like a king for the rest of his life. Unfortunately, Miltiades was a gambler, and a bad one. He once bet a drinking companion a thousand drachmae that the sun wouldn't rise the next day, then just laughed—and paid up—when it did. He would bet on anything, the weather, chariot races, athletic contests, and he seemed pathologically incapable of picking a winner. He'd not only lost his fortune, but he now needed the Parian expedition to clear his debts. Instead, it only increased them, as the Athenian assembly ordered him to replace the ships that were lost. The order seemed absurd—a penniless dying man could never repay such a debt—but after Miltiades died, the assembly went after his nineteen-year-old son Kimon. I would, unfortunately, get to know Kimon over the next few years. An angry young man, crushed by a huge debt, one that he did not even incur himself, is rarely someone you're glad to know. But more about him later, Ephander.

"How did you get off of the island?" said an angelic voice I'd never heard before. We all turned towards it. The voice, itself a thing of mellifluous pleasure, came from the most beautiful woman I'd ever seen in my life. She'd slipped into the room while we were all so captivated by Simeon's story. Now we were captivated by her large almond eyes and long brown hair that fell forward over lovely breasts. Her skin was absolute perfection. She wore a red wool shawl over her shoulders, and a golden chiton that was far too low-cut for Athenian propriety. Our eyes went to her breasts; young men like us had little choice in the matter. Besides Hyperion, I was the only one here who didn't stare at her cleavage. I wanted to, but I resisted the urge, although with some difficulty, because I thought it rude. The others thought so too, but couldn't help themselves.

"Parthenia!" Hyperion said to his sister. "You know you're not supposed to be here. Leave us."

Hyperion invited me to this symposion, which he declared was in my honour, when he learned I had returned to Athens. He took care to only invite guys who were friends of ours when we were ephebes together. Here in Athens, it was considered improper for a woman to be present at a symposion, even when it was in her own home. Hyperion was a fine man, I loved him dearly as a friend, and he was no fool about most things, but he failed to grasp that his sister Parthenia was so stupefyingly beautiful that she did not need to follow rules like other women did. Their father had died the year before, so Hyperion was now responsible for her. He took this very seriously, but never understood that the more he railed against Parthenia's behaviour, the more she would defy him.

"I want to hear the rest of the story," Parthenia said with a butter-melting smile. We all just gawked at her like she was Aphrodite in the sea foam, even though I was the only one of Hyperion's friends who'd never met her before.

Then she turned to me. "And I want to meet Elektros. I've heard all about you. You're even handsomer up close than you are from afar. Most men are the opposite."

She reached out to shake my hand, utterly scandalous behaviour in Athens, as was speaking to me without a formal introduction and calling me by my first name. I was okay with this, though. I'm not Athenian, so I'm less bound by their social conventions.

I took her hand—mine was sweaty, although I

imagined she was used to men being nervous around her—but I mostly maintained my composure, an accomplishment in itself. "Pleased to meet you, Parthenia," I said. "By the gods, you're beautiful, and I hope you don't mind me saying so."

"I don't mind compliments," she laughed. "Is it true that you killed a giant?"

"The real story," I said, "is not as fanciful as that."

"Then you must visit me sometime and tell it to me," she said. "I must leave now for the good of my brother's health. He looks like he'll give birth to puppies if I stay." We all laughed, except for Hyperion, who turned red as blood.

"Good night, gentlemen," she said. "Resume your drinking—or in your case, Elektros, your non-drinking."

She turned and walked away, no more quickly than she had to, and all of our eyes followed her magnificent backside. She had the curves men dream about. Her breasts were full but not freakishly large. Her hips were wide and delightfully rounded, and they narrowed to a slim waist. I could barely tear my eyes away.

Hyperion, as a good host, had drunk almost no wine this evening because he wanted me, a non-drinker, to have some sober company. But now he poured himself a full cup of unwatered wine and drank half of it in a single gulp. None of us envied him the responsibility of having to control Parthenia.

"Sorry for the interruption, my friends," he said. "Let's hear the rest of the story. Simeon, please tell us, if you will, how you managed to escape."

"I shook off the other bodies and stood up," Simeon said. "But that made my head hurt even worse, and I fell over again. I heard laughter. Two Parian soldiers were drunk and stripping armour from the Athenian bodies.

They'd already taken mine, so I now wore only my tattered shit-stained tunic. It was just past sunset. I got up again and began to walk towards a strand of alder trees that had hidden some of the slingers during the battle.

"'There's one still kickin',' said one of the soldiers. 'Betcha two darics he don't make it to them trees.'

"'You're on,' said the other. *Them trees* were only thirty feet away, but there was a good chance the first soldier would win the bet. My balance was off. I fell down several times, and passed out at least once, but I finally made it to the trees, with no idea how long it took me. Might have been five minutes, might have been an hour.

"'Har!' said the first soldier. 'Pay up!'

"'Okay, okay,' said the second soldier. 'Should we go after 'im?'

"'Naw, he won't get far. Half his head's stove in.'

"I kept moving. I had no idea where I was going, but it seemed a good idea to get away from the soldiers. I fell down a few more times, and then passed out again. When I awoke, I was still under the alders. I'd been out for hours, because the sun now rose. Somebody tried to pick me up off the ground. I tried to punch him in the face, but I was seeing double and my fist missed him completely. 'Don't fight me!' the man said. 'It's me, Phrynikos!'

"I knew Phrynikos well. He grew up in the house across the street from mine. But I barely recognized him. One of his eyes was gone, the socket just a pulpy mess, and one of his ears was gone too. His nose was broken and his good eye was almost swollen shut.

"'Can you walk?' he said.

"'If you help me,' I said. 'Can you see?'

"'About as well as you can walk,' he said.

"'Where we going?' I asked.

"'We're close to the water,' he said. 'Let's see if we can find a small boat and escape this hellhole.'

"We didn't know what side of the island we were on, or what direction we should take, but getting off the island, even without food or water, seemed a better idea than staying here. We staggered towards the beach and found a small fishing skiff. I didn't know if I could even row, but we had to try. Any Parians who found us would kill us on the spot. We started to climb into the boat, then its owner showed up. We never saw him coming and didn't even know he was there until he bashed Phrynikos' head in with a rock. Phrynikos crumpled and fell face down, dead before he hit the water.

"I would dearly love to tell you, friends, that I bathed myself in glory here and fought for my life like a hero. I was very willing to fight, but very far from able. I couldn't even stand up on my own. When Phrynikos let go of me, I fell into the water and couldn't get back up. If the fisherman had just left me there, there was a good chance I'd have just drowned. The fisherman looked at me and laughed. He was about to duck my head underwater, and I didn't have the strength to stop him. My choices were to beg for my life, or to die.

"Everybody see the irony here? That was pretty much the same choice the Parians had when the Persians came.

"'Mercy, sir,' I managed to say. I never felt more cowardly in my life, but when you think about it, the fisherman was a coward too. He attacked two of us, it's true, but neither Phrynikos nor I was well. It was like he fought two toddlers. He wouldn't have come at us if we were strong enough to fight back.

"Even speech was difficult for me. 'My father will pay for my safe return,' I finally blurted out. 'My friend's father would have too, if you'd spared him. He might still pay something for his bones.'

"The fisherman thought this over, but not for long. He

gave me a big black-toothed grin, then picked me up and carried me, like I was a sick child, back to his shack, where his wife nursed me back to health and his children taunted me every day. His shack reeked of rotting fish. So did his wife. So did his grunion-faced brood. My father eventually gave the man fifty thousand drachmae, and here I am.

"To this day, I can't stand to eat fish."

"You weren't cowardly," said Hyperion. "A coward refuses to fight, or runs from it. You were not capable of fighting, so negotiating was your only choice. In the same situation, I would have done the same." We all agreed. We'd all fought beside Simeon in the phalanx, and he'd proven his courage.

Simeon never fully recovered from his head injury. There was now a dullness behind his eyes, a grey nothing, that wasn't there before. He would forget the name of anyone he hadn't seen for a while, even people he'd known all his life—including, more than once, his own sister. His sense of balance would never completely return. He'd walk with a cane to the end of his days. He could no longer stand in the phalanx with the rest of us. This pained him more than anything else.

Then it was my turn to tell stories. I told my friends about Halicarnassus and how I rescued the love of my life from the wealthy sociopath who held her there. I told of our journey to Scythia, where I found myself embroiled in a political power struggle, and was advised by King Koraltes to leave. I'd forgotten, Ephander, that even though my friends were men now, who'd all trained as hoplites and had now fought real battles, they were Athenians, not Scythians. Their fighting experiences were very limited. They did not *live* for war as the Scythians did. Scythian warriors their age would have already fought twenty battles. None of these young men had fought more than three, and all of those, with the exception of Simeon's fight at Paria, were relatively safe hoplite battles. They were amazed that I'd trained as a Scythian warrior and learned to fight on horseback. They actually looked terrified when I told them about my huge Uncle Borysthenes, and how he threw a spear so hard into a man's stomach that the whole spear passed completely through him. My Athenian friends regarded me as the best fighter they'd ever seen, and did not believe me when I told them that the Scythians considered me adequate at best.

When I told them about my departure from the Sea of Grass and my chance encounter with the man who murdered my mother, they had tears in their eyes.

Krios asked about what happened to the woman I'd rescued from Halicarnassus. He regretted the words the moment they left his mouth. Now it was my turn to hold back tears. I told him that she remained in Scythia. My friends saw that the topic pained me and no one pressed for details.

I'm not a particularly good storyteller, Ephander, not like my brother Phylo, but somehow Hyperion had focused so much on my tales that he forgot he'd hired a kithara player and singers to entertain us. My friends had been drinking for several hours. All of them, including Hyperion, now slurred their words and began to make less and less sense when they spoke. I've always said, Ephander, that a roomful of drunks is no place for a sober man. Just as Hyperion summoned the singers, I took my leave. Thinking about Kandra, even after many months, still made me tense. A good five-mile night run would relax me.

"I'm the worst host in the world!" Hyperion said. "I planned to stay sober for you, and here I'm as kerfluggered as the others."

I laughed. "The food was great and the company greater," I said. "And only a barbarian would expect a man to stay sober at a symposion. No, Hyperion, you've been the best of hosts."

"You've been the best of guests," he said. "Your stories amazed us. Simeon's too. We may never hear better ones."

My friends all embraced me. I said my goodbyes, thanked my host, and left the house.

Or at least I tried to. Parthenia had other ideas.

The front door to Hyperion's house was thirty feet from the street. I was almost at the gate when a voice, a honeyed melody, said, "I can make you forget her."

I turned around and there was Parthenia looking even better than she did earlier when I thought she was the most beautiful woman I'd ever seen. She'd taken off the red shawl but still wore the low-cut golden chiton. The effect was deliberate. The cool night air put goosebumps on her shoulders, and through her chiton her nipples were large and visibly erect.

Here was a woman who could turn a man into mush in seconds. I was almost there myself, but I prided myself on my discipline and mostly avoided looking at anything but her face. That alone almost unmanned me. By the gods, she was a feast for the eyes.

"Who is it," I said, "that you can make me forget?"

"The woman you lost," she said.

"It's that obvious?" I asked. "You can tell just by looking at me?" I knew this was a game, but now I wanted to play.

"No, Elektros of Skiathos," she said. "It is not. You're a hard man to read."

"Well, you're right me being a hard man," I said. "Especially right now."

I know, Ephander, it was unworthy of me, a juvenile

pun, but she laughed louder and longer than she should have and put her hand on my arm. Her goose-bumped skin looked cold, but her touch was warm, almost feverish. Then she said, "I only know what you told the others."

"So you were listening."

"I have a hiding place where I can hear everything. You won't tell, will you?"

"No. Even if I did, would it stop you?"

She laughed and asked me to come back with her to a private room, but as much as I wanted to, I declined out of respect for Hyperion. If I stayed here with her, I would only do it openly, where everyone could see that we did nothing but talk. She actually pouted, like a child, but in an exaggerated way that made me laugh. She laughed too, but she was clearly unaccustomed to not having a man do exactly what she wanted him to do.

We sat on a stone bench just outside the front door. I insisted that we have a slave present, because I wanted a witness to my inactions. She had her slave bring her shawl out to her, then she told the slave, whose name was Lydiana, to remain on the stone bench on the other side of the door.

I don't know how long we talked, Ephander. When you were with Parthenia, you invariably lost some of your senses, including your ability to gauge the passage of time. I asked her to tell me about herself, but she declined, insisting she'd had a sheltered life and there wasn't much to tell. I knew this wasn't true. The gods had blessed her with unearthly beauty and a keen mind which, when combined with her mischievous nature, would guarantee that she would *never* have a dull life. She was nineteen years old and already knew that I, like all men, liked to talk about myself. Who could resist such a listener?

She'd already heard about my Scythian misadventures,

so I told her about the time I was captured by the Persians. I had no experience with a woman like her—mostly because there are no women like her—so at the time I wasn't yet aware of how masterfully she'd manipulated me. Her eyes brimmed with tears at all the right times, and she laughed at all the right times. When she found something particularly funny, she laughed her calliope laugh, rolled her head back, her breasts jiggled, and my eyes lost all pretense of courtesy.

She'd already heard an exaggerated story that I'd killed a giant, so I told her the true one. It was no giant, I said, just a very large man named Firuz. I'd defeated him but didn't kill him. I told her how Firuz was so busy trying to think up taunts for me that his concentration lapsed, which is dangerous no matter how big or ferocious you are. When he looked away from me, I kicked him in the pinkberries. When I told her that his scrotum was so big that my foot actually got trapped between his huge balls for a couple of seconds, she laughed so hard that Hyperion came running out of the house to see what was going on.

He glared at her, then at me, then back at her. She was still helpless with laughter. She controlled herself, then laughed again. "I'm sorry," she said, "but I can't stop picturing you with your leg knee-deep in a giant's nutsack. Were you both naked?"

"No," I said.

"Well, I'm going to imagine you were anyway." Then she winked at me.

Hyperion was shocked into temporary speechlessness. That was a most inappropriate remark for an Athenian lady. The wink was scandalous.

I wanted to stay—by the gods, Ephander, I'd still be there right now if it were possible. I knew, though, out of respect for my dear friend Hyperion, that I'd already stayed too long.

"The hour is late, Parthenia," I said. "I must go."

She was still a little giggly—and jiggly—from my story. "I understand," she said, her face still blushed from laughter. "But you must return at a more respectful hour and tell me the rest of that story."

"I will, dear lady," I said. I bowed slightly to her, but she stepped forward, put her arms around my neck and kissed me on the cheek.

"Yes," she whispered. "You will." It was almost a command.

She went back into the house. Hyperion walked me to the gate, probably just to make sure I really left this time.

"Your sister," I said, "is the most charming woman in Athens. And an excellent listener."

"To *you*, maybe," said Hyperion. "Doesn't listen to a word *I* say."

2—ASSEMBLY

The smell of the fried breaded fish made me hungry, even though I knew what kind of fish it really was. Stavros had his little wheeled table set up at the rear edge of the Pnyx. As a freedman and a *metic,* a non-Athenian, he could not participate in the Assembly, and had to leave the area once the Assembly formally began, which would be in a half-hour. The Assembly drew thousands of men from the countryside. Some brought food, but none brought fried breaded fish, an Athenian delicacy. It was breaded, spiced with grated cheese and garlic, then fried in olive oil. Few rural customers knew that the fish was tentacled blenny, which fishermen cursed when they netted. It looked like a demon's nightmare, tasted like mud and was impossible to sell as food to anyone who knew what it really was. So Stavros got it cheap, directly from the fishermen, along with hagfish, morays and the other shit-fish no one else wanted, and sold it on Assembly days to unsuspecting yokels. When asked what kind of fish it was, Stavros always said it was river tuna from sacred Delos. Few of his customers were travelers, so they did not know that river tuna does not exist, and even if it did, it would spoil on the ship from Delos long before it got anywhere near Athens. As far as I knew, no one died from eating Stavros' breaded fish.

As far as I knew.

Pudgy Stavros was my friend. When I first got to Athens, he paid me and another man to guard him on Assembly days. Competition for prime spots around the Pnyx was fierce, and some vendors hired thugs to intimidate and beat up their competitors. Even though I no longer worked for Stavros—I worked for Themistocles now—he still gave me money sometimes. My reputation as an enforcer had grown, and if people merely *thought* I still worked for him, it had the desired effect. To perpetuate the illusion, I would stop by his table before every Assembly and say hello.

I too was a freedman and a metic, so I had to leave when Stavros did. The Assembly automatically included Athenian citizens and automatically excluded everyone else. Themistocles had several times offered to use his influence to get me Athenian citizenship—citizenship can be granted easily if you pay the right people—but I always refused. From what I saw of Athenian citizens, and the theatrical screeching matches they called democratic discourse, I had little desire to join their ranks.

Besides Stavros, twenty-five or thirty other opportunists had tables, tents and stalls on the outer perimeter of the Pnyx. Other food vendors, who sold honeycakes, fried goat, flavoured breads and an assortment of mystery meats—usually rat—did well here too.

There was a festive atmosphere before Assemblies, even when the upcoming topic of discussion was grave. Singers and tumblers performed for coins. A man juggled four swords, always catching them by the handles, and I had to admit I was impressed. One vendor had, amongst his cheap polished glass jewelry, some metal shards that he'd painted gold and claimed were fragments of the Great King's crown. He sold each piece for a few obols. Most people scoffed, even most of the farmboys, but he always had a few buyers, usually new citizens who hadn't been coming to the Assembly long enough to know that the vendor had been selling these for years. If these were truly pieces of the Great King's crown, then the Great King's head must have been the size of a small mountain. Several vendors sold small statues of the gods—some farmboys prided themselves on having the whole Olympian set—as well as amulets, charms, and cheap jewelry that they overcharged for on Assembly days.

Even the whores got into the act. Several of them had curtained off a section of a nearby alley and laid straw mattresses on the ground. Farmboys loved coming to Athens for this reason alone.

I've concluded, Ephander, that the primary purpose of the Assembly is to bring rural people into the city to be fleeced by city-dwellers. Any legislative function is secondary and, at times, entirely coincidental.

The aristocrats always sat at the front of the Assembly as a matter of custom and expectation. The entire semicircular front row of the Pnyx was theirs, and theirs alone. Occasionally, a new rural citizen would sit in one of those seats, only to have everyone else yell at him.

The priest of Athena sacrificed the lamb and declared the omens propitious. The herald declared that the Assembly had officially begun. Suddenly there was a racket and clamour in the high back rows of the Pnyx, applause, cheers, shouts. Themistocles had arrived. He was an important man, the most important man in Athens, but he was not an aristocrat and he felt no obligation to sit at the front. He never asked anyone to hold a seat for him, either, but he didn't need to. As he entered the Pnyx and climbed up to the twenty-eighth row, the commoners tripped over each other, almost literally, to get his attention.

"Themistocles!" they called. "Archon! I saved you a seat!" They called him Archon even though it had been several years since he'd last held the office. The aristocrats scowled and rolled their eyes as he came in, annoyed because they thought it was typical Themistoclean grandstanding to arrive late and draw such attention to himself. The aristocrats did not understand that Themistocles *had to* sit with the commoners now. They were his main supporters and would consider it abandonment if he chose to sit elsewhere, especially with the aristocrats.

Another thing the aristocrats did not understand was that Themistocles did not intentionally arrive late. It always took him a long time to get anywhere in Athens because he was constantly stopped by people who wanted to shake his hand or ask his advice. None of the aristocrats had ever experienced popularity and therefore did not understand its demands. For Themistocles, it bordered on mania. I once saw it take more than an hour for him to walk the few city blocks from his house to the agora. Themistocles was unfailingly patient, and once he learned a man's name, he never forgot it.

"Euthymos," he said to one such man, a potter who had approached him on the street, as he firmly grasped the man's hand and looked him in the eye. "How are the twins doing?"

Euthymos' eyes widened with joy. The great man had remembered their last conversation, even though it had been months earlier. "They're household terrors, sir," said Euthymos. "If I ever need to have my house torn down, I can just get them to do it. But I thank the gods they're healthy and strong." Themistocles had just made the man's day.

During the Assemblies, I stood on the side of the hill beside the Pnyx, as close to the Assembly as I could possibly be without actually being in it. I could see Themistocles, but couldn't do a thing if he had any trouble.

He wasn't worried. "I have nothing to fear," he'd said more than once, "from my people."

This was true, but it would take only one desperate man in the pay of the aristocrats to stick a knife into him, after which the desperate man would likely be torn to pieces by the mob before he could tell anyone who had hired him. Themistocles did eventually take my advice to always have two strong citizens, armed with concealed knives, on either side of him at every Assembly.

But neither of us could do anything to stop Basileides from taking the floor.

Since the Battle of Marathon, Themistocles had insisted that Athens needed a fleet of warships to defend itself from the next Persian invasion. The aristocrats dismissed this. We never needed warships before, they said. We beat the Persians with infantry at Marathon and we'll beat them with infantry again when they return. *If* they return. So Themistocles had two major obstacles of belief to overcome. Many people, including most of the commoners who thought he was a genius and a hero, were not convinced that the Persians would ever return. They didn't understand, as I did, as Themistocles and a few others did, that Marathon did not finish the Persians. It was, if anything, a prime motivator for them to return. The Great King did not take defeat lightly. He would be back with an even larger army. Our sources told us that some minor rebellions inside his empire required his immediate attention, but once he'd becalmed those hotspots, he'd refocus on Hellas again, especially Athens. Themistocles was convinced that the next assault would be from a combination of naval and land forces. To defend against it, Athens would need to build a war fleet, even though the city had few shipyards and no great forests for the necessary lumber. At the same time, Athens would need as large an army of hoplites as it could muster. Themistocles insisted that Athens had to have a hundred warships. The crews would need to be trained and paid. As much as the commoners loved Themistocles, they still saw it as a financial impossibility. And few people knew that a hundred warships was, in the mind of Themistocles, only the beginning. Privately, he said that Athens wouldn't be completely safe until it had *three hundred* warships.

Basileides was one of Themistocles' most passionate supporters. He accepted Themistocles' assessment of the situation and spoke loudly in support of the shipbuilding venture. The problem was that Basileides had no credibility. He owned a shipyard, and would profit enormously if Athens built warships. So his support of Themistocles was viewed as completely self-serving, and also drew suspicion about the motivations of Themistocles, whose father Neocles had also owned shipyards. Basileides' support did Themistocles' cause more harm than good, and Themistocles told him so several times, but Basileides insisted on addressing the Assembly anyway.

"Who wishes to address the Assembly?" cried the herald.

"I do," shouted Basileides. "Basileides son of Mentor."

"Speak, Basileides," said the herald.

"My fellow citizens," Basileides began after he'd strode to the front of the Assembly. "Doom impends. How we choose to face it is critical. A fleet of warships would enable us to attack the Great King in his own waters instead of waiting meekly for him to attack us." I was too far away to actually see Themistocles roll his eyes, but I pictured it easily enough. At no time did he ever advocate an invasion of Persia, which he knew to be impractical.

"Sit down, lardy arse!" came a shout from somewhere.

"You don't know what the fuck you're talking about, Basileides!" shouted someone else.

A dozen fierce shouters finally forced Basileides to sit down. Officially, he was supposed to be allowed to say his piece without interruption, but when Solon the lawgiver created that rule for the Assembly, he misunderstood the basic nature of his fellow Athenians. They spoke their minds. It was never customary or natural for them to hold back, and the existence of the Assembly only fortified their belief that it was okay to shriek their opinions whenever they wanted to.

The shout-down was no accident. Basileides trudged off the stage. Themistocles had arranged for a handful of his supporters to shout Basileides down every time he rose to speak in the assembly. They had to let him say a few words before they began—it was always possible, though unlikely, that he wanted to speak on another subject—but the shout-down worked and minimized the damage Basileides' words could do.

In the Assembly, matters great and small were discussed and voted on. On this day, the road in the Ceramicus needed repair. The hinges on the great doors of the Piraean Gate were cracked and had to be replaced. The Bluebeard Temple needed to be repainted. Someone proposed that vendors who set up around the Pnyx should be made to pay an annual fee for the privilege. Someone else proposed an increase in the annual tax collected from metics for the privilege of living in Athens. Repairs to this bridge and that temple were also discussed.

After about three hours, when all the minor maintenance discussions had ended, Themistocles addressed the Assembly. He once again stressed the need for an Athenian war fleet, but knew not to bring it to a vote that he would not win. He put into voters' minds the idea that the fleet would be essential in the long term, even after the Persian threat was eliminated. "Athens grows," he said, "right before our very eyes. Before long, we'll need to expand into colonies, which we cannot currently protect." But Themistocles knew not to speak for too long on the subject, because he still did not know how Athens could financially support a fleet, apart from the political suicide of jacking up taxes.

As he thanked the Assembly for its attention and started toward his seat, Kimon took the floor. "This man," he shouted, pointing at Themistocles, "this man, your *hero*, wants to piss on the memory of the brave men who died at Marathon. And he never fought there himself! He watched from a position of safety."

This was as utterly untrue, Ephander, as it was foolish to publicly challenge Themistocles on a matter of honour. I was at Marathon. I saw Themistocles fight like a fire-demon in the front line. I saw him kill no less than five Persian soldiers with his own spear, and I only saw what he did for part of the battle.

Themistocles, who'd begun to climb the stairs back to his seat, now returned to the floor and stood about ten feet away from Kimon. Kimon was smart enough to be a nuisance for Themistocles, but not smart enough to be a threat. A nuisance could cost him votes, though, so Themistocles retook the floor beside Kimon.

"You claim, Kimon, that I did not fight the Persians at Marathon," he said. Then he paused for effect and added, "Did *you*?"

Themistocles' supporters hooted and hollered and laughed. It was well known that Kimon had been too young to fight at Marathon. It was less known that he was offered the opportunity to serve as a messenger and runner during the battle, but turned it down because he considered such work beneath him. That job that was then given to me.

"You know as well as I do, Themistocles," Kimon

said, "that I was underage. I would have fought gladly."

"Would have, should have, could have," said Themistocles. I knew by the hardness of his gaze that he was extremely angry, but only those closest to him could see it. He controlled it so well that most people weren't aware that something even needed to be controlled. "For whatever reason, when spear clashed with shield, when sword clashed with armour, you weren't there. I would like to ask the men who *were* there to raise their hands if they saw me fight at Marathon. Raise your hands, men of Attica, but only if you saw me fight during the battle."

There were about seven thousand present, and close to half of them raised their hands. Aristides, who sat with the aristocrats in his tattered cloak, raised his hand but did not do so happily. He did not like to draw attention to his rival's heroism but was too principled *not* to raise his hand.

"Oddly enough, you're right about one thing, boy," said Themistocles. Kimon, always ready to take offense, bristled at being called *boy*. "I did in fact spend the entire battle in a position of safety—standing in the phalanx with my fellow Athenians. At Marathon, that was the safest place to be! If you don't believe me, ask the Persians."

The entire Assembly cheered and applauded. Kimon's face turned redder than Hades' arse. He should have quit right there, but Kimon was a complex and bitter young man who didn't understand how foolish he'd just made himself look, and wasn't smart enough to know that if he continued, he'd only make it worse.

"I still say," he crowed, "that your idea to build a fleet disrespects the memory of the brave men who fell at Marathon. Our army saved us then, and our army will save us if the Persians or anyone else attack us again! Plus we already have an army, so we don't have to bankrupt ourselves to create one."

This drew much more applause than Themistocles

liked. Too many people thought the Persian threat was over.

Themistocles rarely lost his temper, but this was too much. "Listen, you little knob-polisher," he bellowed. "If you ever say again that I didn't fight at Marathon and that I don't respect the men who fell there, then I'll have to decide whether to sue your sorry ass for slander, or to just beat the living shit out of you."

"I'm not afraid of you, old man," Kimon said. "Let's go. Right here. Right now."

The herald jumped between them. "You will *not* fight here," he said. "If you do, you disrespect this Assembly and will both be banned from attending for one year."

Both Themistocles and Kimon muttered apologies and promised not to fight, at least not here. The pause was long enough for Themistocles to calm down and try another approach.

"If you have such great love for the men who fell at Marathon," he said to Kimon, "then name one."

"What?" said Kimon.

"It's not exactly a Pythagorean tetractys," said Themistocles. "Recite for us, if you will, the name of one man who died at Marathon, and the name of his father."

Kimon looked like he wanted to fight again. "This is nonsense," he said. "Themistocles wastes our time with childish word-play."

"So you won't name one man?"

"Is that why we're here tonight? To play whatever stupid game you've concocted?"

"So you won't do it? Or you can't do it? I ask only for one name."

"I'll not stand before this Assembly and engage in such foolishness."

Kimon stalked off the floor, right through the crowd

and out to the street. Eight or nine of his friends and hangers-on followed.

Themistocles smiled. "He claimed that I disrespect the heroes of Marathon," he said, "yet he cannot name one, even though his own cousin died bravely in the battle. I, on the other hand, can name *every* man who fell, all one hundred and ninety two of them."

"Do it!" shouted one of the aristocrats. I couldn't see who it was, but the fool had just taken the bait.

"I will not," said Themistocles. "This Assembly is for pressing business. Reciting the names of the fallen is not a priority right now."

"You can't do it!" shouted someone. "You're bluffing!"

"Oh, I can," said Themistocles. "And I will, but only if the herald gives his permission."

The herald looked like he didn't want to allow this, but now seven thousand voices demanded it. Themistocles' opponents wanted to see him try and fail. How was it possible that they did not yet know who they were dealing with?

"Proceed, Themistocles," said the herald.

"I, Themistocles son of Neocles, will commemorate the fallen at Marathon by reciting their names, and the names of their fathers. I recite the names in no particular order. All are heroes, therefore no man among them should be considered more heroic than another simply because I name him sooner. And men of Attica, if I get a name wrong, even slightly, it is your duty to correct me. I will also ask my friend and colleague Aristides, the most honest man in all Hellas, to keep count. Do you agree, sir?"

Aristides rose, unhappy that he'd just been made part of this pageant. "I do not agree that I am your friend," he said, "or your colleague. I do not even welcome your claim that I'm an honest man, because if Themistocles declares a man honest, it is often the surest sign that he is not." This got a few laughs. Even Themistocles chuckled. "But I do agree to keep count."

For effect, Themistocles paused, closed his eyes, then took a few deep breaths.

"Daedalos son of Heron," he said.

"One!" said Aristides.

"Amphitor son of Amphitor."

"Two!" said Aristides. Some other voices joined him.

"Koros son of Phillipos."

"Three!" said Aristides, and now a hundred voices joined in.

"Alas, brave Phillipos also fell. Phillipos son of Phaedes."

"Four!" said Aristides, but it was no longer necessary for him to speak at all because now almost the entire Assembly was counting and did so right to the end.

I won't repeat all of the names, Ephander. I couldn't if I tried. Themistocles named all one hundred and ninety-two men and every single one of their fathers. When he finished, about a half hour later, the Assembly stood and cheered. Or at least the commoners did. The aristocrats looked irritated, but none of them could leave the recital without appearing disrespectful of the Marathon war dead. So they ground their teeth and watched Themistocles make himself even more popular than he already was.

Men had wagered on the outcome. I wished that I had too. Themistocles was too masterful a statesman to say he could recite all the names if he wasn't one hundred percent certain he would succeed.

Impressive as this was, though, none of it made the Athenians want to build a war fleet.

3—LANIKE

A couple of months earlier, when I'd first arrived in Athens, I rented a room at an inn, then went looking for Themistocles. I found him at a table outside a wine shop near the agora. He spoke animatedly to a group of men. He appeared to be just relaxing with friends over a few cups, but I knew even then that the Archon *never* completely relaxed. He was driven by the idea that the Persians would be back and that Athens would be helpless against them without a war fleet. At the time, Athens had maybe six rundown biremes and a few smaller merchant vessels. Themistocles had a Sisyphean task: he had to persuade his fellow Athenians that a victory like Marathon, a winner-take-all land battle, could not happen again because next time the Persians would attack us by land and by sea. The Great King had the measure of our troops now, and he was smart enough to recognize that his army of slaves and conscripts would not defeat an army of Hellene hoplites, even if he had them outnumbered. At Marathon, the Persians used their ships mostly to supply their land army. When they returned—and it was *when*, not *if*—they would blockade all of our ports and choke all of our trade. They would use their ships to transport troops quickly to wherever our armies were not. They would sack our cities and ravage our farmlands and be gone before our land-bound troops could get anywhere close to them.

As popular as Themistocles was, few listened when he spoke of warships. Athenians were still too impressed by their own performance at Marathon. Even the men at his table in this wine shop dismissed his concerns. Few men anywhere saw the world as Themistocles did, mainly because few knew as much as he did. He had spies everywhere, including at the court of the Great King. He knew the political situations in Susa, Aegyptos, Sardis, Sparta, Thebes, and everywhere else. His aristocratic rivals in Athens did not have anything remotely close to his level of information. A moralist like Aristides, for example, would be a very ethical and capable leader, but he would myopically concern himself only with Athens. He would refuse to believe that Athens' future was being determined anywhere but here. He would not consider the intrigues at the court of the Great King to be relevant, and would therefore see no reason to have an observer there.

So part of Themistocles' problem was that his opinions were based on facts that no other Athenian had. His opponents always labelled him a power-hungry tyrant-in-waiting who would stretch the truth as it suited him. There was validity to this claim, especially the truth-stretching part. His grand plan, so said his detractors, was impossible. Most people believed that Athens could have either a land army or a fleet, but not both. Themistocles insisted that it was possible for Athens to have both, but when asked how Athens would pay for it, even he did not yet have a convincing answer.

As I approached the wine shop, he had his back to me as he spoke to the man across the table. "I say again, Aklepiades," he said, "that we'll pay for the fleet *after* we defeat the Persians because we'll then be able to build a trade empire. We'll get the money by borrowing it from other poleis. *But if that Elektros fucker ever shows his face in Athens again, I'll string him up by the nuts!*"

Stunned, I was. Why would he say such a thing? He had his back to me and I never saw him turn around, so how did he even know I was here?

Then the men at the table all laughed, and I realized it

was the rough soldiers' humour that Themistocles knew I liked. He stood up, turned around, gave me a big grin and crushed me in a bear hug. "Good to see you, Lex," he said. "Apollo's balls, have you gotten taller? Sorry to hear about your father. A great man."

I was glad he didn't ask how Father died. I couldn't speak of it yet.

"You looking for work?" he then asked.

"I am, sir," I said.

"Look no further," he said. "I have need of your talents. Where you staying?"

"Hera's," I said. Hera's Retreat was Attica's finest inn.

"Not anymore," he said. "As of now, you live at my house."

So I moved my few belongings, my weapons, armour, and clothing, from my room at Hera's into a smaller one in the house of Themistocles.

It was a mistake. Themistocles' heart was bigger than his house. The house was the smallest one in the Virgin Quarter, the aristocrats' neighbourhood, but it still had three storeys and fourteen rooms. Even so, it was nowhere near large enough for all the people who currently lived there. I arrived in late afternoon, so it was no surprise that the place was noisy at that time of day. I would soon learn that it was noisy most of the time, even in the wee hours of the night. Themistocles offered his hospitality freely. He had nine or ten other guests, plus his wife, his three boys, a few slaves, and his widowed sister and her two kids. The boys were whirlwinds, little hurricanes between the ages of seven and eleven, who seemed to chase each other and fight every waking moment. I rarely saw Archippe, Themistocles' wife, who spent most of her time upstairs in the *gynaikeion*, the women's quarters. Themistocles' sister Lanike greeted me at the door.

"Elektros of Skiathos," she said as she shook my hand.

"My brother told me that if you were to ever show up here, I was to take you in immediately—and use leg irons, if I had to, to keep you here. Welcome!" Then she hugged me.

Athenian women weren't supposed to be so outgoing, but Lanike had her brother's boldness. She was younger than Themistocles, a little past thirty, and pretty—she shared her brother's wit but, luckily for her, not his face. You knew immediately that there was a quick mind behind those big brown eyes. She tied her long dark hair in a single braid and wore a dark blue linen chiton. Tall and proud and confident, the overall effect was regal. She'd been married and widowed twice. She spoke her mind. Themistocles encouraged her to do so. Most Athenian men wanted their sisters to smile much and say little, but Themistocles wisely recognized that Lanike was always worth listening to. She shared his great memory for names and grasped the depth of political situations without needing much explanation. She was quicker to laugh than Themistocles. She understood that an offer of hospitality was the best way to make political connections, so she supervised the slaves who prepared meals for twenty or twenty-five people every single day. I liked her immediately.

My first night in the house of Themistocles, I shared a room with two other men, a merchant from Ephesus and an ambassador from Corcyra. There were only two beds, so I, as the new guy, slept on the floor. The next night, neither of them were at the house, but more men had arrived, two shipbuilders from Phoenicia, the son of an aristocrat from Lesbos, an ambassador from Megara, Themistocles' old friend from Plataea, and one or two more. Now there were five of us in the room, so three of us slept on the floor. It must have cost Themistocles a fortune to feed so many people every day, but it was also brilliant diplomacy. All of these men from all of those places were now his guest-friends, and he'd set the example of never turning anyone away. They would be inclined to favour his proposals, and might even feel obliged to do so, when it was time to form alliances against the Persians. Lanike was a key part of the plan because she discussed politics with everyone who came to the house and reported everything to her brother. She would identify which poleis would ally with Athens, which ones inclined towards the Persians, and perhaps most important of all, which ones were undecided. Her role in forming the great alliance against the Persians was mostly unknown but that didn't make it any less important. And unlike most Hellenes, she knew the same facts that Themistocles did.

My third day in the house of Themistocles, I saw an old man on a couch groping a pretty dark-haired slave girl, no older than fifteen, whom he'd pulled onto his lap. She had to pretend she was happy about it. The old man, fat and bald and unacquainted with personal hygiene—I could smell him from across the room—shoved his hands under her tunic and licked her breasts. Her smile was forced. She hated this but feared that if she resisted, the punishment, probably a beating, would be worse. Slaves and whores often distance their minds from what is being done to their bodies, but this girl had had not been an object of desire long enough to have learned this survival technique. Her smile looked like a stage mask, stuck to her face like it had been painted there, but the eyes did not fake anything. She wanted to cry but dared not.

"You disapprove, Scythian?" the old man said after I'd looked at him and the girl for a few seconds too long.

"Would it matter if I did, sir?" I said.

"Not a hog fart," he said. Then he laughed, lifted his leg, and farted loudly. Which of course only made it worse for the poor girl. He squeezed one of her breasts so hard that her flesh was red when he removed his hand.

Lanike rescued the girl. She took her hand and pulled her off the old man's lap. "Ismene is needed in the kitchen right now," she said. "Elektros, this is Mnesiphilos, Themistocles' tutor."

"Themistocles gets tutored?" I said.

"No," said Lanike. "Mnesiphilos was his tutor when he was a boy, and he thought it would be a good idea if Mnesiphilos tutored his own children. Except he only tutors them in drinking wine all day and pawing the slave girls. I suspect my brother keeps him around to show the kids what becomes of the indolent."

Mnesiphilos pinched Lanike's buttocks as she walked by. She wheeled around and punched him in the face. Blood dripped from one of his nostrils. He just laughed and poured himself another cup of wine.

"I heard o' you, Elektros," he then said to me. "Rumour is that you're an even bigger prig than Aristides."

"If you've heard that," I said, "then why haven't you also heard that I'm much more vicious than Aristides? He would never beat the shit out of someone who insulted him. But I would."

"Bet you feel proud of yourself," he said, "threatening an old man."

"I see old," I said, "but I don't see a man. You must also feel proud of *your*self, tormenting a slave."

A quirk of the house of Themistocles was the rarity of his actual presence there. Every two or three days, he would show up in the early morning, and apologize for waking people, even though it was usually his apology that woke them, then he would sleep for a couple of hours and put on fresh clothing. Then he'd leave and you wouldn't see him there again for a few more days.

His boys you saw every minute. They were wild, just short of feral. They fought. They yelled. They broke things. They were not shy about speaking their minds. The aristocrats would have been appalled. The adults who lived in the house were too busy to control the boys, and the guests found their rambunctiousness amusing.

I did too, Ephander. The oldest boy, named Neocles after Themistocles' father, began to follow me around. "I've heard all about you, sir," he said. "Father says you're the best swordsman in all Hellas."

"That's nice of him to say," I said, "but it's not true. Even if it was, it would be impossible to prove. I was taught by Xenocrates, who actually *was* the best swordsman in all Hellas. But he's gone now, so the title is vacant."

I liked the lad. He had Archippe's dark eyes and his father's work ethic. He was naturally curious and asked many questions. Lanike told me it was okay to teach him the basics of swordsmanship, so Neocles and I practiced for an hour or two every day. If it had been up to the boy, it would have been twelve hours a day. He was a fast learner and he worked hard. After two days, he'd improved noticeably. He had some trouble at first with the weighted wooden practice swords we used, but he'd seen the regular exercises that I did to keep my upper body strong, so he started to do them himself, without any prompting from me. At eleven years old, I marked him as a future leader of men, smart, hardworking, and aware of all things, big and small, spoken and unspoken, that went on around him.

Alas, I couldn't stay in the house of Themistocles any longer. It was too damned noisy. Nobody slept much here. That wasn't the main issue for me, Ephander, because I never slept more than two or three hours a night anyway.

But I liked to practice my sword-work in the quiet hours, and in the house of Themistocles, there were no quiet hours.

I told Lanike that I needed a space of my own. "I understand," she said. "This isn't a house of peace or privacy."

"How do you manage to get any sleep?" I asked her.

"Like Odysseus' crewmen," she said with a laugh. It took me a few seconds to realize that she referred to the part in *The Odyssey* where Odysseus had himself lashed to the mainmast as his ship passed the island of the Sirens. He ordered his crewmen to seal their ears with beeswax so they wouldn't hear the Sirens' irresistible song, which would draw their ship to its doom on the rocky coast. Lanike used beeswax in her ears every night just to get some sleep.

"I'll rent a room," I said.

"No," she said. "There's a house two streets over that's perfect."

"How much is the rent?" I asked.

"Doesn't matter," she said. "You're going to buy it."

I laughed at the way she'd just made up my mind. Turned out she was right. The house was close enough that I could quickly get to the house of Themistocles, not to mention the agora and the Pnyx, but also far enough away that I would have peace and privacy. The house was a single floor with five rooms. The previous owner, an older man, had died. His sons, who didn't live in Athens, wanted to sell it quickly. The place had no gynaikon and no separate slave quarters, but I didn't need them. It had a small courtyard behind it and my neighbours were tradesmen and their families. I liked the neighbourhood, liked the house, and bought it immediately.

All of the previous occupant's furniture was included

in the purchase price. "Thanks, Lanike," I said. "I have everything I need now, thanks to you."

"Not quite everything," she said. By the suggestive look in her eye I thought she wanted to sleep with me. Before I could misread her meaning any further and make a complete ass of myself, she introduced me to a small grey-haired woman, who smiled shyly at me.

"This is Phaedra," Lanike said. "She is the sister of the previous owner. She took care of the house for him and she'll do the same for you. She'll keep the place clean and she's an excellent cook. You don't have to pay her apart from letting her live here rent-free, although you will need to give her grocery money. You will often be away from Athens on my brother's business, so she will tend to the place when you're not here."

I bought the house, took in the housekeeper, and everything was as Lanike said it would be. A few days after I moved in, Lanike came to me one night. It was well past midnight, a highly unusual time for a woman to be out. The suggestive look in her eye was there again. I hadn't misread her intentions after all. She would join me almost every night, but would stay no more than two or three hours.

On the fifth or sixth night, after we'd made love, and we lolled, sweaty and giddy, in each other's arms, she said, "You're not like other men."

I felt so good at that moment it was hard to think straight, even harder to talk coherently. Lanike had just fucked me silly. I'd tried to return the favour.

"I'm half Saka," I said. "Once you go Sak, you don't go back."

She laughed. "No, that's not what I meant," she said. "You actually listen to me. Most men just stare at my ass."

"Well, if it makes you feel better, I stare at your ass sometimes too."

She laughed again. Loved that sound, full and throaty. "No, thanks for the compliment, but most men smirk when I speak to them. They can't take a woman seriously, even when I'm much smarter than them and understand politics ten times better than they do."

I'd seen this. When she spoke about politics or war, many men smiled indulgently, as if she was a child reciting a poem. They didn't listen. But it wasn't true that they all stared at her ass—some stared at her breasts.

"I don't have a lot of experience with women," I said, "but I've had the good fortune to know smart ones. Plus both my father and my grandfather always told me that when you hear wise words, you don't question their source."

She insisted that Themistocles must not know about her nightly visits. It was the only time I'd heard her say something stupid. "He knows," I said. "Never underestimate your brother's ability to know things. He hasn't said anything to me about it, but he knows. He *always* knows." I also knew that when you take a secret lover, it's never a secret for as long as you think it is. When you hear your lover's name, maybe you smile a little. You might even blush. People spot these little clues and talk behind your back, and figure it out long before they say anything to your face.

I also knew this couldn't last. Once people began to talk about me and his sister, Themistocles would put a stop to it. Themistocles needed to find Lanike a politically advantageous husband, and could not afford for her to have a wanton reputation. He knew that with her sharp mind, she would not be a good match for any man who wanted his wife to just shut up and let the men speak. This alone eliminated most of the eligible aristocrats in Athens. Themistocles had even speculated about marrying Lanike into the family of an aristocratic Persian family that was close to the Great King, although he dropped this subject when he realized his fellow Athenians would consider this treasonous. Plus it would in effect give the Great King a valuable hostage without Themistocles getting one in exchange. Nothing good would come of it.

I enjoyed my nights with Lanike while I could. Lanike was no maiden, she was a grown woman with needs, and by the gods, she knew how to please a man. So I did everything I could to please her.

At the time, I often appeared with Themistocles in public but wasn't required to actually do much. Another bodyguard, Dexicos, was usually present too. The sight of us was a deterrent. So was Themistocles' popularity. Anyone who tried to assault Themistocles would be torn to pieces by the mob. When Themistocles attended the Assembly, Dexicos, a free Athenian citizen with voting rights, went with him. My job was to patrol the perimeter.

One fine summer evening, after the Assembly had ended and Themistocles went with his usual retinue of friends to *The Golden Shield*, his favourite wine shop, he dismissed me for the evening. I'd barely left him when I heard shouts and screams coming from the direction of *The Golden Shield*.

I turned around and sprinted back to the wine shop, and saw a crowd gathered, but it was a block up the street from the *Shield*. Themistocles was safe. He too ran towards the scene, with Dexicos right beside him.

"What's happened?" I asked.

"Old Neocles, I heard," Dexicos said. "Dead. Horse kicked him. That's all I know."

Old Neocles was Themistocles' father. I'd met him a few times. He was a nice old guy, a shipbuilder, as proud of his daughter as he was of his son. He liked to laugh but would not put up with any shit from people. He reminded me of Grandfather.

I reached the scene and pushed my way through the crowd. It was no time for delicacy. I grabbed people and shoved them aside. They looked like they wanted to hit me until they saw who I was. I'd apologize later. Right now, I had to clear a path for Themistocles.

When I finally got close, the body was in a pool of blood that had formed around its head. It was too small to be Old Neocles, who sat beside the body and wept.

The body, whose skull had been caved in on one side, was the other Neocles. Themistocles' son.

4—EKPHORA

"Please, sirs," the man begged. He was on his knees in the stable, eyes red from his own tears and the fist I'd just driven into his face. I kicked him in the ribs. "Mercy, sirs."

"We don't want to hurt you," Dexicos said. "We want to help you. But only if you help us. Tell us who paid you to do it, or I'll sic this Scythian on you. You don't want that."

I tried to look maniacal as I grinned at the man. Dexicos was the good guy today. I was the bad guy. The man, a carter named Kleitos, owned the mule that had killed young Neocles. Dexicos and I had to find out, beyond all doubt, if it was truly an accident.

"I don't know what you're talking about," Kleitos said. "Nobody paid me to do anything except move things with my cart."

We were in the small stable behind Kleitos' house. Dexicos and I waited until he'd put his mules into their stalls for the evening before we burst in on him. If he cried out, we told him, we'd kill his wife and kids.

"Give me the name," said Dexicos.

"There is no name," he said. "By all the gods, I swear it!"

I gave him a backhand smack in the face that knocked him down on the dirt floor again. I was pretty sure by now that he told the truth, but we had to be absolutely certain. Themistocles would insist on no less. I did not care for this, Ephander, tormenting the clearly innocent, but I accepted it as an occasional necessity.

The man's fear and grief were real. He wailed and wept at the scene when he found out what his mule had done to young Neocles. I'd seen him then, as he sat in the street and cried. He wasn't play-acting, then or now.

"I'll ask you one last time," said Dexicos. "Who paid you to kill Themistocles' son?"

"Nobody!" wept Kleitos. "I would never! He was my boy's play-friend. I didn't even know about it until after it happened."

He told us, again, that he didn't actually see it happen. His two mules were hitched to his wagon on the street, not far from *The Golden Shield*. He'd just delivered furniture to a house nearby. When he came out of the house, he saw a dog sniffing around his wagon. One of his mules became skittish—it always did around dogs—and he quickly shooed away the dog, then took the mule's traces in one hand as he spoke softly to the animal and patted its muzzle. He did this, he said, so the mule would close its eyes and forget about the dog. He'd succeeded in calming the mule, but its agitation had made the other mule skittish too. Before he could calm the second mule, it had kicked little Neocles. The boy had been playing with a leather ball, tossing it high in the air and catching it himself, as he and his grandfather walked down the street. He missed a catch and the ball bounced away from him towards the front wheels of the wagon. He retrieved it when the second mule happened to be skittish. The carter could not have prevented it. No one could have planned it.

Dexicos and I looked at each other. We were done here.

I pulled Kleitos to his feet. I reached into my tunic pocket. He cringed, like he thought I was going for a knife. I pulled out some coins and held them out to him. He looked at the money in disbelief.

"For your trouble," I said. "And your pain."

"Themistocles doesn't know we're here," Dexicos said, "so don't go around telling people he sent us. In fact, we weren't even here. Got it?" He also handed the man some coins.

It took a few seconds for the man to realize we were serious. Then relief flowed over his face like water from a burst dam. He pocketed the coins.

When I got back home, my house was dark, but I made out the figure of a man sitting in the darkness at my table. I immediately drew my sword. If he'd harmed Phaedra, I'd make him pay.

"Phaedra's asleep, Elektros."

Themistocles sat alone in the dark, waiting. That was rarely a good thing.

"Why didn't you light a lamp?" I said.

"Why waste oil?" he said. "I'm here alone with my thoughts. I don't need to see anything." I wondered why he was here instead of with his family. The death of young Neocles must have devastated his wife. Then I realized that if he wanted a few minutes of peace, he couldn't find it in his own house at the best of times.

"You think it's wise to break into somebody's house?" I said as I lit a lamp. "If you were closer to the door when I came in, I might've killed you."

"That's why I didn't sit closer to the door," he said. "And I didn't break in. Phaedra let me in."

"Well, since you're here, will you have some wine?" I said, before I noticed that he'd already found the wine and had poured himself a cup. He drank it unwatered, unusual for him.

He sat silently for a minute or two. Themistocles was here for a reason. He didn't need to be in my house for some quiet time, as he had many friends with houses as quiet as mine.

"You know my father, right?" he said suddenly.

"Yes," I said. "A fine old fellow."

"Did I ever tell you how he made his money?"

"He's a shipbuilder. Everybody knows that."

"No, there's more to it. When I was a boy, he struggled. Business wasn't good. There were four shipyards near Athens, and none of them was particularly profitable. So my father burned his down. All his precious lumber, all his tools, all his frames went up in smoke."

Themistocles was silent again. He was blurry eyed, drunker than I'd ever seen him before. On the day his boy died, it was no surprise.

"For the insurance money?" I finally asked.

"No," he said. "He had no insurance. The fire almost ruined us. He ended up heavily in debt."

"Then why did he do it?"

"To deflect suspicion. He burnt his own shipyard down first so no one would suspect him when he burnt down his competitors' shipyards one by one. His operation was up and running again by the time the last one burned down, and by the time his competitors had rebuilt, he'd snapped up all the available lumber for five hundred miles in any direction. If the other shipyards wanted lumber, they'd either have to get it from across the Euxine—ridiculously expensive—or buy it from my father. Two of them went out of business, and the third one sold his shipyard cheap to my father."

His eyes were glazed and brimmed with tears, from a combination of grief, fatigue, and too much to drink. He was not himself. He was usually a focused speaker, even after many drinks, but here he kept drifting away and I had to keep bringing him back. I also couldn't figure out why he was talking about his father when his son had died. Perhaps it was because they were both named Neocles.

"Is there a reason you're telling me this?" I finally asked.

"Yes," he said. "My father was ruthless. I am too. He

found a way to crush his rivals into the ground without them even knowing he'd done it. *As I will do to you if you don't stop fucking my sister!*"

The glassiness in his eyes was suddenly gone, and now he looked like he was ready to kill me. Even drunk and weaponless, he was always dangerous.

"She's no blushing maiden," I said. "She's a grown woman who makes her own choices."

"The sister of Themistocles does *not* make her own choices," he said. It was the first time I'd ever heard him refer to himself in the third person. Over the years, he would do it more and more.

"We are discrete," I said.

"You are," he said, "but it's not enough. One of the slave-girls noticed two nights ago that Lanike was not in her bed and was not in the house. House-slaves always know their masters' secrets, and they always talk. The slave-girl has already deduced that Lanike has a lover, and now all the slaves speculate about who it is. They will eventually learn it is you, if they don't know already. So this stops now. Lanike's reputation must remain intact because I need to find her a husband.

"I'll marry her. She's quite a woman."

"Do not joke about this."

"I'm not joking. We'll do it at the feast of Tyche." Tyche was the Hellene goddess of fortune. Her feast day was in less than a month. Athenians considered it the luckiest day of the year to take wedding vows.

Themistocles was a master of masking his emotions, but now his eyebrows shot up and his mouth dropped open before he could regain control of himself. I wasn't completely serious about marrying Lanike because I knew Themistocles would never allow it. For one thing, as I was already his ally, so he did not need a marriage alliance to bind me to him. My family, what was left of it, was also not important enough. He had only one sister, and he would use her to make a key political alliance. He would marry her to a man from a prominent family and not necessarily one from Athens.

"She's fond of you," he said, "and she would not object to the match, but I already have a husband in mind for her. Negotiations are ongoing. I will not tell you who it is until I confirm it. If, however, you want a high-born Athenian wife, I'll find you one. From this moment on, though, you stop fucking my sister!"

Themistocles had an unmistakably bullish look in his eyes once he'd decided there would be no more debate on a matter. At this point, only a fool would cross him.

"She cannot marry for love," he went on. "None of us can, including myself. My father married for love, and I'm still digging my family out of the hole that put us into." Themistocles had never revealed such personal details to me before. It was the wine talking.

"Surely your mother," I said, "must have been a worthy woman to have produced a son like you and a daughter like Lanike."

"My mother was saintly," he said. "Her mind amazed me. I truly loved her, but she was slave-born, and these prissy Athenian pickle-arses have never let me forget it. And they never will."

The *prissy Athenian pickle-arses* were the aristocrats, of course, the well-born men who considered themselves, with little evidence, beacons of virtue and wisdom, and the only men capable of ruling Athens. Few were virtuous. Fewer still were wise. They were often as petty and argumentative as Theban fishwives on market day. Their main complaint about Themistocles was that he was popular. They scoffed at popularity, but in truth they were envious, though none could ever admit it.

A minute later, Themistocles put his head down on the table and wept. Then he nodded off. I let him sleep. I went outside and exercised with my weighted swords. After a couple of hours, I came back into the house. Themistocles still sat at my table, head down, snoring like a drunk bear. I put a blanket over his shoulders. I went to my own bed and slept a little. When I awoke at dawn, the blanket was still there but Themistocles was not.

* * * * * *

Polydora was acknowledged as the best professional mourner in Athens, and today she proved it yet again. When she howled her grief, she made sounds that I never thought a human could make. Her wail chilled me. For a few moments, I truly felt that her pain was real.

A dozen other professionals adorned this procession, and they were all pretty good, but there was only one Polydora. They all wore black robes and black veils. All I could see of Polydora was her hands and part of her face. The best mourners approached the job like stage actors and got into character many hours before the funeral began. Polydora interviewed members of Themistocles' household to learn as much as she could about the dead boy. She'd stayed up all of the previous night weeping, and as a result she looked convincingly red-eyed for the funeral. In fact, she looked much sadder than Themistocles and Lanike, who had to comport themselves in public with some restraint, even at this sad time. Their faces remained stern and solemn but not grief-stricken. Neither wept, although Lanike occasionally brushed away a tear.

There was blood on both of Polydora's cheeks. She'd

scratched her face, or so it appeared. It was actually animal blood that she'd concealed in a small leather pouch in each hand. Professional mourners faked the scratches because if they did it for real at every funeral, their faces would soon be disfigured with scars. I wouldn't have known she was faking, though, if I hadn't been looking for it. She tore her hair out, too, which she also somehow faked just as convincingly.

The professional mourners surprised me. Themistocles was so popular that there was no shortage of actual mourners, women who genuinely grieved for little Neocles. They scratched their faces and tore their hair out for real. Lanike hired the professionals because it was the tradition, the done thing. Some of the aristocrats would later claim it was unnecessary, and further proof of how Themistocles liked to waste money, but those same people would probably call Themistocles miserly if the professionals weren't here today. Themistocles and Lanike knew this was a spectacle. The real grief would take place privately. Almost every Athenian was here, either in the procession or out on the street to watch it.

Even Themistocles' enemies were here. Aristides stood in the street and bowed his head as the wagon that bore the body passed by. Aristides showed up at the *prothesis*, the laying out of the body in Themistocles' house in the days before the funeral, which was done so friends and relatives could express their condolences. Aristides looked sad, and he never faked emotions. "It is always tragic," I heard him say to Themistocles, "when a young life ends so abruptly. My prayers are with you and your family." Themistocles was moved. He wept after Aristides left. Other aristocrats had shown up, too, but some of them were only there because they'd never seen the inside of Themistocles' house, and they probably also hoped there would be free food. Which, of course, there was.

The procession, the *ekphora*, would normally go straight from the home of the deceased to the cemetery, but nothing was ever normal for Themistocles. Today the ekphora headed to the Pnyx first. Themistocles would speak to the crowd, and ask them to join him in mourning hymns and prayers. Only then could the ekphora proceed to the family tomb just outside the city.

Themistocles, Lanike, and Neocles the Elder, who had all shaved half their heads, as tradition required, were at the front of the procession. The other children from the household, at least the ones old enough to understand what was going on, were also near the front. Archippe, the boy's mother, was notably absent. She'd been sickly for months, rarely leaving the gynaikon, but the death of young Neocles would, eventually, destroy her. When she learned of it a few days earlier, she wailed and took to her bed, and hadn't left it since.

There were thousands of people in this procession. Most meant well, but I hated this. I appreciated the honest support they all gave Themistocles in this difficult time, but their presence made him much harder to protect. Make no mistake, Ephander: his enemies would have no qualms about using a solemn occasion to kill him. That's why their claims to aristocratic virtuousness were always so laughable. The only good thing about this situation was that unlike the Assembly, slaves and freedmen were allowed to join in, and even attend the speeches at the Pnyx. Dexicos and I could stay close to Themistocles.

When the procession reached the Pnyx, I spotted a man whose eyes were wide and wild and constantly in motion. I'd seen this lunatic around the city before. People called him *Pygolampída*, 'firefly,' because his eyes always looked combustible, like flames would shoot out of them at any moment. He was tall, thin from malnutrition, and his moth-eaten robe, a mix of brown, green, and grey, was so filthy that it was impossible to guess its original colour. His hair and beard were matted filth. You could smell him from ten yards away. He muttered and cursed, and shouted things to people who were not there. As Themistocles took his place on the podium to speak, Pygolampída elbowed his way to the front of the crowd. "If it rains, we die!" he screamed. "Demons! Everywhere demons! Kill the slaves but spare the horses!" Then he pulled a knife out of his tattered robe, shouted, "Fuck you, Achilles," then sliced the man next to him for no apparent reason, cutting the poor fellow's arm.

The madman then moved towards Themistocles. I don't know if murder was his intention. He was probably incapable of focusing on such a task, but now he was ten feet away from the podium and swinging a knife around. He never actually looked at Themistocles. I was on Pygolampída like a sling-stone. I grabbed his left wrist, his knife-hand, twisted his arm and punched him hard in the ribs. Dexicos grabbed him by the neck from behind. The madman dropped the weapon. Dexicos twisted the man's arm around his back. Themistocles had hired extra bodyguards for the occasion, and two of them very quickly rushed to him and put themselves between Themistocles and the deranged man.

Two Scythian archers came forward and hauled the man away to the city lockup. The man was dead by morning. I never found out if it was suicide or if the Scythians killed him. He was so weak from starvation that a naturally-caused death was also possible.

Do you see, Ephander, why I was so worried? I would normally have spotted this man long before he was anywhere near Themistocles, but concealed by this crowd, he was able to get close. A professional assassin could too, and he'd finish the job.

Once the madman was taken away, Themistocles ascended the platform and stood at the podium.

"Well, that concludes," he said, "the entertainment portion of today's program."

This got a mild laugh. Themistocles could not speak loudly enough to reach even halfway to the back of this huge crowd, which filled the Pnyx and spread to the surrounding streets, so his words were repeated by six heralds, each placed at two hundred yard intervals in the crowd. Themistocles would say a couple of sentences, then pause to allow the first herald to repeat the words, which the second would repeat, then the third, and so on. As a result, the laughter from Themistocles' little joke susurrated back to us in diminishing waves, which sounded like real ocean waves.

"People of Athens," Themistocles said, "my family and I cannot thank you enough for the support you've given us these difficult past few days. In gratitude, I will sponsor games three days hence." This drew applause, which like the laughter also came in waves.

"I would also like to thank," he continued, "the men who are generally regarded as my political opponents. Most of them are here today. They've put politics aside to show support for my family and me. These are true gentlemen. True Athenians. Please, let's give them a round of applause."

Most Athenians would not normally applaud aristocrats unless they'd done something heroic, but urged on by Themistocles, the crowd cheered loudly, although this was partly because Themistocles' announcement of games had already cheered them a little. The applause served another purpose for Themistocles. His political rivals were here not because they wanted to be but because they'd be thought impious and callous if they failed to show. By having the crowd applaud them, Themistocles showed the aristocrats the depth of his power. The commoners of Athens would kill the aristocrats right now if Themistocles told them to. He owned this crowd in a way the aristocrats never could. The people were his, always his, never theirs. All the aristocrats could do here is bow their heads modestly as they were being applauded, even though the applause pained them. If they reacted any other way, they'd just look like assholes.

After the last waves of applause faded away, Themistocles began his proper speech. He said that the death of his son was contrary to the natural order of life. In peace, he said, sons bury their fathers, but in war, fathers bury their sons. That delusional slubberdegullion Herodotus claims to have come up with this line, but Athenians have been saying it for centuries. Themistocles went on to say that a father who buries his son during peacetime does not even have the consolation that it was a noble death. Tears formed in his eyes, and many people in the crowd wept too.

That's when I saw a man, only a few rows back from the platform, in a dark grey robe, with the hood over part of his face. He did not look right. It was too hot to dress like that. There were thieves and cutpurses in the crowd, but this man was neither. He was sweating. He looked around nervously. Why would he be nervous at a funeral oration?

As I moved closer, I recognized him. His name was Anakletos. I knew him to be the worst slave tracker in the known world. Xenocrates had once given him money to track down an escaped slave, and Anakletos had spent it all on wine and whores. Of course he didn't find the slave. His search method was not to go to where the escaped slave would go, but to hope the slave would show up at whatever wine-shop or brothel Anakletos happened to patronize. I'd tipped off the slave, who was my friend Krites, and he'd left Athens that same day. Long after Krites had left, Anakletos insisted he'd catch him in Athens. He was lucky Xenocrates had died. People who cheated Xenocrates rarely lived long enough to enjoy it.

Anakletos was no better an assassin than he was a slave tracker. The bulge of the dagger under his robe was so obvious that a blind man would have known about it. Anakletos didn't see much more than a blind man would, because the hood limited his peripheral vision. It also made him conspicuous. I was able to slip into the crowd, push my way a few rows back, then come up behind him.

"Give me the dagger, asshole," I whispered in his ear, "and maybe I won't kill you."

He jumped. He turned around, terror in his eyes. He'd gotten fatter in the few years since I'd seen him, and he now lacked front teeth.

"Oh, hi there, Elektros," he said, forcing a smile. "What are you talking about? I don't have a dagger."

I punched him hard in the ribs. "Give me the weapon," I said. "*Now.*" He sighed, groan, then handed me the dagger.

"Who hired you?" I asked.

"Ain't it obvious?"

"Just fucking tell me. Who hired you to kill Themistocles?"

"Nobody."

I punched him in the ribs again. He yowled like a bee-stung child. "Wrong answer," I said.

"I'm not lying. Nobody paid me to kill Themistocles."

I suddenly realized he was right. Some of Themistocles' biggest enemies were foolish, but none were stupid enough to hire Anakletos as an assassin. Whoever paid him had only wanted him to create a distraction—

and I fell for it. The real assassin was someone else.

"I was hired," said Anakletos, "to kill *you*."

I looked him in the eye. He wasn't lying. I heard the rustle of robes behind me and the *swoosh* of a dagger being pulled from its small scabbard. I turned quickly, and ducked to one side. The dagger got me just below the right shoulder. If I hadn't moved, it would have gone through my heart. The man who wielded the dagger was dark-haired, maybe forty years old, unsmiling, calm, and clearly a pro. He wore a plain grey tunic and fit into the crowd so well that I hadn't noticed him earlier. He pulled his dagger out of my shoulder and kicked my legs out from under me. As I went down, I grabbed at his right hand with my left, but I was off balance and I missed. My right arm was useless, paralyzed with pain, so all I was able to do was pull the man down on top of me. He sat on my stomach and punched me in the jaw with his free hand. I saw stars for a second, dazed, helpless. He raised his dagger to plunge it into my throat, then he suddenly stopped. His own eyes widened, his body froze, and blood dripped from his mouth.

Someone in the crowd pushed the man off of me. Themistocles' old tutor, Mnesiphilos, stood over him, then reached down to check the man's pulse. Satisfied that the man was dead, he used the man's tunic to wipe the blood from his own dagger.

Mnesiphilos was a drunkard, a lecher. I'd thought him worthless. We didn't like each other. If our situations had been reversed, I don't know if I would have helped him.

He looked at my shoulder wound. He pulled a small flask of wine from inside his old grey robe, pulled out the stopper, took a healthy swig, then turned me on my side and poured a bit of it over my wound. It stung like blessed Hades.

"Ain't too bad, lad," he said to me. "The wound ain't deep. You're a healthy young buck, so you'll be on your feet in a few days." He then ripped a swathe from my tunic, poured some wine over it, took another drink himself, then pressed the swathe onto the back of my shoulder. Then he poured more wine over the cloth.

"Are you a healer?" I managed to gasp.

"Fuck no," he said. He then tore another strip from my tunic and used it to tie the wound-dressing in place. "Okay, lad, let's get you out of here."

Mnesiphilos then got four men in the crowd to carry me. They each grabbed an arm or a leg, although Mnesiphilos made sure the man who took my right arm was extra careful.

I just gawked at Mnesiphilos. He guessed what I was thinking. "It's true, Elektros, we ain't exactly pals," he said, "but you're important to the Archon, so that makes you important to me. Let's get him home, gentlemen."

They carried me away to the sound of a ruckus behind us. I found out later that the crowd had swarmed Anakletos and beaten him to death.

5—LAURION

Ever been stabbed, Ephander? No? Feels like you'd expect it to feel. Sharp pain, yes, a stabbing pain that remains long after the blade is pulled out and the wound is cleaned. Mnesiphilos and the four men carried me to my house. They put me into my bed. Mnesiphilos thanked them, gave each man a silver coin, then told them to go back to the funeral. Soon afterwards, two other armed men walked into my front door. I froze. Even if I could defend myself, my sword was a dozen feet away, leaning against the wall where Mnesiphilos had put it.

"Relax, Elektros," said Mnesiphilos. "Carneades and Nomion will stay with you night and day until you're up and around again. Themistocles' orders."

"I don't need guards," I said.

"From what's just happened," Mnesiphilos said, "I'd say you do. But it don't matter what you'n'me think. The Archon says you need guards, so you get guards. That's the end of it."

Then he relayed Themistocles' other order to me: stay in bed until I was better. I groaned. I hated inactivity, even when I so clearly needed it.

When Phaedra saw the men carry me in, she wept. Mnesiphilos looked at her—lewdly I thought, he wasn't capable of looking at a woman, even an older one, any other way. He put his hand on her shoulder. If he harassed her, I'd beat the shit out of him, somehow. I still had one good arm and my legs still worked.

"It's Phaedra, right?" he said, with a gentleness I didn't expect. "I knew your brother. A fine man. Sorry for his passing. But we'll talk about him later. Right now, is there any chance you could bring Elektros some of your legendary lentil soup? And after you do that, I'd like some too, if it's not too much trouble. Him first, though. If you hafta force-feed this stubborn fucker, pardon my Phoenician, I'll hold him down for you."

Phaedra calmed down immediately. A minute later, she brought me soup in a cup, with bread still warm from the oven. I wouldn't let her spoon the soup into my mouth for me, so she rolled her eyes and put the cup into my left hand.

Her lentil soup, by the way, was magical. It had a sharp but pleasant aftertaste and made your lips tingle a little, but in a good way. Two of her secret ingredients were asphodel extract and honey, but I don't know what else was in it. What I do know is that I've never tasted better. It always filled you more than you expected it to.

Once Mnesiphilos saw me eating, he turned to Phaedra and said, "My turn!" She laughed and went to fetch him his soup.

He sat at the table. When she brought the soup to him, he tasted it, then jumped to his feet. He moved so quickly, so violently, that I thought he was angry.

"Holy fuck!" he cried out. "Uh, pardon my Phoenician, Phaedra, but this soup is amazing! And I don't normally get excited about any liquids that ain't wine. You should be selling this."

After I finished eating, Mnesiphilos brought me a small vial. "Drink this," he said. "Poppy juice. For the pain. You'll sleep some, too."

I drank the white liquid. Within minutes, I felt no pain. I was giggly. I felt so good I almost wished I had more stab wounds. While I was in this accommodating state of mind, Mnesiphilos asked me if he could go into business with Phaedra and me. Every day, they would fill an amphora with lentil soup and take it down to the agora around midday. We'd split the profits three ways. I agreed to it. In my drug-addled state, I didn't consider that it meant I'd have to see Mnesiphilos every day, although I had to admit I liked him better now.

Then I fell asleep, and dreamt of ladies and lightning. And soup.

For the next two days, Carneades and Nomion slept in turns but never left my side. Mnesiphilos came to my house first thing in the morning each day, gave me another vial of poppy juice, then he and Phaedra went to the agora to buy ingredients for the soup. The lentils and the asphodel and the honey and the other ingredients needed time, at least twelve hours, to meld into the magic soup, so they didn't take soup to the agora the first day. On the second, they went to the agora to get more ingredients, came back to the house to make the soup, then took the batch they'd made the previous day back to the agora around midday. They returned an hour later with an empty amphora, big smiles, and pockets full of silver.

"We coulda sold twice as much," Mnesiphilos said, beaming, "if we had it."

Phaedra was a shy woman who rarely spoke, and when she did, her voice was so soft that you had to listen very carefully. "Master Mnesiphilos," she said, "is a master salesman."

"Well, I'll take a little credit," he said, "but this fucking soup—pardon my Phoenician—is very easy to sell. All of today's customers'll be back tomorrow."

He then asked me if we could use the first day's profits to buy two larger amphorae. He'd given me poppy juice first, so of course I agreed. He also had a woodworker make some hinged wooden handles that functioned like a litter for the large amphorae. The handles enabled him and Phaedra to carry the soup to the agora while it was still hot.

On the third day, after Phaedra and Mnesiphilos had left, Carneades came to my bed. "There's a lady here, Elektros," he said. "Says she knows you."

Nomion stood at my open front door. Outside was a figure in a long grey hooded robe, with the hood over her head, on a day far too hot for that. She wore a veil that revealed only her eyes, which I recognized immediately.

"Let me in, boys," she said. "I'm an old friend of Lex's."

"It's okay, lads," I said. "She's a friend, though far from old."

She laughed, too loudly. It wasn't *that* funny.

She came in, still covered, and looked at me. Carneades and Nomion just gawped like gargoyles at her. Even though they couldn't see much more than her eyes, her nectarous voice had paralyzed them. Then she said, "Gentlemen? A little privacy?"

I nodded to Carneades and Nomion. They understood, and posted themselves outside the house, one at the front door, the other at the back.

Parthenia lowered the veil but kept the robe on. Her face was angelic, and perfect. "I'm a little disappointed," she said, "that neither of those handsome fellows offered to frisk me."

"I can do that, if you insist," I said.

"You should. You just never know what I might have hidden in here."

I sat up. She stood beside the bed. My shoulder still hurt when I moved, but not as much as it did the day before, and there wasn't anything wrong with the rest of me. I began to pat her down, like I was searching for a weapon. I put my hands under her robe, started at her right ankle, moved up her leg, and soon discovered that she wasn't wearing anything under the robe.

What happened next, Ephander, I will keep to myself, although I will confess that I didn't find any weapons on her and I looked *everywhere* twice. Sorry, you depraved bastard, I know you want details, but how can you not know by now that it's not my style?

This was far from our first time together. I'd visited Parthenia several times at her home when Hyperion was away. I never spent the night, mostly because I didn't want her servants to see me, even though they knew not to ask questions. Once we met in a room at Hera's Retreat, Athens' finest inn. Another time, we met outside the walls of the city. Other times, she had her slave-woman Lydiana rent a room for us at one of the shit-hole inns near the Phaleron. One time we rented a small boat, rowed a half-mile off shore, and made love under the stars amid the danger of the waves. She liked the forbiddenness, the constant risk of these secret meetings, and I must admit that I did too. If Hyperion found out, he and I would cease to be friends. High-born Athenians had the silly notion that women lacked the reasoning capabilities to make good decisions when it came to lovers, so if a wife or a daughter or a sister slept with a man, it was always the man's fault.

With Parthenia, however, it was clearly the men who lost the ability to make good decisions. She turned us into quivering jelly in seconds. Her parents had named her Parthenia, 'virgin,' never dreaming of the mockery she'd make of that name. She was also called Siren. It fit. She caused shipwrecks. She ruined marriages. Soldiers who have fought a hundred battles turned into babbling ninnies if she smiled at them. Men who have loved a hundred women followed her like lost puppies. She was the most desired woman in Athens, perhaps in all Hellas. She knew it, too.

Parthenia visited me every day while I recuperated.

She helped to speed my recovery and at the same time gave me motivation to remain laid up. I expected her to get tired of me—apart from a desire for each other's bodies, we didn't have much in common—but it just didn't seem to happen. I lived in dread that Hyperion would find out. That didn't seem to happen either.

On the fourth morning of my recuperation, I woke up to shouting outside. It was two hours past dawn, Mnesiphilos and Phaedra had just left for the agora, and Parthenia had not yet arrived. The shouters sounded drunk. I was groggy, from my poppy-induced sleep, but I managed to stumble to the door to see what was going on. Carneades came with me. There was a group of a dozen men on the street. They all looked pretty happy.

"Somebody get married?" I asked one of them.

"Elektros!" one of the men shouted. "Have some wine." I didn't recognize him. He brought a jar of wine over to me.

"No thanks," I said. "What's the occasion?"

"You didn't hear?" said the man. "A new vein's been found at Laurion. It's so rich that every citizen of Athens gets a million drachmae!"

Athens had been mining silver at Laurion since the-gods-know-when. It was southeast of the city, a dozen miles from the sea. It had always been profitable, but lately the returns had been diminishing. If news of the new vein was true, then it was indeed cause for celebration, although I doubted it would make every Athenian rich.

It didn't take a Pythagorean meta-mathematician to guess what Themistocles would want to do with the new silver.

* * * * * *

"Who wishes to address this Assembly?" the herald called out to the gathering at the Pnyx, which was packed to standing room only. Thousands more citizens spilled out into the nearby streets. The new silver strike at Laurion had been confirmed and today we would find out how much silver it would yield. An Assembly usually drew six or seven thousand citizens, but at least twice that many were here today. The food and trinket vendors brought extra stock but still ran out early. The Pnyx whores were happy too, or at least would be in a couple of days, once the swelling had subsided.

"I, Diotrephes, son of Doros," said a short fat man, "will speak if I may." Diotrephes was a freeborn Athenian, and had lived here all his life, but he was not a citizen. Born with a club foot, he'd never had the mandatory ephebe training. He'd used a walking stick all his life. He always had a good head for numbers, though, so he was given the job as Athens' accounts manager. A non-citizen could address the Assembly, but only if invited to do so, which Diotrephes had been. I stood so far away that all I saw was a dark distant figure with a walking stick, but I could still see that Diotrephes enjoyed this attention. The most important men in Athens would now gladly listen to every word he said.

"My fellow citizens," Diotrephes called out in a surprisingly deep and robust voice that echoed around the Pnyx. "My fellow citizens," he repeated, even though it was technically untrue, but no one said anything. "There have been wild speculations about the discovery of a second vein of silver at Laurion. I have gone with the mining engineers to the site, and I can confirm that it is true. There is a second vein, only a few hundred yards from the first one." Cheers erupted. Diotrephes paused to let them die down.

"Once we get new shafts dug and fortified," he continued, "we can begin to mine. This will take some time. Then the mined ore needs to be refined before it becomes money in our pockets, but we will start seeing profits in a few months. And when I say profits, the engineers think we can mine ten talents a day."

There was a collective gasp. People chattered excitedly to each other. Laurion's output, before this new discovery, had fallen to less than two talents a day.

"We will not abandon the first vein," he continued. "It's still profitable, so we'll keep most of its slaves there. For the new vein we need to buy another sixty slaves. And we still don't know how deep the new vein goes. It's possible that it's a surface vein, which means it will get mined out after a few months. But at the very least, we'll get over one hundred talents total."

This brought a roar of applause. Men embraced each other. Tears of joy soaked men's tunics.

The party had begun. From this point on, I didn't hear a word Diotrephes said. No one did. People were so happy that it would have been a perfect moment for Diotrephes to ask the Assembly to grant him citizenship. I think that's actually what he was trying to do when twenty-five or thirty men rushed the floor of the Pnyx. I thought Diotrephes was a dead man—he thought so too, as he desperately tried to hobble away—and the men tore his tunic almost completely off of him. That, it turned out, was an accident. The men picked him up and carried him, half naked now, over their shoulders, like he was a hero, like he'd personally discovered the new silver and had made them all rich. Diotrephes' face was white with terror, but all the men did was get him drunk and take him to a whorehouse.

He'd have a lot of company there on this day.

Men sang, danced, sang some more. The aristocrats shook their heads, rolled their eyes, looked disgusted by this display, which had proven to them yet again that commoners were rabble, unfit to make important political decisions. Themistocles, who sat with these people, the tradesmen and the farmers and the labourers, sang with them. He too knew that order would not be restored today, but unlike the aristocrats, he joined in on the fun. When the herald declared that the Assembly was dissolved, and would meet again the next day to discuss how the money would be spent, almost no one heard him.

The next day, when the Assembly met again, stupidity reigned.

It was unusual for the Assembly to meet on consecutive days unless there was war or another national emergency. The food and trinket sellers had restocked, and the whores did their usual good trade, although I heard one man complain that he had to settle for a handjob because his whore was too sore from the night before for anything else.

"Who wishes to address this Assembly?" asked the herald.

Forty-eight men came forward.

It would be a long and silly night. I won't bore you with all of the suggestions, Ephander. I'll only tell you about the dumbest ones, just to give you an idea of the mindset that the sudden discovery of a huge amount of silver can create.

One man proposed that we hire five hundred thousand mercenaries and station them permanently in Athens.

Idiocy. If we did that, the Great King would laugh and sit back and wait for the mercenaries to bankrupt us.

Mercenaries can easily be made to change sides, too, so this would give Xerxes the option of paying the soldiers in our midst to conquer us.

Another man suggested that we build a wall of solid iron around Athens. Then his friend said we had enough money to build a wall of iron around every house in Athens. The two men left the floor arguing loudly about which of their idiotic ideas was the better one.

Another man said we could just pay the Great King to not attack us. He was booed off the floor. Rotten fruit was thrown at him as he skulked back to his seat. I was always amazed that people carried rotten fruit around with them in the event they'd find a suitable target for it.

One man proposed that we just divide up the money amongst the citizens. He cited Diotrephes' claim that there was enough money to give each man an annuity of twenty thousand drachmae. This idea was popular enough to be supported by a majority, and truly worried Themistocles. It would leave no money to improve the defenses of Athens. It also implied that Athenians either did not believe the Great King would invade again or that they put their own enrichment ahead of the city's defense.

Another man got up and suggested that we use the money to dig a massive trench around Athens, a trench so great that it couldn't be bridged. He did not consider that if the Persians couldn't cross the trench, then we couldn't either. Like the iron walls, the trench would enable the Persians to starve us out in a siege.

Another man suggested we bring fifty African elephants to Athens. In peacetime, they'd be a profitable tourist attraction. They could be trained to do tricks and people would pay good money to ride on them. In wartime, they'd be turned on the Persians or any other invader. The beauty of it, the man said, is that their population would be self-perpetuating because they'd breed. It was one of the more novel ideas, but the man admitted that he'd never seen an elephant and didn't know how much it would cost to feed one, let alone fifty. I'd never seen one either, but Grandfather, who'd been a mercenary in Asia as a young man, had seen elephants in battle. He'd told me that they were not reliable in war. They will scare the bejeekers out of the enemy, and a single rampaging elephant can kill fifty men in a matter of minutes, but elephants will not run into flames or a spear phalanx, and they usually reach a point where they lose interest in killing enemies. When this happens, they simply leave the field by the most direct route. They become uncontrollable and will trample anyone, friend or foe, who gets in their way. Grandfather said it was never clear if the elephants did more harm to their own armies or to the enemy's. The Persians used elephants sometimes, so they would probably also know the best counter-strategies against them.

One man suggested that we use the money to invade Persia. And why stop there? We could hire all the mercenaries we needed to not only defeat the Great King, but to take over the Persian Empire *in its entirety*. This was yet another man who misunderstood mercenaries. They are not slaves. They will fight for you as long as you pay them, but will just as easily fight for somebody else, including your enemy, who pays them more. For an army large enough to invade Persia, the mercenaries would outnumber the Hellene soldiers.

Many more ludicrous ideas were suggested, including a bizarre plan to kidnap the Great King and another to infect the Persian Empire with plague. It was evening, the sun was close to the horizon, and most of the men here were tired from a long day. It appeared that no one else would speak, and most of us were okay with this.

Then Kimon rose and addressed the Assembly. He was, on this evening, the representative of the aristocratic faction. When he spoke, I usually rolled my eyes and hoped he didn't yammer on for too long because he rarely said anything worth hearing. He'd listened to the earlier suggestions, advised everyone to disregard the sillier ones, and then combined the few sensible ones. He suggested that a portion of the new silver be used to build new stone walls around Athens. The current ones had weak points that needed refortification, and he suggested that we design new walls that were thirty feet high and included slinger and archer turrets.

This actually made sense. Even Themistocles had acknowledged that upgraded fortifications were necessary because the Persians were not the only enemies of Athens.

Kimon then suggested something that no one else had thought of: the mines of Laurion had a perimeter fence around it, and a few dozen armed guards, but no defensive wall. The mines were vulnerable. Preparations for a proper stone wall around Laurion should be begun there immediately. It would only require a small percentage of the new silver. Our engineers should survey the area, and Kimon asked the Assembly to put this to a vote without delay. The herald did so, and the motion was approved almost unanimously. Engineers and surveyors would be dispatched to Laurion the next day.

It was the first time I'd ever seen Kimon not be obnoxious. I hadn't known it was possible for him. While other men spouted unrealistic nonsense and squirrel-brained lunacy, Kimon, of all people, had been the voice of reason. Instead of his usual schoolboy taunting of Themistocles, he'd shown himself capable of clear and rational thought when other men had gone silver-mad.

It was a political triumph for him—or it would have

been if he'd had the sense to quit while he was ahead.

He should've thanked the Assembly and graciously returned to his seat, but Kimon, being Kimon, chose to gloat.

"My learned colleague Themistocles," he said, "has chosen not to speak on this day. Why the sudden silence? Every day for years, we've had to listen to his delusional carping about the Persians and their mighty fleet—their mighty *invisible* fleet, I might add, because no one here has ever seen it. Well, I have to give the man credit to finally recognize that he's beaten—that his fleet of warships is, pardon the pun, *dead in the water*."

A few people from the aristocratic faction chuckled at this, but most people did not. The other aristocrats knew what Kimon never seemed to comprehend: a verbal attack on Themistocles would only provoke a counterattack that Kimon would lose handily.

Themistocles had not intended to speak today, but he had to answer this challenge. He calmly made his way down from the high seats, where he always sat, and took the floor of the Pnyx. He asked for permission to address the Assembly. This drew attention to the fact that Kimon had not done so—he'd just gotten up and started speaking, as if an aristocrat did not need to observe the formalities of the Assembly. A minor point, maybe, but it didn't go unnoticed.

When permission to speak was granted, Themistocles paused for effect. "A long day for all of us," he said. "Everybody get enough to drink last night?"

This drew a mild laugh. Then Themistocles turned serious. "I will not criticize my young colleague's plan to fortify Laurion," he said. "In fact, it's an excellent idea. I'm all for it. I also support his proposal to upgrade the wall around Athens. We should start on this as soon as possible.

"But these two worthy projects will take less than one-fiftieth of our confirmed output from the new mines—and a much smaller fraction if the new vein runs deep. We will still have to make an important decision about the rest of the money. Building warships is an option, and one that I still support."

"Ha!" shouted Kimon. "I knew it. Themistocles is like a sick old starling that has learned to mimic one sound, and *only* one sound. Is anyone surprised that he proposes that we build him a fleet of ships to play with?"

"You are mistaken, Kimon," said Themistocles, "as you so often are. I have not proposed anything at all yet."

"But we all know what's coming," said Kimon. "So go ahead and propose that we build warships, so the rest of us can go ahead and laugh you off the stage."

Themistocles shook his head and smiled. "Ah, my young friend," he said calmly. "So inexperienced at warfare, and equally inexperienced at peace. I will make a proposal right now, but not the one you expect."

Themistocles paused for effect. There were about fourteen thousand men here, but not a single man spoke. Even Kimon hung on Themistocles' words.

"I believe this new wealth is a sign that the gods have favoured us," said Themistocles. "Does anyone here say otherwise?"

No one did. Everyone agreed, or at least pretended to. Anyone who contradicted this would seem impious. Not even Kimon was stupid enough to do that.

"I therefore propose that we do not make an impulsive decision about the silver," said Themistocles.

"Here comes the big load," cried Kimon. A few people chuckled, but most people, including his fellow aristocrats, really just wanted him to sit the fuck down and shut the fuck up.

"The gods have favoured us," Themistocles repeated, "with this new silver, so we should consult them about how to spend it. We must send a delegation to the Pythia as soon as possible."

Nobody expected this. The crowd murmured. Few men knew what to make of it.

"It will take at least a month," Themistocles continued, once everyone had settled down, "to get to Mount Parnassos and back. But Diotrephes told us yesterday that it will be several months before we get any of the new silver, so we've got time.

"And I volunteer to go."

Aristides jumped to his feet. With his threadbare cloak and his unkempt hair, he always looked a little like a lunatic, but his voice was loud and clear.

"Out of the question!" Aristides said. "While I generally endorse any plan that would take Themistocles away from us for a month,"—this drew some laughs, even from Themistocles' people—"we cannot trust him to report the Oracle's words accurately. Themistocles must *not* be part of the delegation."

"Do you call me a liar?" asked Themistocles, glaring at Aristides. "Or a blasphemer? Or both? You slander me, sir."

"Let me rephrase, Themistocles," Aristides said. "Far be it from me to slander my honey-tongued adversary. Maybe you would never sink so low that you'd misreport the Oracle's actual words, but I am certain that by the time her prophesy was reported to this Assembly, you would have had plenty of time to cook up a highly creative, and highly self-serving, interpretation of it. And you would use the time away to plot and manipulate the situation."

Aristides was an intelligent man who might make a good leader, but he was a poor politician. He did not understand that if Themistocles went to Parnassos for a month, it would give his opponents time to plot and manipulate. It was actually the last thing Themistocles wanted.

Aristides also failed to see that Themistocles plotted against and manipulated *him* at this very moment.

"Did you just make a half-assed apology for slandering me?" asked Themistocles with a grin. "If so, then I half-assedly accept. But enough about me. I put this question to the Assembly: can anybody here think of someone who is ethically without flaw? Someone who is honest and honourable at all times, yet has the weight of ancestral authority? Can you think of anyone at all who should lead our delegation to the Oracle?"

"Aristides!" someone shouted. "He'd be perfect!"

"Aristides the Just!" someone else cried out.

Before long, the Assembly was chanting *Aristides the Just! Aristides the Just!*

Aristides was paralyzed into silence. His face was white, like he would faint, then suddenly red with rage. He looked like he really wanted to punch Themistocles in the face, but was far too ethical to do so.

When the chants finally subsided, Themistocles spoke. "It's settled, then. Good Aristides will lead the delegation. I propose that we also include someone who represents the tradesmen, someone who represents the merchants, and someone else to represent the farmers. Make no mistake, though: Aristides will lead. He must be the one who hears the Pythia's words. Any of the others *can* also be present, but Aristides is the one who *must* be present."

We found out later that Aristides was honoured to be chosen for the delegation—but he also thought he'd have to pay for it himself. His rage came because he was broke—his tattered tunic was a sign of poverty, not virtuous asceticism—and he thought he'd have to confess this in front of the Assembly. Being Aristides, he would not lie, he would not say that he had an urgent family matter or a serious health issue to prevent him from going.

Themistocles went to shake Aristides' hand to congratulate him, but Aristides refused. He simply glared at Themistocles. Then Themistocles quietly told him that the delegation was city business, so Athens would pay for provisions, slaves, horses and wagons, and armed guards for the journey. Only then did Aristides relax, smile, and shake Themistocles' hand.

Themistocles personally selected some of the armed guards who would accompany Aristides. And the gods be damned, Ephander, if I wasn't one of them.

6—PARNASSOS

"There's a problem with the horses, sir," I said to Aristides.

"They look healthy enough to me," he said.

"Oh, they're all healthy, sir," I said. "Well cared for. Well fed."

"Then what's the problem?"

Aristides glared at me. He was all about decorum and appearances. He did not like me to report a problem to him with so many people watching. We were at the Thriasian Gate, ready to take the northwest road from Athens to Mount Parnassos. We had four wagons, twelve horses, eight armed guards and eight other men, counting the slaves. Several hundred well-wishers had come to cheer us and see us off.

"Four of these horses are unsuitable for this journey, sir," I told him.

"You just said they were all healthy," he said.

"They are. The eight horses hitched to the wagons are fine, but the other four are high-strung stallions. They're war chargers, strong and fast, but they lack stamina. Plus they're temperamental. The big one just bit me. If anything happens to one of the wagon horses, we can't use any of the stallions to take its place. We need mares or geldings, which are calmer."

"We can deal with them later," said Aristides. He was too proper to even acknowledge the people who called out and wished him well. He was nonetheless pleased with all the attention, even as he was irritated with me.

"Begging your pardon, sir," I said, "but we can't deal with them later." His jaw clenched as he bit back his anger. I'd spoken out of turn, and much worse, I just contradicted him.

"And why not?" he snapped. He looked at me like I'd just slapped his face and pissed on his feet.

"We must replace these horses before we leave the city. It will delay us an hour or two, but it will save us problems later."

He looked me in the eye, cold as death. "You press your luck, Scythian," he said to me. "I am in command of this delegation. I will not tolerate my orders being questioned."

"Acknowledged, sir," I said, "but if I see a problem that endangers the delegation, is it not my duty to report it to you?"

"It is," he said. "And you have done so. I thank you for it. We leave immediately, with the horses Athens has so graciously provided us."

It was Aesop who said familiarity breeds contempt. From afar, I'd always admired Aristides the Just, the most honest and ethical man I'd ever known, but now I saw a stubborn fool who would not listen to good advice. He commanded infantry in battle—superbly, I might add, he was inspirational at Marathon—but he didn't know spadiddly about horses.

It was a clear morning. We looked like a merchants' caravan. The wagons were loaded with supplies and food for the journey, including fodder for the horses. The plan was to have one guard on each of the wagons, while the other four guards each rode a horse. The crowd cheered for us. Women wept and gave us gifts of food and drink, and hugged us like they were mothers seeing sons off to war.

The original plan was to rotate the guards between the wagons and the horses, but four of the guards were poor riders and felt more comfortable on foot or on the wagons. So I would ride a horse every day, mostly because I was the only one in the party who could handle the biggest warhorse, the one that had bitten me. It was no comfort to learn that his name was Deathblow. The other three stallions were only slightly less volatile. These four magnificent beasts were powerful and proud, and they all hated each other. We had to keep them apart at all times, not easy in a small caravan.

Deathblow bit anyone who came near the front of him and kicked anyone who wandered behind him. He'd already broken the arm of one of Aristides' slaves with a vicious kick. All the man had done was walk behind the horse. Deathblow particularly hated Lightning, the fastest horse here. Whoever chose these animals was unaware that stallions form rivalries and friendships with each other, just as men do, and no matter how well trained they are, they never cease to hate their horse enemies and love their horse friends.

There were sometimes bandits on the road to Mount Parnassus. If they attacked us, we'd have to worry about our own horses as much as the bandits. Plus we would not be able to fight them as a group, because each of our warhorses would be distracted by the other three.

On the Sea of Grass, I'd had some experience with a headstrong stallion similar to Deathblow. Before I mounted Deathblow for the first time, just outside the Thriasian Gate, I grabbed his reins and pulled his face towards mine. I looked him in the eye. He looked like he wanted to kill me, but I didn't waver, didn't blink. I stared him down. You have to show a horse like this that you are not afraid of him, but you also do not want to break him completely because his high-spiritedness can be useful in a fight.

I also saw that the traces were too tight around his

jaw. They caused him pain and increased his orneriness. By the end of the day, he'd have chafing and open sores that would bother him for the rest of the journey. So after I mounted him—and it's important with a horse like this to get on his back in a single swift motion—I reached forward and loosened the traces a little. Now he knew that I could bring pain but also make it go away.

The next thing I did was have him gallop. As the caravan started rolling slowly, I took off ahead of the others. The other stallions whinnied. They wanted to gallop too, so later I would make sure the other three riders did this at least once a day. The other people in the caravan thought I was nuts. They didn't understand that a spirited horse who wants to run must be allowed to so. He will be calmer afterwards, and it's not a bad idea to tire him out a little. It will also keep him fit.

"You see?" Aristides said when I returned. "The horses are not a problem."

Aristides sat in the lead wagon. A slave with a bandaged and splinted arm held the reins beside him.

It was true that Deathblow, sweaty from the exertion, was a little calmer now, and slightly less dangerous, but this wouldn't last. "What makes you say that, sir?" I said.

"You've just tamed him," he said.

"Not true, sir," I said. "He considers me less of an enemy than he did before, but he still needs to be kept away from the other horses. He will still kick anyone who walks behind him. By the way, sir, who chose these horses?"

"Audax here," said Aristides, nodding towards the man next to him. He was ten years older than Aristides, with much grey in his close-cropped hair and beard. He was fit and strong, despite his age. To rest his broken arm, he handled the reins with one hand. That took skill and made me wonder how he'd learned to do it.

"Who'd you get them from?" I said to Audax. He did not answer me right away. Aristides observed every little social protocol and courtesy, even when it was impractical to do so, as it was right now. His slaves were not permitted to reply to free men, when the master was present, without his permission. Aristides nodded to Audax, who then spoke.

"There is a man who leases horses, sir," he said.

"What's his name?" I asked.

"I do not know his real name, sir," he said. "I only know his nickname, which is disrespectful and beyond my station to repeat."

Aristides smiled. The sendoff had lifted his spirits, and he seemed to have forgiven me for contradicting him earlier. "I believe the man is known to you, Elektros," he said.

"Pudge?" I asked.

"Yes, sir," said Audax. "I have never called him that, though."

I smiled at this. Pudge, or Pudger, was my brother Phylo's nickname as a boy on Skiathos, and the epithet had followed him to Athens. When he trained as an ephebe, he became leaner than I'd ever seen him, but once the training was over, he didn't keep it up and was soon pudgy again. He now leased horses with his Athenian business partner Epictetos, and he also arranged for the Scythians in Athens to do demonstrations of their horsemanship. These were popular and lucrative, but Phylo, the gods love him, hated riding and didn't know spadiddly about horses either. If he did, he wouldn't have given us these ones. Horses know when they're being ridden by good riders, and these four stallions had been ridden mostly by Scythians, the best horsemen in the world. As riders, none of us on this journey was anywhere close to the Scythians, not even me.

I didn't blame Audax. He was city born and bred and knew nothing about horses, and of course Aristides would not allow his slave to seek advice. In his mind, that would be improper. Slaves on errands do not question or negotiate. Audax would have been forbidden from merely asking about the horses, even if he'd known what to ask.

"You could've asked one of the Scythians for advice, Audax," I said.

"Even if my master permitted that, sir," Audax said, "the Scythians have been known to beat slaves who speak to them uninvited."

"True," I said. "So if you ever have to select horses again, come and talk to me. I will either help you choose them, or I will introduce you to one of the Scythians. Most of them are friends of mine."

"Thank you, sir, that's a kind offer," said Audax.

"Which we will *not* accept," Aristides put in quickly. "I'll not have my slave pestering free men."

I just stared at Aristides because I wasn't sure if he meant it. He was dead serious, though.

"I've just given Audax permission to speak to me, sir," I said, "so it would not be pestering."

Aristides just shook his head. The conversation was over.

We rode the rest of that day without incident. As the sun started to sink, we were near no towns, so we camped beside the road, close to a stream. We made a rough square out of the four wagons and pitched our leather tents inside the square. I had my gorytos with me, so I went into the woods and brought us back three rabbits to add to our meal of dried fruit and hard bread. After I'd handed the rabbits to Audax to clean and roast—I would have done it myself, as Audax had other duties, but Aristides insisted that it was slaves' work—Aristides invited me to sit beside him.

As Themistocles had proposed in the Assembly, we had representatives of the tradesmen, the farmers, and the merchants with us, although their presence was more symbolic than functional. With no actual duties, this journey was a little holiday for them. The tradesmen were represented by Aberkios, a white-haired and mostly retired cobbler. I loved talking to him. He often forgot what he was saying in mid-sentence, but made so many jokes and puns that he would have made an excellent comic playwright. The farmers were represented by Kaletor, who was also mostly retired, as his sons now ran the farm that was the one of the biggest producers of olives in Attica. Kaletor spoke little. His prime role on this journey was to remind Aberkios what he'd been talking about.

The most pleasant surprise for me was that the merchants were represented by my friend Simeon. His father imported silk, amber, faience, and other things from the Far East, and he was somehow able to continue his trade even while we were at war with Persia and most eastern trade routes were blocked to us. Simeon, who was no longer physically able to fight in the phalanx, was now devoted to learning the business, although this journey was a holiday for him too.

The aristocrats were represented by Aristides, of course, even though he was not truly representative of anyone other than himself. Aristides never had more than one cup of well-watered wine with meals, never got drunk, never ate to excess, never went to a brothel. He wore the same tattered cloak every day. He retired early every night and rose with the sun every morning.

"You're here to spy on me," he said. I sat next to him at his camp table as we waited for the rabbits to finish roasting. "You're Themistocles' man through and through."

"You're partly right, sir," I said. "I am Themistocles' man. I will report anything that happens on this journey. But I'm not here to spy on you. Why would I be? You are the most honest and ethical man in all Hellas. You do not participate in plots or intrigues. You do not keep a mistress. You do not get drunk and say stupid things, as most men, including Themistocles, do on occasion. Beg pardon, sir, but anybody sent to spy on *you* would die of boredom."

He actually laughed. He was proud of his upright reputation.

"I had heard that you speak plainly, Elektros of Skiathos," he said. "And I thank you for it. We'd all be better off if everyone spoke so truthfully."

It was a veiled dig at Themistocles. After we'd eaten, Aristides wanted to hear about my experiences in Scythia, as did other members of the party, so I told a few stories. Any of the Scythian archers in Athens would have had better ones, and more of them, but Aristides deemed it improper to speak to men who were slaves, which the Scythians of Athens were in theory, though not in practice. Most Athenians were actually afraid of them. According to Simeon, my friendship with the Scythians made me an object of fascination and more than a little awe to the other members of this party.

Nothing happened on the second day of our journey, apart from a little rain. I'd galloped Deathblow twice that day. I'd been with him almost every waking moment. He now allowed me to rub his muzzle and no longer tried to bite me, although he still tried to bite any other man or horse who came near him. The other three guards on horseback now galloped their mounts twice a day, and the exertion calmed those horses down a little too.

When we camped on the second night, I took my bow into the brush and came back an hour later with two pheasants and two rock partridges. This was a spectacular success. These birds, not common around Athens, would only be found on a wealthy man's table. The other members of the delegation were thrilled. Some had never tasted pheasant or partridge before.

Aristides, however, would not allow me to sit with him now, or even near him.

"I have been told," he said, "that you were born a slave."

"True, sir," I said, "but I was freed when I was still a child."

"It makes no difference," he said. "I am an aristocrat. It is not proper for me to associate with freedmen."

"Are you fucking kidding me?" I said. Aristides the Just? Well, that's true enough, but Aristides the Narrow-Minded Humourless Nit-Picking Asshole would have been more accurate.

The birds, which Audax had already cleaned and dressed, roasted on two spits over the fire in front of Aristides. I grabbed both spits. "I will share these, sir," I said, "only with those who consider me fit company." Then I stomped off to build my own fire.

I know, Ephander, this was petty of me. Grandfather had always told me that you shouldn't let small men drag you down to their level, and I've always tried to live up to that. But Aristides was impossible. His insistence on observing every little rule of etiquette was damned silly. A half hour later, when I'd built my fire and finished roasting the birds, I was joined by everyone except for Aristides, Audax, and the other three slaves. The slaves would have been welcome at my fire, but Aristides wouldn't allow it.

On the third day, Aristides tried to assert himself as a cavalry commander, even though he himself did not ride but sat in the wagon, with Audax at the reins. Earlier in the journey, when Aristides tried to tell us how to handle our horses, we generally said *yes sir, as you say, sir,* then ignored him completely. He designated Timoleon, one of the other horsemen, as guard commander. Timoleon said *yes sir, as you say, sir,* then just ignored Aristides' commands.

When we'd stopped to rest and take a midday meal, Timoleon came up to me and clapped me on the shoulder. "Let's humour the old fart," he said quietly. "I'll pretend to be your commanding officer, even though you know way more about horses than I do. The upside is that you won't have to talk to His Exalted Fucking Majesty anymore. The downside is that *I* will."

I laughed. Everyone in this delegation, besides Aristides, was born either a commoner or a slave. Aristides thought his noble lineage automatically made him our superior in every respect. This attitude had made him as many friends here as his insistence on meaningless protocols.

When we saddled up to move again, Aristides ordered Timoleon and one of the other horsemen to ride beside the lead wagon, one on each side, which he declared was the proper formation for an official delegation. "We need to practice," he said, "for our entry into the town of Delphi."

"Bad idea, sir," I said.

"Did I ask your opinion, Scythian?" Aristides snapped at me.

"You did not, sir," I said, "but I still must report it. These stallions are—"

"Silence!" Aristides shouted. "I am in command here."

When a man constantly reminds you that he is in command, it is usually a clear indication that he is not.

"But sir, those horses—"

"SILENCE!" Aristides shouted. "One more word and I'll put you in chains for insubordination!"

It would have been laughable if it wasn't so foolish. We had no chains, and if any of the other guards tried to put ropes on me, I'd knock him on his ass.

We were on a stretch of good road, with few hills and no mud patches, so we should have made good time, but Timoleon and Isidoros, the rider on the other side of the wagon, both had trouble controlling their mounts. Even though there was a wagon between the two horses, they were never less than ten feet apart, so the stallions were still keenly aware of each other. Timoleon knew this, and kept trying to quietly nudge his horse, the speedy but hot-tempered Lightning, farther away from the wagon. Unfortunately, Aristides noticed it and ordered him to return to proper formation beside the lead wagon. I rode on fifty yards ahead, and every time I looked back, both Lightning and the other horse, Whirlwind, were looking at each other instead of the road ahead. Blinders wouldn't have helped because they were close enough to smell each other.

Then a hare ran across the road in front of the wagon. It startled both horses, who were already on edge. Lightning reared, and Timoleon managed to stay on him, but Timoleon knew he needed to gallop his mount for a minute or two to calm him down. He'd need to come forward, close to where I was, so I galloped Deathblow farther ahead to maintain a distance between us.

Isidoros was not so lucky. When the hare startled the horses, Whirlwind kicked the front wagon wheel so hard that he broke it. Then he bucked and threw Isidoros, who landed on his back. Whirlwind kicked at the air with his back legs, missed Isidoros' head by inches, then took off, riderless.

"Stop the wagons!" Aristides yelled unnecessarily, as Audax had already done so, as had the wagons behind.

"What kind of inept horsemen have I been saddled with?" Aristides whined, probably unaware of the pun. "Audax, replace that wheel."

Each wagon, luckily, carried a spare wheel. As Audax and one of the other slaves saw to the replacement, I rode back to the wagon, making sure that I avoided Timoleon and Lightning on the way back.

I didn't say *I told you so*. I didn't need to. Aristides glared at me with antarctic hatred.

"Spare me your gloating, Scythian," he said.

"That's not why I'm here, sir," I said. "We need to get that horse back, and if I take Deathblow after him, they'll only fight. While the wheel is replaced, I request permission to take one of the wagon horses."

Aristides told me to go ahead. He decided to make camp here, even though it was late afternoon and we'd still have a good three hours of daylight left after we replaced the wagon wheel and calmed the horses down. We stopped because Isidoros was in bad shape. He didn't break any bones when he landed, but he had a slightly dislocated shoulder, with cuts and bruises on his back. His neck was so sore that he couldn't turn his head more than a few degrees. If we were lucky, he'd be able to ride the next day.

I tied Deathblow's reins to a tree a hundred yards away from the road and hobbled him. I then came back to the wagon, took the mare, and retrieved Whirlwind easily. The mare wasn't in heat, but Whirlwind still liked being close to her. We found him a half mile up the road, drinking water from a small pond. He caught the mare's scent and trotted towards us. He was relaxed and nuzzled the mare. I quickly but quietly slipped off the mare and onto Whirlwind's back before he even knew it. As I walked him back to the camp, with the mare following happily, I saw three deer in a meadow on the edge of a small forest. Once we got the horses calmed down again, I'd come back here to hunt. A single deer would provide meat for days.

After I returned Whirlwind and the mare, I galloped Deathblow up the road to the meadow. The areas that the caravan had passed that day were mostly rocky with no good hunting in sight.

In riding ahead to the meadow, I'd made a big mistake—I was on a part of the road we hadn't travelled yet. The hunting would be better here, but not just for me.

I was a quarter of a mile away from help.

I tied Deathblow's reins to a tree. His ears flickered and he snorted. He jerked his head back a few times. He was agitated. I thought it was because he'd smelled or seen the deer. I would gallop him again after I'd gotten one.

I was crouched behind a bush. I spotted the deer. There were now six of them, upwind and in bow range. I had an arrow nocked, and just as I was about to raise the bow to shoot, a gruff voice spoke.

"Whoa right there, boy," the voice said. Two horsemen came up from a thicket in front of me and stood in front of Deathblow, who now whinnied in rage. The deer fled.

"Don't fight us, sonny," said one of the horsemen, a gaunt older man with matted hair and a filthy beard. His smile had more gaps than teeth. His leather corselet must have been twenty years old. "Give us your bow and your sword, and maybe we won't string you up by the nuts."

"What about the horse?" said the man beside him.

"Yup, we'll take that too," said the older man with a cackle. "If we can't train it or sell it, we'll just eat it." Both men laughed. There also was laughter behind me, at least two more men.

I didn't move. I stayed crouched. I made the mistake of being here, but these bandits made the mistake of not killing me while they had the chance. They saw me long before I saw them, so it would have been easy.

I cursed myself. We'd seen desperate-looking men on this journey, but always in the distance and never more than two of them. We'd spot them on high hills, far enough away that we didn't worry about them. But I still should have known we were being watched.

I didn't believe they'd be merciful if I handed over my weapons, so that was never a consideration.

While still crouched, I shot an arrow through the older man's chest, then quickly pulled out another arrow—something I'd practiced for hundreds of hours in Scythia—and shot the second man through the neck. When he toppled to the ground, his horse took off, as did the older man's mount. Deathblow had spooked them.

Then I untied Deathblow's reins from the tree and was on his back in two blinks. An arrow whizzed past my ear. I did not intend to fight the men behind me. They had at least one bow and would kill me pretty easily if I turned around to face them. So I spurred Deathblow to a gallop. He could easily outrun the bandits' skinny nags. He'd just sprinted, but his blood was up, so he charged like the magnificent gods-blessed creature that he was.

Except he did not run in the direction I commanded him to.

He turned around one hundred and eighty degrees, with a quickness I never imagined possible for a big horse, then he charged at the other two bandits.

I have never before told this to another living soul, Ephander. Almost everyone in the caravan would swear afterwards that I was truly heroic that day, but the truth is that I lost control of my horse. Deathblow was no ordinary creature, but he, not I, dictated the actions that followed. On the Sea of Grass, this would be the ultimate disgrace. A Scythian warrior who lost control of his mount would be humiliated. His woman wouldn't sleep with him for days afterwards, and it would take years for him to live it down, if he lived it down at all. *Ord-darg* they would call him, horse's bitch. In the Scythians' minds, you never ride a horse into battle unless you're absolutely, completely, one hundred percent certain you can control him in all situations.

Deathblow shrieked his rage and almost threw me when he reared up. He didn't give a shit about the men with the weapons. It was their horses he hated. He was territorial, and these scrawny nags were in his space. The two remaining bandits fought to control their panicked mounts. Deathblow charged and bit the ear off one of the horses.

Consider this, Ephander: horse teeth are dull, meant for grinding fodder, not for tearing meat, so Deathblow must've had some massively powerful jaws to take another horse's ear clean off like that. The rider was so concerned with his own horse, all frothing panic and blood and pain, that he didn't even raise his sword to me, so he was helpless as the Sword of Oiorpata hacked his head off with a single swipe. A gout of blood spurted from his neck before the headless body fell to the ground and the panicked horse bolted up the road.

Deathblow, now with horse blood on his muzzle, turned to the final horse and reared up again, using his front hooves to punch the air in front of the other horse's face, just like an Olympic boxer practicing on a punching bag. The Scythians must have taught him this, because it's not something horses do naturally. The other horse screeched in blind terror, then turned and ran. As it turned, the rider fell off, but one of his hands was tangled in the reins. The horse dragged him as it ran, as the man's screams increased the horse's panic. The gravel and stone on the road first shredded the man's thin leather corselet and then the skin beneath it. Even from a distance, I could see that he left a trail of blood. After the horse had dragged him a quarter mile, the screaming stopped. Whether the man had died, or if the reins had just snapped, we never found out.

Deathblow, satisfied that his work was done, was calm now. I had an apple in my pocket, which I gave to him. He accepted it gladly and walked calmly back to the caravan. If horses purred, he would have done so now.

"Holy fuck," said Timoleon when I reached the camp. "I'm sorry I wasn't close enough to help you—but I'm not sorry to have seen *that*! Four of 'em!"

"I've seen Elektros fight before," said Simeon, "so I'm less surprised than you, Timoleon. I'm still impressed, though."

"Do you know about that?" asked Timoleon as he pointed at Deathblow's right haunch. An arrow was stuck there. Blood had run down his entire leg. It's probably what enraged him.

I dismounted and quickly pulled the arrow out, which luckily had not gone in too deep. Deathblow flinched a little but did not otherwise react.

Before I'd even asked for it, Audax brought me a small vial with a salve for Deathblow's wound.

"Thanks, Audax," I said. "Now stand clear. This salve will sting a little, and you know what Deathblow is like." Audax bowed and quickly moved away.

I gently put the salve on the wound and waited for Deathblow's fierce reaction. He didn't even twitch. He bore the pain like he'd taken a hundred battle wounds in his life and understood that pain was part of war, and that it was always necessary to disinfect wounds.

I'd never seen him calmer.

This was a warrior.

Just as some men are born to war and are never truly content during peacetime, so Deathblow craved combat. He should've been on the Sea of Grass, where he'd be ridden into battle regularly, not here in Athens where he almost never got to fight. Deathblow would want to fight again tomorrow, and possibly even later today. It's hard to know for sure what a horse thinks, but I truly believe that Deathblow, like a Spartan, craved battle more than he feared death. Regardless of where he came from, he was, at heart, a Scythian.

Aristides was miffed, of course. Miffed was his natural state. "Did I authorize any of you," he said, as I brushed down Deathblow, "to engage with the locals?"

He actually spoke not to me but to Timoleon, who stood next to me. As the guard commander, Timoleon was, in Aristides' eyes, responsible for my actions.

I just shook my head and went back to brushing Deathblow.

"Beg pardon, sir," said Timoleon, "but the locals engaged with *him*. They were going to kill him."

"You don't know that," said Aristides. "Did Elektros even attempt to negotiate with those men?"

"Sir, they were brigands," said Timoleon. "Negotiation was never an option."

"Elektros may have just drawn us into a blood feud," said Aristides. "Did you even think of that? Every bandit in the hills will be on us now."

Aristides, yet again, showed how little he knew of men and the world around him. If any other bandits saw what had just happened, they would now be *less* likely to tangle with us.

"Well, I suppose it's possible," said Timoleon, "but there aren't many more bandits around, certainly no large groups of them. If there were, sir, they would've attacked us long before now. We've been in the middle of nowhere for two days. We've passed a dozen places where they could have ambushed us."

"How can you be so sure?" said Aristides.

"They waited until Elektros was alone, sir, before they approached him."

"When we reach the next town," said Aristides, "none of us is to speak of this. The bandits may have relatives there."

"Understood, sir," said Timoleon, "but it's more likely that Elektros just did the townsfolk a huge favour."

"You will reprimand him," said Aristides.

"Are you serious, sir?" said Timoleon.

"I am," said Aristides. "He acted without orders. Twenty lashes would be appropriate."

"I'll do no such thing, sir," said Timoleon. "If he'd waited for orders, he'd be dead, and the bandits would stalk us for the rest of this journey."

"Then if you're not man enough to give the lashes," said Aristides, his face red from trying to maintain his patrician self-control, "then I'll do it myself."

I hadn't intended to speak here—anything I said would only anger Aristides more—but he was no longer being rational.

"We must tell him, Timoleon," I said.

Aristides turned on me, eyes wide and rage-crazed. "Who told you to speak?" he blurted. "And what must you tell me?"

"You can't command us, sir," said Timoleon, "because we don't actually work for you."

"What nonsense do you speak?" said Aristides. "I

command this delegation."

"You do, sir," said Timoleon, "but the four horsemen, and the horses they ride, are not officially part of the delegation. Athens only provided you with four guards and eight wagon-horses."

Aristides just gawked at us. He wasn't a total fool, despite all the times on this journey he'd acted like one. He stared at Timoleon and me with confusion and a fire-brick fury that changed, in only a few moments, to sudden realization.

"Themistocles," he said. "Themistocles hired you."

"True, sir," I said. I still called him *sir* to preserve his dignity and pride. "He felt that this delegation was too important to have only four guards. So he paid for the extra men and horses out of his own pocket."

"Why didn't he ask the treasurer to supply more?" said Aristides. "He could have persuaded them—never mind, I just figured it out. He wanted his own men on this journey."

Like I said, Aristides wasn't a fool unless he chose to be.

"True, sir," said Timoleon.

"Who else knows about this?" Aristides asked.

"Just the mounted guards, sir," I said, "and now you. The plan was to not tell anyone, not even you, unless it was absolutely necessary. You gave us an order that we cannot obey, so we had to tell you."

"Regardless of who pays us, sir," said Timoleon, "we still consider it an honour to guard you on this journey."

"Out of the question," said Aristides. "You were not chosen for this delegation, so you cannot be part of it." In an instant, he'd gone back to being a fool. Hadn't the incident with the bandits just proven to him that this road was potentially dangerous? We weren't even a quarter of the way to Delphi yet.

The next day, and for the rest of the journey, we four horsemen continued to guard Aristides as he pretended we weren't there. Two of us rode ahead of the caravan, the other two behind. When the caravan camped, or stopped for a midday rest, we did too. In the evening, two of us pitched a tent in front of the caravan and the other two put their tent behind it. We posted sentries throughout the night, as if we were still on official duty.

Timoleon and I rode ahead of the delegation, keeping our horses a safe distance apart, while Isidoros and Doryssos rode behind. The slow pace of the wagons suited Isidoros, who was still in significant pain but never complained of it, even though he still could not get on or off of his horse without help, and slept poorly from the pain.

We were no longer allowed food or drink from the delegation's supplies. I expected no less from Aristides, but we four horsemen actually ate better than the delegation did. While they ate salted meat, hard bread, and dried fruit, we horsemen had fresh meat and fish every night, and we bought bread and fresh fruit whenever we passed through a village. In fact, we had a surplus most nights. Doryssos and I hunted every evening. Isidoros, despite his bruises, remained adept at setting snares, and always caught us a bird or two. We camped near creeks or streams, and Timoleon almost always caught us a brown trout or a gudgeon to roast. Aberkios, Kaletor, and Simeon joined us at our fire every night. Aristides had initially tried to forbid this, but he eventually recognized that he did not have the authority to control who the three men socialized with. The four other guardsmen, the ones who rode on the wagons, also joined us, but they had rotating sentry duty so we never had more than two of them with us at any time. This really burned Aristides' arse. He considered them disloyal, but also knew there was nothing he could do to stop them when they weren't actually on duty.

Two days after we'd revealed to Aristides the big secret, Audax appeared at our fire. He looked scared.

"He figured it out, sirs," he said.

"Surprised it took him so long," said Timoleon.

We gave Audax some of the rabbit we'd just roasted. His eyes widened and he literally drooled a little. He'd smelled the meat from our cook-fires every night. Aristides wouldn't let him eat any, even though we had plenty and had offered it. It must have been torture for Audax and the other slaves. Aristides fed them boiled beans and hard bread, and had a strict notion of what a slave's rations should be every day, exactly two-thirds of what he himself ate—and he never ate that much. His slaves were always hungry, even after they'd just eaten.

Simeon was with us and asked what we were talking about. "When Audax leased the horses," I said, "he'd only been authorized to get eight horses to pull four wagons. To get the extra four horses, he had to use money that was given to him by one of Themistocles' men. Aristides would never have allowed this, so he wasn't told about it. When Aristides figured it out, he immediately dismissed Audax from his service."

Aristides called Audax a traitor and refused to utter his name, or allow it to be spoken in his presence, to the end of his days. Audax was lucky he wasn't flogged.

"He may change his mind," I told Audax. It had not been a formal manumission, so Aristides could legally reclaim Audax at any time. "So don't do anything else that he can call treachery, and don't tell us anything he wouldn't want you to reveal."

"I know one thing for certain, sir," said Audax. "My master—that is, my former master—will *not* change his mind. He never changes his mind about anything."

"So you're a free man," said Timoleon. "Congratulations!"

Audax did not jump for joy. He forced a smile and a thank you, but he was now homeless and penniless. He didn't even have sandals. Aristides claimed them as his property and took them before he sent Audax away. He didn't take Audax's coarse grey slave's tunic from him, because he didn't feel it was right to send a man away naked, but he told Audax that he wanted it back later.

For the moment, Audax tore enthusiastically through the rabbit meat, and gladly took the second helping we offered him.

Fear and uncertainty never left his eyes. I'd seen this before. There were two older slaves in my father's house, Ergos and Adina, that my father once offered to manumit. Ergos and Adina considered it a punishment, not a reward. Freedom was the frightening unknown to them. They'd been slaves for so long that they didn't know how to live free. They thought they'd end up as beggars. They wept, and not tears of joy, so Father quickly rescinded the manumission offer.

"You can stay with us for the rest of the journey," said Timoleon. "And the return, of course."

"Do you have anywhere to go," I asked, "when we get back to Athens?"

"No, sir," said Audax. He was past fifty, younger than Ergos and Adina had been, but he'd been a slave since he was a boy. He had no family in Athens. His only options were probably beggary or to become someone else's slave.

"Then I'll find you a place somewhere," I said. "We'll get you some sandals, and your own tunic, in the next town."

"You are most kind, sir," said Audax.

"Would you like to learn how to ride a horse?" I asked him.

Audax went white. "No, sir," he said quickly. "The way the big one looks at me, I'm glad horses aren't carnivorous." Timoleon and I laughed. Audax did not.

We continued to unofficially guard the delegation for the rest of the journey. We tried several times to make peace with Aristides, but he would not even speak to us.

When we were a day away from Delphi, we met two horsemen on the road headed in the direction of Athens. When they got close, I recognized Carneades and Nomion, the two men Themistocles had assigned to guard me after I'd been stabbed.

As soon as I saw them, I knew why they'd gone to Delphi. Aristides, of course, missed it.

"I'm getting married in the spring," said Nomion, when Aristides asked him why he'd been to Delphi. "I had some free time, so I sought the Pythia's advice."

Aristides actually believed this.

When we finally arrived at the village of Delphi, we were almost swarmed by peddlers, mostly charlatans who tried to sell us mangy sacrificial goats or badly rendered statuettes of Apollo. But Deathblow, who had been unusually well-behaved since the incident with the bandits, reared up and shrieked at one of the peddlers, who literally pissed himself, then ran away as fast as his fat wet legs would carry him. The others backed away and didn't bother us again.

I was really starting to love this horse. When we got back to Athens, I would buy him from Phylo.

There were a lot of tourists in Delphi, mostly affluent people. The shrine is sacred to all Hellenes, so visitors come from as far away as Sikelia and Sinope. Aristides was told when he arrived that it would be at least four days before he could see the Pythia.

He was willing to wait. I wasn't. I asked myself, what would Themistocles do?

I went to the shrine alone, paid off the priests who manned the doorway to the shrine, and payed them extra to tell Aristides that he was being advanced to the front of the line because of the blessed importance of his mission. Themistocles had given me money for exactly this purpose. The priests sent a slave to tell Aristides that the Pythia would see him later that afternoon. We never told Aristides the truth. If we did, he would have insisted on waiting the four days.

Aristides still had four guards, the ones who rode in the wagons, and two of them accompanied him to the entrance of the shrine. Armed men were not allowed to enter, so they waited at the doorway while Aristides visited the Pythia. He did not allow Simeon, Aberkios and Kaletor to accompany him inside. They would have been permitted, but Aristides claimed that he alone had been chosen for this mission, so he alone must hear the Oracle's words. This was nonsense, of course. He was just being spiteful because on the journey here Simeon, Aberkios and Kaletor had joined the horsemen's fire every night. Aristides said he would reveal the words of the Oracle to them afterwards.

Then when he came away from the Pythia, he refused to speak. He looked stricken. In fact, he did not speak, apart from terse commands to the slaves, for most of the journey home.

7—AEGINETES

"Put the knife down, Parthenia," I said. We were in a room in a dockside inn, a shit-hole with walls so porous you felt the wind blow through them.

Parthenia often told me that what we had together was a bit of fun, nothing serious, and that it would end when she needed it to. I accepted this, but I also thought it meant it might end if *I* needed it to. I'd just told her that Themistocles had ordered me to stay away from her, and she didn't say anything. She just pulled out her knife.

"I said, put the fucking knife down!"

"Okay," she said. She remained tensed up, so I wasn't fooled when she pretended to put the knife down on the bedside table, then suddenly flung it at me. I'd taught her how to use the knife to defend herself, but she ignored the first thing I told her, which was *never throw your knife*. If you do, you won't incapacitate your attacker, you end up weaponless, and if your attacker is weaponless, you've just given him your knife. The exception to that advice would be only if she practiced and practiced and practiced her knife-throwing until she was absolutely certain she could incapacitate her opponent on the first throw. She never did that, of course, and when the knife came at my face, I blocked it easily with my forearm. The knife clattered harmlessly to the floor.

The water jug was next. She grabbed it and flung it at my head, but I ducked it and it shattered against the wall behind me. Her knife-throwing wasn't good, but she threw things with such determined accuracy that I wondered how often she'd done this before. The next thing she threw was her sandal, and it too came straight for my face, as did the other sandal a few seconds later.

She was now out of things to throw at me, and I thought maybe she would be calm enough to talk about this. Unfortunately, this was true.

"You were never any good anyway," she said. "Most of the time, I just wanted a good hard fuck, and it always took you a half hour to give it to me. You had to do all that kissing and fondling shit first. Kid stuff."

This I knew to be untrue—she enjoyed the fact that I didn't rush things, and we wouldn't have lasted this long if she didn't like it—but it was pointless to argue.

I also knew not to tell her that Hyperion must never know about her and me, because if I did so it would be the first thing she'd say to him when she saw him next.

"Thena, I just—"

"If Themistocles told you to suck his dick, would you do it?"

"Come on, Thena, you knew as well as I did that you and I were temporary. You said so many times."

The previous night, Themistocles visited my house again. The last time he'd done this, he told me to stop fucking his sister. This time, he told me to stop seeing Parthenia.

"You seem to take a lot of interest," I said, "in where I put the little fella."

He chuckled. "That's because you stick the little guy into places that fall into my sphere of interest."

"How could this possibly interest you, sir? Parthenia and I are consenting adults. Neither of us is related to you, and neither of us is betrothed."

"For now," said Themistocles. "Parthenia will be betrothed soon. I'm negotiating a marriage for her that will make a valuable alliance, one that will help Athens in the coming war." This meant that the groom would be from a powerful family in one of the poleis that had not yet committed to the Hellenic Coalition.

"*You* are negotiating?" I said. "Isn't that Hyperion's responsibility?"

"I do it with his blessing," he said. "I also want Hyperion clear-headed and focused on his upcoming tasks. He can't be distracted because one of his best friends is screwing his sister. It stops now."

Once Themistocles decided on something, you couldn't change his mind with an army of berserker elephants. I'd already planned to meet Parthenia this day, in this shit-hole near the docks, and I told her as soon as I got there.

Seconds later, her knife flew towards my face. When she ran out of things to throw, she wouldn't even look at me.

"Just get the fuck out of my sight," she said. Our dalliance had lasted more than two years. And still—amazingly—Hyperion didn't know about it.

* * * * * * *

Aristides had been back in Athens for a few days and still had said not a word about the divine message. In two days, the Assembly would meet. Only then would Aristides report the Pythia's words.

The day before the Assembly, someone came to my door in the early morning. It was Lampon, one of Themistocles' slaves, who pounded on my door like the hounds of Hades were snapping at his arse. I heard shouting outside, the sounds of running footsteps, sandals slapping cobblestones.

"Master Elektros, sir!" Lampon said. "Please wake up, sir! It's an emergency!"

"Quiet, Lampon," I hissed at him. "You'll cause a panic."

"Beg pardon, sir," he said, "but the panic has already begun."

He was right. The shouts and clatter outside had already gotten louder in the few seconds since Lampon came to my door.

"Is the city under attack?" I asked him.

"Not the city, sir," he said. "The harbour."

"Persians?"

"No, sir. The raiders are Hellenes."

Lots of Hellenes fought for the Persians on land and sea, so an attack might be on the Great King's orders.

"Where's Themistocles?"

"Already at the Phaleron, sir. The Archon wants you down there on the fastest horse you can find."

Themistocles, though not the archon that year, was still called that by his followers. It was significant that he was the one down at the Phaleron dealing with the crisis. He did not have official authority, but the current war archon, Brontes, spoke boldly but in a crisis couldn't find his own arse without a detailed map and someone to read it to him.

I quickly drank some water and ate some cheese and hard bread as Lampon helped me get my armour on. Then I ran to Kleitos' stable to get a horse.

He was outside his front door, expecting me. "I would have picked one for you, sir," he said, "but I know you like to choose your own."

"You are right again, Kleitos," I said as I handed him some coins. "I need a calm one today. The grey gelding, please." Kleitos nodded and went inside to get the horse for me.

A mile from the Phaleron, I could hear the screams, smell the smoke, and I saw what seemed like an early sunrise but was actually the dull glow of burning buildings and burning ships. By the time I reached the harbour, the worst of it was over. Five or six dead men were on the ground in various places. Most of the docks were burnt. Only two remained useable. Two big Scythians, the biggest and toughest men here, knelt weeping beside a third Scythian, dead on the ground. An arrow had hit him in the back, and its head still protruded through his chest. I knew him. Dorak was a good man.

Themistocles stood with a group of about twenty hoplites, all of them in full armour. They were tired and smoke stained. Five buildings had been torched. The hoplites had managed to get those fires out, but now these men looked defeated, too tired to even speak much. Some of the ships still burned, but they were in the water where the fire couldn't spread, and they were all ruined now anyway, so Themistocles and his men just let them burn.

"Who did this?" I asked Themistocles.

"Not the Persians," said Themistocles. "Pirates, probably from Aegina. That's probably where they're headed now."

I could see distant ships as they sailed away. Some of them towed other ships, our ships, which they'd just stolen right out of our harbour. Those ships were lost for good. We couldn't pursue them because we now had no ships.

Sentries always patrolled the Phaleron at night, but only four of them. They could prevent vandalism or theft, but four men could not withstand an organized attack by a fleet of thirty warships.

Themistocles just sat down on the ground, too tired to even speak. He drank from a flask someone passed to him.

Dexicos, one of the men with Themistocles, told me

what had happened. "The ships rolled into the port while it was still dark," he said. "They were almost at our docks before anyone on shore even noticed them. Someone torched a few buildings"—he gestured towards the charred heap of ash that was once Dio's, the Scythians' favourite tavern—"as a diversion, then set fire to the ships. They only burnt ships without cargos. They towed away the ones with cargos loaded."

This was most disturbing of all. In order for them to know which ships had cargos worth stealing, they had someone working for them onshore, probably the same person or persons who torched the buildings.

Dexicos went on to explain that Dorak was on duty here, and had drawn his bow to shoot the captain of one of the raider ships when someone on land shot him in the back. "That guy there," said Dexicos, pointing at a headless naked corpse forty feet away from Dorak and the Scythians. The man's head was missing, tossed to the dogs. His body would be thrown into the sea. In Athens, it was illegal to bury or burn a traitor's body in the city.

Athens had been helpless against this attack. We all felt it.

The next day, that helplessness came out as impotent rage in the Assembly.

"I say we crucify every fucking man, woman, child, dog, chicken, goat, and horse in Aegina. The fuckers deserve no better."

These were the words of Gauanes, a merchant who owned eight of the thirty-four ships that had been either stolen or destroyed in the attack.

Everyone let Gauanes rant. Angry men splutter and blither and fume. Gauanes had not been the first man, nor the last, to rise in the Assembly this day and propose that we turn Aegina into a ghost polis.

We could do no more than let these men vent their anger. In a land battle, Athens could crush Aegina into the ground twenty times over. Athens could raise twenty thousand hoplites ready to fight. Aegina would be lucky to raise a thousand. But Aegina was an island, just across the Saronic Gulf, only twenty miles away, and on clear days, frustratingly visible. It may as well have been a million miles away. Athens did not have ships to transport troops, and the Aeginetes knew it. The Aeginetes always denied that they allowed pirates to use their harbours, but everyone knew that they did. When we sent envoys to ask them to control their pirates, they laughed at us. They'd often preyed on Athenian ships, but this was the first time they'd ever launched a full-scale attack.

This was war.

Even Themistocles' usual enemies could no longer deny that Athens needed warships.

Finally, after the angry men had finished ranting, Themistocles took the floor.

"We will have our revenge," he said. "We will have justice. But I must counsel patience."

This actually drew boos. Helpless rage had made men unreasonable. They were even angrier now than they'd been right after the raid because bread prices had already spiked. The raiders, after they'd ravaged the Phaleron, had captured six grain ships from Sicily that had been headed to Athens.

"You know as well as I do that we can't do anything right now," said Themistocles, scolding like a schoolmaster. "We do not have warships. If we tried to transport troops to Aegina on our remaining merchant ships, the Aeginetes would sink them. We have only four shipyards. If we start building today, it will still take us months to build the ships we need to attack Aegina. Plus we need to train crews."

At this point, Aristides rose. "Themistocles," he said. "Please allow me to speak."

"I have the goddamn floor now, Aristides," said Themistocles. "You'll get your turn."

"True," said Aristides. "But the Oracle is quite relevant to what you now say. Please allow me the floor."

Themistocles stared hard at Aristides, then gave Aristides the floor.

Aristides stood calmly. "My fellow citizens," he said. "The Oracle seems to have known in advance about the attack on our harbour. I must therefore tarry no longer. I will reveal the words of the Pythia now."

Aristides was trained in oratory and had a magnificent speaking voice. This is what he reported:

The savage foe comes
But not like before
Peace means enslavement
Freedom means war
Fight, sons of Pallas
The hour is at hand
If you rule on the water
You'll salvage your lands.

Aristides remained silent for a couple of minutes, just to let the words of the Pythia sink in. "I was commissioned only to report to you the Pythia's words," he finally said, "but I will interpret them for you, if you so desire. May I continue?"

Agreement was unanimous. "Continue, Aristides," said the herald.

"Unlike some oracles we've heard," said Aristides, "this one is not cryptic—so much so that it's almost out of character for an Oracle. This is because the god advises us to act quickly. A clear message will garner less debate amongst us, so we can act on it sooner. 'The savage foe comes, but not like before.' This means that the Great King will invade us again, but he will not try to defeat us solely on land. Last time he brought a supply and transport fleet. This time he will bring a war fleet. He will strangle our sea trade and sink or capture all of our trading ships.

"'Peace means enslavement, freedom means war.' Again, this is clear. If we offer earth and water to the Great King now, he will not show Athenians the mercy he has shown other poleis. He would kill all the men and enslave all the women and children.

"'If you rule on the water, you'll salvage your lands.' With these words, the Pythia practically commands us to build a war fleet. The events of two days ago prove that Persia isn't our only threat from the sea."

Aristides bowed his head, thanked the Assembly for hearing him out, then quietly took his seat at the front with the other aristocrats. Themistocles kept it to himself, but he was very, very happy with Aristides' interpretation of the Oracle because it was almost precisely what he was about to say himself. Despite his popularity and persuasiveness, Themistocles did not have the credibility of Aristides the Just, a man who always told the truth, even when it was politically disadvantageous to do so.

Themistocles hoped he could get the Assembly to agree to build fifty warships. So he was doubly pleased when they shouted down his proposal to build fifty because no less than a hundred would do. The new vein at Laurion, which the engineers had confirmed was a deep one, would pay for them.

Themistocles had planned for years to build ships, so it was only natural for him to take the lead here. Athens would buy lumber from Thessaly, he said, which would be expensive but could be brought to Athens entirely by land—any ships that carried lumber could be taken by the Aeginetes or even the Persians. He had already secured some lumber before the raid, enough for all four Athenian shipyards to get started. He'd found some land on the coast, near the Phaleron, where his two houseguests, the Phoenician shipwrights, had already begun to build a new shipyard. They'd start to build ships in a matter of days.

Finding crews was more difficult. "Where will we possibly get enough slaves to row, row, row your goddamn boats?" Brontes thundered at Themistocles. Brontes was, quite frankly, a loud idiot. He thought of problems but never made any attempt to think of solutions.

"No slaves," said Themistocles. "Slaves will not row any harder than they have to. Wage-earning free men, defending their homeland, make better oarsmen." He then went on to explain how there were thousands of landless and unemployed men in Athens and the surrounding countryside who would be paid oarsmen's wages. The beauty of Themistocles' plan was that his hired oarsmen would not thin the ranks of Athenian hoplites. The oarsmen would be men who could not afford armour and were not of the hoplite class. Freedmen and non-citizens would also be welcome to man the oars.

Themistocles' aristocratic rivals had thought of none of this. They had not planned for this moment, so even they had to look, begrudgingly, to Themistocles for guidance on the subject.

The Assembly then voted to give Themistocles special status as Navarch General, which would enable him to take as much money from the treasury as he needed.

8—MELI

The young man tripped the old woman while his two friends laughed. I recognized her. She sold small wooden statuettes of the Olympian gods in the agora. As she fell, her tray of little statues flew across the ground and the young man grabbed her coin purse.

"Why, thank you, old hag," said the young man. He then grabbed a small cloth sack from her. It contained her evening meal, bread and cheese.

"Please, young sir," she said. "Take my money, if you must. But I'll go hungry if you take my food."

"Too fucking bad," said the young man. He tossed the sack to one of his friends, who caught it, and put the coin purse in the pocket of his tunic—a silk tunic, a sign that he was a rich man's son.

"You young shits," said the old woman, emboldened with rage and with nothing else to lose.

"Shut it, Medusa," said one of the other young men, "or we'll take your cheap-ass little statues too."

A small crowd had gathered. Some people were amused, most were disgusted, but no one did anything. Perhaps Athenians had become so accustomed to letting the Scythians handle these situations that they'd lost the impetus to intervene. No Scythians were nearby at the moment.

The young man who'd tripped the woman was their leader. He had a thick head of black curly hair. They didn't need her money, and they probably wouldn't even eat the food. They'd robbed her because they wanted to and she was there and they figured they'd get away with it.

"I apologize," said the old woman.

"That's more like it," said the curly haired-man.

"I'm not apologizing to you," she said. "I'm apologizing to shit. Because by calling you shit, I have insulted all the shit in the world. You're worse than shit! I could make better men out of steaming lumps of pig dung. Useless, gutless, cowardly lowlifes. Go suck a dead dog's asshole, every one of you!"

She was braver than the three young men. Some in the crowd laughed at her colourful invective, but still no one stepped in. The three young men clearly scared them.

They didn't scare me, though. It was no coincidence that they'd chosen to rough the old lady up when the Scythians weren't around, which, considering their victim, made it doubly gutless. The lady was right, these guys gave shit a bad name. Some behaviour can be excused as the foolishness of youth, but not this purposeless cruelty.

I just happened to be passing by. I'd gone out for a run, followed by a swim in the river. My hair and beard were still damp as I walked back to my house. I wore a light tunic and sandals.

These highborn lowlifes needed a lesson. I had no weapon, but I didn't need one against these lightweights.

"I told you to shut it!" Curly Hair said to the old woman. He pulled his fist back to punch her, but before he threw it, I punched him in the lower back, a kidney shot. He threw his head back in pain, and I kicked his feet out from under him. He fell, then looked up at me, scared now, confused.

"Fucking stay down!" I growled at him, unnecessarily. Xenocrates had taught me the exact spot to land a kidney punch that would cause the most pain and incapacitate your opponent for the longest time. It worked here. Curly Hair wasn't going anywhere for a while.

Then I turned to the other two. They also wore expensive tunics of silk and brushed linen. They advanced towards me. I looked to the one on the right, saw fear in his eyes, even though there were two of them and one of me, then I stomped on the toes of the guy to my left, an old trick. These were bullies, not fighters. As the guy on the left hopped on one foot, the one on the right threw a punch at my head, but he was not used to punching upwards—I was a good six inches taller than him—and I ducked aside. His punch grazed my shoulder. I landed a solid left to his nose, then a right into his ribs. He was still on his feet, but dazed now, helpless. The fight was already over.

Curly Hair was still on the ground. I'd hurt him more than I intended to. Can't say I regretted it.

"Give me the money and the sack," I said to these guys. "Then pick up your heroic friend and get the fuck out of here before I lose my temper. You don't want that."

"You're a metic!" Curly Hair hissed at me between grimaces. "You can't assault citizens. I'll sue your barbarian ass off."

"Well, in that case," I said, "I better just fucking kill you now. In for an obol, in for a drachma, as my grandad used to say."

Curly Hair looked even more scared than he already was. "I've got witnesses!" he blurted.

"Really?" I said. I turned to the crowd. "Anyone here see anything?"

No one would look me in the eye. They were embarrassed because a metic had helped the old woman when they had not, but I now saw that they were women, children, and a couple of old men, people you wouldn't expect to step in against three young thugs. I thought less harshly of them. One old man who walked with a cane said, "I didn't see anything, young sir. In fact, I'm not even here." Then he turned his back on me and Curly Hair. Slowly everyone else did too.

Curly Hair scrambled to his feet, even though it pained him to move, then he and his two friends skedaddled like burnt rats.

I didn't know the old woman's name, although I always said hello when I passed her in the agora. She'd been selling her little figurines in the agora for years. I remembered her from when I first arrived in Athens, before the Battle of Marathon. She carved the figurines herself, out of scrap wood—broken wagon wheels, old spade handles, even shields that had been splintered in battle—then painted them. She wasn't getting rich, but she did well enough to keep at it for many years. She'd never been heavy, but now seemed thinner than usual, frailer. She'd aged a decade in the last two or three years.

"You okay?" I said. She was unhurt, apart from a little swelling on her face where Curly Hair had slapped her. As I handed her the coin-purse and sack of food, someone jumped on my back.

A high voice screeched into my ear. "Asshole! Picking on an old lady! Make you feel like a big man?"

It was a woman. She had her thighs wrapped around my mid-section, one hand around my neck, choking me, as her other hand clawed at my eyes. I grabbed her by the wrists, pried her off me, then swung her around so that I was behind her. As I held her arm behind her back, she tried to butt me in the face with the back of her head. I turned my head down and away to avoid it. If she'd made contact, she would have broken my nose. She knew how to fight.

"Meli!" said the old woman. "Stop! He helped me!"

"But I heard you were being robbed," Meli said. "I saw your purse and your sack in his hand, so I thought it was him."

"No, it was three others," said the old woman. "This

young gentleman drove them off."

The young woman stopped struggling. She was tall and blonde, and very pretty. Her green eyes, wide with rage a moment ago, now narrowed in confusion.

"I will let you go," I said to her, "if you promise not to head butt me again."

She nodded, embarrassed now that she'd attacked me. I let her go.

"I can't thank you enough, young sir," the old woman said as I helped her up. The young woman and I then retrieved her little statues for her.

"It was nothing," I said. "Those were boys, not men."

"My name is Khlöe," said the old woman.

"Elektros," I said.

"How did you learn to fight like that?" asked Khlöe.

"Trained by Xenocrates," I said.

"*Marg Tufan* himself," said the old woman. "I'm impressed."

"And I'm sorry," said the young woman.

"It's okay," I said. "Both of you are spirited. That's a good thing these days." Meli had given me a slight scratch under my left eye that bled a little.

They accepted my offer to walk them home. Meli said she had a salve there to put on my scratch. I wanted to see them off safely, but I won't deny, Ephander, that I was quite interested in Meli. She was a few years older than me and had a scar across her cheekbone that stopped at her nose. It gave her face a rough edge, and there was a hardness in her eyes, but the beauty was still there, enhanced rather than diminished by the scar. The more we chatted, the more I learned that the interest was mutual.

Before the young men accosted Khlöe, Meli had gone to fetch her a vial of 'dream tonic.' The woman who sold it in the agora claimed that it cured arthritis and other chronic afflictions. It consisted of poppy juice, wine, and a few spices to give it an exotic taste, but almost no one, probably not even Khlöe, believed it actually cured anything. It relieved pain but was also highly addictive. The vendor's customers became customers for life.

Both women said they knew of me, though not my name. "You work for Themistocles," said Khlöe.

"You're kind of hard to miss," said Meli. "You have a lot of female admirers in the city, Elektros."

Meli was also hard to miss. She was an inch or two under six feet, the tallest woman I'd seen in Athens, and although Khlöe was hunched over with age now, I could see that at one time she too had been taller than most women. They both had green eyes and the same honey shade of blonde hair, although most of Khlöe's was grey now. The resemblance was clear.

When I commented on Meli's height, and how it made her even more beautiful, she smiled and said, "Thank you. It runs in the family. Phye was my great-grandmother."

Phye.

Phye?

Phye!

I stopped walking. Hera's tits, Ephander, I almost stopped breathing. Kandra had claimed that the legendary Phye was her great-grandmother. Both of these women resembled Kandra a little. Same eyes. Same height. Same natural regality.

When I finally regained my composure, I asked Khlöe if she had another daughter.

"No," she said. "Just the one daughter. I had a son, but he's gone now." That made her sad, so I dropped the subject.

I liked the way Meli looked at me. When we reached the small house they rented in the Ceramicus, the potters' quarter, she ran inside and soon came back with a smile and a vial of a chamomile ointment. She used a clean cloth to clean to gently dab the ointment on the scratch on my cheek. She leaned in close to me and smelled of asphodels. She was quite comfortable with a big half-Scythian right next to her. I wanted to stay, but Themistocles expected me at his house that evening—he'd invited me to a dinner party as a guest, not a guard, a rare invitation only a fool would miss. So I bid the ladies good night. Khlöe shook my hand. Meli kissed me on the cheek.

I called on Meli the next day. She was glad to see me. We went horseback riding outside the city. I rented the horses from Phylo, or tried to. He wouldn't take my money. He also greeted Meli by name. Meli means 'honey,' but Phylo called her Melicheilia, 'honey lips,' a name that advertised an erotic specialty. It was a whore's name. I expected her to take offense, but she did not. She greeted Phylo with a little hug and a kiss on the cheek.

As his liveryman fetched the horses, Phylo took me aside, just out of Meli's hearing. "She's a beauty," he said. "Gonna marry her?"

"I met her yesterday," I laughed. "Let's not get ahead of ourselves here."

"Just asking," said Phylo. "I know you. When you have a girlfriend, you always want her to be your wife."

He was right, of course. "Wouldn't rule it out," I said. "Too early to say, though."

"She's still a prostitute sometimes, you know," he said. "She's been with a lot of men in the city. As far as I know, she's good-hearted, but she'll never be respectable. Don't get angry, I just wanted you to know."

I didn't get angry because I already knew. When we'd walked from Meli's house to Phylo's stable, some of the women who passed us gave her black looks, the angry glares they reserve for whores and traitors. Several men looked like they wanted to say something lewd, but stayed their tongues when I looked them in the eye.

I still liked Meli's eyes on me, and mine on her. Whatever would happen would happen. Neither of us had mentioned money, but it was possible that she considered me a customer rather than a man who was interested in her. Overall, though, her respectability, or lack thereof, didn't concern me, because Athenians didn't consider me respectable either. This may be why I never insisted on it in others. Good-heartedness was more important to me. Some 'respectable' men were cruel assholes, and I knew 'respectable' women who were just horrendous to people. Respectability was illusory and superficial, and didn't truly define character, so it never counted much for me.

Meli had ridden before. It had been a few years, so she was out of practice, but she still wasn't half bad as a rider. She knew that you must let the horse know who's in charge, but also that you must do it without cruelty. You wanted the horse to respect rather than hate you. She mounted her pony quickly and firmly.

We rode steppe ponies, which I'd convinced Phylo to acquire. They were small, slow, and bug-eyed, and their looks impressed no one, but Phylo thanked me for the advice because they were hardy and calm, and the best horses for inexperienced riders, or for one who was rusty.

I taught Meli a few things about riding. When we stopped in a secluded spot for a picnic, she taught me a few things about a different kind of riding. Sorry, Ephander, no details, you dirty bugger.

Before we became lovers, Meli had two conditions. "You will be honest with me," she said. "And you will not judge me."

Those were fair. I agreed to them if she would also be honest and non-judgmental towards me. She'd been with a lot of men. Athenian society did not forgive that in a woman, although it was perfectly acceptable for an unmarried man to rut with any man, woman or beast who would have him, and only slightly less acceptable for a married man to do so. I was not Athenian, I told her, I was from a small island where a woman's character was more important than her past. I was slave-born and half Scythian, so her lack of respectability could hardly be worse than mine. It wasn't my nature to judge people based on circumstances of their births or the vagaries of where their lives had taken them. I was, however, extremely judgmental towards aristocrats who behaved like gutter rats but still claimed themselves virtuous because of their high birth. Meli was glad to hear that.

We had a magnificent afternoon, and several equally magnificent evenings afterwards. Besides being beautiful, Meli was intelligent and easy-going company. Her experience as a lover, far more extensive than mine, was a new education for me. Within a few days, she began to greet me at my door at the end of a long day and stay until morning, although she didn't technically live with me. I worried that Khlöe was left alone at night. Meli said no, Khlöe had a man of her own, a good man close to her own age who doted on her. Khlöe had taken to her bed by that time. She would not leave it again.

We each spoke of our pasts. We'd both had our share of heartache. We'd both met the loves of our lives and lost them. When Meli was nineteen, she married a handsome and charming soldier named Kalliaros who planned to settle down with her in Athens. He apprenticed to a potter and tried to learn the trade, but he absolutely hated it. He had no knack for it, he told her, and soon began to hate his employer. After a few months, he quit pottery and was hired as a mercenary. Soldiering, he said, was truer to his nature than pottery could ever be.

As much as he loved her, he had to leave Athens. Meli

decided to go with him.

It wasn't unheard of. Many mercenaries had camp wives, although they were usually widowed or displaced women they'd met in the areas where they fought, and who often had nowhere else to go. Kalliaros wasn't thrilled by the idea—finding new women was the best part of the soldier's life, and he'd have to limit this if his wife was around—but Meli was determined to go, so he accepted it. She also thought that if she didn't like that life, she could just return to Athens and start over. She was young, beautiful, smart. She'd survive, and whatever happened, it would be an adventure. In Athens, to supplement Kalliaros' apprentice wages, she'd been doing people's laundry for a pittance. The lot of a mercenary's wife, she figured, couldn't have been a whole lot worse.

This I understood. Kalliaros I also understood. At one time, I too had the same strong desire for adventure.

Long story short, Ephander: they travelled to Sikelia, where Kalliaros joined the armies of King Gelon in his war against the Carthaginians. Gelon's forces came from all over, but much of Sikelia was Hellenic, so Hellenic was the language used in the army, which had literally thousands of men from mainland Hellas. Gelon paid well. For more than a year, Kalliaros fought for Gelon, who expanded his forces constantly and soon dominated Sikelia. Meli and Kalliaros were together every night, except when he was on guard duty. But Meli found the life dull. Camp wives had little to do other than pack up their tents to move with the army and be ready to greet their men at night. She didn't plan to do this forever. Kalliaros made so much money, with occasional plundered gold and jewelry to go with his wages, that they'd have enough in another year to buy a farm. This was Kalliaros' stated plan. He understood that the mercenary life wasn't a permanent one. Meli knew nothing about being a farm wife but would learn. It was a realistic plan. It would work.

Then Kalliaros died.

Gelon's army conquered Syracuse easily. His forces were so superior that the city surrendered in a matter of hours, with almost no fighting. Kalliaros actually died after the battle. While on sentry duty, he stumbled off the city wall in the dark and fell to his death.

Meli was jolted but determined to live on. As the widow, she tried to collect her husband's unpaid wages, only to find that the paymaster had no record of Kalliaros ever having married. Camp wives were not considered legal wives and had no spousal inheritance rights. She and Kalliaros had been legally married in Athens, but Kalliaros had never informed the army. He'd also gambled away all of the extra money he'd earned from plunder. He told her that he'd banked it but would never go into details. The army had a banking system, which would hold money for soldiers so they didn't have to carry it around with them, but Kalliaros never used it. Now Meli had no money, no family, no trade, and no man to protect her in a strange land.

She did the only thing she could do. She became a whore.

"You will not judge me for this," she said as we lay in each other's arm one night, "because you would never be in that situation. You're a swordsman. If you were penniless and hungry in a foreign land, someone would take one look at you and hire you as a soldier. I became a whore because my only other option was camp wife. A camp wife ends up with any man who will have her. If her man dies, or leaves, she is without protection of any kind. She can be raped, beaten, or killed with impunity. When a soldier retires, he almost never takes his camp wife back home with him. As a whore, I could at least choose my clients. I went for officers because I was pretty enough to charge prices only they could afford. Most of my men treated me well. One did not. This," she said, indicating her scar, "came from a man who was Gelon's cousin. He sliced me simply because he could. I screamed. I bled. I thought he was going to cut me up, but he just laughed and said, 'You're damaged goods now, girl. Next time you give me a blowjob, you can only charge me half as much.' There was nothing I could do about it."

I touched her scar. "It gives your face its own personality," I said. "And it doesn't ruin your looks. In fact, I kind of like it."

"You are kind," she said.

"I am honest," I replied.

She knew she had to leave Sikelia. The scar became infected and the infection had spread to her eye, which she had to cover with an eyepatch. The eye eventually healed, but no one would pay top dollar for her anymore. This made her just another camp whore. She had enough money now to get back to Athens, but not much more. She'd hoped to make enough to start a business or buy a shop in Athens—she had some skill as a seamstress, and planned to buy and sell imported textiles—but she knew she had to get out of Sikelia while she could. She'd been gone less than three years. The first thing she learned when she returned to Athens was that her mother had died.

A tear rolled down one cheek. I held her close to me, kissed her tears, tried to kiss her pain away.

She wanted me to tell her about my own mother. I'd begun to describe how Roxella Oiorpata had been attacked by four men, and how she had killed three of them and injured the fourth, but then I stopped cold.

"Wait a minute," I said. "Your mother *died?* So Khlöe

isn't your mother?"

"No," she said. "People assume she is because of the resemblance. She's my aunt."

Phye was my great-grandmother.

"She said she had 'just the one daughter,'" I said. "What was the daughter's name?"

"She doesn't speak of her much, but I've heard her weep about 'my Kannie.' Her father seized her from Khlöe a few months after she was born."

"Was the father Simonides?"

"Yes. How did you know that?"

"I've met Simonides many times," I said. "Kandra was the woman I lost."

"*Was*? She no longer lives?"

"She lives," I said. "In Scythia, last I heard."

Meli knew I'd been to Scythia, but she had no idea I'd taken Kandra, the cousin she'd never met, with me. So I told her the story. I left out the most disturbing parts.

Even so, Meli cried when my story was done. I did too.

*   *   *   *   *   *   *

"I am old, Elektros, sick, and not long for this world," Khlöe said, her voice a delicate rasp, her face grey as death. "I'm barely here. When you first arrived today, I'd forgotten your name, although it came back to me after a minute. I'm addle-headed from opium and pain. My vision blurs, my hearing is weak. I cannot walk, cannot sing. I can barely speak. My thoughts crash into one another, like horses on fire, panicky and terror-stricken.

'But I was once the highest paid hetaera in Athens. I

know men. I've seen them at their best and at their worst and at all points in between. Even now, as I lay here in death's dark shadow, I can read a man's face the instant I see it. I know immediately if he is a good man or evil, a kind man or cruel, a gentleman or a brute. I know if he tries to conceal his fear, or if he has dangerous thoughts and *I* should be the one afraid.

"*And I know when a man is lying.* Now tell me the *truth* about my daughter, or I swear by all the gods my shade will haunt you to your grave. And beyond!"

I'd wanted to spare her the sad parts of Kandra's life, so I told her a half-truth, that Kandra was married to a good man in Halicarnassus. It was true at one time, and I figured Khlöe would have no choice but to believe me. It's not like she could disprove it. But all I did here was prove once again how poor a liar I am. I can't even tell a half-truth to a half-blind old woman on her deathbed.

From this moment on, I would omit a few things but tell no more lies to Khlöe.

I would not tell her that Kandra had been raped on Skiathos by four men. This would only add to a dying woman's despair, even though she might be pleased to hear that within a year, Kandra had hunted down and killed each of the four men.

I told Khlöe that I had asked Kandra's father to let me marry her. He said I'd been a good friend to her and he'd consider it, and that he'd talk to my father about it. He never did, though. He'd sent Kandra off to an arranged marriage far, far away, without a word to anyone.

"If you knew that Keossian cocksucker like I did," she said, "you'd've known not to believe him." When she spoke of Simonides, her voice was suddenly clear. Anger gave it strength, if only for a few moments.

"Please, tell me more," she said, her voice again a raspy whisper thin as dragonfly wings.

I told her that Simonides had betrothed Kandra to a nice older man in Halicarnassus, a wealthy widower. Kandra quite liked the man and was happier with him than she ever expected to be. Then the man died suddenly, and his deranged son claimed her as his wife. He had no legal right to do so, but he was wealthy enough to ignore inconvenient laws. Kandra also had nowhere else to go. She couldn't return to her father because no one knew where he was.

Khlöe groaned when I told her that. "Typical," she muttered.

The son, Kratisto, kept her under guard night and day, and had even sliced her Achilles' tendon so she couldn't run away. She wrote to me to ask for help. When the letter eventually reached me in Athens, I went to Halicarnassus and infiltrated the household of Kratisto as one of his bodyguards. Kandra and I devised a plot to murder Kratisto during a festival, when the city watch would have thousands of drunks on their hands and it would be easier for us to sneak out of the city. We didn't kill Kratisto, but only because someone else beat us to it. Yet we knew we'd be blamed for it, and Kratisto's sister, who hated him as much as anyone, offered, for appearances' sake, a huge reward for our capture. So we decided to go to Scythia, where bounty hunters were less likely to follow us. I had relatives there. She was there, alive and well, the last time I saw her.

"Scythia!" she said. "You took my Kannie to the Sea of Grass—*and you left her there?!?*"

"Not willingly," I said. "I had to leave Scythia. I asked Kandra to come with me. She refused. I would have had to chain her to a wagon. I didn't even have a wagon. Or a chain."

"She left you?"

I nodded, tears in my eyes. "She had a very powerful protector there," I said.

"Well, what do you expect?" said Khlöe. "You were screwing those Scythian girls. Island boy meets these wild barbarian women, I'm not surprised she found another man."

"That's not even close to the truth!" I said. "You may be dying, but that doesn't mean you can say that kind of shit to me! I wasn't screwing anybody! Not even Kandra." I was on my feet, didn't remember rising.

"Okay, I'm sorry, I'm sorry," she said. "Please sit down. That's what most young men in that situation would do. I know men, but I never claimed infallibility."

"Well, you're way off here," I said. "I said Kandra had a powerful protector. I did not say it was a man."

Now Khlöe didn't know what to say and just gawked at me with her mouth open.

"Tabiri was a powerful warrior," I went on, "like the Amazons of legend. In Scythia, some women fight. I could have challenged Tabiri, but even if I won, I would not have ended up with Kandra. She did not want to be with a man anymore. And Tabiri probably would have killed me."

"A fighter like you? Defeated by a woman?"

"I am considered an elite fighter in Hellas, but to the Scythians, I'm barely adequate, with the exception of my sword work. They tolerated me because I rode into battle with them. I was their worst horseman, but to the Scythians, I showed courage, which they prize above all. But I would have stood no chance in a duel against Tabiri."

Khlöe was silent now, tears in her eyes. "This

Kratisto," she finally said. "What did he do to put her off men?

"Apart from the cut Achilles' tendon, I don't know," I said. "She wouldn't tell me. It must have been horrible, though. She had nightmares about it."

Khlöe sobbed, and Faenus came running into the room. He was Khlöe's faithful freedman, who looked after her.

"What in Hades are you saying to her?" he said. He was a sad-faced older man whose hair was trying to evacuate his head.

"It's okay, Faenus," she said. "He's telling me about my Kannie. I insisted that he tell me everything." Once Faenus saw that she was okay, he left the room.

"So far, I've told you mostly bad things," I said. "Now I'll tell you good things. There are many."

I told Khlöe how, when we were fourteen years old, Kandra once tricked me into thinking she couldn't run, then beat me in a foot race, even though I was the fastest runner on Skiathos, and how my brother then arranged for her to run against the boys at the Artemisia, a race which she also won. Khlöe had tears in her eyes again, happy ones this time.

"I ran well as a girl, too," she rasped, her voice weak now.

I told her about how Kandra was tall and strong and beautiful and intelligent. "And witty," I said. "I can't tell you how many times she made me laugh."

I told her that I'd taught Kandra to read and write, and that she was determined to learn everything about herblore. Her father taught her a little but she learned more on her own. Any time we encountered a healer, Kandra would ask many questions about medicinal herbs. She never wrote any of it down but always remembered it. Her mind was keen, her body strong, her face a vision. The Scythians, who ordinarily consider Hellene women to be good for only one thing, were impressed by her skills as a healer, although Kandra herself thought her medical education was far from complete.

"She'd also learned the Scythian language," I said, "before we ever got there. My aunt Gia, also a healer, became her mentor. And that's even better than it sounds, because it means Gia's brother, my Uncle Borysthenes, who is almost seven feet tall and a leading nobleman, will consider it an affront if anyone mistreats Kandra. So you do not need to worry about Kandra's safety in Scythia."

I didn't tell Khlöe that I counted on Borysthenes' protection more than Tabiri's, because Tabiri never stayed with one woman for a long time.

Now I was teary too. These reminiscences of Kandra tired me, more than running did, more than battle. Khlöe looked worn out, even more than usual, so I ended the conversation. Before I left, she clasped my hand, her flesh cold as death but her grip surprisingly strong.

"Thank you," she said. "My girl had a hard life. There are things you do not tell me, but now I can die knowing that my Kannie became a woman of honour, someone I can be proud of. And I know this wasn't easy for you."

Khlöe slept. Meli, who'd been in the next room, came in and sat beside the bed. I offered to stay, too, but she insisted I go back home. So I did, slept all night, rare for me. When I awoke, Meli was beside me. She didn't wake me when she arrived.

"Thank you," she said softly.
"For what?" I said.

"For answering Khlöe's final question. She can die in peace now."

For a moment, I considered the idea of taking Khlöe to Scythia so she could meet her daughter. Why not? Athens wasn't my city, and the Persians would still be around when I got back. Then I immediately saw the impossibility. Khlöe could not travel anymore. Even if she lived long enough for a months-long journey, the journey itself would probably kill her. In fact, any day now could be her last.

9—PHAEDRA

As the men who thought themselves important had decided that Athens must build warships, Phaedra made soup.

She made money, too. Her soup was so popular that when she and Mnesiphilos took their two amphorae to the agora every day, they sold out in minutes. Several upper-class women had even hired her to make some for their private parties, and paid her well for it.

Did I mention this before, Ephander? Phaedra was married now.

The day before I'd left for Delphi, I came home in the afternoon and heard a man's moans of pleasure. They came from the direction of Phaedra's room. I did not hesitate for a moment. I burst into her room, sword drawn, ready to kill whoever was raping her, but the look on her face was purest ecstasy, or at least it was until she realized I was in the room. She was on her back, naked, on the bed. A flabby naked man thrust furiously between her legs, which were wrapped around his lower back. She'd been moaning too. I didn't hear it at first because the man's moans had drowned hers out.

The man was Mnesiphilos, of course. His pasty arse-flesh, his hairy reptilian back, his jiggling flab—Ephander, that's a sight that will haunt me to the end of my days.

He stopped thrusting but did not disengage when he turned his head towards me and said, "Is there a problem, pal?"

I'd always assumed that Phaedra, well past fifty and unmarried, was virginal. I knew little about her, but there was nothing in her speech or manner to suggest she was sexually active—just as there was nothing here to suggest that she wasn't enjoying this. It had never occurred to me that she would take a lover, or even want one. Or that it would be troll-like Mnesiphilos.

Now that I thought about it, I had to admit that Phaedra was pleasant looking, with pure skin and a healthy bosom, and it was wrong for me to assume she wouldn't want a man in her bed. She had a wrinkle or two here, her flesh sagged a little there, but all in all she was an attractive woman.

"Sorry," I said, red-faced. "Carry on."

I went outside and sat at the table in the small courtyard behind my house. Twenty minutes later, Mnesiphilos came and joined me. He was, thank every god, clothed again.

"Sorry, Elektros," he said. "We didn't expect you home."

"Have you two been doing this for a while?" I asked.

"We have. It's not what you think."

"What do you think I think?"

"I'd like to marry Phaedra. With your permission, of course."

"She's not my slave. You don't need my permission."

"We'd still like your blessing."

"Go tell Phaedra that I'd like to speak to her alone."

Mnesiphilos nodded and went back inside. A minute later, Phaedra came out and sat at the table. She wore a white chiton, and her hair was all over the place. She had a pinkish glow to her face, a faint trace of sweat, and slightly dopey eyes—that freshly fucked look. She also looked more defiant than embarrassed.

"Mnesiphilos says he wants to marry you," I said. "How do you like that idea?"

"I like it just fine," she said.

"He's not coercing you in any way?"

"Not at all. He brought it up after the first time we'd gone to bed together."

"You know he's just marrying you for your soup?"

She laughed. "Know you, young sir, that making soup is not the only thing I do well. He and I are good together. We're both old enough to know when someone is right for us, so the decision to marry, though made quickly, was not made rashly. Unlike you youngsters, we don't have time to wait, so we don't waste any." I'd previously noticed that there was an ease to their conversations. He made her laugh, even when he said slightly lewd things that I thought were inappropriate.

"Why don't you just keep doing what you're doing?" I said. "Skip marriage altogether. Then if it goes sour, you can just walk away."

"In Athens, if an unmarried woman sleeps with a man, she's a whore. It shouldn't matter at my age, but it does. So we will marry."

There was no doubt in her eyes. She was my live-in housekeeper, so I considered her to be under my protection, but she was always free. Our contract, unwritten, could be terminated at any time. If she wanted to marry, she was free to do so.

I wanted her to be happy. I congratulated her on her upcoming marriage. There was no denying that since Mnesiphilos started helping Phaedra with her soup business, she'd been happier. I still didn't like Mnesiphilos much, even though he'd saved my life, but I found that I now hated him less. I'd once thought him a useless drunken lecher, but he'd proven himself capable. He'd convinced Phaedra to sell her marvelous soup, and now both of them had a profitable daily activity. He even smelled better these days. He bathed regularly and drank less. Without her, he'd been directionless, like a feather floating on the wind. He still spent some evenings in the house of Themistocles, and he still pawed slave girls but, according to Lanike, not nearly as often as before. And pawing them was all he did now. His enthusiastic wife was much better than any slave girl, no matter how pretty, who merely endured his attentions.

"Her first husband was the same," Lanike told me.

"She was married once before?" I asked.

"Thrice before," said Lanike. "One husband died in battle, one died of natural causes, and the other was lost at sea. But all of them swore off other women after they'd been with Phaedra. She has Aphrodite's gift. More than one upper class lady has sought her advice on how to please a husband."

Mnesiphilos and Phaedra were married in Themistocles' garden while I was on the mission to Delphi. Themistocles gave them a small house as a wedding present. He'd known Mnesiphilos all his life. After they were married, Phaedra no longer lived with me but still insisted on taking care of my house, and she still made me soup. I still paid her a wage, and with the profits from the soup, Phaedra and Mnesiphilos did all right.

When I returned from Delphi, Audax came with me. Unceremoniously manumitted by Aristides, he was now homeless and penniless, with no trade and no family. If I didn't take him in, he'd become a beggar. Sometimes beggars were kidnapped and forced to work in the mines. He deserved better.

In my house, he was restless. He was a free man now, which meant for the first time in his life he did not have his entire day planned out for him. Phaedra still took care of my house, and since I'd always oiled and polished my own armour and weapons, Audax couldn't even do that for me. One morning I found him in bed—he'd taken Phaedra's room—lying flat on his back, wide awake, staring at the ceiling.

He had no idea what to do with himself, and no reason to get out of bed.

Athens' hundred warships needed oarsmen—seventeen thousand altogether—and even though no ships had yet been built, Themistocles had already begun to hire and train crews. They would train on merchant ships, just to get a feel for the oars, but not before every man learned to swim. I thought this would be an opportunity for Audax to learn a skill that was in high demand.

While Athenians make excellent oarsmen and sailors, they're not natural swimmers. The mere idea scared them. Some even believed that a sailor who learns to swim implicitly dares Poseidon to sink his ship, and that it's a form of hubris to think that you deserve to survive when your ship goes down. It was widely believed that a man who attempts to swim to safety would probably still die anyway from exposure, starvation, or shark attacks. Rescue, if it happened, would likely be by the enemy, which meant enslavement. Drowning was the quicker and more merciful end. Still, everyone knew someone who'd survived a shipwreck. I'd survived one myself. On top of this, Themistocles insisted that the sea battles against the Persians would take place within sight of shore, and he planned to have ships patrol battle areas with the specific purpose of collecting oarsmen whose ships went down.

This stopped most of the grumbling, but not all of it.

I was one of the swimming instructors. There were twenty men in my first group of students.

"Fuckin' easy for you," said one of my students, a sturdy farm labourer who was terrified of the water and made no attempt to conceal it.

"Why do you say that?" I said.

"You're Scythian, ain't ya?" he said. "You people come from the Sea of Grass."

I laughed out loud. Several others did too. Then I realized he was serious.

"That's a figure of speech, my friend," I said. "The Sea of Grass is thousands of miles of grazing land. It's called a sea because when you look across it, you see no end to it, just like the ocean. Scythians are even lousier swimmers than Athenians."

"Then why the fuck are *you* teaching us?" asked another man.

"Because if *I* can learn," I replied, "then anyone can."

We practiced at the beach just south of the Phaleron, where we could actually hear the hammers and saws of the shipbuilders. I had each man stand in waist-deep water, in a small cove where there was no current, and literally held him in place as he laid across the water and moved his arms and legs in swimming motions. At the end of the morning, all but one of the men could swim and tread water. Then I had the men race each other the fifty yards across the cove. Men who feared the water at the start of the day now whooped and hollered and dove in like schoolboys. I gave a gold daric to the winner.

The one man I could not teach to swim was Audax. Like a horse panicked by lightning, he could not be calmed down with reason or threats. All I could do was let the panic run its course, then try again. When he came back into the water, the result was always the same. After eight attempts, with no progress whatsoever, I realized I was only traumatizing the poor bugger. If he could not swim, he could not be an oarsman. I had to find him another job.

Audax moped around the house like a ghost, a shadow. I'm not sure that he liked freedom. I didn't agree with Aristides and others who insisted that non-aristocrats were naturally inclined to servitude, but Audax had been a slave for decades, since before Aristides was born, and he knew no other life. Even when he had no specific tasks, he'd always been at his master's side, ready to do as ordered. I insisted that he not call me master, but he still did sometimes. It was a reflex, as was rising early every day to prepare his master's breakfast. I let him do this for me because it made him feel a little better.

"You could take a wife," I said, "if you're interested. Have a family. Do you have any experience with women?"

"Once a year, on his birthday," said Audax, "Lysimachus would take all the male slaves to the whorehouse. He didn't know when any of our birthdays were, so he just made his ours."

Lysimachus was Aristides' late father. "Did Aristides continue the tradition?"

"What do you think, sir?"

"Well, I'll get you a whore for your birthday," I said, "but do you want a wife?"

"Not sure, master," he said. "I wouldn't be able to support her."

This was the crux of the problem. Audax had no trade. He could do house repairs, use a hammer and a saw, but not well enough to be a carpenter. He could fix sandals and even make them, but not well enough to be a sandal-maker. He could calculate household finances, but wealthy men had slaves to do that, or just did it themselves. He could cook, sew, clean, launder, shop, but most households had slaves for those tasks. He was an intelligent man, capable and fit, but too old for any tradesman to take on as an apprentice. He could tutor children in music and poetry, but Athens was already plagued with tutors.

He was, more than anything else, afraid.

I asked Phylo if he could use Audax in his armaments factory. Audax only had experience with maintaining weaponry, but he could run errands and learn whatever he needed to in the factory.

"It would be okay with me," said Phylo, "but Epictetos will not have it."

"Why the hell not?" I asked. "And how does he even know who Audax is?"

"Aristides, for all his pretensions of propriety, has one of the biggest mouths in Athens. He gossips like a Theban fishwife. He's told everyone about his former slave who went behind his back to hire the extra horses. Epictetos was outraged when he heard about it."

So I taught Athenians how to swim in the morning, guarded Themistocles in the afternoon and evenings, worked out in the wee hours of the morning, and had no idea what to do with Audax at any time of the day.

Two months later, when Athens was building ships and training oarsmen and Themistocles was everywhere at once, I went to the agora to give Phaedra her wages. It was midday, the time she and Mnesiphilos did their best business, but they weren't there. I wasn't terribly alarmed. They were late sometimes. Like young newlyweds, they were spontaneous and energetic in their lovemaking, and occasionally they lost track of time.

So I went to their house, which was on the same street as mine. I was about to knock on the door when I heard a wail of pain and grief and shock, all at the same time.

I knew immediately what it was. I went into the house, smelled something burning. It was the soup, left unattended on the cooking brazier. I used the wooden handles, the ones Mnesiphilos had designed, to lift the two amphorae off the brazier and onto the floor. The soup could be dealt with later.

I went into the bedroom. What I saw was worse than I expected. Phaedra knelt on the floor beside the bed, naked, weeping. Mnesiphilos, also naked, lay on the bed on his side, eyes and mouth wide open. He wasn't breathing.

"His heart?" I asked quietly.

Phaedra nodded. I picked up a blanket and wrapped it around her.

Mnesiphilos' penis was still erect, gorged with blood. Once his heart stopped beating, there was nothing to draw the blood away from it.

I swear, Ephander, he had a smile on his face. Phaedra had just fucked him to death. There are worse ways to go.

Come to think of it, *every other way to die* is a worse way to go.

This was no time to joke, though. Phaedra was inconsolable. I led her to the other room, sat her down, poured her a mug of unwatered wine. Then I went back to the bedroom and turned Mnesiphilos onto his back. His erection disappeared as gravity drained the blood from his penis. If gravity was a goddess, I would have sacrificed a bull to her at that moment. I positioned him on his back with his hands folded over his chest and covered him with a blanket.

After the funeral a few days later, I told Phaedra that she could stay at my house if she didn't want to be alone. I'd once again underestimated her. I'd always found her likeable, so I shouldn't have been surprised to learn that she had dozens of friends. During her period of grief, she was never alone. Then we learned that Mnesiphilos had nearly fifty thousand drachmae in an Athenian bank account that was now hers.

She wanted to continue her soup business, but she had difficulty getting her two full amphorae down to the agora by herself. She asked me if I knew anyone who could help her.

It just so happened that I did.

10—NOBILITY

One early afternoon, I went to the agora, bought some fresh bread and sweet cheese, and sat to eat it against the side wall of the baker's stall. I'd just finished eating when I heard two men talking.

"Aristides campaigns," said one of them, "to have Themistocles ostracized."

"Think he'll succeed?" said the other.

"It's possible," said the first man. "The man tends to be believed by people."

If the Assembly voted to ostracize Themistocles, he would be required by law to leave Athens for ten years. It wouldn't be personally disastrous for him—he'd be permitted to keep his properties and his business interests—but it would be disastrous for all Hellas, which would have to somehow defeat the Persians without his leadership. He was the only man who fully understood the degree, and the inevitability, of the threat that faced us. There was still an influential party of aristocrats who insisted that the Persians learned their lesson from the humiliation at Marathon and wouldn't dare attack Athens again. These noble twits failed to understand that the humiliation made the proud Great King *more* likely to attack Athens, not less.

I walked calmly until I was outside of the agora, then I sprinted all the way to Themistocles' house. I tromped right through his front door, brushed past a couple of house slaves. Otreus, Themistocles' secretary, tried to prevent me from entering Themistocles' study, where he and two other men studied a map on the table.

"Archon!" Otreus shouted. "Intruder! Intruder!" He stepped in front of me, which was brave of him. He knew me, but not well enough to understand that I was unfailingly loyal to Themistocles. Otreus was a small, thin man, so I just picked him up like a straw doll and set him down out of my way.

"It's okay, Otreus," said Themistocles. "I believe Lexo has news."

I stood in the study, out of breath—I'd sprinted all the way from the agora, a quarter-mile—and struggled for a few moments to form words.

"Well, out with it, Lexo," said Themistocles. "Have the fucking Persians attacked?"

"No, sir," I glubbered. "It's Aristides. He campaigns to have you ostracized."

"And?"

"And what, sir? Isn't that enough?"

Themistocles broke into a broad smile. The two men with him laughed aloud.

"Gentlemen, gentlemen," said Themistocles. "Go easy on our young friend. He is occupied with other matters, so he doesn't know that Aristides tries to have me ostracized at least once a year. This is, what, the sixth time?"

"Eighth," said one of the other men.

"So it's no new thing, lad," Themistocles continued. "He'll never succeed. Aristides doesn't understand democracy very well. He tries to have me ostracized by talking to the aristocrats, who already hate me, and makes little effort to persuade my fellow commoners, whom he needs because the aristocrats are too few to carry a vote."

"Well, sir, I feel like a complete idiot now," I said.

"Forget it, Lexo," said Themistocles. "You were mistaken about the urgency of this news, but you were right to bring it to me quickly."

I felt slightly less foolish. On my way out, I apologized to Otreus. "No harm done, sir," he said. "Just remind me to never get on your bad side."

Themistocles walked me out the front door of his house and told me there was a situation with Phylo that had to be dealt with before it escalated.

Two nights later, I had dinner with Phylo at his house. I'd offered to take him to Hera's Retreat, Athens' finest inn, famous for its mutton pie, but Phylo wanted me to meet his wife and see his house. I'd been back in Athens for several years now, and I'd spoken to Phylo many times, but we were both so busy that we'd only had snippet conversations on the street. I'd passed his house many times but had never been inside, even though he'd given me a standing invitation. He was always so busy. He was away from Athens frequently, for both business and diplomacy. Themistocles sometimes sent him to other cities to gauge the residents' receptiveness to a military coalition of Hellene poleis against the Persians. Phylo was a natural diplomat. His particular skill was finding out where people stood on particular issues without them actually knowing he'd done so. I wasn't surprised. He'd always been like that, great with words, great with people, great at reading between the lines, even when the lines weren't written down.

Athens had been very good to him. His house, which was larger than the one we'd grown up in on Skiathos, was in the aristocratic neighbourhood, the Virgin Quarter, so called because it was believed to be especially favoured by grey-eyed Athena, and also because prostitutes and hetaerae were not allowed to live there. It was unlikely that the area was home to more virgins than any other part of the city, but the aristocrats who called it home felt entitled to many things, including this delusion.

Phylo had several businesses in Athens. Father sent him here when he was eighteen for ephebe training. He was barely off the boat when he'd bought part-ownership of a smithy that produced quality swords and armour—he'd foreseen that Athens would soon be at war. The Battle of Marathon made him a lot of money, as Athenians scrambled to buy new arms and replace old ones. He owned a stable that leased horses, and he also arranged horsemanship shows by the Scythians. They were the best horsemen in the world, and while the popularity of these demonstrations ebbed and flowed as popular tastes fluctuated, there were at least a few horse-shows every year, and the stable was continuously profitable. It had recently become popular for the wealthier classes to lease horses for an afternoon to go riding, and they loved being able to do it right from Athens, without having to make the day-long journey to their countryside estates where they kept their own horses.

Phylo was the first man in the history of Athens to find a way to profit from leasing horses to rich Athenians who already had horses of their own.

He'd also inherited our father's farm and the shipping business. He sold both of them because he did not have the time or inclination to travel back and forth to Skiathos to monitor them. He gave me a quarter of the sale price of the farm and the shipping business. By rights, as the eldest son, he wasn't obliged to give me anything at all, but he always had a generous nature. He then invested in another shipping business based in Athens. It too thrived. He'd bought an olive farm ten miles north of Athens, as well as a potters' workshop that produced the new Attic red-figure pottery, which had become so popular as an export commodity that Phylo could not keep up with foreign demand for it. He now sought to expand his workshop into a factory.

On top of all this, Themistocles had gotten him Athenian citizenship. Phylo had completed his ephebe training, and people liked him, so it wasn't terribly difficult to make him a citizen. He spoke differently now. He'd hired a diction tutor when he first got to Athens, and now, unlike me, there were few traces of Skiathan twang when he spoke. He now sounded more like an Athenian aristocrat, and less like the son of an island farmer. In fact, he sounded more Athenian than most Athenians. He voted in the Assembly. While he aspired to join the elite citizens, the aristocrats, they would have thought him a presumptuous island hucklebuck if he sat with them now. Maybe in a few years it would be okay, but for now he sat a row or two behind them at the Assembly, not actually with them but close enough to speak with them.

His marriage reflected his ambition. His wife's father was an aristocrat.

In one way, his house reminded me of Themistocles' place. When you entered, the first thing you heard was an array of voices. My house was usually quiet, but here there were at least a dozen people inside, not counting the slaves. Men lounged on couches and drank wine as pretty young slave girls poured it for them. The mood, though festive, was not an orgy or a symposium, but I still saw trouble here. Every single slave was an attractive young woman. When we were boys, Phylo always said that when he had his own house, he'd fill it with pretty girls, but I always thought it was a boy's idle boast. While it was socially acceptable for a married Athenian man to screw his slave girls, this did not mean that his wife liked it—and no man could call his home happy if his wife was not. I knew Phylo. He would charm and cajole his wife when she was displeased with him, and he would calm her anxieties and soothe her wounded pride with kind words and honeyed promises to change his ways, then two days later he'd be banging his slave-girls again. One of the ones who poured the wine was visibly pregnant.

Before he was married, Phylo was often involved with more than one woman at the same time. The women were slaves or freewomen, and sometimes other men's wives.

I never did this. My first sexual experiences were with women who made me want to be with them exclusively. When I had a girlfriend, it felt wrong to dally with another woman, so I didn't do it.

Yet Phylo was the respectable Athenian citizen and I was the one called barbarian. Infer from that, Ephander, what you will.

"I'm having dinner with my little brother tonight," said Phylo to his guests, who all looked like they were ready to settle in for the night. "We have a lot of catching up to do. So you mad drunk buggers all have to leave."

I was worried that this might be similar to Odysseus' return to Ithaka, where he found dozens of nobly born layabouts who abused his hospitality, but the men here all laughed. They were in high spirits, but none was actually drunk, and they all got up and left. I recognized a few whom I'd seen around Athens. On the way out, one of them invited Phylo to his house for dinner the next evening, which Phylo accepted. "Bring your little brother too," he said. Several shook my hand before they left and said they were pleased to meet me.

When they were all gone, Phylo summoned his wife. She was a small pale woman, thin and sad-eyed, who wore a partial veil in her own house and mostly kept her eyes lowered to the floor, even when she spoke directly to me. This was Athenian propriety at its silliest.

"Pleased to meet you, sir," she said. "My husband's brother is always welcome here." The veil prevented me from completely seeing what she looked like. If I saw her without it, I doubted if I would recognize her.

"No need to be so formal with me, dear lady," I said.

"My name is Elektros, but call me Lex, like your husband does. What's your name?"

Phylo had introduced her as *my wife*. Her words seemed scripted. When I deviated from the script, she was confused for a moment and looked at Phylo for permission to speak. Phylo nodded to her.

"Cythereia," she said.

"Pleased to meet you, Cythereia," I said, and offered my hand to her. She looked terrified by this too.

"It's okay, Cythi," said Phylo.

She shook my hand but the fear never left her eyes. While I didn't expect this small woman to have a strong grip, it was still weaker than I'd expected. Her hand was moist with fear, and cold to the touch. I terrified her.

"Please," I said. "Relax. I'm quite civilized. You're my brother's wife, so I'm honour-bound to protect you as a sister."

"It's true," said Phylo. "Lex is notoriously kind to women. I've never been able to cure him of that."

I think Cythi smiled, but with the veil I couldn't be sure. All I saw were her eyes, and they were distinctly unjoyful. She would not dine with us. She left, politely and demurely, to return to the gynaikeion, where she would eat with her house girls. She probably felt like she'd just escaped Hades.

Phylo and I dined alone. We lounged on the couches in his dining room as his pretty slave girls brought us olives, bread, cheese, grilled swordfish, roast pork, apricots, apples, pomegranates and honey-roasted almonds. The food was excellent. Phylo's cook was an older woman, the only slave in the house who wasn't young and pretty. Phylo wanted to rise socially in Athens and understood that it was crucial to serve first-rate meals to important citizens. One of the girls played the lute as we dined, as another sang softly.

"If any of my girls strike your fancy," he said after we'd eaten, "just help yourself."

Had to admit, Ephander, I was tempted. Their eyes were invitations and all of their tunics were just a little too short.

"I will pass, brother," I said. "I'm more interested in learning how you got the shiner."

He'd rubbed some powder on his face to cover a bruised eye, and he'd intentionally kept the lamps down low, but he'd failed to completely reduce the swelling. I've seen many fights, so I spot their after-effects better than most.

"You should see the other guy," said Phylo. After a pause, he added, "Not a mark on him!"

I laughed. Then I said, "Tell me what really happened."

"It was foolish," he said. "I was in a wine-shop a few days ago. I said something about a man's wife, not realizing he was at the next table. He challenged me to a fight. I could've just apologized, but I was a little drunk, so I took him up on it. Big mistake. He was old, almost sixty, but he knew how to fight. I was flat on my ass in less than ten seconds. I tried to conceal my bruise because I'm embarrassed about it."

"Nice little story," I said. "Now tell me what *really* happened."

"Fuck you, little brother," he said, the smile vanishing. "You already know."

I did. Themistocles had told me. Cythereia had told her mother all about Phylo's behaviour. The mother told her husband, who had his men give Phylo a beating, a light one, to send him a message.

Cythereia's father was Pankratios, who was, as his name suggested, a fighter. He had five daughters. He was able to place the four eldest girls in favourable marriages that connected him to three aristocratic families in Athens and one in Plataea. The youngest, Cythereia, was small and had some health problems. From what I saw of her, she was pretty enough but looked like a stiff wind could carry her away.

Phylo slept with his slave girls and rarely touched his wife. The worst thing he did, which aroused the ire of Pankratios, was that he spent too much time with a hetaera named Red Issa. He'd even appeared at the theatre with her on his arm.

This is what Themistocles told me I had to fix. Phylo was making no attempt to impregnate his wife. The public appearance with Red Issa was foolish. Pankratios wouldn't stand for it. This wasn't about marital fidelity. Athenian aristocrats didn't know the meaning of the term, and Pankratios was himself one of Red Issa's occasional customers. The problem was that Phylo had appeared *in public* with her. Phylo, to his credit, recognized afterwards how foolish this was if he wanted to rise in Athenian society. He promised to keep his visits to Red Issa private, although this would not completely solve the problem.

"The next beating," I said to him, "will be much worse."

"Begging your pardon, little brother," he said, "but I can't believe you're giving me marital advice. You've never been married, and what the fuck do you know about Athenian society?"

"Compared to you? Next to nothing. But if somebody beats on my brother, even if they have a good reason, I get involved."

Phylo scowled at me. He was in the wrong here and he knew it, but he hated having it pointed out like this.

"Listen to me," I said. "All you have to do is get your wife pregnant. How hard can that be?"

"It's not hard for me," he said, "but it's extremely hard for her. She's Sapphic. Whenever I lay with her, she cringes like she's being raped, even though I'm gentle with her. She cries and moans, not with pleasure but with pain. She hates every second of it. I do love her, you know. She's sweet natured. That's why I don't force myself on her anymore."

"So you screw your slave girls because you love your wife too much?"

"Absurd as that sounds, yes, it's true."

"Have you tried giving her some wine first?"

"First thing I thought of," he said. "It makes her puke."

"The gods have given you this problem," I said, "because they know you have the ability to solve it."

"Don't make me laugh, Lex," he said. "You don't believe that gods intervene in human lives. You stopped believing the day your mother died. Oh, I'm sorry, I shouldn't have said that."

He used a common debating tactic, one that Themistocles used all the time—say something peripherally relevant to distract your opponent. I wasn't offended, mostly because Phylo was right. The gods, if they exist at all, have little interest in us mortals.

"Okay, forget the gods," I said. "If anyone has the brains to solve this problem, it's you."

"Poppy juice might work," he said.

"So you'll drug her?"

"If necessary. It might be the only way."

"I know someone," I said, "who might help you."

Later, when I left Phylo's house, I went to visit Pankratios, who lived nearby. Pankratios was not the one who would help Phylo's dilemma, but I had to make some kind of truce with him as soon as possible. Phylo was the only Hellenic family I had now. Whether he was right or wrong, I would defend him.

There was no need to tell Pankratios that his daughter was Sapphic. He already knew, or at least suspected. It's probably why she was available to marry a commoner from Skiathos. I felt sorry for her. If a man only loved other men, he could get away with it, but a woman who only loved women still had to marry a man, especially if she was highborn. Her family would insist on it. Such a marriage is rarely happy.

Pankratios came to his front door with two armed men. "If Themistocles has something to say to me," he growled, "he can damned well come and tell me himself."

"This is not a matter of state," I said. "I'm here on a private matter."

He nodded. He probably expected me at some point. He invited me in very warily, and kept his two guards in the room with us. They were probably the ones who'd beaten Phylo. All four of us remained standing.

I turned down the wine he offered. "I won't stay long," I said. "I will come to the point. I am aware of your displeasure with my brother. He has behaved dishonourably, so the light beating you gave him was justified."

"I don't know what you're talking about," said Pankratios.

"We will not resolve this situation to anyone's satisfaction," I said, "*if you insult my fucking intelligence!* I know he was beaten at your order, and these two guys did it. I'm here to tell you that I will not retaliate for it. He deserved it. He's not seriously hurt, and he's gotten the message. But you will not do it again. If that happens, I *will* retaliate."

His two men smirked at me, then at each other. "I haven't come here to fight, gentlemen," I said to them, "but I will gladly demonstrate my capabilities. Right now, if you want. I'm not terribly concerned that there are two of you."

I held a firm gaze. The two guards tried to do the same, but after a few seconds both men wavered. I was much taller than either of them, had better weapons, was in better condition, and being half-Scythian does wonders for a man's reputation as a fighter. It wasn't bluff or bluster. If it came to a fight, I would incapacitate the man on my left with a hard punch to the throat. Then I would knee the other man in the nuts before he had a chance to react. It would be no contest.

"Stand down, boys," said Pankratios. "Elektros is here to speak. So that's what we will do." He then turned to me. "Your brother's behaviour must change. If he screws his slave-girls at home, that's one thing. We all do that. When he parades Red Issa at the theatre, however, he goes too far."

"Agreed," I said. "It won't happen again. Phylo will apologize to you, if you'll let him. If you have further complaints about his behaviour, I ask you to talk to me first. Such conduct dishonours me as much as it does you."

Pankratios was past sixty, but he was fit and sharp-eyed, with an intelligence in his eyes that you grasped immediately. He had one of those noses that made you think of an eagle—a predator, a fighter, a creature capable of sudden attack. He still fought in the phalanx, and by all accounts fought well. He was not a man to cross.

"I will agree to that," he said, "if you promise me that Phylo will treat my daughter better."

"I cannot promise," I said, "what another man will do, not even my own brother. Phylo has always been his own man. But I promise you this: if he does not change his behaviour, the next beating he gets will come from me."

We shook hands. "I like you," he said. "You come to me and talk man-to-man. Sometimes that takes more courage than fighting."

"I appreciate your plain speech too, sir," I said. "I do believe we'll resolve this problem."

I went home. In the days that followed, Phylo still screwed his slave girls. He still visited Red Issa, but not as often as before, and now they met in private.

Shortly after I'd spoken with Pankratios, Phaedra had visited Cythi several times. A month later, Phylo announced that his wife was pregnant.

Phylo invited me to dinner to celebrate the news. Once again, it was only the two of us. He insisted that I tell him what happened to our father.

He only knew part of the story. It pained me to tell him all of it, but he deserved to know.

11—ATHANATOS

When I arrived home from Scythia, Phylo, our bireme rowed into the north port of Skiathos, which was too small to have a proper harbourmaster. Old Hestios sometimes acted like one. He ran towards us, shouting and flailing his arms, but he wouldn't come anywhere near the ship. From a hundred yards away, he yelled *Eritrea* and *a curse* and *stay on the goddamn ship* and *go back, go back!* He wouldn't come close enough to talk to us properly. It was odd behaviour, even for this odd man. In the past, he'd tried to get us to pay him harbour fees, and we'd always just told him to go fuck himself. We ignored him now, a longstanding and well-respected tradition here.

I'd been away from Skiathos for more than three years. I was bone tired, and I wasn't in the mood for any nonsense from Hestios. This ship had indeed come from Eritrea. A few hours after we left port, I felt sick, nothing serious, a slight fever. A couple of the others on board felt it too. It made me more tired than usual, and short-tempered.

"Get back on the ship, Elektros!" Hestios yelled. What little sense he ever had seemed to have left him. "You too, Athanatos!"

Athanatos was as anxious to get home as I was, but when he tried to approach Hestios, to see what all the yammering was about, Hestios ran away.

"Fucking idiot," Athanatos muttered. "He's finally snapped."

"No surprise," I said. "He's always been a few arrows short of a quiver."

Ah, but we should have listened to Hestios.

Instead, I stretched my legs and shook off the stiffness

from the boat trip. I shouldered my travel-sack, held my sword up so I wouldn't trip on it, and jogged towards home, a couple miles away. Hestios still yammered and yawed from somewhere. *Death. Eritrea. A black curse. Go back, go back! Death! Eritrea! Death! Death!*

As I jogged on, Hestios' voice faded to nothing. A good run usually made me feel better, but this time it made me dizzy. I stopped, puked up the water I'd drunk on the ship, then continued at a rapid walk. My legs ached, so I slowed down. I was definitely sick, but it was just a cold, so I didn't give it a lot of thought, even though it took me close to an hour to get home.

Father was working in the fields when someone told him of my approach, and he actually ran to the house to wait for me and have food prepared. When I arrived, he stood at the front door with a big smile on his face, then he hugged me for maybe the third or fourth time in my life. He fought back tears.

"I bet you have stories to tell," he said, beaming.

"I do, sir," I said. "Right now, though, I must rest."

He nodded. "You look like something the dog buried," he said. "You okay?"

"Caught a cold on the boat," I said. "I'll lie down for a bit and I'll be okay."

Old Adina came and gave me a hug and a nearly toothless smile. When I saw her last, her hair still had traces of its original black, but now it was completely white. "You sick," she said. "You lying down. I give soup."

Adina was a slave, but when she told you to do something, it was always the smartest thing to do. I went to my old bedroom and laid down. A few minutes later, she came back with bread and a bowl of warm lentil soup, then she sat beside the bed and spooned the soup into my mouth. I could barely taste it. It wasn't long before I puked up every spoonful. She cleaned it up.

"You should leave," I said. "You don't want to catch my cold."

"I no get cold," she said. "Not never." It was true. I couldn't remember her ever being sick. "I leave it soup," she added. "Feel better later, you finish. Now sleep you."

Adina was my virtual mother when I was a kid. I thought for the longest time that she didn't like me. She called me *Freakboy* when Father wasn't around. She later confessed she did it because I was mute and she thought it would induce me to speak. She always made sure I was well fed and warmly dressed. You and I played rough, Phylo, and Adina always tended our cuts and bruises, new ones almost every day. When she made honeycakes, she always made a few extra ones for me, and whenever she had fresh fruit, dates or plums or apricots, she always called me right away because she knew how much I liked them. Little things, it's true, but she always did more than her duties required. It was love, whether I was aware of it or not.

So I felt that much worse when I learned that she'd taken to her bed within hours of my arrival at the house. She was light-headed and feverish and had collapsed in the kitchen, but true to her nature, she still wanted to do her work. Father led her to her bed and literally held her down while he explained that she was sick and had to rest and that was an order.

I felt even worse the next day. I was awakened by the sound of wailing. We had only four slaves in the household—Adina, her husband Ergos, and two slave girls—but they sounded like a herd of harpies.

I rose from my bed, or tried to. I fell down immediately, sicker than I'd ever felt, dizzy and rubber-legged. My head felt like a hammer was being driven into it. I managed to crawl to the bedroom door and open it.

"What's going on?" I tried to yell. "Ergos! What's happening?" But my voice was a sad squawk, and the slaves couldn't hear me over their own howls. One of the slave girls, Otonia, finally came to check on me. She wept.

"Help me back to bed, Otonia," I said. "What's going on?"

"The mistress Adina," she said between sobs.

Ergos found Adina dead in her bed. Ergos, a quiet man who'd been old and white-haired for as long as I could remember, shrieked his grief so loudly that our six farm labourers—four slaves, two free men—came running from the fields into the house to see what was happening. They found Ergos crying over Adina's lifeless body in the bed.

"Where's Father?" I asked Otonia.

"I do not know, master," she said. "I have not seen him this morning."

This wasn't unusual. Father was a notorious early riser. Like me, he slept little. Even now, past fifty, he rarely slept more than four hours a night, and often got by with only two. He would usually be out in the fields before the sun rose, before the slaves were up. On a hunch, I sent Otonia to check his bedroom, and she came back and told me that Father was still in bed, unable to rise. He was weak but awake. I told her to fetch him some water from the well, bring me some too, then to go into town to fetch Simmios, the best physician on Skiathos. Anything that could make Father and Adina sick had to be pretty serious.

She brought us the water, then left the house. I don't know if she found Simmios, or even tried to, because I never saw her again. Simmios never came.

We had two other farmhands, the brothers Gorgias and Lycophon, who now arrived at the house in a mule wagon. They were free men and did not live in the slave barrack beside our barn. They'd taken the wagon home with them the previous day because Father told them to go to the village this morning to buy supplies.

I heard them talking outside to the other farmhands, who'd left Ergos to his grief and waited behind the house, uncertain what to do next.

"The old lady's gone," I heard one of the men say. "Died in her sleep."

"A sad day," said Lycophon. "She'd been with them fifty years. How's Belkos?"

"Otonia said he was sick in bed," said the first man. "We haven't actually seen him."

Lycophon came into the house. "Hello?" he called. "Belkos? Anybody?"

"In here," I croaked from my bed.

Lycophon heard me. The door was open. He stepped in, took one look at me and stepped back. He was well tanned from working the fields, but his face suddenly went milky with horror.

"Plague!" he called out. "Nobody else come into the house!"

"What are you talking about?" I said. "It's just a cold. Adina died because she was old."

Lycophon pulled the top of his tunic front up over his mouth and nose, hoping to filter out whatever evil was in the air.

"I've seen it before, Lex, in Sikelia," he said. "That lump on your neck is black. You've got the plague."

I put my hand on my neck, felt nothing. "Other side," said Lycophon.

I found a lump there the size of an apricot. It was painful to the touch. Whatever it was, it felt like it would burst soon.

Lycophon was scared, but not too scared to steal. My

sword was in its scabbard, leaning against the wall inside the door to my room. He picked it up, still holding his tunic front over his lower face. It muffled his voice a little when he spoke. "This is nice," he said.

"Fucking put that down!" I skrawked. It was the Sword of Oiorpata. It belonged to my mother. I brought it back from Scythia.

"I think I'll keep it. You're a dead man, so it's not like you'll ever use it again."

"I'm not dead yet, asshole."

"You will be soon enough. Nobody survives the plague. Besides, I never liked you much anyway. Where does your father keep his gold?"

He left me. I heard things in the house getting thrown around. Pottery was smashed on the floor. Lycophon ransacked every room in the house that didn't have a sick person in it. I was delirious by now, and I shouted vows of revenge, and invoked every god I could think of to strike him down. Lycophon, if he heard me, ignored it.

"Ah! Found it!" he finally said. He'd found the small jar of coins Father kept in the pantry off the kitchen. He did not find the main coin hoard under the kitchen floorboards. After this, Lycophon left the house. I'm not sure what happened next. All I could hear was Ergos weeping. Our other slave-girl vanished. Can't say I blamed her, she must have been terrified. So were the other farmhands. They too disappeared. I don't know if any of them survived.

Ergos never again rose from Adina's bed. The plague took him before the next sunrise. He died with his arms around Adina's lifeless body.

Father died, too, alone in his own bed.

I was now a patricide.

I'd brought this pestilence into my father's house and

killed him, and felt just as guilty as if I'd slain him with a sword. Death was what I wanted now, too, and what I deserved.

The gods, Phylo, if they truly exist, have an annoying habit of keeping me alive so they can torment me further.

I laid there for three more days without water, without food. I shat and puked where I lay, too weak to even climb out of my own filth. There were more black pustules on my neck, and under my armpits. They all burst and oozed a foul pus that smelled of rot, of death. The stink made me retch, even though my stomach was empty and nothing came up.

I slept and woke and slept and woke, I don't know how many times. Our chickens squawked and the goats bleated endlessly, because they were penned in without anyone to feed them. I tried to get up, to go open their pens and give them a fighting chance, but I was so weak I didn't even make it to the bedroom door. I couldn't get back into bed, either, so I just laid on the floor.

The nights were black. I was too weak to light a candle or a lamp. Flies buzzed around me and my bodily wastes every minute of the day or night.

On the fourth night, I awoke to the sight of a perfect young man looking down at me. His golden curls shone, almost as if they radiated light, and fell to his shoulders. He was beardless, and shirtless too. His body, though slender, was well-developed, muscular in the arms and shoulders, lean in the waist, rippled in the abdomen. He smiled as I awoke, then turned his nose up.

"*Phewww!* You reek, boy," he said to me. He looked younger than me. Why would he call me *boy*?

Then I suddenly knew.

"Forgive me, Lord Hermes," I said. "I cannot bow before you. I'm too weak to move."

He ignored this. "Did you know," he continued, "that

we gods don't piss or shit? Ambrosia and nektar nourish us exactly the right amount, so there's no bodily waste. We never vomit, either. We perspire a little, but even that smells like asphodels. Sometimes I start to feel kindly towards mortals, then I get a whiff of one and despise them anew."

He stared at me. I actually smelled asphodels, a scent so sweet and strong that it overpowered the rot and vomit and shit. I was transfixed by those golden eyes. I couldn't speak.

"Egads, boy, you look hideous," he went on. "I won't stay any longer than I have to. I'm here to deliver a message from my brother. It is this: you will live. Everyone around you will die but you will survive."

He turned and left. I smelled asphodels for several minutes afterwards, then the reek of pus and vomit and shit returned. I dry-heaved until I fell asleep again.

I know, Phylo, that the god Hermes did not really visit my sickbed to deliver a message from Apollo. I hallucinated the whole thing, even though it seemed so real at the time.

Two days later, I was finally able to walk again. I was wobblier, weaker, thirstier, hungrier and sadder than I'd ever been.

The house was full of flies, beetles, wasps, and every other kind of bug that fed on dead flesh. I was lucky that neither of the outside doors had been left open, otherwise I would have had vultures, crows and stray dogs to deal with.

Despite the rot and the smell of dead flesh, I had to eat and drink. I didn't want to live, but my body did. I found some dried meat in the kitchen. It was difficult to chew, but this was probably a good thing because it meant I wouldn't eat more than my tortured stomach could handle. I went to the well outside, drew some water, drank too much of it, spewed it up, drank some more. I found a sack of chicken feed in the barn, but I was too weak to lift or even drag it. So I tipped it over, took a handful of seed, went to the chicken pen, let the chickens out, then left a trail of seed that led to the overturned sack. Several of the chickens had died. The seed would last them a few weeks. Then I released the goats. They were bone-thin, but none had died. I didn't need to do anything else because goats, once they're unpenned, always find their way to food. There was a stream nearby and they'd find that too.

We had two plough mules and Father's riding horse. One of the mules was too weak to stand. I would take the horse—I was too weak to walk into town—but first I had to feed it, to let it regain some of its strength. I brought hay from the barn, and water from the well. I wouldn't be able to ride the skinny mare into town today, she probably wouldn't be able to handle it, but she was in better shape then I'd expected. She'd been able to reach weeds and grass outside her pen.

Then I went back into the house. I'd dreaded this most of all, but I couldn't put it off any longer. I couldn't leave Father and Adina and Ergos to rot like dead dogs.

Father laid in bed, eyes and mouth wide open, his face covered in flies. His skin was waxy, wet, still in the first stages of decay. He hadn't been dead more than two or three days. His face was a sickly green. I wept, although I was still too dehydrated for tears to come. He was a physically strong man, very hardy, and until that moment I'd maintained a dim hope that, like me, he'd survived the plague.

Afterwards, I went to look in on Adina and Ergos. Adina had been dead the longest, and it showed. There was almost no flesh left on her face, most of it already eaten away by maggots. There were maggots on her hands and under her clothing, and they'd started on Ergos too.

I rushed out of the house. I couldn't deal with this. The house belonged to you and me now, Phylo. Before the plague, it would have been valuable. Father had hired the best carpenters to build it. It could be cleaned up, but I couldn't live in it again. If I did, I would always be reminded of this day, and the death I'd brought to the people I loved. It was accursed now. Contaminated. Polluted. No one else would want to live in it either. We would sell the farm. Even without the house, it was valuable. Over the years, Father had expanded his farm. He'd bought two adjacent farms and cultivated every square inch of the land.

There was still several days' worth of unspoiled food in the pantry. The barley flour had gone wormy, but there were dried beans, some dried fruit, dried meat, and several sealed jars of fish pickled in brine. I carried the salvageable food outside. Then I went back into the house for Father's coin hoard under the kitchen floorboards, the one Lycophon had missed. I also took Father's old sword, which was still in pretty good shape, even though he hadn't used it in years, and I went into my room and found a drawing of my mother. It was a rolled up scroll tucked into the bottom of a cupboard. Ergos had hidden it there because Father would probably have destroyed it if he'd ever found it. Ergos had copied it from an original he'd made when my mother was still alive. Now that her sword was lost, it was all I had left of her.

I spread lamp oil on the floors and walls of every room, and doused all three of the bodies.

Then I torched the place. I ate pickled mullet, sipped water from the well, and watched it burn.

I went to the stream and washed the filth from myself. I slept in the farmhands' barrack that night.

The next morning, I fed the horse and the remaining mule—one of the mules had died overnight. The house was now a heap of smoldering ash. I dragged the charred remains of Father and Adina and Ergos out of the ruins and buried them. I was weak, so it took me all afternoon to dig a single shallow grave. I'd originally planned to dig three graves, but I was physically unable to. I was exhausted after digging just the one. The three of them would remain together in death.

That evening, I killed one of the chickens. I was lucky that they hadn't strayed far from the seed bag in the barn. I plucked and cleaned the bird, but it was so damned thin that I had to kill another one just to get a decent meal.

I rested for two days. I fed the horse and mule at proper intervals and they recovered well. So did I. I tried to run. It felt odd at first. I had cramps in my legs because the muscles had atrophied a little, but the cramps faded as I ran. I moved slowly and couldn't go more than half a mile, but I was happy with my progress.

If I needed to fight, now I could.

I rode the mare into the village, but also dismounted a few times and walked beside her because I needed to rebuild the strength in my legs.

On the way, I passed dead bodies in three different places. They looked like they'd dropped dead where they laid. By their state of decay, with bones showing through very little remaining flesh, they all must have died shortly after I arrived on Skiathos. I didn't recognize any of them, but then again, there was so little left of their faces that their own mothers wouldn't have recognized them. I knew one was a woman only because her skeleton had a pink bow in its long curly hair. The hair hadn't decayed and actually would have looked perfectly fine on a living person. That made it doubly disturbing.

When I reached the village, it was quiet. Half the

people on Skiathos had died, including most of the old people and children. The plague had now passed. I spoke to a scrawny survivor I met in the village, and he told me no one else was known to be sick. The slaves and freedmen who'd fled to the hills had all died there.

The thin man who told me all this was our old friend Epimenes. I didn't recognize him. He'd been quite fat the last time I saw him, and now his beard was mostly white. He'd organized some of the survivors, women as well as men, into work parties to dig pits. Epimenes and I would drag bodies out of houses, load them onto a wagon and unload them into the pits. The diggers all had scarves covering their mouths and noses. The bodies would be burned.

"As far I know," said Epimenes, "you and I are the only ones who had the plague and lived. How fares Belkos?"

"Dead," I said. "He was a strong man. He might have lived if there'd been someone to take care of him, but everyone else in the house was sick too. How are your boys?"

He bit back a sob. He didn't say a word. It was a bad idea, I now knew, to ask anyone on Skiathos how their family was doing.

Epimenes then told me how heroic my uncle Damon had been. He had tended to his wife and his sons, who were all stricken early, and he looked after his neighbours too. But he saved no one, and then he took to his bed and never left it again. He'd died just two days earlier.

"You'll find Lycophon down by the docks," Epimenes said, without me asking about him. "After you're done with him, I could use your help here."

I told him I'd return as soon as I could. I found Lycophon at a dockside wine shop. There was no one else around. There was an ancient ash tree outside the shop that shaded some of the tables. Lycophon laid on the ground under the tree.

He looked awful, smelled worse. He had two black lumps on his neck. He was deathly still as he laid in his own shit. His face was greenish, like he'd already begun to decompose. I thought he was dead, then he moaned. He had my sword-belt, with the Sword of Oiorpata in its sheath, buckled around his waist.

He looked up at me. "Aww, fuck," he rasped weakly. "I'm sorry, man."

I said nothing. I just stared at him.

"Are you a ghost?" he said. "A nightmare? Since I saw you last, I've had nothing but nightmares."

I still said nothing. I was in no hurry. He wasn't going anywhere. It pained him to talk, his voice barely audible, but he couldn't stop himself. "I tried to sell the sword. No one would buy it. Someone recognized it as yours. Then when I tried to spend the money I took, nobody would accept it because they knew I stole it from your house. Here, you can have it back."

He tried to pull a money pouch out of his tunic, but was too weak to do so.

"Then when I took sick," he went on, "no one would help me. I've wronged you, Lex, but you can see that the gods didn't let me get away with it."

I still said nothing to this piss-poor excuse for a man. My silence terrified him. I unbuckled the sword-belt, pulled it off of him, then buckled it around my waist. I reached down into his pocket and took the money-pouch. Then I drew the Sword of Oiorpata and put the point to his throat. He was too weak to do anything but lie there.

"Please do it," he said. "Do me this last mercy."

I resheathed my sword and laughed at him. "If the gods punish you," I said, "it would be impious of me to deny them the joy they take in your suffering."

"You evil cunt!" he screamed, much more loudly than I could have done when I was as sick as he was now. "You can't leave me like this!"

"I can," I said, "and I will. I never did like you either, Lycophon."

"You owe me! I didn't kill you when I had the chance."

I laughed again. "You didn't kill me, asshole, because you were afraid to come near me."

I left him there. I went back to Epimenes in the village and helped him collect bodies. He and I had survived the plague, so it was commonly believed that we would be immune to it for the rest of our lives. I couldn't decide if that was a blessing or a curse. We would now grieve for the friends and families we lost. I envied the dead at that moment. None of the other people with us had actually gotten the plague, so they weren't immune. They would dig a large funeral pit, but only if the bodies weren't present when they did so. None of them would go into houses to fetch bodies, so this task fell to Epimenes and me. We'd go into a house, collect the bodies one at a time, and pitch them into the back of a mule-wagon. Old Alastor drove the wagon. He was not strong enough to heft bodies, but we were glad for his help. I asked him why he wasn't afraid of catching the plague.

"I'm seventy-four years old, son," he said. "The gods have had all kinds of chances to kill me and have chosen not to. If they change their minds, I'm ready."

Epimenes and I did not go into every house on Skiathos because we didn't need to. Some families were completely wiped out, while others lost only one or two members. Some houses were bypassed completely by the pestilence.

Even so, there were literally hundreds of bodies. At the end of each day, we'd throw them in the pit, add wood and straw, douse them with lamp oil, and set fire to them. Some of the survivors objected, claiming that the burning bodies would contaminate the very air we all breathed. We'd considered this, but eventually decided that leaving the bodies to rot, even if we buried them, was more likely to bring the plague back than burning them would. So we told people to remain indoors after sundown and keep their noses and mouths covered. Skiathos is an island, and we were close to a shore, so it was always breezy here. The winds would quickly disperse whatever foul things were in the air.

Each morning, Epimenes and I would return to the previous day's pit and bury the charred remains. Then we'd get the other survivors to dig a new pit as the two of us went looking for more dead.

Five days later, when all of the houses and streets were finally clear of bodies, I went to the dockside wine shop. Lycophon was dead, although by the looks of him, not for more than a day or two. A sickly dog had torn one of his arms off and now gnawed on the bone. When I shooed the dog away, he took the arm with him.

While Lycophon got what he deserved, I took no joy from it. I wondered if I'd ever again be able to take joy in anything. I did not want to live, but my vision of Hermes had told me that I had no choice. I'd have cursed the gods if I thought it would do me any good.

Then I remembered you, big brother. The gods had given me one small mercy. When the plague struck Skiathos, you were in Athens.

The only thing I could do now was come here and give you the bad news.

12—OSTRAKOPHORIA

I sat in a chair as many thousands of eyes were on me. I wore a blue tunic, like a true Athenian, which of course I wasn't. Weapons weren't allowed, but I sure wished I had my sword with me now. I wouldn't have used it here in the Assembly, of course, but I always felt better just having the Sword of Oiorpata within reach. I sat in an ancient Anatolian oak chair and hoped it would all be over soon. I had to speak to this huge crowd, and had to resist the urge to run away as fast as I could. I never felt that way in battle.

"State your name before the gods and the Assembly," the herald said to me in a loud clear voice. The man was gifted. He should have been a soldier. Such a voice would cut through the din of a battle.

"Elektros of Skiathos," I said as loudly as I could. As a *metic*, a foreign born non-citizen, I could only appear in the Assembly by special invitation. I'd been made to swear an oath to fair-visaged Athena that I would tell the truth. Citizens were not required to swear this oath, which may explain why so few of them told the truth here.

I had already told Themistocles that I would not lie. If words that I did not say were attributed to me, I would correct the questioner.

"You are inept at untruth, Lexo," Themistocles had agreed. "If you lie, you won't get away with it. But when it comes to the truth, no one tells it better." I wasn't sure if that was a compliment or an insult. Either way, though, it was true.

Solon the Lawgiver had decreed a century earlier that if any Athenian man became too powerful, he could be ostracized by a majority vote in the Assembly and banished from the city for ten years. He would not lose his citizenship, properties, or businesses. He simply had to go away. His family was not required to leave with him. Wives and young children almost always did, but usually a brother, an uncle, or an adult son remained in Athens to mind the family businesses. A couple of months earlier, Brontes had been ostracized. He was a loud aristocratic dolt whose power was limited because no one took him seriously, even when he'd been elected archon. *Ostrakophoria* was a means for Themistocles to rid himself of political nuisances, like Brontes, as well as men who posed actual threats.

Two men were candidates for ostracism today. Themistocles was one. Aristides was the other.

Themistocles claimed that Aristides wanted to set himself up as king of Athens. Aristides made the same claim about Themistocles. Each man accused the other of sedition, of treason, of damaging the reputation of the Assembly by tyrannically manipulating its voters.

I hated all this. Aristides was foolish at times and politically unskilled, and not without ambition, but he did not want to be king of Athens. He couldn't manipulate the voters to gain such power because he simply didn't know how. Even if he did, he'd be too principled to do it.

The herald announced that the floor was open. Any citizen had the right to ask me questions.

Kimon was first. This was a paradox of the Assembly: all citizens were theoretically equal here, and no man's vote counted for more than any other man's, but the aristocrats were still the leaders and the commoners deferred to them. The aristocrats were a minority but addressed the Assembly the most often. They were also most likely to be ostracized.

Themistocles had warned me that Kimon would try to

twist my words. I would have to be careful.

"You are not a citizen of Athens?" Kimon said.

"True, sir," I said. "We've already established that."

"Why not?" said Kimon. "Athens not good enough for you?"

"It's not that, sir," I said. I called him 'sir' out of courtesy. Kimon was my age. If I was polite and Kimon was not, most of the men here today would notice that the half barbarian had better manners than the aristocrat. Kimon never seemed to get this.

"I never completed the ephebe training," I went on. "I will eventually apply for citizenship, once I've provided some years of service to the city."

"Service to Themistocles, you mean."

"Themistocles has official authority right now, so if I serve him, I serve Athens."

"Tell the Assembly why you didn't finish ephebe training. You left under mysterious circumstances."

"Nothing mysterious about them, sir. I was expelled on a technicality. I was born a slave. I was manumitted as a child, but the Ephebe College is open to only the freeborn." Most of the young men who'd been my fellow ephebes were present today. This was good. They could be called upon, if necessary, to vouch for my courage in battle.

"So you lied to get in?"

"No, sir, at no time did I deny my slave birth, as I don't deny it now. I didn't speak of it much because I wasn't aware that it mattered. I grew up on Skiathos, where the details of a man's birth are not as important as his character. My fellow ephebes and our trainers and officers all knew I was born a slave."

"So you're only half an ephebe?" This drew chuckles, although not as many as Kimon had hoped.

"No, sir, I was a damned good one."

"Legally, though, you never completed the training, so Athens cannot officially consider you a soldier."

Kimon was just being an asshole here. It was a matter of pride now, time to go on the offensive. I stood up and looked him in the eye. Tall as he was, I was taller.

"Do *you* actually question my skill as a soldier?" I said. "*You?* I don't have a boastful nature, but as an ephebe I could outrun and outfight any man in my unit. I was by far the best swordsman. Ask around if you don't believe me."

Kimon tried to interrupt me but I wouldn't let him. I spoke with the momentum of a charging bull, quickly, loudly, unstoppably. It was a trick I'd seen Themistocles use often.

"When our soldiers were all at Marathon," I continued, "I led forty-eight first-year ephebes against a hundred barbarian raiders. Most of the men I commanded are here today and will vouch for me. We defeated the barbarians handily, with few casualties. Afterwards, I was summoned to Marathon to act as a runner for the strategoi. I wanted to fight in the phalanx, but Miltiades wouldn't let me because he had another job for me. So I scouted the enemy and the terrain, I provided intelligence about the number and disposition of the Persian forces, and I was on hand at the battle itself to help any way I could. I delivered messages between Miltiades and the other strategoi. I killed five Persian soldiers with javelins. While I was doing all that, where were you?"

"It does not matter where I was," Kimon blurted out. "I'm not the one being questioned here."

I laughed. "That's an excellent way to evade the question, Kimon. So I'll answer it for the Assembly. Kimon was in Athens during the battle. Before the runner's job was offered to me, it was first offered to

Kimon, but he turned it down. He spent the battle cowering in his mommy's gynaikeion, with a sudden case of Mede fever."

This drew laughter and some shocked gasps. It was no lightweight accusation. *Mede fever* was a well-known term for cowardice, like *Spartan chilblains.* If I'd said this to someone on the street or in a wine-shop, fists would fly. Kimon at that moment looked, I had to admit, decidedly non-cowardly. His face was red, his fists were clenched, and he was breathing hard. He wanted to fight me right here, right now. I sized him up, got myself ready, just in case he tried.

"So are we done talking about me?" I asked him. "Or shall we talk about you some more? Or is there a chance we can get down to our real business today?"

Kimon was very relieved to change the subject. "You were one of the men hired to guard Aristides," he said, "on the journey to Parnassos."

"Yes sir, I was," I said. I'd sat back down.

"Did you at any time," said Kimon, "hear good Aristides say that he wanted to rule Athens?"

"No sir, I did not."

"So he never said he wanted to be the king of Athens?"

"I never heard him say so."

"So he never said anything like that?"

"I don't know about 'never.' I didn't spend every minute with him. I can only tell you what he said in my presence. I cannot offer opinions on things he didn't say."

"Did Aristides say he planned to raise an army and take Athens by force?"

"Not that I heard."

"Did he say he thought himself the true king of Athens?"

"No."

"Did he say he planned to have his rivals rounded up

and executed?"

"No."

"Did he ever say that he would provide intelligence to the Great King in return for governorship of Athens?"

"No." That was an unbelievably stupid question. No one had accused Aristides of complicity with the enemy, but now Kimon had put it into people's minds.

"I'm done," Kimon said to the Assembly. "I see no reason to ask this man anything else. If anyone else wants to, it's your time to waste."

Kimon made so many mistakes here that he did Aristides more harm than good. First he tried to discredit my character, and then have me vouch for Aristides' words. The biggest mistake, though, was his focus on words Aristides hadn't said. His opponents today, starting with Themistocles, would ask about Aristides' actual words. Those would be the spades that buried him.

Themistocles took the floor. Kimon had made it easy for him.

"Someone just asked me," said Themistocles to me, "if you were the son of the late Belkos the Olympian. Is this true?"

"I have that privilege, sir," I said. There were a few murmurs, as well as muttered comments about how little I resembled my father, but Themistocles' intent was clear. Belkos was an athletic hero everywhere in Hellas. Many Athenians hadn't known he was my father. Many of the men here had seen him run to victory in Athens and elsewhere. It made me a little less foreign in their eyes.

Themistocles began again. "Unlike my learned colleague, I—"

"I'm not your colleague, *commoner*," Kimon shouted.

"I stand corrected," said Themistocles. "The previous questioner and I are not colleagues. In fact, we're not in the same league at all." This drew a few chuckles.

"Unlike the previous questioner," Themistocles went on, "I do not believe there's any reason to discuss what Aristides did *not* say. I will focus on what he *did* say. Elektros, did he ever offer an opinion of this Assembly as a political institution?"

"Yes, sir," I said. "On several occasions, I heard him call it 'a congregation of apes.' Another time he referred to it as 'the moron symposium.'"

"Did he ever say why he thought this?"

"Yes sir. He said that instead of a property qualification or an age qualification, the Assembly should have a knowledge qualification. Citizens' intelligence should be tested, and the qualifying standard should be high. While I never heard him go into the specifics of how the tests should be administered, he did say that uneducated men and 'idiot farmers'—his term, not mine—should not be allowed to vote in the Assembly because they will only pursue their tiny ranges of personal interest. He said farmers lack the foresight to see the larger picture, and will invariably fail to make sensible political decisions." As I said this, I almost laughed. Aristides himself was conspicuously incapable of seeing the larger picture. And Athenian aristocrats were as likely as anyone else to make political decisions that supported their own narrow interests.

"So a man who works hard and is a law-abiding citizen should not have any say in how Athens is run?"

"I never heard him say those words, sir, but he certainly implied that being hard-working and law-abiding isn't enough."

"Did he ever say who he thought should govern Athens?"

"His exact words were 'the better men of Athens.'"

"Meaning the aristocrats?"

"That's what I took it to mean, sir, but you'd have to ask him if you want to know for sure."

"Did he say that the aristocrats would also be given the intelligence test?"

"Not that I heard."

This was a clever question. There was no shortage of unintelligent men in the aristocratic faction. Themistocles put that thought into everyone's minds without actually calling the aristocrats anything.

"Did he say what his role would be in this ideal government of his?" he continued.

"He said that Athens should be ruled by a council of 'better men.' He would automatically be included, because of his education and noble birth. You, Themistocles, despite your acknowledged abilities, would automatically be excluded due to your non-aristocratic birth."

"So I wouldn't pass his intelligence test?" Themistocles chuckled. Others laughed too. Many negative words could be used to describe Themistocles—ruthless, power-hungry, deceitful—but even his bitterest enemies acknowledged that *stupid* was not one of them.

That was pretty much all I said. No one else questioned me—which meant that I, as a non-citizen, had to leave the Pnyx. I could not legally be present during the ostrakophoria vote.

Afterwards, Phylo told me what happened. Six other men were called forward to be questioned. I told no lies, but they told no truths. One man, a fisherman, claimed that Aristides told him that he planned to become king of Athens. Once he was in power, he would execute Themistocles and outlaw the Assembly. If Aristides had ever said such a thing, which I seriously doubted, he was far too snobbish to confide it to a common fisherman.

Ironically, the Assembly on this night confirmed

Aristides' main criticism of it, which was that it could, and often did, degenerate into mob rule.

After the last man had finished lying to the Assembly, Aristides took the floor to speak on his own behalf. He tried to laugh off the absurd words that had been attributed to him. "King of Athens?" he said. "I'm not even king of my own house. Just ask my wife." He did not deny any of the words I'd attributed to him. In fact, he admitted he'd said many of them. "I have distinguished lineage," he said. "My ancestors were here when Athens was founded. Several served with King Menestheus and died before the walls of Troy. So I am entitled, as much as anyone, in fact more than most, to my opinion. I am also entitled to speak it, even when it is unpopular. If I'm not free to say what I want, then the only tyrant here is the Assembly itself. If you vote to ostracize me, you only prove my claim that self-serving demagogues can coerce the Assembly into making foolish and dangerous decisions."

I found that hard to argue with, Ephander, but no one rose to speak on Aristides' behalf. He was respected by his fellow aristocrats, but not particularly well-liked. I would have thought they'd at least object to the precedent that was about to be set here, that an aristocrat could be ostracized based on accusations that were patently untrue, but the real truth here was that Aristides irritated people, even his friends, with his unfailing righteousness. The epithet *Aristides the Just* was based as much on disdain as it was on respect.

Aristides called no witnesses other than the gods. They failed him. He questioned no one. It was not his way. It was beneath him. He considered himself a beacon of aristocratic virtue, and he thought that this, along with the clear untruth of his accusers' claims, would save him. He tried to point out that he could never be king of Athens because its current king, Themistocles, wasn't ready to abdicate. He had admitted early that he didn't respect the Assembly. He insisted that he'd done nothing wrong—and I agreed, all he'd done was speak his mind—but the mob's blood was up. By the end of his speech, when he pointed out that Themistocles manipulated the Assembly and was a tyrant in all but name—again, mostly true—the citizens of Athens didn't hear him.

When the vote for the ostracism was done, it was no contest. Most of the aristocrats, and a few commoners that probably owed them favours, voted to ostracize Themistocles, but an overall majority of eighty-five percent voted to banish Aristides.

The theoretical purpose of ostracism was to check tyranny. In practice, it banished unpopular people. An archon who proposed tax increases, no matter how badly they were needed, was just as likely to be ostracized as someone with monarchic intent.

The story went around that when it was time to vote on the ostracism, an illiterate farmer, who had arrived late at the Assembly and missed the speakers, asked an Athenian to write Aristides' name on his clay shard for him.

"What have you got against Aristides?" the Athenian asked him.

"Anyone nicknamed 'the Just,'" said the farmer, "has got to be an asshole."

The Athenian marked Aristides' name on the shard and handed it back to the farmer. The Athenian, if you haven't guessed it already, was Aristides himself, so infallibly honest that he'd help a man vote even if the result was his own banishment.

Alas, Ephander, only part of that story is true. There was an illiterate farmer, and he did ask Aristides to help write a name on his shard. My friend Timoleon was near

Aristides when it happened.

"Could you help me here, bud?" the farmer said to Aristides. "I don't write so good."

"If you can't read or write," Aristides snapped at him, "then why in the names of all the gods should you be permitted to vote in the Assembly? Go slop your hogs, you ignorant clod, and leave politics to better men!"

According to Timoleon, the farmer never actually told Aristides who he wanted to vote for, and Aristides didn't mark the shard for him, but he was still foolish here. Farmers made up the majority of the Assembly. A tirade against them, which was heard by dozens of men besides Timoleon, some of whom hadn't voted yet, was more damaging to Aristides than a single vote against him could ever be.

Honesty is one thing. Stupidity is another. Aristides demonstrated, yet again, how little he understood the political process, and how easy it was for Themistocles to use that against him.

13—SLINGER

It was past midnight. I was in my back courtyard exercising with a weighted wooden sword in each hand when I heard the knock on my door. It was Balak, one of the Scythian archers who policed the streets of Athens. He wore the Scythians' customary patterned orange long-sleeved tunic and trousers. He was armed to the tits, sword, gorytos, dagger, spear, and whip.

"Fuckingpersia spy we capture, Lectoros," he said.

"You don't need my help, Balak," I said. "You deal with spies much better than I ever could."

"Is true," said Balak. Scythians do not believe in false modesty. "Spy say knowing you. Name Sominios. Maybe not lying. So come getting you."

I didn't recognize the name, but the Scythians were famous for their inability to get Hellenic names right. Almost all of them called me Lectoros, *lecturer*, which was as close as they could get to Elektros. So I went with Balak to the lockups, which were in a drab grey building near the agora, right beside the Scythians' barracks, only a few streets away from my house.

Athenians paint their houses and public buildings bright colours, blue, green, red, yellow, so this building, unpainted grey stone, stood out for its dullness. Other Scythians nodded to Balak and me as we walked in. Inside was a central corridor with a dozen cells on both sides of it. Only four of the cells were occupied. One of the occupants wept to himself, while two others snored away, passed out drunk.

The fourth cell was lit with a dim lamp. A small naked man laid on the floor with his hands tied behind his back.

Blood ran from his nose, and his eyes were swollen almost completely shut.

A Scythian with blood on his fists stood over him. "Is man you knowing?" said the Scythian, a new man I didn't know. "If lying is, I cut off balls."

I didn't recognize the prisoner. His face was so red and purple and swollen that if he had a mirror, he probably wouldn't have recognized himself.

"What's your name?" I asked him.

He looked up at me, his face a purple nightmare, swollen lips, blood in his mouth. He tried to smile. He had some trouble speaking. The cuts over both eyes had bled so much that his face was completely red in the few places where it wasn't bruised purple. Most of the blood was caked dry, so this had begun at least an hour ago.

I couldn't understand his first few attempts at speech. He'd been hit in the throat, which made his voice a thin rasp.

"Zosi—Zosi—uhhh," he said. He coughed and blood came up.

"Zosimos?" I suddenly realized. The man on the floor nodded and stopped trying to speak.

"You've done some job on his face," I said to the Scythians, "so I can't tell for sure if he's the man he claims to be, but if he is, you were right to come and get me. He's a friend, and Themistocles will definitely want to speak to him."

The little man groaned in pain as I picked him up by the shoulders and sat him on the stone bench in his cell.

"I'm going to untie you, buddy," I said, "but I need to confirm who you are. If you try anything stupid, I'll fucking kill you myself." He nodded.

We gave him bread, cheese, and a mug of watered wine. After he'd eaten and drunk a little, his voice was still raspy but at least now we could understand him. I still didn't recognize his face, though. "Tell me about how you and I met," I said.

"In the mines," he rasped, "at Thasos." He coughed again, but no blood came up this time.

"That's *where* we met," I said. "Lots of people know I was there. Tell me about the first conversation you and I ever had."

He coughed some more, then paused for a full minute before he spoke again. "You and Andronicus had started the revolt. You started to fight your way out of the mines, but I wanted to go back inside because I had a brother, a cousin, my uncle and some Rhodian friends still locked up. You and Andronicus had two swords. I asked you for one of them. You didn't give it to me, but you let me have a dagger."

It was all true. Even with his tortured voice, the Rhodian accent was clear. He had the slight physique and small voice that I remembered of Zosimos.

"Zosimos," I said, "I will do what I can for you—and right now, it's not much. You'll stay here overnight, and the Scythians will leave you alone. Get some sleep, if you can. Tomorrow, I'll take you to Themistocles."

I had the Scythians bring Zosimos a blanket and a pillow. Hard to tell with all the blood and bruising, but the tears in his eyes were not of pain, not of joy, but of blessed relief.

The next morning, Zosimos and I were at Themistocles' house. Zosimos had been given a rough but clean tunic, and the Scythians allowed him to wash up a little, but they still insisted that Zosimos' hands be bound behind his back. If anything happened, they would be responsible, so I agreed to it, though not to the leg irons they'd also wanted on him. As soon as we were out of the Scythians' sight, I took the cords off Zosimos' wrists.

Themistocles sat at a table in his dining room eating cheese and bread and sausage. He stopped chewing when he saw Zosimos, whose entire face was swollen and purple now.

"You should see the *other* guy," Zosimos said.

Themistocles smiled. "So this is our Persian spy?" he said.

"Sir, let me introduce you," I said, "to Zosimos, son of—"

"Aklepiades," said Themistocles. "Aklepiades of Rhodes. I know your father well, Zosimos. Does the old bugger still raise his pheasants?"

"Yes, sir," said Zosimos. "I haven't been home in years, but I heard that he finally learned how to make a profit from them." His voice was clearer now, and much closer to the one I remembered from Thasos.

"Really?" said Themistocles. "How?"

"He'd been selling them as game for hunting, and getting nowhere. He finally figured out that people just want to eat them."

"That's a great idea," Themistocles said. "In fact, I might try something like that myself? What do you think, Lex?"

"All I know about pheasant, sir," I said, "is that many Athenians will pay dearly to eat it."

Themistocles nodded and wrote something on a wax tablet. Then he said, "Zosimos, you and I have met before."

"I don't think so, sir," said Zosimos. "I would remember you."

Themistocles laughed. "You were an infant," he said, "still at your mother's tit. Literally. I'm sorry to hear about Xandros. A good man, by all accounts."

"Thank you, sir," said Zosimos, who then turned to

me and explained that Xandros was his older brother, who'd been accused by the Persians of leading a revolt. The Persians crucified Xandros. It took him eight days to die. Crows pecked out his eyes while he was still alive.

Zosimos then told us about how he'd arrived at the Phaleron and gone to an inn, the Ganymede, to eat. He didn't know that the Ganymede accommodated to the tastes of a specific clientele, men who sought male prostitutes, and later he cursed himself for not figuring it out from the inn's name. I've told you before, Ephander, that Zosimos, though brave, was pretty, or at least he was before the beating, with flawless alabaster skin, soft black hair, and a face that would never sprout a beard. Girls loved him at first sight. Unfortunately, some men did too. At Thasos, the guards buggered him nightly. At the Ganymede, he'd caught the eye of a rich old man who refused to believe that Zosimos *wasn't* a prostitute. The fat man thought Zosimos' protestations were a ploy to raise his price, so he made a final offer, then tried to rape Zosimos, who, despite his delicate features, could fight. He hit the man several times and broke a water jug over his head. Then the man's two bodyguards beat Zosimos senseless. Most of the previous night's beating, he said, had been from the bodyguards, not the Scythians. The fat man, once he'd recovered his senses, denounced Zosimos as a Persian spy. The Scythians were called in and Zosimos was arrested.

This explained how he ended up in the lockups, but not what he was doing in Athens, although I'd already guessed. At Thasos, he swore vengeance on the man who'd kidnapped him and sold him to Aegean pirates, who then sold him to the Persians as a slave. My guess was that he thought that man was here.

After his escape from the mines, Zosimos could never return home. The Persians, who controlled Rhodes, considered him not only a runaway slave but also a criminal for his role in the revolt at Thasos. If he made it back home, he would only endanger his family and probably end up on a cross.

Themistocles now had that glow in his eyes that he got when he suddenly had a grand idea. The energy jumped out of him, almost lifted him right off the ground. My brother Phylo did the same thing sometimes.

"I don't know why you're in Athens," Themistocles said, even though he probably *did* know, "but I can give you an excellent reason to stay. It will be difficult work, but I'll find you a place to live and I'll pay you for your troubles. Plus it will be one more way we can fuck with the Persians. Interested?"

Zosimos' grotesquely purple smile was all the answer Themistocles needed.

A few nights later, I hosted a dinner for a few friends. The occasion was that my cousin Thoas would soon finish his five-year obligation to the city of Athens and would return to the Sea of Grass. Most Scythians did not miss Athens after they left. They rarely stayed here when their terms of service were up. They were feared here, even respected, but not particularly well liked, mostly because their reputations as fighters made Athenians uncomfortable. They were almost never invited into people's homes. In fact, this was the first time Thoas had been a houseguest in Athens. He'd been inside houses before, but only to deal with crimes. Athenians generally treated him kindly. He was often given gifts, and many Athenians greeted him on the street with a handshake and a smile, but no Athenian wanted a Scythian in his house if he didn't need to be there. Athenians still considered the Scythians savages who, if given half a chance, would murder all the men in the household and then rape all the women.

Few Hellenes understand that Scythians hold guest-friendship as sacred as we do. It was a high crime to assault your host or his family or his slaves, or to steal anything. They considered such behaviour so odious that any Scythian who behaved like that would have the shit beaten out of him by the other Scythians.

I wasn't worried that they'd harass the only woman present. The odd thing was that she wasn't worried either.

It was Phaedra, of course. She'd prepared a big meal for us. Audax helped her. He'd been helping her with her soup business for a month now. They got along splendidly. Phaedra was glad of the help and Audax was keen to be useful again. He still lived with me but wouldn't for much longer.

I told Phaedra it wasn't necessary to do this, she owed me nothing, but she insisted. I offered to pay her. She refused.

"You are a gentleman, young sir," she said. "You've always treated me with respect, and when my husband died, you found me another good man to help me with my soup business. This meal is a token of my appreciation. If you and your beastly friends enjoy it, that will be payment enough."

I didn't know at the time that when she said 'beastly,' she was being sarcastic. When the Scythians arrived at my house, she greeted them at the door with me.

"Thank you, Lectoros," said Thoas in Scythian. "Thank you for invitation." He seemed a little nervous, probably because he wasn't sure *how* to be a houseguest in Athens. That was typically Scythian. He'd fearlessly fight a dozen Sarmatians, but worried himself sick that he might inadvertently do something impolite in my home.

One of the other Scythians, Gral—nicknamed Gral the Tall, because he was almost as big as my Uncle

Borysthenes—asked me in Scythian if the pretty lady, meaning Phaedra, was also on the menu. The Scythians considered it dishonourable to take their host's women unwilling, but there was nothing wrong with asking. He was, after all, asking politely.

Unlike the other Scythians, who wore long hair and full beards, Gral shaved his head and kept his beard short. I'd invited him because he was Thoas' blood brother, but I didn't know him well and couldn't guess how serious he was. I put my arm around Phaedra's shoulders and said, in Scythian, "No. She is free, not a slave, but this good woman is under my protection."

Gral nodded. End of conversation. He would violate the code of hospitality if he tried anything with Phaedra, so he put it out of his mind.

"You are kind, Elektros," said Phaedra. "But I'm only a good woman when I need to be." She'd understood every word we'd said. She winked at Gral, then she added, in perfect Scythian, "After dinner, boys, if you need something besides food, maybe Lectoros will take you to a whorehouse."

The Scythians laughed. I did too. "Phaedra," I said, "I didn't know you spoke Scythian."

"My first husband was Saka," she said. "So was my third."

I just gawked at her. The Scythians looked at her with something approaching amazement. The more I learned about Phaedra, the more I realized how little I knew about her. And to think that when I first met her, I'd assumed she was a prissy spinster who'd led a sheltered life.

It was a warm night, so before dinner we lounged in my back courtyard. The Scythians were on their second cup of watered wine when the final guest arrived. It was Zosimos. The swelling in his face had almost completely disappeared, but he still had facial bruises and two black eyes, which added some ruggedness to his face. It actually made him handsomer.

I introduced him to the Scythians. "I hope you don't mind," I said, "that I invited an old friend of mine." None of the Scythians knew him, but they knew who he was. Themistocles suggested I invite him so that there would be no trouble between Zosimos and the men who had none-too-kindly detained him.

Gral looked at Zosimos and stood in front of him. "Is Fuckingpersian spy?" he said. He'd been one of the men who arrested Zosimos. He'd been told that Zosimos was a Persian spy, and so far no one had told him otherwise. He put his hand on his sword.

"Definitely not," I said. "He was falsely accused. Zosimos is wanted by the Persians. He helped lead a slave revolt and is now the Great King's enemy."

Gral glared at Zosimos who, though more than a foot shorter and unarmed, didn't flinch. He glared right back. This was an important moment. Scythians respect courage and despise cowardice. A man who faced them without fear, especially in a situation like this, where if it came to a fight he would probably die, earned their respect. The other Scythians rose too, ready to restrain Gral if necessary, but they too hated Persian spies.

Then Gral offered his hand to Zosimos and grinned. "Friend of Lectoros," he said, "friend of Gral. Enemy of Fuckingpersia also friend of Gral. We drink twice!"

Phaedra filled a cup with unwatered wine, then passed it around, twice. And just like that, they were friends. Scythians are quick to fight but also quick to make peace. For Zosimos, a courageous moment was all it took.

It was no coincidence that the dinner included pheasant. Themistocles did this for us. Pheasant was uncommon in Athens, not to mention expensive. Phaedra probably wouldn't have been able to find it on her own, let alone afford it, but once Themistocles had the idea to raise pheasants to sell to rich Athenians, he'd started immediately. He'd somehow acquired four breeding pairs and already had pens set up. He also acquired a dozen other pheasants for immediate sale. Then he hired Audax, whose work with Phaedra only filled part of his day, to tend them. Rich men were already asking Themistocles when he would have more.

Phaedra knew that the Scythians did not like meals with numerous courses, which they considered wasteful. It was contrary to their steppe upbringing to have a dozen dishes to choose from. If there were eight dishes in a meal, they would leave half of them untouched. Instead, they thought it the height of luxury to have two kinds of meat—Phaedra had roasted a suckling pig along with the pheasant—with several vegetables. They disdained cakes and sweet pastries, though they liked the fig-sweetened bread Phaedra had baked for them, and the fresh fruit she served them as dessert. I may have lived among the Scythians, but she'd been married to two of them and knew their eating habits better than I did. The Scythians had big smiles on their faces throughout the entire meal.

After we'd eaten our fill, Phaedra had a special treat: three skins of *koumiss*, fermented mare's milk, the Scythians' beverage of choice, which none of them had tasted since they'd left the Sea of Grass. They accepted the koumiss politely, initially unable to believe that it was real, or if it was, that it would be any good. But after they'd all tasted it, they gaped at Phaedra in astonishment. She made it herself, she said. Her first Saka husband's mother taught her how. Gral said that when he went back to the Sea of Grass, he wanted to take Phaedra with him as his wife, the ultimate compliment. He wasn't entirely serious—she was thirty years older than him—but he wasn't entirely *not* serious either.

I took a couple of sips of koumiss to be a good host, but I never much cared for it and left it for those who did.

One of them was Zosimos. It was the first time he'd ever had it. "I love this stuff!" he said. "If I drank it when I was younger, maybe I'd be as big as you ugly fuckers."

Thoas laughed so hard that he actually sprayed koumiss out his nose. Gral roared—if a bear laughed, that's what it would sound like—and clapped Zosimos hard on the shoulder. Then when he saw that he'd hurt Zosimos, who was still sore from the beating a few days earlier, Gral almost wept. "Am sorry, Sominios," he said. "I forgetting."

"Well, it's nothing," said Zosimos, grimacing, "that another snootful of koumiss wouldn't cure."

Gral again roared, then almost clapped Zosimos on the back again, but stopped himself just in time.

After the food was eaten and the wine was drunk and the koumiss was gone, when it was time for the Scythians to go home—not as late as you'd think, Ephander, Scythians are very sensitive about overstaying their welcome—Zosimos and I walked the Scythians back to their barracks. They were in excellent spirits. They'd eaten the best meal of their lives and had koumiss and wine. They were happy drunks, too, who sang lewd songs and made bad jokes.

All evening, Thoas had avoided mentioning his mother and step-father, Gia and Sevan, and his younger brother Korat, all of whom he missed severely. He wanted more than anything to see them again, and the sooner the better, but the return home was always a dilemma for the Scythians. They had all undergone the rites of manhood back on the Sea of Grass, they were all respected warriors before they left, but a Scythian considered himself a failure if he returned home without horses. This was compounded by the fact that they usually left Athens without money or even a single horse. They had their weapons, so they could hunt to survive the journey, but without a horse, it could take two years to get home. Some worked as mercenaries to get enough money for a horse or two, some simply stole horses, but both soldiering and horse-theft had associated risks. Some Scythians never made it back.

On the way back to the barracks, we stopped at Kleitos' stables. Kleitos knew we'd be stopping by late at night, so earlier that day he'd given me a key. As I was unlocking the stable doors, Deathblow whinnied. Even though I was fifty feet away from him, and on the other side of a wooden door, he knew I was there. I'd bought him from Phylo, who refused to take more than one-tenth of the horse's market price, and moved him to Kleitos' stable because there were only mares and geldings here, and no stallions, which made Deathblow a little calmer.

"Thoas," I said. "I have a problem and I need your help."

"You family," he said. "I helping, yes."

We went in to the stalls. Deathblow snorted, glared at everyone but me, then calmed down a little when I gave him an apple and rubbed his muzzle. "This fine animal should not be in a city. Deathblow is a warrior. He likes battle. In Athens, I can only ride him into battle once a year—if I'm lucky—but he wants to fight all the time. I swear, he wants to die gloriously on the battlefield. He should be on the Sea of Grass, where he'll get that chance. Please take him there."

Thoas was stunned. Unlike a Hellene, who would probably consider Deathblow an untamable problem, a Scythian would consider him a worthy challenge, one he could boast about afterwards.

"How much you wanting for him?" said Thoas.

"We're family, Thoas," I said. "This is a gift. That is, if you want him. I realize that Deathblow is not a great travel horse and he'll probably bite you at first, but he is a one man horse who, once he accepts you, becomes fiercely loyal. If you take him home with you, it will be a great favour for me. For Deathblow, too."

I'd worried that Thoas would not want to take a difficult horse that lacked stamina on a long journey, but he wept with joy, then hugged me long and hard. The other Scythians gave me bone-crushing hugs too. Never befriend Scythians, Ephander, unless you're absolutely sure you're strong enough to withstand their affection. Gral the Tall beamed and said I could marry his sister if I wanted to. This was a compliment of regal proportions.

The very next day, Thoas began to ride Deathblow daily, two or three times if he could. He took him outside the city and galloped him until he frothed. A month later, as Thoas led Deathblow out of Athens for the last time, Deathblow seemed to know that he wasn't coming back. I'd gone to the Acharnian Gate to see Thoas off. Deathblow stopped dead. He refused to budge. He stood and stared at me.

He was saying goodbye, almost like he knew he was going to a place where he could fight often and wanted to thank me for it. When I approached him, he nuzzled me and let me rub his mane. He looked at me one last time, then turned away. Horses don't cry, so he didn't turn away to hide his tears.

I did, though.

*   *   *   *   *   *

"I suspect," said Zosimos, "that Themistocles has rounded up every degenerate and deviant in Athens and sent them all to me."

I laughed. He and I were running outside the city. Every day, I taught oarsmen to swim. I had a few degenerates too, but most were fit and able. Only a handful of them did not learn how to swim a little after their first day with me. Zosimos, at Themistocles' behest, trained a unit of slingers. At the end of each day, Zosimos and I would go for a long run. His slight build and ingrained hardiness made him a natural distance runner.

Every Hellene knows how devastating slingers can be if properly deployed in battle. Miltiades learned it the hard way at Paros. If slingers get behind hoplites, or even beside them, they can destroy them. If they run out of lead sling bullets, they can use stones. At Paros, my friend Simeon had his skull fractured by a sling bullet that went right through his helmet. Slingers are vulnerable to cavalry on an open plain, but they can scramble over rough terrain where horses cannot follow, and they can easily outrun armoured hoplites.

Athenians, for some reason, are attitudinally hostile to slinging. They think it unmanly, bordering on cowardly. A real man faces his enemies up close, armed as a hoplite, face to face with shield and spear and sword. Standing in the phalanx confirms an Athenian's citizenship and, even though the Scythians might not agree, his manhood. Slinging is for goat boys. Or the poor. Everyone loved having slingers on the battlefield to weaken their enemies, but in Athens, no one wanted to be one.

Few of Zosimos' twenty-two trainees had volunteered. They were mostly harassed or cajoled by their families to learn a useful combat skill. Half of them were from families that had several sons and could not afford hoplite armour for all of them. Some of these guys accepted their role, although few actually liked it. Their parents were grateful that Themistocles had found a useful role for their sons in the upcoming war.

The few who did volunteer had physical limitations that made them unable to stand in the phalanx. One man's left arm was paralyzed, a battle injury that was, ironically, caused by a sling bullet. He could still hold a shield but couldn't move it. No one wanted to stand next to him in the phalanx, but his paralyzed arm could hold a pouch of sling shot well enough, and he really worked hard to learn how to load and sling with one hand. Another man had a leg injury that made him unable to carry the weight of his own armour. Another man was blind, but could shoot in whatever direction Zosimos told him to.

On the first day of training, Zosimos and his unhappy charges met outside the Piraean Gate, where Zosimos had drawn man-sized targets on the city wall. One of the trainees, Ezekias, showed up late, took one look at Zosimos and decided that he didn't like him. Ezekias was six feet tall and flabby. He already stunk of wine.

"Fuckin' wonderful," he said when Zosimos introduced himself to the group. "We're learning to fight like girls, so they got a girl to teach us."

Zosimos just smiled. He'd heard that sort of thing all his life.

"Your name?" he said to Exekias.

"None of your fucking business, little girl," said Ezekias. A few of the others laughed.

"Odd name," said Zosimos, "but I'll make you a deal, Noneofyourfuckingbusinesslittlegirl. If you learn how to sling passably well, I'll teach you how to fight like a man."

Ezekias laughed. "I know how to fight like a man, sweetheart," he said.

"Really?" said Zosimos. "I'd guess that you can drink

passably well, but a fucking *toddler* could probably kick your ass."

Ezekias threw an overhand punch at Zosimos, who ducked it and then countered with a hard shot into Ezekias' ribs. Then he stunned Ezekias with a hard left to the head, and dropped him with a kick in the balls. It took maybe six seconds.

"Does anyone else have any objections to being taught to sling today?" asked Zosimos. "Speak up now so we can get it out of the way."

None of the others laughed now. Eventually, Ezekias soon stopped drinking in the morning, then he worked hard enough at slinging that Zosimos made him his second-in-command. The others had started to call Ezekias *Nunno*, an abbreviation of Noneofyourfuckingbusinesslittlegirl, until Zosimos made them knock it off.

The trainees respected Zosimos now, but that didn't make them respect slinging, and it definitely didn't make them any better at it. None of them had even known how to hold a sling. Themistocles had warned Zosimos of this.

Zosimos had a sling and a pouch of sling bullets for every man. He'd made all the slings himself out of leather—he believed, rightly, that no one in Athens could make one properly—and he showed every man how to hold the sling properly. Then when the actual slinging began, none of the Athenians had even rudimentary skill.

"I'd assumed that an Athenian man," Zosimos later told me, "would sling about as well as a Rhodian four-year-old. That was an over-generous prediction. A Rhodian four-year-old can at least send the bullet in the direction he wants it to go. When the Athenians released their shots that first day, they flew in all directions, including straight up."

Zosimos lifted the side of his tunic to show me a

vicious welt on his rib cage. "I was *beside* the guy who did this to me," he said. "Apollo's balls, on the second day I was tempted to wear armour. As it was, I had to clear out onlookers. Anyone within a couple hundred yards was not safe from my wild Athenians. Six of them were wounded by errant shots from the other slingers, even though they were standing nowhere near the target—which was a fucking stone wall. One man managed to sling a stone into his own foot. Broke his toe."

Zosimos laughed, despite his frustration. Years ago, Kandra had taught me how to use a sling in a couple of hours. I wasn't a particularly good shot—by Rhodian standards, neither was Kandra—but at least I could send the stone in the direction of the target, and I never actually hit myself.

"So far, my best shooter," said Zosimos, "is the blind guy. When I got him, he already knew how to hold the sling and could send it in the direction of the target. The poor bugger can't actually *see* the target, so if the target moves, he can't adjust. Did you know Themistocles wants my slingers on the ships?"

"No," I said. This meant I'd probably have to teach these guys how to swim. The one-armed man would be a special challenge.

After our run, Zosimos and I plunged ourselves into the River Ilissos, just south of the city's Acharnian Gate, to rinse off the day's sweat and grime and dust. The River Eridanos, which ran right through Athens, was closer but the water was unclean. It was illegal to dump human waste into the Eridanos, but the law was unenforceable and generally ignored. The lawmakers had hoped people would just use common sense and not pour shit into their own drinking water. You know as well as I do, Ephander, how well *that* ever works. So Zosimos and I went the extra couple of miles to the cleaner Ilissos.

We walked back to the city. It was still warm in the early evening sun. As we approached the Agora, where Zosimos and I would split up, me to my house and Zosimos to the family that billeted him, I heard a familiar voice.

"This savage fucker," the voice said, "took my daughter to fucking Scythia, then left her there."

"She's much safer there," I said, "than she was in Halicarnassus—where *you* left her."

Simonides hadn't changed much since I'd last seen him. His hair was a little thinner and a little whiter. He reeked of garum. He was drunk, or pretended to be. The two men with him were bodyguards. Each man put a hand on the dagger in his belt. Simonides did not appear to have a weapon, but was an expert at concealing one.

"Forget this clown, boys," Simonides said. "The Archon says I'm not allowed to kill him."

"You couldn't if you tried, old man," I said.

Simonides was about to say something else, but took one look at Zosimos and the colour suddenly drained from his face, like he'd just seen a demon.

"And if you check with the Archon," Simonides spluttered, "he'll tell you that you're not allowed to kill me either."

In a single breath Simonides went from bullish to cowed. He and his companions quickly moved on.

I didn't know why he said I wasn't allowed to kill him. I didn't particularly want to, and even if I did, I wouldn't do it because his daughter still loved him. I wouldn't add to all the suffering she'd already had.

"What the fuck was *that* all about?" I said to Zosimos. Then I saw his eyes, angrier than I'd ever seen, even back in the mines.

"I didn't know you knew Simonides," Zosimos said.

"Yes," I said. "Long story. I wanted to marry his daughter, but he didn't think I was good enough. Where do you know him from?"

"Simonides of Keos was guest-friend to my father," he said. "He dined at my father's house many times. You cannot kill him."

"I don't intend to."

"Good. I must kill him myself. He's the man who sold me to the pirates."

14—KORINTHOS

Dymnos gasped and grunted as the lash bit into the flesh on his back. He was hunched over, shoulder against a tree trunk, while Timoleon and I each held one of his arms. He looked at me, a silent plea to make it stop, but it wasn't my decision. The fifth and final lash was the first to draw blood, only a little. The flogging was flawlessly executed. The wielder of the whip knew what he was doing. The purpose was to punish and set an example, not render Dymnos unfit for duty. He would feel the pain for a few days, but the last lash had barely left his skin before a slave jumped forward and put a salve on the bleeding welt to curtail infection. Dymnos' grimace was tighter than a Scythian bowstring, but he remained conscious and stayed on his feet after we let him go.

Themistocles whipped expertly. When this caravan, headed to Korinthos, camped our first night, Dymnos had been drunk on sentry duty. We travelled all of the next day, and Themistocles had done or said nothing about it. Some of the guards thought Themistocles would let it go, but I knew him too well. If he allowed one of us to be drunk on duty, the others would have no reason to restrain themselves. So after we'd set up camp at the end of the second day and had our evening meal, and after the men who had sentry duty took their stations, Themistocles, exactly as I'd expected, ordered Timoleon and me to bring Dymnos to him.

As a commander, how different Themistocles was from Aristides. He didn't bluster, didn't make threats that he couldn't act upon. Men followed Themistocles' commands but still loved him, even Dymnos after the flogging, which Themistocles never again mentioned to him or to anyone else. As long as men did their duty, maintained their armour and weapons, and showed up sober for sentry shifts, he was satisfied. He did not constantly remind us that he was in command. He didn't need to. Themistocles assumed command naturally, rarely raising his voice, and often said nothing at all. Men who were older than him, even officers, deferred to him without debate. He was hard but fair—the flogging, painful but not debilitating, served its exact purpose. Around his campfire at night, he laughed and joked and sang with the men, and all were welcome, slave or free, as long as they didn't have duties. The two slaves on the journey rode in our supply wagon, and at the end of the day, they ate what we ate. They, too, loved Themistocles.

Themistocles even took a turn as a sentry, but after his first shift, Timoleon convinced him not to take another.

"You're too valuable, sir," Timoleon said. "You never ask gold to guard itself. You must leave this to us."

Themistocles relented, but word got around that he'd volunteered for sentry duty and the men were impressed that he wanted to share their hardships. He would sometimes stand with one of the sentries and chat with him for half an hour. It was one of those little ways that Themistocles got to know all of his men. Whenever he was in command, morale was high.

We were headed to Korinthos for a summit meeting of Hellenic leaders. The objective, at least for Themistocles, was to form a military and naval coalition against the Persians. Despite the fact that we had twenty-four armed horsemen—half that number would have been enough to discourage the few bandits on this road—this was a peace mission, an exercise in high diplomacy, headed by the most persuasive man in all Hellas.

"Walk with me," Themistocles said to me around

midnight of the third day out from Athens. I was outside my leather tent, exercising with weighted wooden swords, as I usually did at night. Themistocles had something important to say, so I just walked beside him in silence. He would pick the moment to speak and would not be rushed. We stopped about a quarter mile up the road.

"Dymnos thinks you snitched on him," Themistocles said.

"I didn't, sir," I said. "As you know." I'd been the other sentry on duty with Dymnos when he was drunk. Themistocles had spoken to Dymnos that night. He couldn't have failed to notice Dymnos' bleary eyes and wine-stink.

"And why not?" he said. "A drunken sentry endangers us all. It was your duty to report him."

"He's a friend, sir, so I let it go once. I told him he was a fool, and that if he ever did it again, I'd not only report him but beat the shit out of him. Plus I didn't see the need to tell you what you already knew."

"You are merciless to men who succumb to a vice that never tempts you."

"Hardly merciless, sir. I did let it go once."

"True."

We sat on a large stone at the side of the road. This was just the prelude, and not what he really wanted to talk about. He looked up at the sky, clear and clean and full of stars, on one of those gentle nights you wish you could bottle and preserve.

"I have a dilemma, Lexo," he finally said.

"I would think, sir," I said, "that this mission consists of a hundred dilemmas. Maybe a thousand."

"You got that right," he said with a laugh. "But this dilemma involves you. I found out who tried to kill you."

"But you won't tell me who it is," I said. "At least, not right now."

He just gawked at me, a little stunned. "That's exactly right," he said. "How did you know that?"

"Not hard to figure out, sir," I said, trying not to get a swelled head. Praise from Themistocles was a golden breeze. "If you wanted me to know, you would have told me by now. You know I want my revenge. If it's someone back in Athens, you won't tell me because I'll be so distracted that I'll ask you to let me go back home and deal with him. If it's someone who will be at Korinthos, you won't tell me because if I take my revenge there, it will jeopardize our shaky coalition before it even begins."

"You're unbelievable sometimes," he said. "I don't think you actually read my mind, but you definitely think along with me. Phylo does it too."

"And you won't tell me after we get back to Athens, either, sir," I said.

"Right again, Lexo," he said. "In fact, the one who wanted you dead must remain alive for a while longer. So I won't give you the name until after the Persians are dealt with."

"That could take years," I said.

"True. But you are young and have those years ahead of you. So I have to ask you to put the future of Hellas ahead of personal revenge, however justified it may be."

I knew the look. He wasn't asking. "I have made your would-be killer swear an oath," he said, "to not make an attempt on your life again."

"You think an oath will protect me?"

"Yes. An oath will protect you, but not the assassin's oath, which ain't worth a horse-fart in a hurricane. *My* oath will protect you. I swore I'd kill the assassin's entire family if any of them even blinks at you."

This was ruthless Themistocles, the inhuman terror that only a fool would provoke. His eyes were wide, his jaw clenched, his voice strained and tense. He meant every word. It wasn't directed at me but still gave me chills.

Then he smiled and patted me on the knee. "I have also had a similar conversation with Zosimos about Simonides."

"So Simonides isn't the one who wants me dead."

"No. He might not admit it, but he's grateful that you got his daughter out of Halicarnassus."

"You won't be able to threaten Zosimos' family to encourage his oath-keeping. They're too far away. Plus Simonides deserves to die for what he did to Zosimos."

"Do you want to kill him yourself?"

"No. My grudges against him are small, and it would not make me happy to make his daughter sad. She's suffered enough. I do not, however, have any great desire to protect Simonides from enemies he deserves to have."

"When we return to Athens, I want you to keep an eye on Zosimos. I don't know him as well as I know you, so I need you to make sure he doesn't go after Simonides against my orders. You and Zosimos will have your revenge. I promise you that. But both of you must wait. If you don't, there will be consequences. I promise you that, too."

Once Simonides was no longer useful, Themistocles would throw him under the chariot wheels, so to speak. I couldn't help but wonder if someday he'd do the same to me, but I agreed to watch Zosimos for him. Themistocles had probably also asked Zosimos, or somebody else, to keep an eye on me.

In the early afternoon of our fifth day out from Athens, we entered Korinthos through its northern gate, which the locals called the Horse Gate for the magnificent carvings of winged Pegasus on both of the great wooden doors. Pegasus was Korinthos' symbol, like the owl of Athens, and there were winged horses everywhere, including on their coins, which led the Korinthians to call drachmae *pegs*. A cheap whore, for example, was called a half-pegger, meaning that she only cost half a drachmae, while a young and beautiful one was an eight-pegger. Rooms at the best inns were ten-peggers.

Korinthos was a blessed place. Fresh water was plentiful because the city was built around half a dozen natural springs. As we approached from the north, the road took us through plains that were among the most fertile in all Hellas. In some places, the vineyards and barley and olives started right beside the roadway and stretched beyond the horizon. The locals there claimed that the farmlands south of the city were even better.

Korinthos had been a centre of trade for centuries. It was on an isthmus and controlled the ports on both sides of it. Many importers and exporters brought their wares through Korinthos, unloading their goods and transporting them overland across the isthmus, and even though they had to pay fees at both harbours and another for crossing the city, they still preferred it to the risky sea voyage around the rocky Peloponnese.

As a result, Korinthos was one of the richest cities in the world. One of the first things I noticed was that most people here were fat. Even the slaves. The beggars too.

Many of the young people, the ones who still engaged in athletic activities, were not as fat as their parents, but they were still noticeably chubbier here than their counterparts in Athens. We didn't notice it so much in farm country, where farmers and their families still worked their own land, but it was obvious in the city proper.

We teased Dymnos, who was a little pudgy. "If you lived here, Dym," Timoleon said, "you'd be one of the thinnest people in town."

"Not for long," said Dymnos, eyeing some fig cakes,

still steaming from the oven, on a vendor's cart that had been set up just inside the Horse Gate.

The fig cakes would have to wait. Themistocles understood the importance of a grand entrance. Once we entered the city, we rode in formation—in Korinthos, unlike Athens, we were allowed to ride our horses inside the city walls as long as we didn't gallop them—and as long as we paid the two-pegs-per-horse riding fee. We'd actually rehearsed our entrance. It was nothing elaborate, but Themistocles wanted us to look powerful but not tyrannical, military but not unduly aggressive, confident but not cocky. He wanted us to look like ideal allies.

Our bronze armour gleamed in the sunlight. It didn't matter that it was hoplite armour, made for men who fought on foot rather than horseback. We'd all removed our greaves, which would chafe our horses' sides if we rode any distance while wearing them. The hinged face-plates on our helmets impeded our vision, but Themistocles insisted that all of us, himself included, wear them down because it made us look more fearsome. We laughed when Dymnos said Themistocles just wanted to conceal my face so all the whores in Korinthos wouldn't flee the city in terror.

The Korinthians are worldly. So many people from so many places pass through their city, especially during peacetime, that they become accustomed to things that other Hellenes would find extraordinary. Even so, most people stopped and looked at our little parade.

When the Korinthians saw our silver owl banners, which identified us as Athenian, they knew the man who led us was Themistocles, and some called out greetings. They applauded too. The applause continued, however, after we'd passed, and we could see that the people on the street now looked behind us.

I lifted my face-plate and looked back. The spectacle

there would turn anyone's head. Twenty horsemen in golden armour rode huge white stallions, war steeds that were two hands taller than the biggest of our horses. They flanked a great golden coach pulled by four immaculate white mares. A beautiful woman, tall and black-haired and curvy and barefoot, in a yellow tunic that was way too short at the bottom and too skimpy at the top, stood on the roof of the coach and threw handfuls of gold coins to the crowd. After each throw there was a frenzy as people scrambled after the money and pushed others out of the way to get at it. A fist-fight broke out, but even those two men recognized that they wouldn't get any more of the free money if they kept fighting.

The people putting on this little spectacle were as rich as Persians. In fact, the display was so consistent with fabled Persian lavishness that for a tiny moment that's who I thought it was. Even Themistocles wasn't immediately sure who these people were, but then he saw that their banners bore a golden gryphon on a green background.

"Son of a bitch," said Themistocles. "I invited King Gelon of Syracuse, but he never replied, so I didn't know he was sending anyone."

Instead of being miffed at being upstaged, Themistocles smiled, and it wasn't the fake smile he was forced to use in the Assembly. Themistocles had two smiles. One was ceremonial, the other genuine. Over the years, I'd learned to spot the way the skin beside his left eye crinkled when the smile was real, which didn't occur when the smile was forced. He probably did not know about it, because if he did, he'd fix it.

I never told him about it because it was good to know one thing that Themistocles did not.

Themistocles understood political performances and

admired the calculated pageantry of the Syracusan entrance. The Korinthians would remember Gelon's delegation long after they'd forgotten ours.

"What do you think Athenians would say," Themistocles asked us, "if I threw money around like that?"

"Some think you already do, sir," said Timoleon, "so they wouldn't say anything they don't say now."

We laughed, Themistocles too, the genuine laugh, not the fake one.

"I wonder what Gelon wants," Themistocles said. We'd pulled off to the side of the wide street to let the Syracusans pass. "He has a large army and a larger navy. His support would be invaluable, but if he helps us against the Persians, he'll want us to join him against the Carthaginians. We don't have the men or ships to spare. Even so, this summit just got a lot more interesting."

As the coach passed us, the woman on the coach smiled and waved at us. She was the kind of black-haired, dark-skinned, curvy woman that most men dream about. "If you throw me any money, Jocasta," Themistocles called out to her, "you know you'll just get it back from me later!"

The woman laughed, not offended in the least that Themistocles had just publicly called her a whore. "Ah, Themistocles," she said in a throaty Carthaginian accent. "Some men no change. But I change. You no afford me now!"

Themistocles laughed. "Good health, dear lady," he called as the spectacle moved up the street. Jocasta smiled, bowed just enough to reveal more deep cleavage, then threw more money at the crowd.

Anyone who'd seen the Syracusans was no longer interested in us. Our moment had passed, so we rode on, observed by almost no one, to the inn Themistocles had reserved for us.

Innkeepers did well in Korinthos. There were entire streets of inns and they all stayed in business. Somebody said there were over a hundred in the city, and while I couldn't verify that, I couldn't deny it either. There were certainly more than I've ever seen anywhere else.

When we first got into Korinthos, I asked Themistocles if we were going to The Silver Owl, the inn preferred by most Athenians, famous for its quail pie, which I had a hankering for.

"That is exactly," he said, "where my enemies expect me to go. So no."

I wasn't terribly disappointed. If I had any free time, I could slip over to The Silver Owl for the famous pie. We went to The Dancing Dolphin, only two streets away from the Owl.

The Dolphin was not the most expensive inn here, but it was clean and airy and had its own reputation for outstanding food, especially the grilled goose. After we fed and watered our horses in the Dolphin's stables, we settled in, all of us on the inn's third floor, two men to a room. Most of us were able to get some sleep, but even here Themistocles posted sentries.

The innkeeper, a fat sweaty man who would have looked like an innkeeper anywhere if he wasn't wearing so much gold jewelry, took offense at this. "You are safe in The Dancing Dolphin, sir," he said. "I have guards on duty at all times."

His old and fat and wheezy guards hardly inspired feelings of security, but Themistocles reassured the innkeeper. "I don't doubt you or your men," he said, "but I want my own men to remain alert at all times. In a fine city like Korinthos, they could easily become distracted. I'm posting sentries to maintain discipline, not because we need protection here. Think nothing of it."

The innkeeper, satisfied with this explanation, sent a pretty girl up to Themistocles' room shortly afterwards.

That evening, the Dolphin's large dining hall was packed. Themistocles had invited all summit delegates to a banquet that was not officially part of the summit itself. Otreus, Themistocles' secretary, had arrived in the city a few days ahead of us to make all the arrangements.

There was some risk having all of these men, over a hundred altogether, in the same room. The first thing Themistocles did was make everyone swear an oath not to violate his hospitality with violence. An oath would not stop anyone who was determined, but would at least make it impossible to violate the peace without looking like a blasphemous asshole. Themistocles also specified that delegates could not bring weapons to the banquet.

Themistocles could not have a head table, as was customary for the host of a diplomatic banquet, because whoever sat at that table would be resented by everyone else. If he tried to appease hostile delegates by having them at this table, he could alienate friendly ones. Even the delegates at the head table would feel slighted if they did not sit in the places of honour next to Themistocles. So the only men at Themistocles' table were Timoleon, as a show of security, and small hairless Otreus, who had at least one wax tablet on him at all times. Throughout the banquet, Otreus listened to Themistocles and wrote almost continuously, even while both men ate.

All other seating was on a first come, first served basis. A few delegations, like the Plataeans, were offended by this because they had been faithful allies to Athens for decades and thought they deserved to be at the head table. They had a point, so Themistocles spoke to them to soften their hard feelings. I couldn't hear what he said, but at the end of it they laughed and shared wine.

The purpose of this banquet was to gauge the political atmosphere of other poleis, especially the ones who had so far not committed one way or the other to the Hellenic coalition. Themistocles had initially assumed that if any polis that failed to send a delegate to the banquet, then that polis was an enemy of Athens. But when everyone showed up, including the Thebans, who hated Athens in general and Themistocles in particular, he knew that attendance or non-attendance was not a reliable indicator of hostility. The Thebans, and a few others, liked free food and free wine more than they hated Athens.

When everyone was seated, the Korinthian delegate, Adeimanthos, stood up and proposed a toast to his host.

"I will drink your fine Chian, Themistocles," said Adeimanthos, well into his fourth cup, "and I'll eat your pleasant pheasant, but if I had my way, I'd have you strung up by the nuts in the public square." There was laughter and a sprinkle of applause. A troublingly high number of men drank to this as though they genuinely seconded the motion.

Themistocles laughed. He rose and raised his cup. "Well, in that case, Adeimanthos," he said, "I don't feel so bad now about poisoning your wine."

Horror flashed across Adeimanthos' face, but only for a split-second as he quickly realized it was a joke and laughed with everyone else.

Themistocles continued: "I jest, sir. I would never poison your wine. I want you to die in your own bed, at the age of ninety, surrounded by your flute-boys and butter-tarts and your hundred bastard children, and I want your last words in this life to be, 'Thank the gods I listened to Themistocles and didn't spread my arse-cheeks for the Great King like I did for every other man in Hellas! And now every one of my hundred bastards will live free and beget a hundred bastards of his own!'"

All laughed, even Adeimanthos, who stood up and bowed, raised his glass to Themistocles and declared another toast. He was laughing still, and had trouble getting the words out, but finally spoke.

"Well said, sir, well said. May our bastard children thrive when we ourselves are gone! By the time you're done, son of Neocles, you'll probably have more of them than I will." I have to credit the man for being a good sport. When he sat back down, he was still laughing at Themistocles' words.

Adeimanthos had previously claimed that he did not want Korinthos to join any alliance with Athens. Themistocles believed this to be a negotiating ploy. Korinthos was already allied to Sparta, but any alliance with those grim fuckers was always more beneficial for the Spartans than it was for the allies—and never entirely voluntary. If Korinthos was attacked, the Spartans might—*might*—send troops. The Spartans, despite their proven courage and legendary fighting skill, are always reluctant to send troops out of their own lands, even for sworn allies. They were Athens' allies the last time the Persians invaded, and how did that work out? They eventually sent a force to Marathon, but they refused to mobilize until a religious festival, the Carneia, had ended. By the time the Spartans got to Marathon, the battle was over and the deflated Persians were gone, so the Spartans just surveyed the battlefield and then marched home. Adeimanthos knew he could not rely on the Spartans. Once they took up arms, they could be counted on to fight well, but if Korinthos was invaded, it might be rubble by the time the Spartans got there.

At the banquet, the two Spartan delegates sat off by themselves, rarely speaking, making sure their wine was precisely watered, and they even ordered the serving girls to take it back if it wasn't. The Plataeans shared their table. No one envied the Plataeans. Spartans commanded an aura of superiority in the presence of other Hellenes, and did not consider conversation terribly important. They were famous for one-word answers to long questions. They say little, almost none of it worth hearing, and act like they expect a god to strike them down if they laugh at anything. They weren't stupid, just dull. It was said that if you locked a Spartan in a room with a lump of stone, the lump of stone would die of boredom. Both of the Plataeans looked like they envied lumps of stone, and they'd already abandoned any attempt to converse with the Spartans. Eventually, they began conversations with the men at other tables as if the Spartans weren't there. The Spartans cared not.

This summit was actually the second attempt to get Hellenes to ally against the Persians. The first summit, a year earlier, came at a time when Themistocles had just gotten Athenians to agree to build ships. He could not leave the city at the time—he had a thousand things to do, not only shipbuilding but training oarsmen and making sure the silver from Laurion got to the shipbuilders—and there was still a chance that Athenians might be persuaded to abandon shipbuilding if he left the city for more than a few days. The Athenian delegation at the first summit was headed by the wealthy aristocrat Epicydes, a gifted speaker. Kimon accompanied him. Themistocles knew it was a good thing to get Kimon out of Athens for a while, and was confident that Epicydes, one of the few aristocrats whose abilities were matched by his own opinion of them, would keep the younger man's abrasive manner under control.

That first summit was almost fatal. Things went wrong from the start. The Argives walked out almost the moment they arrived in Korinthos when they learned that Thebes had been invited. The Thebans weren't actually there—they never showed up or responded to the invitation—but at the time, the Argives thought they'd arrive at any moment. The Spartans, whom Themistocles believed had not fully understood the magnitude and imminence of the Persian threat, said at the start of that summit that they did not favour coalition. Themistocles was certain that they didn't make themselves clear—Spartans are not known for their communication skills—and in fact favoured the coalition but had just explained their position poorly. They'd informally told him earlier that they *were* in favour, and it wasn't like them to change their minds. On the second day of that summit, the Spartans left. They saw all the other poleis bickering like wharf-rats and thought it pointless to remain.

Once the Spartans left, everyone else did too. Instead of forming a coalition, Hellenes were more divided than ever. It had taken Themistocles a year of determined persuasion to get all the poleis to agree to try again. Incidentally, Ephander, my brother Phylo was instrumental in bringing several of the more hesitant and hostile cities to the negotiating table. He was the one who'd persuaded the Thebans to send a representative. Themistocles said he doubted he could have done it himself, and while this may have been flattery, there was little doubt about Phylo's persuasion skills. The Thebans now called him Chrysaphenios, 'the golden one,' and said with admiration that Phylo could stand in a shit-storm and convince you it was a nice day.

Themistocles' greatest task at the second summit would be to undo the damage done by the first. He did not blame Epicydes or Kimon for the previous failure. Both men represented Athens well enough—Themistocles, of course, had someone there to watch them—but neither man had the ability to lead the coalition or persuade the most hostile delegates.

Hostility was a natural state for Hellenes, who were almost always in a state of prickly distrust, if not outright war, with other Hellene city-states. Total peace was unknown in Hellas. At any given moment, at least a few poleis were at war with each other. This climate had existed for centuries. An external power threatened the liberty of all Hellas and, if victorious, would massacre or enslave entire cities, but that was not enough to make Hellenes forget their little squabbles with each other. Themistocles knew that the choice Hellenes had to make now was not between war and peace but between war against Persia as part of a coalition, or war against Persia one polis at a time. A huge obstacle for Themistocles was that some Hellenes, like the Thebans, hated the poleis that bordered their territory more than they hated the Persians. Siding with the Great King was not seen as any worse, and in many ways much better, than joining a coalition of Hellenes that was doomed to defeat. In fact, the Thebans had already declared that they planned to side with the Persians when the big invasion came, and they weren't the only ones.

There were visitors at the Syracusan table the entire evening. The two Syracusan delegates, who'd shed their golden armour and now wore gold trimmed red and green tunics, were the friendliest men here and the most popular, but the least likely to provide meaningful help against the Persians. They had the best wine and shared it freely. Themistocles muttered that some of the other delegates hung around the Syracusans because they hoped money would start getting thrown around again.

One surprising guest was Alexander, the king of Thessaly. The Thessalians had been invited to the summit but were not expected to attend. They'd sided with the Persians before Marathon, and still remained subjects of the Persian empire. I wondered about Alexander. He wore fine purple silk, and had a witticism or a wisecrack for everyone, and seemed determined to make as many friends as possible. He was bloated from too much wine, too many rich meals, and too little exercise, but he seemed harmless enough, although I wasn't the only one to suspect that he was here to act as Xerxes' spy.

This banquet seemed like a social occasion, but Themistocles never did anything that was solely social. In the course of the evening, he would speak to every man here. Amazingly, he knew everyone's name, including men he'd never met before. He did not make new allies that night, but the hostile poleis at least were willing to talk to him now.

As the evening wound down, and the delegates had eaten their fill and gotten sleepy from wine, the serving girls removed food, bowls and plates from the tables, and dodged the grasping hands of the randier delegates. The serving girls wore baggy long tunics, all grey, with white head-scarfs. One of them looked odd to me, particularly because I hadn't seen her earlier in the evening. It may have been because she'd had duties elsewhere during the meal, but as she cleared the tables with the others, I noticed she wasn't very good at it. She was probably the oldest servant here, but one of the other girls had to show her how to wipe a tabletop clean. Herakles' arse, even *I* know how to do that. Something wasn't right here.

She had sidled over to Themistocles' table, where Themistocles sipped wine and laughed at something Timoleon had just said. She used a cloth to clean the top of Themistocles' table, even though one of the other girls had just done this.

I crept up behind her. "Don't even think it, little

bitch," I said in Persian.

She flinched, a light flinch, so slight that you'd miss it if you weren't looking for it. She understood what I'd just said.

It was all the proof I needed. I grabbed her right arm, twisted it behind her back, which made her drop the dagger in her hand, but I couldn't prevent her left hand from quickly putting something into her mouth.

"Spit it out!" I said. I twisted her arm hard so that she almost collapsed from the pain. I slapped her hard on the back. She moaned, but still swallowed whatever it was.

By now, Themistocles was on his feet. Timoleon and Dymnos stood at either side of him, swords drawn.

The serving girl was still alive but had sunk to her knees. Whatever poison she'd just swallowed was fast-acting. Blood already trickled from one of her eyes, which I'd heard will happen if you're bitten by a puff adder, an African snake. She wouldn't live long enough to tell us much. In less than a minute, she was moaning and delirious. We probably wouldn't even be able to find out who hired her. We couldn't threaten her with any pain worse than what she already suffered, and she was already past the point where she could speak coherently.

She also wasn't a she. He was a man, small and clean-shaven.

We watched him die. He vomited, evacuated his bowels, and blood came out of his other eye, his nose, his mouth. It took only a few minutes for him to breathe his last.

"Report," Themistocles said to me.

"Not much to tell, sir," I said. "I noticed her, or rather him, because he wasn't a very good serving girl. I spoke Persian to him and he understood it."

"So the Great King sent him," Themistocles said.

"Possibly," I said. "How'd he even get in here?"

It was easy to understand the Great King's motivation to eliminate Themistocles. If the assassination had succeeded, the Athenians would accuse other poleis of complicity. We already knew there were men here who would approve of a dead Themistocles. I firmly believed it then, Ephander, just as I firmly believe it now, that no other man had the ability to unite the Hellenes against the Persians. If Themistocles died, we'd be divided and leaderless. This alone could win the war for the Persians. We'd been very, very lucky. I wouldn't have even spotted the assassin if I happened to be on the other side of the dining hall.

We returned to the inn's third floor to the sound of the innkeeper wailing and weeping. The man's jowls jiggled red as he apologized at least a dozen times. He screamed at his flabby old guardsmen, who'd been watching the doors during the banquet. Then he groveled to Themistocles. *Please, sir, I don't know the dead man, he was a guest at my inn, sir, but he was quiet, even when he was alive, sir, and clean and polite and didn't cause any problems, sir, and seemed like such a nice man, sir, I don't know his name, I didn't ask, sir, it wouldn't have been polite, but there was no reason to suspect him of anything, sir, and with all the new strange faces in Korinthos tonight he was just one more but now I'm ruined, sir, ruined, if word gets out that my guests try to murder each other do you know, kind sir, how hard it is to operate a fine inn in Korinthos where all the best innkeepers in the world operate and you could be ruined by just a single incident, not my fault, sir, not remotely my fault, and even if it was, sir, you and your men look like you can take care of yourselves, which you have, sir, so no harm done, sir, plus your guardsmen have had an opportunity to prove to you how good they are, sir, how really good they are at their jobs.*

The man should have just stopped talking, because the

more he proclaimed his innocence, the less we believed him. If he wasn't in on the plot, he at least knew about it.

The innkeeper begged Themistocles for forgiveness. Themistocles forgave him, or said he did, but still made the innkeeper his personal food and wine taster for the rest of his time in Korinthos. Nothing passed Themistocles' lips unless the innkeeper tried it first. Themistocles also told the innkeeper that we would not be billed for our stay. The innkeeper barely protested. This too mitigated against him. It suggested that the plotters had paid him so well that he could suffer the loss of our hefty bill, which he must have anticipated wouldn't get paid if Themistocles had been killed.

15—ALLIANCES

"We Hellenes are the only ones," thundered Adeimanthos, pounding his fist on the table, "with the right to murder Themistocles!"

The laughter was strained, the joke grim, but the point well understood. The Great King must not be permitted to interfere in the affairs of free Hellenes. On this, and probably only on this, there was unanimity, even though there was still no consensus on who sent the assassin.

We were at The Blue Eagle, the finest inn in Korinthos. Its huge dining room had been taken over for the summit negotiations. The piglet was sacrificed, the auspices taken, the oaths sworn. The summit had officially begun.

The first order of business was to determine the identity or at least the origin of the assassin, now dead and cold, dumped without ceremony outside the city for the kites and the crows and the dogs. The serving girls from the Dancing Dolphin were questioned, but none of them had seen the assassin before. Only two of them had even spoken to the man, who didn't say more than one or two words as they'd instructed him on how to clear a table. Serving women came and went frequently at The Dancing Dolphin, they said. Sometimes they had no previous experience, particularly if they'd been high-born and fairly recently enslaved, so there was nothing too unusual about a new servant who didn't know how to clear a table properly.

The innkeeper was hauled before the delegates. He said, yet again, that the assassin seemed a nice man, had paid in advance and had given him no cause for suspicion.

Themistocles was the official host of this conference,

but because this was a legal matter, Adeimanthos of Korinthos had jurisdiction here and now asked the questions. "Did the man," he asked, "ever say where he was from?"

"Miletus," the innkeeper replied. "He said he was here on business."

"Did he say what his business was?"

"He did not."

"Did he tell you his name?"

"Demetrius."

Earlier, the innkeeper had told us that he didn't know the man's name or where he'd come from. Themistocles took note of this. Adeimanthos asked more questions, but the innkeeper had nothing more to tell us. He claimed that it was not his practice to interrogate his guests, that their privacy was sacred, as was his hospitality, although if there had been even a little truth to that statement, he would never have told the assassin that Themistocles was staying at the Dolphin.

"Lock him alone in a room with me," Timoleon said quietly to me, as he tapped the handle of the dagger in his belt. "I'll learn all we need to know in five minutes or less."

I chuckled and didn't doubt it.

The next person Adeimanthos questioned was me. I stood in front of the head table, where Adeimanthos and two other Korinthians glared at me like I was their worst enemy.

"It is customary, *boy*," huffed the oldest of the three, a fat wheezing man who looked like every breath he took might be his last, "to remove one's helmet when addressing a formal inquiry."

"I didn't realize this was a formal inquiry, *old man*," I said as I removed my helmet and held it under my left arm.

"Mind your place, *boy*," the wheezy man said. "It is customary to speak courteously here."

"I always speak courteously, *old man*," I said, "to those who speak courteously to me. You spoke first, so you established today's courtesy level. I simply followed your lead."

The other old man at the table was amused by this. "The young man is a soldier," he said with a smile, "but clearly no politician."

"Unlike you old wheeze-buckets," I shot back. "Politicians, but clearly no soldiers."

Adeimanthos laughed, as did everyone else except the two old Korinthians. Old Wheezer looked like he was passing a fist-sized kidney stone.

At this point, Themistocles, who sat at an adjacent table, stood up and spoke. He tried not to laugh. "Forgive me for speaking out of turn, gentlemen, but trading insults with Elektros is not a particularly good use of our time. As you've just learned, it's also not a battle you'll easily win."

"Agreed," said Adeimanthos. "So let's start. You say, Elektros, that the assassin spoke Persian?"

"I never said that, sir. I said that he *understood* Persian."

"How do you know that?"

"I spoke Persian to him, just to see if he'd react to it."

"And did he?"

"Yes, sir."

"What did you say to him?"

"I said, 'Don't even *think* it, little bitch." I said this in Persian, and there were a few chuckles around the room, and a few more when the words were translated.

"How did he react?" asked Adeimanthos.

"He flinched, his eyes widened, then he reached into his tunic for a weapon. I grabbed his arm and twisted it behind his back until he dropped the dagger, but he'd also gone for a vial of poison with his other hand. Even though I had him down on the ground with my knee in his back within seconds, he still managed to pop the cork and swallow the poison before I could stop him."

"How does that prove that he understood Persian?" asked Old Wheezer.

"Once he knew I was on to him, he knew his mission had failed, so he chose to end his life rather than let us interrogate him."

"Are you one hundred percent certain," said Adeimanthos, "that he was Persian?"

"I never said he was Persian, sir," I said. "I said only that he understood the Persian language. I'm one hundred percent certain of *that*."

That the assassin was conversant in Persian did not make him terribly rare in Hellas. Many Hellenes had traded in Persian-held ports, with Persian-speaking toll collectors and harbourmasters, so it was advantageous to know the language. Themistocles and probably fifteen or twenty of the other men here spoke it.

There was nothing to be done now about the assassination attempt. Themistocles knew the innkeeper was involved but doubted the man could provide much detail. The assassin was likely too shrewd to have told the innkeeper any more than was necessary.

Adeimanthos thanked me for my time. The coalition negotiations could now begin.

How tough would it be to unite Hellenes? At the time, and I exaggerate not, Ephander, Athens had a small fleet of warships ready to attack Aegina, Megara was at war with Salamis, Korinthos was at war with the Argives, Thebes was at war with almost everyone, particularly Plataea and Thespiae, Leuctra was at war with Chaeronea,

Orchomenos was at war with Leuctra and Thespiae, Elis was at war with Opus, Panormos was at war with Aegion, which had just made peace with the Aegirans, who were now at war with Pellene, which had just made peace with the Sykyonians, who were now at war with Nemea, which was also at war with the Argives, who were at war with Sparta and the Mantineans, who had just made peace with Tegea, which was now allied with the Thyrians against Lerna, which was at war with Tyrins, which was now allied with the Argives against Asini, which had just made peace with Epidavros, which was in peace negotiations with Ermione that would probably fail, while Oropos fought Ramnous in an alliance with Styra, which was still at war with Karystos, while Potidania fought with the Herakleians and Trachians, who were now on the verge of war with each other, as Amfissa fought the Kirrans, who were no longer at war with Nafpaktos but now fought Thermos, as Calydon and Pleuron formed an alliance to fight the Thermians, while Astakos fought Oenidaem, Thyrium fought both Alyzia and Medion, and Stratos fought Agrinion.

Got all that, Ephander?

And that's not even all of them.

Many other small wars had just ended and others would soon begin. If I simply told you that every polis was at war with every other polis, it wouldn't be too far from wrong. Almost all of these little wars were over good farmland, so precious and so scarce in Hellas, although several were over mining resources, and a few others were fought because of tradition and sheer spite. Some of these little wars would go on for decades with occasional ceasefires as both sides regained their strength. There was an undercurrent in Hellenic thought that war was both bad and good. It was bad because young men died and trade was disrupted, but it was good because it kept a city's soldiers sharp, so that if they ever needed to fight something more than just a border dispute, such as a Persian invasion, they'd be experienced, fit and battle ready. This was why we won at Marathon; the Athenian and Plataean troops were amateurs, mostly farmers by profession, but they fought well because both cities had fought recent battles with their neighbours. Soldiering was a part of their lives. An army, like an athlete, needs to work out regularly to remain competitive. That's what our little wars did for us. In general, prolonged war was not a good thing, but neither was prolonged peace, which led to complacency. As war goes, the battles between poleis were relatively civilized. The object was to win the battle, not wipe out the opponent to the last man. Sometimes two poleis would negotiate before a battle and make not a peace treaty but a war treaty, which would specify where, when and how the battle would be fought. Both sides might agree in advance not to use missile troops, for example, or cavalry. The battle would then be fought between massed phalanxes of heavy infantry, hoplites only, and would end when one side fled the battlefield. Phylo joked that before a battle was fought, grandstands should be constructed so non-participants could watch it and wager on the outcome.

That's not as far-fetched as you might think, Ephander. When the losing side sent a herald to the victors to request permission to remove their dead, it was almost always granted because it was deemed a formal admission that the battle was lost. Casualties were relatively low, too, even for the losers, who rarely lost more than one man in ten. More than once, an army that faced Spartans fled before the sides had even engaged. This too was accepted by both sides as an admission of defeat and an end to the battle. Hellenes easily made war with each other, but almost as easily saw the advantages of peace with each other. This is what Themistocles would work with at Korinthos.

At the end of the summit's first day, the delegates had accomplished little more than introductions. Two incidents required the guards' intervention. A fistfight erupted between a Theban delegate and a Thespian, but it was easy to break up. Both men were past sixty years old and flabby. Timoleon and I jumped in, and the men, who'd been lamely slapping at each other—to call it girl fighting would needlessly insult girls—froze when they heard the *raaasp* of our swords being drawn. The Thebans and Thespians had been sitting near each other, so we moved each group to opposite sides of the room. We found out later that the fight had nothing to do with politics. It was over an incident, decades past, which involved the Theban delegate and the Thespian's wife.

Another fight broke out later that day, on the other side of the room, and it also involved the Thebans. When we moved them, we'd mistakenly put them too close to the Plataeans, who had never forgiven them for medizing before Marathon, and had always been their traditional enemies. The two groups traded a few insults, then one of the Plataeans lost his temper and tried to brain one of the Thebans with a water jug. The Theban, whose head bled now, laughed and taunted the Plataean, a hothead named Arimnestos, who was more a soldier than a diplomat and probably would have killed the Theban if we hadn't broken it up. We moved the Thebans and Plataeans away from each other, and this time made sure we didn't put either group close to any of their other enemies.

I won't bore you with all the details of the talks, Ephander, partly because even though I was there, I did not pay much attention to the delegates' words, so few of which were worth hearing, let alone repeating. But there were no more incidents that first day. With only a couple of daylight hours left, Dymnos came and relieved me at my post near the front doors.

"You're early," I said to him.

"You have a visitor," he said. "He waits for you in the dining room of the Blue Spear."

"Any idea who it is?" I asked.

"Hyperion," he said.

I looked forward to seeing my friend, but when I got to the Blue Spear's dining room, I saw Hyperion at a table in an intense conversation with Parthenia. From fifty paces, he seemed angry. She looked defiant. I was sure she'd just told him about our dalliance, and I wanted to be anywhere but here. I thought of coming back later, to perhaps give him time to calm down, but then realized that would only make things worse. Plus he'd now spotted me. I couldn't turn back. I had to face him.

When I got close, he jumped to his feet and gave me a big hug and a big smile. "Great to see you, old buddy!" he said. It was genuine. Sarcasm wasn't in him. "You remember Parthenia?"

"Of course," I said. "What man could forget her? Hello, dear lady."

She smiled. "Elektros!" she said. "I didn't know you were in Korinthos!" Then she rose and hugged me too, and kissed me on the cheek. Just as she broke it off, she squeezed my right buttock, on the side of me that Hyperion couldn't see.

"Oh come now, Thena," said Hyperion. "Where Themistocles goes, Elektros goes too."

"Mostly true," I said.

I still wasn't sure what was going on here. "That looked like a pretty serious discussion you two were having," I said.

"Ah, yes, politics," said Hyperion. "I say Thebes should be brought into the coalition, or at least be given that chance. Thena says it's impossible because the Thebans can never be trusted now, and the coalition, once it's made, should attack Thebes and take control of it so we don't have a potential enemy at our backs when we face the Persians."

What a relief. They weren't discussing Parthenia and me. I'd known that Hyperion would be in Korinthos, but not that Parthenia would come with him. Hyperion was part of the diplomatic mission. He'd come by ship and arrived two days before we did. Parthenia had begged him to take her with him to Korinthos, and he reluctantly agreed, although he probably did it only because he thought he could keep an eye on her more easily if the two of them were in the same city.

They'd spent the previous day visiting Korinthian aristocrats, to try and make them amenable to an alliance with Athens. Hyperion had impressed them, Parthenia even more so. She flirted without saying a word. Some of the aristocrats barely even noticed Hyperion, whose great failing, one that he shared with Aristides the Just, was that he never understood how few people were as proper as he was in their thoughts and actions.

Parthenia could destroy my friendship with her brother at any moment. Right now, if she chose. I was tempted to just tell Hyperion myself. It would take that power away from her. During dinner, she removed one of her sandals and put her bare foot into my groin. She massaged me, and I immediately got hard—I was at that age, Ephander, when I really didn't have much choice in the matter. Nor could I stop it. If I tried, she'd tell Hyperion about her and me. It didn't matter that our dalliance ended years ago.

When we finished dinner, I told them that I had to check in with Themistocles to see if he had any orders for me. It wasn't true, I still had a couple of hours of liberty, but I had to get away from that agonizing situation. As we said our goodbyes for the night, I had to move my sword-belt from my side to my front so my erection wouldn't show. I thanked Hyperion for dinner, which he insisted on paying for, and it wasn't cheap, so I told him that the next one was on me. As I left, Parthenia winked at me and smiled at my discomfiture. She kissed me on the cheek, 'accidentally' brushed her thigh against mine, and grabbed my right buttock again.

On the second day of the conference, there was another incident. A man tried to kill one of the two Spartan delegates. One Spartan was an older man, maybe sixty, while the other was no more than thirty. The assassin pretended to be one of the slaves who refilled the water pitchers on all of the tables. He pulled a concealed knife and attempted to stab the older Spartan, and none of the guards was close enough to intervene. Spartans are disgustingly fit, however, even at sixty, and the older man grabbed the assassin's wrist, kicked him in the balls, and threw him to the floor. Then the younger Spartan was on him quick as a wildcat, and before the assassin knew what was happening, he was flat on his stomach with his arm twisted behind his back. It turned out the assassin was an escaped helot with a private grudge against Arcas, the older Spartan, who suffered a cut arm in the attack but would not leave his table to get it treated. A slave was summoned to clean and bind the wound. Adeimanthos offered to execute the helot forthwith, but the Spartans asked that he be kept in chains, alive. They would take him back to Sparta and administer their own punishment. If the helot was smart, he would find a way to end his own life rather than face that horror.

It probably wasn't the helot's intention, but he would

have ended these negotiations if he'd succeeded. If the older Spartan was killed, the younger man would not have had the authority to approve the terms of the coalition. The Spartans would send a messenger back to their polis to request that the Gerousia, their council of elders, select another delegate. The Spartans were notoriously slow to make such decisions, so with travel time it would be at least a month before negotiations could resume. There was no way in Hades or heaven that all the other delegates would wait in Korinthos for the Spartans to return, and few would join a military coalition that didn't include the Spartans.

"We really dodged the poison arrow on that one," Themistocles said quietly to Timoleon and me, after the assassin was taken away in chains.

The summit ran for six days altogether. There were no more incidents. It took five days to decide who would and who would not join the coalition. The conversations were fractious and accusatory at times, and in the end only a little more than half of the poleis joined the coalition. When you consider how divided the Hellenes were when the summit began, this was outstanding diplomacy by Themistocles, ably assisted by Hyperion who, in the absence of the ostracized Aristides the Just, filled the role of the honourable aristocrat, the man of character and principle who impressed people with his upright thinking and plain speech. And unlike Aristides, Hyperion supported both Themistocles' policies and the man himself. If anyone doubted Themistocles' overall intentions, few doubted that Hyperion, as honest as the sea is wet, sincerely believed that the coalition was good for all Hellas and not just for Athens. His support of the coalition made others want to support it too.

When we set out for Korinthos, Themistocles had hoped to get ten or twelve poleis to join the fight and contribute ships. He was ecstatic that thirty-one had joined. Some were small states that could only contribute a couple of ships and a few hundred men. Most importantly, Sparta was in. They too had been impressed by Hyperion.

I was proud that my home polis, little Skiathos, would send three ships and two hundred men. We had no more than that, and while our force would make little difference to the total war effort, it was symbolically important because we gave all we had. Plus we'd been one of the first poleis to join.

All the poleis who did not join the alliance left Korinthos, except for the Syracusans, who had not committed either way. On the last day, the coalition members debated who would command in battle. It was agreed by all of the remaining delegates that united command had a better chance of success than a scattered command. So it was quickly decided that there should be two overall commanders, one for the fleet and one for the land troops. It was also agreed that the commander of the land forces, in the event of a disagreement, would have the authority to overrule the fleet commander.

The Syracusan delegates, easily the most popular men here since the summit began, now promised that their King Gelon would come in person and bring a fleet of forty warships and eight thousand battle-hardened infantry and skirmishers—but only if Gelon was given overall command on both land and sea.

There were advantages to this. The Syracusans had more experience fighting at sea than almost anyone else, Gelon was known as a savvy strategist, and those extra ships and troops were sadly needed. We couldn't accept, though. If Gelon commanded, he'd further his own interests and not those of all Hellas. No one here, not even Themistocles, knew Gelon particularly well, so we would in effect give command, and the responsibility for our very survival, to a near stranger. Hellenes also inherently fear monarchs. All of the poleis here, with only two exceptions, had ousted their tyrants and despots in favour of some form of democratic government. The exceptions were the Spartans, with their two kings, and the Syracusans themselves. We could not defend ourselves against a foreign king by putting our forces in the hands of a slightly less foreign king.

The Spartans immediately said they would leave the coalition if Syracuse was given command of anything. Spartans don't bluff. Their style of 'negotiation' is to state clearly what they consider acceptable. Compromise is not their way, so no one was surprised when the Spartans said that they would command all the land forces. Themistocles had always known that the Spartans would not ally with Athens unless they were given command, but he knew it was worth it. In battle, they would lead bravely.

The Syracusans then said they would still send the ships, but not the troops, if they were given command of the fleet. Gelon would not come in person, but he would send his best admiral. Both the Spartans and the Athenians absolutely refused this condition. The Syracusans, once they learned that any troops or ships they contributed would be commanded by others, left the conference.

Then the Spartans demanded command of the fleet. While it made sense for the best soldiers in the world to command on land, it made little sense for them to command at sea. They had no sea battle experience and no warships of their own. Their general Eurybiades would be, for the first time in his life, an admiral. Even so, Themistocles had no choice but to accept this.

There was now little left to discuss. Adeimanthos made an impassioned oration about how he would be the best commander of the land forces, even though the

Spartan Pausanias had already been given command. Adeimanthos believed that the Persian land forces would force battle shortly after they arrived because their army would be too big to live off the land for long, and their supply lines, which would be by sea, could be cut if the Hellenes focused their warships on this specific task. This showed that he understood what the coming war would be like, and that if the Persians fought by land and sea, we had to be ready on both land and sea. I wasn't the only one who believed he would have made good commander, but even Adeimanthos did not press his argument too far because the Spartans would not relinquish command under any circumstances. He knew this, of course, and wanted only to make an impression. The Spartans, even if they didn't comprehend the strategy he endorsed, were now aware of his value as a strategist. When the war came, his advice could be useful.

Once the question of command had been settled, the summit ended with pledges and oaths. We would all go back home and organize our armies and navies. The next day, we left Korinthos. The Athenian diplomats who'd arrived by ship, including Hyperion and Parthenia, returned by ship. Themistocles led his band of horsemen out of the Horse Gate. We were just about to pass through the gates when a dozen armed horsemen galloped towards us from the centre of the city, led by Adeimanthos.

"Is there a problem?" Themistocles asked.

"Yes," said Adeimanthos. "And you know exactly what it is."

"Here's a fair conundrum, lads," Themistocles said to us. "Adeimanthos knows what I know more than I myself know what I know."

We laughed, but only a little because we knew by the grim expressions of Adeimanthos and his men that this, whatever it was, was serious. A few hundred yards up the street, another forty armed horsemen galloped towards us. If it came to a fight, we'd be outnumbered.

"It's Karopophores," said Adeimanthos.

"The innkeeper?" said Themistocles. "Does that little fat fuck now claim that I stiffed him for the bill? He agreed to waive it."

"He claims nothing," said Adeimanthos. "He's dead."

"Can't say I'm sorry," said Themistocles. "He was in cahoots with the guy who tried to kill me. May his shade never know peace, and wander lost for eternity."

He paused. Adeimanthos said nothing.

Then Themistocles said, "Are you fucking kidding me, Adeimanthos? Do you think I'm stupid enough to kill a man that everyone in Hellas knew I had a grievance with?"

"You've got to admit, it looks suspicious," said Adeimanthos.

"It does. So anyone else who had a grievance with that sweaty shit-sack would see it as an opportune time to kill him and have it blamed on me."

"Themistocles, I've always liked you," said Adeimanthos. "You're full of shit and only a complete moron would trust you, but I still like you. So if you look me in the eye and tell me you didn't kill Karopophores, I'll take your word for it."

Themistocles looked Adeimanthos in the eye, unblinking, unwavering, unsmiling, and said, "I did not kill him or order any of my men to do so. As much as I approve of his death, I do not claim credit for it."

Adeimanthos was no fool. He still suspected Themistocles but knew there was no evidence to connect him to the murder. Pursuit of the matter would be futile. Karopophores' death could have been accidental. He was found at the bottom of his cellar stairs, stinking of wine, with a broken neck and other bruises consistent with a drunken fall.

And Herakles' arse, Ephander, please don't ask me how I knew that.

16—WALLS

Before we left for Korinthos, Themistocles dispatched another delegation to the Oracle at Delphi.

Aristides was unavailable, of course, exiled from Athens and rumoured to be in Aegina, yet again proving how poorly he understood politics. He'd insisted, after his ostrakophoria, that he was free to go anywhere he chose. This was true, technically, but he chose to go to our enemies, the Aeginetes, which left himself open to accusations of treason. Treasonous intent was never in him, but that's not how many others might see it.

So the man chosen to lead the delegation was Megakles, Aristides' uncle, brother of his late father. While Megakles did not have quite the credibility of his better known nephew, he was every bit as prissy and snobbish and loudly critical of the Assembly. If Megakles instead of Aristides had been called the Just, with all the good and bad implications of the epithet, it would have been just as accurate.

A few days after we'd returned to Athens from Korinthos, Megakles returned from Delphi. Like his nephew, he uttered not a word of the divine message to any of his travelling companions or slaves. He, too, would reveal the message only to the Assembly.

I've never been a great believer in cryptic divine messages, Ephander. Do you believe that the all-powerful gods are idiots when it comes to basic communication? If they want to tell us something, why don't they just say it straight out? Why would they put their messages in a goat's internal organs, or a bird's flight, or the way a bull bleeds to death when its throat is cut? Why would they expect us to know that the way a cloud passes in front of the sun just before a battle is a good sign for us but a bad one for our enemies? They do not communicate with each other like this, so why would they do so with us, their acknowledged mental inferiors? And when they decide to send messages through a human intermediary, why do they always choose lunatics, the people least likely to be believed?

There are two logical explanations. The first is that they laugh at us, and always have. As a practical joke, they convinced our ancestors to search for divine favour in animal guts and the sky, and the gods howl with laughter at us every time we do it.

The second explanation is that the gods don't exist. Men created them out of their own imaginations. If that's true, then trying to read the future in goat guts is too absurd to think about.

As for priests and priestesses, they either believe all this horseshit or they're charlatans who recognize the advantage of pretending they do. Don't get me started on *that*.

I am not foolish enough, Ephander, to tell people what I really think of the gods. When people invoke the gods to bless their ventures or their hearths, I do not point out their silliness. I nod and bow my head solemnly like everyone else. It is dangerous to screw with people's beliefs, no matter how inane they may be.

This was doubly true on the day Megakles revealed the words of the Pythia to the people of Athens.

Heralds had been sent out to tell everyone in the city and in the countryside that the words of the Pythia would be revealed in the Assembly on this day. I swear that twenty thousand people showed up. They crammed into the Pnyx and spilled out the sides.

Megakles, so observant of protocols, remained in his

seat in the front row with the other aristocrats. After the ceremonial sacrifice, he rose and asked the herald for permission to address the Assembly. He looked like an older version of Aristides, tall and slender and ramrod straight, although he was twenty years older with more grey in his hair. And he didn't wear rags. His tunic, unadorned blue linen, was fairly new.

When he began to speak, his voice had, despite his age, the same power that Aristides had as a speaker. He, too, had been formally trained in rhetoric.

"My fellow citizens," he began. "As you know, I was appointed by this Assembly to hear the sacred words of the Pythia at Delphi. My mission was to seek divine guidance on the matter of the war which will soon be upon us. This I have done." Megakles' smooth baritone, deeper than Aristides' voice, washed over the audience like warm sweet rain.

"You may also have heard," he went on, "that I have not yet revealed the sacred words to anyone else, including the men who accompanied me on the mission. They expected me to report the Oracle to them the moment after I received them. I knew that if I told these men what the Pythia had said, her words would have travelled to Athens ahead of us, swiftly, on the wings of rumour, in the voices of the wind. You would have received a distorted version of the Oracle, and some among us today would have persuaded you of self-serving interpretations of the sacred words."

It was a dig at Themistocles.

Megakles didn't know the half of it. Themistocles nominated him for the oracle mission because he could be counted on to do exactly what Aristides would have done, and could be manipulated just as easily as his nephew.

"Oh, don't get me wrong, the men who accompanied me on the sacred journey were no more or no less untrustworthy than most men, but even if I'd sworn them to secrecy, the slaves with us would have found out, as slaves inevitably do, and you know as well as I do that there's no point in swearing slaves to secrecy. Slaves talk. It is beyond their station to keep confidences, and the more important the news, the more likely they'll blab to friend and foe alike.

"So you must agree that I've done the right thing. Every citizen of Athens, with the exception of myself of course, will hear the words of the Oracle at the same time."

The Assembly applauded, but I suspected they did so just to get Megakles to reveal the damned Oracle. They wanted him to shut up and speak.

Megakles pulled a small scroll from his tunic pocket and read aloud:

> *Men of the Owl, steadfast and steady,*
> *Great war will come, if it's not here already*
> *Await not in silence the coming of horses,*
> *Of enemy ships and evil black forces*
> *Your walls of stone are under construction*
> *But a wall of wood saves you from destruction.*

The words were relayed to the higher seats of the Pnyx and to the people outside who were too far away to hear Megakles' voice.

Amidst the din of bewildered voices, Themistocles rose from his seat and began to make the climb down to the stage. But Megakles stopped him. "Return to your seat, son of Neocles," he said. "You'll get your turn, when I surrender the floor. Which I have not yet done."

He glared at Themistocles and said not another word to him. Themistocles held his gaze for a few moments, then nodded and went back to his seat.

Megakles then said almost everything Themistocles had planned to say.

"The first two lines of the Oracle are straightforward," he said. "We cannot avoid war with Persia. King Darius was proud. We defeated him, which his son Xerxes cannot overlook. He would consider it a taint on the honour of his family and his throne. He will not spare us if we surrender. If we want to live, we must fight.

"The words 'wall of wood' confused me. The Oracle knew that we'd already begun a wall of stone, so why would the priestess tell us to build a wall of wood? A wall of stone is far superior to a wall of wood. Wood can be burned. Stone cannot. Wood can be broken. Stone can be too, but with much more difficulty. Any part of a wooden wall can be broken by a battering ram, but against a stone wall, the ram could only be used effectively at the gates, which is where we'll have trenches and traps and most of our soldiers. So it is unimaginable that great Apollo would advise us to build a weaker wall in place of a stronger one.

"It then occurred to me that maybe we should build a second wall around the city, maybe a hundred yards outside the first wall. Think of that: if invaders were to breach the first wall, they'd have to cross an exposed killing ground. If we had archers or slingers on the inner walls, enemy casualties would be uncountable. So this is what I thought great Apollo told us to do.

"Then I realized there is no sensible reason for the outer wall to be made of wood. It, too, should be stone, especially when we consider the practical difficulties of getting good lumber and how much stone we already have. The one advantage of a wooden wall is that it can be built more quickly than a stone wall—but only if you have the lumber to hand, which we do not. In the time it would take us to find, purchase, and transport all that wood, the stone wall would probably be finished.

"Two days after I left Delphi, the god woke me from a deep sleep in the middle of the night and put the meaning into my mind. The words *wall of wood* are both plain speech and metaphor at the same time. We have already begun this barrier of wood that will confound our enemies. It is a wall, but a mobile wall.

"It is a wall of ships.

"When the Great King comes, he will have the primary goal of destroying Athens. Last time, he had other goals, such as capturing Thessaly and a few island poleis. This time, he will focus on us, and he will attack by sea. If there are land battles, the Persian soldiers will be supported and supplied by their ships.

"And no, my colleague Themistocles has not coerced me to say this. You all know how much I despise the man."

The crowd was stunned. Even though Themistocles was the hero of working men, he did not have the credibility of the uncle of Aristides the Just. Few men did.

The Assembly broke up shortly afterwards, once it was agreed that it would meet again in five days to decide how many more ships Athens would need to build. There were other details to work out, too, such as how many extra shipbuilders we would need.

As Megakles left the Assembly and headed for home, Themistocles approached him.

"Thank you, sir," said Themistocles. He held out his hand. Megakles looked at it like it was diseased.

"Do you think I actually did this for you?" Megakles sneered at him. "I do what's best for Athens, not what's best for myself, and certainly not what's best for Themistocles."

Themistocles, momentarily stunned, withdrew his

hand. "I still appreciate it," he said. "You are one of the few men in Athens who is guided solely by his sense of right and wrong, even when it's contrary to what the other aristocrats think. I admire you for it."

"I care," said Megakles, "not a goat's gobbet for what you think of me." Then he turned quickly and strode for home.

I did too. I went home to Meli.

I realize, Ephander, that I have not told you a whole lot about Meli and me. That is because there is little to tell, or at least little that I am inclined to tell. You know me by now, you filthy bugger, so you know I will not taint my lady's honour by giving you erotic details, even though you are my friend and that was another time, and a place thousands of miles from where we now sit.

Here is what I will tell: she and I had an unusually fine physical compatibility. Even after we'd been together for months, and the roses-and-sunshine phase, which all new lovers have, had diminished, we were always able to satisfy each other. Whenever I went away from Athens, I always brought her a gift. In Korinthos, I bought her a silver Pegasus-shaped brooch.

By this time, after the Korinthos mission and the second Oracle, Meli and I had been together for several years. We slept together almost every night, but she wouldn't move into my house. She still had her own house, the one she'd inherited from Khlöe, and continued to live there as she and Khlöe's freedman Faenus did the extensive repairs it needed. The roof leaked, the floorboards had rotted in places, the cellar was simply a hole in the ground, and the whole place needed painting inside and out. It was taking her years to complete. She wouldn't say so, but I believed she was worried about Faenus, who was now frail with age. She looked after him the same way, and with the same love, that Faenus had done with Khlöe.

Even though Meli and I hadn't wed, I considered myself married in all but name. Temptation came my way regularly—hey, Ephander, I was good looking back then, in my prime, and not this grey-bearded hucklebuck you see today—but I did not sleep with or even look at other women. I planned my free time, the little that I had, around Meli. I made no important decisions without her.

"She's got you wrapped around her little finger, brother," Timoleon once teased me.

"You say that," I said, "like it's a bad thing."

Timoleon laughed and said he actually envied me, and half-jokingly asked if Meli had a sister.

Actually, there was one thing we argued about. Meli wanted a child. I did too, but I believed the timing was terrible. We would go to war any day now, which would make it difficult to guarantee the safety of a young child—especially if the war was lost, a stark possibility.

"We are Hellenes," she said. "We are always at war or preparing for war. If you wait for peace, you wait forever."

"Let's deal with this Persian incursion first," I said. "Then I'll spend every waking moment trying to get you pregnant."

She was not the least bit amused. It could take years, she said, even decades, to eliminate the Persian threat. She thought I was stalling, that I did not want to make the ultimate commitment to her, but I knew something I couldn't tell her. Themistocles had sworn me to secrecy about his plan to evacuate the city, and there was a very good chance he'd have to enact it. If that happened, we would be homeless. The Persians would destroy Athens, and we'd live in tents as refugees. I did not want to endanger a child's health by bringing him or her into that situation.

I couldn't tell her this, though. Sure, Ephander, I trusted her, but when Themistocles made you swear an oath to tell no one, you told no one. I didn't take the gods seriously, but oaths were inviolable to me.

There was also a very real chance that the fucking Persians would win this war. If they did, I'd be executed or sent to the mines, Meli would be raped and enslaved, and a child too young to be useful would be killed for being an extra mouth to feed.

Still, Meli wanted a child and I wouldn't let her have one, so she lived in her own house and I lived in mine.

17—TEMPE

We looked magnificent, like twelve thousand demigods, as we stood in our formations on the plain in the Vale of Tempe, five thousand Spartan hoplites, five thousand Athenian hoplites, plus another two thousand skirmishers—helots and landless Athenians who couldn't afford armour and would hurl javelins and sling-stones at the enemy—and two hundred cavalrymen, one of whom was me. The Spartans were spotless, of course, armour glowing, the sparkle on their bronze almost blinding in the afternoon sun, and their confidence contagious as they stood still as stone. The Athenians looked almost as good. We also had another eight thousand local hoplites and skirmishers, which King Alexander of Thessaly had sent to us.

All we lacked was an enemy.

The two-hundred mile march from Athens took fourteen days. We'd met the Spartans at Plataea. They'd arrived two days ahead of us. Spartans on the march do not like to wait. The Spartan *polemarch* Euenetus was furious when the Athenians arrived in mid-afternoon, and even angrier when Themistocles told him the Athenians needed to rest before they could resume the march, which would now have to wait until morning.

"Did you not leave at the appointed time?" he snarled at Themistocles.

"We did, sir," said Themistocles.

"Then what took you so long?" said Euenetus.

"Your men are Spartans," said Themistocles. "Mine are farmers. They are fit, to be sure, and courageous in battle, but they are unaccustomed to walking more than ten or twelve miles a day. By the end of this march, they'll handle twenty a day, but if we march them too far too soon, they'll be exhausted, and militarily useless, when we reach Tempe."

"This will add days to the march," said Euenetus.

"Two days, by my calculations," conceded Themistocles. "But we have time, sir. The Persians crossed the Hellespont six days ago. They're at least twenty-two days away from the Vale."

"And you know this how?" said Euenetus. He clearly had no idea who he was dealing with.

"I have men on land and sea who send me reports, sir."

"I expect full cooperation from you, Themistocles," said Euenetus. "If you do not heed my commands, I will dismiss you from my army."

I must explain, Ephander, that Themistocles commanded the Athenians, but the overall commander here was Euenetus. It had been agreed at Korinthos that when the Spartans took the field with allies, the highest-ranking Spartan would have overall command, regardless of the rank of the allied officers present.

"But I *have* heeded your commands, sir," said Themistocles. "You specified a departure date for the Athenians, and that's when we left. You never said how many miles a day my men were to cover, and you never told me what day we were expected here."

Euenetus smoldered, but said nothing and walked away.

We camped that night outside Plataea, right beside the Spartan camp. The next morning, Euenetus wanted to start marching thirty miles a day, believing it would whip the Athenians into shape, but Themistocles somehow convinced him that a maximum of twenty would be wiser. Euenetus said that twenty miles would be a day of rest for the Spartans. It was an attempted joke, quite possibly the first of his life. He was about thirty years old, a couple of inches under six feet, taller than most Athenians but smallish for a Spartan, and he wore his hair and beard long, with his upper lip shaved, in the Spartan manner. He laughed never, and spoke no more than he had to, except to quote Spartan proverbs and praise Spartan military practices. Once he started on this, it was sometimes hard to shut him up. There was an intensity in his eyes that you normally see only in lunatics, although in the coming months I would learn that a certain controlled lunacy was mandatory for Spartan commanders.

No one doubted Euenetus' competence. What worried me was his attitude. Spartans are brave, and skilled, and so fit that they can fight on long after other troops are exhausted. This alone wins them battles. When you stand in the field with them, you thank every god that they're beside you and not facing you. But Spartans don't believe in retreat, even when it's the only wise option, and they cannot, or will not, alter tactics in the midst of battle, even when it's clear that a current strategy is failing. They have little interest in cavalry, having none of their own, and when they command allied cavalry, they have no idea how to deploy it properly.

They're also not terribly interested in advice, regardless of who gives it or how sensible it may be. In the command tent two nights before we reached the Vale of Tempe, Themistocles warned Euenetus that the Vale was a far from ideal place to fight an army of mixed forces that outnumbered us.

"Spartans ask not how many are the enemy," Euenetus huffed, "but only where they are."

It was an ancient Spartan proverb, one we'd all heard before. Themistocles bristled. Courage alone would not defeat the Persians. Themistocles was a strategist. He went to war to win, not to die gloriously. Proverbs aren't strategy, and this particular one suggested a rigidity of mind that would be fatal against the Persians. Themistocles kept his thoughts to himself, however, and we continued on.

So there we stood, in the plain in the Vale of Tempe. I'd been given a minor command, my very first. I led a scouting party of a dozen horsemen. Euenetus ordered me to take my men up the ridge in front of us. At the crest, we could see the sea. On the coast road, we spotted a small number of horsemen headed our way. They carried banners and wore royal finery, but they didn't look Persian. Even from a half-mile we could see that their horses, garlanded with gold tracings, were better suited for a parade than a battle. By the time I reported back to Euenetus, the horsemen had ridden to the crest we'd just left. They paused to observe us for a few minutes, then started to ride slowly down the ridge towards us, except for several horsemen who stayed on the ridge.

"A war party?" Euenetus asked me.

"No sir," I said. "Too few, and there are no support troops between them and the sea. This is a diplomatic party, probably local."

When the horsemen finished their descent and were on the plain ahead of us, Euenetus ordered me to go ask the horsemen who they were.

"Sir?" I said. "Their leader is an important man, probably royalty. Are you sure you want *me* to speak to him?"

Euenetus' eyes flared. "Question my orders again, Scythian," he growled, "and I'll have you executed. Now go!"

It wasn't the time to point out that I was not a citizen of Athens, and although I worked for Themistocles, I wasn't officially in the Athenian army. I was technically a civilian, so the overall authority of Spartan commanders, or any officer besides Themistocles, did not apply to me. Anyone who tried to execute me would get a sword in his guts.

My men and I approached the newcomers. Their leader, an old but regal man with an ingrained scowl that only an aristocrat could have, halted his dozen horsemen and looked at me with practiced disdain.

"Hail, my lord," I said. "My commander, Euenetus of Sparta, sends greetings. He wishes to know who you are."

The old man spat. "Typical fucking Spartan," he said. "Marches into my lands and acts like I'm the one trespassing. Why does he not ride out to meet me himself?"

"As you just said, sir," I said, "typical fucking Spartan. He doesn't observe diplomatic protocols because he probably doesn't even know they exist. He couldn't ride a horse anyway."

"You're no Spartan," he said. "And by the looks of you, no Athenian either."

"Elektros of Skiathos, sir," I said. "Euenetus sent me because I happened to be standing next to him when he first spotted you, Lord Kadmos."

"How do you know my name?" he said, amused now.

"My regular commander, sir, is Themistocles," I said. "He always knows the names of the people whose lands he enters."

"Themistocles is here?" he said. He looked at his men with alarm, then recovered. "Well, he's always fun to talk to. Full of shit, and you can't believe one word in ten, but still fun. Lead on, lad."

Twenty minutes later, Kadmos and his men were seated on camp stools in front of Euenetus' command tent. They drank sour Spartan wine and ate strips of salted meat and dried apricots. Hardly a feast fit for royalty, but the Spartans don't consider such things. It was actually a huge improvement over the infamous black broth that was their usual fare at home.

"My advice to you, Euenetus, if you'll have it," said Kadmos, "is to turn your troops around right now and march back home."

"We were invited here, Kadmos," said Euenetus, "by your own King Alexander."

"Alexander is no king to me," said Kadmos. "My nephew is barely the king of his own arse. A dangerous fool, to be perfectly honest. Xerxes lets him call himself a king as long as he doesn't actually rule anything."

"Then why did he invite us here?" asked Euenetus.

"Alexander medized years ago," said Kadmos. "He attended the summit at Korinthos as the Great King's emissary. He invited you to march into this trap—which was, in fact, Xerxes' idea."

"Spartans answer threats," said Euenetus, "with steel." Another proverb. By the gods, the man was irritating.

"It's not a threat, Euenetus," said Kadmos. "It's a warning. If you stay here, you'll be massacred. In fact, we've already got you surrounded."

"You joke too much, old man," said Euenetus.

"I joke not at all," said Kadmos. He stood up. "There," he said, as he pointed to the ridge to the east, the one he'd just ridden down, where we could make out a few horsemen. Then he pointed to the roadway north of us, where there were a few more horsemen. "There, too," he said as he pointed to the south. "And there." Then he pointed to the road behind us, to the west. "Back there, too." He'd placed men around us in every direction.

Euenetus glared at me. "Did you not say that Kadmos had no support troops?"

"I saw none, sir," I said, "but I only scouted the terrain ahead of us, as you ordered. Have your other scouts not reported yet?"

Euenetus looked stunned for a moment. That's when I realized that he'd only sent scouts ahead. I never told him that he needed to scout the terrain in all directions because, firstly, he didn't like advice, even when it was wise, and secondly, it never occurred to me that he wouldn't know to do this.

"We may die here," said Euenetus, "but you won't live to see it, old man." He drew his sword and took a step towards Kadmos, who rolled his eyes and laughed. He didn't go for his weapon.

"Are Spartans usually this clueless?" said Kadmos. "Do you really think I'm stupid enough to put myself in an enemy's hands before a battle? Now sit the fuck down, lad, and put your sword back in its sheath. Then have someone get me another cup of this pig-piss you Spartans call wine."

"Sir, please allow me to speak," Themistocles said to Euenetus, "before you do anything rash."

"Speak," said Euenetus, red-faced and still unsure of what was actually happening.

"Lord Kadmos is our friend, not our enemy," said Themistocles. "We should be grateful for his warning. He does not have enough men to attack us. He has stationed them around us to prove that we can't close off all the entry points to the Vale of Tempe. If we fight the Persians here, they'll come at us from all directions. And they *do* have enough men to attack us."

Kadmos nodded in agreement. Euenetus still simmered, but he slowly re-sheathed his sword and sat back down.

Now I understood: Kadmos had been surprised to learn Themistocles was here because he couldn't believe

Themistocles would be stupid enough to march his troops into this grand ambush. Once Kadmos had met Euenetus, though, he clearly saw that the Spartan commander had a limited view of warfare. Shrewd Kadmos also saw that Themistocles went along with the entire Tempe venture just to prove to Euenetus the value of good advice and good intelligence.

"This was my fault, Lord Kadmos," Themistocles continued. "I was responsible for intelligence, and I never informed General Euenetus of the disadvantages of this Vale as a battlefield." This was true, technically, but only because Euenetus had refused to listen to him.

Kadmos sat back down. He did not really believe Themistocles was at fault here, but for diplomatic reasons he pretended to. He was a professional soldier, an officer with almost five decades of experience, and he knew it was the responsibility of the overall commander, not a subordinate, to know exactly where he was taking his men. If Euenetus didn't know, he should have sent scouts ahead before any of his soldiers set foot into the Vale.

Kadmos also told us that once the Persians arrived, Alexander's troops would turn on us. "My nephew," he said, "looks like a king, dresses like a king, occasionally even acts like a king, but he's basically Xerxes' slubberdegullion bumboy. His mother—my dear deluded sister Nemerte—thought the responsibility of kingship, even a phony one propped up by the fucking Persians, would make a better man of him. Alexander doesn't drink all night and sleep all day as often as he used to, and he no longer spends days on end in the brothel, but apart from that, he's no better a man. In most ways, he's worse. He acts like he's earned his throne by the sword. To me, arrogance is ten times worse when it's not based on ability. The truth is that he yips and yammers and makes grand claims, but he can't be a reliable ally to you, or to any Hellenes, because he will follow the dictates of the Great King."

"That is no surprise," said Euenetus. "Thessaly is a natural breeding ground for two creatures: horses and traitors."

Tact is not a Spartan trait.

"Now you listen to me, you fucking toad," said Kadmos, jumping to his feet with an energy I didn't expect from a septuagenarian. I rose to step in front of him, but Themistocles caught my eye and shook his head. I was to let Kadmos have his say. "We submitted to the Great King because our only alternative was to be slaughtered. We were willing to fight, but we have too few men and too much territory to protect. Miltiades promised to send help but never did. We didn't ask the Spartans because it would have been a waste of time. You never considered us allies, so you can't call us traitors. If we fought the Persians, you would have just stood aside and let us die. We did what was best for our own people. So don't judge me, you little prick, until a quarter-million Persians have your rat's-arse of a polis surrounded. I will not be judged by commander who's stupid enough to march his men into an obvious ambush. If you stay to fight the Persians here, not one of your men will ever see home again."

Euenetus was unmoved, his face its usual blank mask. He'd drawn his sword and was ready to kill Kadmos. That would have been a disaster for us, because Kadmos' men, though few in number, knew the terrain and would ambush us repeatedly as we tried to march out of the Vale. I envisioned boulders falling on our heads as we marched below cliffs, which we'd have to do in several places to get out of here.

"Sir, please," said Themistocles, now on his feet. "We've already established that marching into this unscouted plain was my fault." Repeating this didn't make it any truer. "Please be seated again. We're all on the same side here."

Themistocles then invited Kadmos and his party to dinner at his tent. Some of our men had hunted earlier in the day, and venison was on the menu. "That is, if my commander approves," he said to Euemetus.

"Suit yourself," said Euemetus, indifferent to the fact that he'd just alienated a valuable local ally.

I remembered Alexander of Thessaly at the summit in Korinthos. Something wasn't right about him. Oh, he was friendly, Ephander, and he said all the right things, diplomatic niceties, but he greeted Themistocles with too many hugs and too much praise. At the time, Themistocles wondered what game Alexander played with his suspicious agreeability. He asked Themistocles to send troops to Thessaly to fight the Persians. The Thessalians would maintain the façade of alliance with the Persians, to draw them into the heart of Thessaly, but once the Athenians and their allies began the battle, the Thessalians would change sides. Themistocles asked Alexander for a quarter million drachmae to support his troops on the expedition. Alexander agreed. Then Themistocles asked Alexander to provision his troops and provide fodder for his cavalry the entire time they'd be in Thessaly. Again, Alexander agreed, no hesitation. Themistocles asked Alexander to supply two spare horses for each of the two hundred cavalrymen he planned to bring to Thessaly. No problem, said Alexander. He even promised to supply our soldiers with whores and wine, as much as they wanted of both.

Alexander had been far too agreeable. He didn't even pretend to negotiate. Whatever Themistocles asked for, Alexander agreed to provide, without even a pretense of negotiation. It was un-Hellenic. Even backed by the Great King's gold, Alexander promised more than he could deliver. And how much can you ever trust a man who has just promised to betray his current allies, even when those allies are your enemy? The Korinthos summit had been a year before the Persians would invade. Themistocles doubted that Alexander could keep his planned abandonment of the Persians secret for that long. But Themistocles played along.

"What do you think?" Themistocles had asked me in Korinthos, immediately after Alexander had left him to go drink more of the Syracusans' free Chian.

"I trust the man, sir," I said, "about as far as I could hip-toss an ox."

"Agreed. He has an agenda that he does not tell us."

This expedition to the Vale of Tempe should never have begun, but the Spartans would not listen when Themistocles told them that Alexander was untrustworthy. Themistocles insisted that Alexander's son should come to Athens as a hostage, as a guarantee of Alexander's good faith, before the expedition began. The Spartans considered such a request dishonourable, saying that Spartans answered treachery with death. Another fucking useless proverb.

After Euenetus went to confer with the other Spartan officers, as the winds blew warm across the Vale of Tempe in early evening, Kadmos and his men sat at the fire in front of Themistocles' tent and filled themselves with venison and roasted apples. They drank Chian wine. Kadmos smiled contentedly.

"You are, like me," Kadmos said to Themistocles, "a political realist. When the Persians come, the Thessalians must take their side. We will have no choice. I fully understand that you cannot commit troops to our defense without leaving Athens vulnerable. I don't blame you for protecting your own. We would not sacrifice Thessaly to protect Athens."

"Your warning, old friend," said Themistocles, "comes at a significant risk to yourself. Alexander will see it as treachery. Come back with us to Athens. You would be a valuable advisor in the war to come. Plus we can protect you."

Kadmos laughed. "I don't need protection from my idiot nephew," he said. "My place is here. But thanks for the offer, Themistocles. How's Lanike?"

"She's well, sir," Themistocles said. "She sends her regards." Themistocles had almost betrothed his sister to Kadmos, to give Athens an ally in the north. Kadmos had met Lanike, and both of them were agreeable to the marriage. It never happened because it was never clear that Kadmos would become the ruler of Thessaly, and hardy as he was, he was too old.

Before the night was done, a helot messenger arrived to inform Themistocles that the Spartans and Athenians would evacuate the Vale. We would march at dawn.

We would go home. It was a huge relief. Up until this moment, there was still a possibility that Euenetus would stubbornly insist that we remain here to get gloriously massacred. It would have destroyed the coalition, because Themistocles would have defied an order to stay. He would not let half of the Athenian army get annihilated in an unwinnable battle.

Kadmos pointed out that if the Spartans were still determined to stand gloriously against the Persians, there was a place to do it that had strategic value. The Persians planned to march their troops into Thessaly from the northeast. They brought a hundred and fifty thousand men—by the gods, Ephander, that's no exaggeration, Themistocles' sources had confirmed it—far too many to transport by sea, even with their huge fleet. So if they chose to invade Attica by land, they would have to pass through Thermopylae, the Hot Gates, so named for the thermal springs nearby. It was the only pass large enough to allow an army through, but at one point it was only a few dozen yards wide. That chokepoint could be held by a few hundred men. While the Persians had the numbers to overwhelm the defenders, it might take days. The effect this would have on Persian morale could turn the tide of the entire war. It didn't matter how many soldiers the Great King had if their spirits were broken.

The next morning, Themistocles suggested a stand at Thermopylae to Euenetus, taking great care not to reveal that the idea had come from Kadmos. Euenetus' eyes lit up for a second. He almost smiled. He spoke neither for nor against the idea, but you could tell he liked the notion of a few hundred Spartans standing up to the entire Persian army.

To a Spartan, glory, and feats of valour that men would remember for a thousand years, were more important than survival.

18—TRICKSTER

"Themistocles should be tried and convicted of recklessly squandering the resources of Athens!" the speaker told the Assembly. "And once found guilty, as we all know he is, he must be stripped of all public authority and honours, he must repay all the money he wasted, with a substantial fine on top of that, and after two years in prison, he should be ostracized—no, not just ostracized, but banished for life from Athens."

I'd never seen the man before. His name was Diodromes, but the words he spoke were Kimon's. After years of futile tirades against Themistocles, Kimon had finally figured out that the voters in the Assembly didn't like him, and that his cause might be better served if someone else spoke for him.

It didn't work. Diodromes' harangue against Themistocles had the same result it would have had if Kimon had delivered it himself. The men who cheered were outnumbered at least ten-to-one by the men who booed. Even most of the aristocrats thought the proposal was too stupid to pursue.

When Diodromes was done, Themistocles took the floor. He was calm. "I understand Kimon's bitterness," he said. "And make no mistake, my fellow Athenians, Kimon is the one who put those words into Diadromes' mouth. Kimon's father Miltiades, who served Athens so gloriously at Marathon, was severely punished, or would have been if he'd lived long enough, for his failed expedition against Paria. There are men here today who survived that failure, but not many. So few returned.

"If a commander gets to bask in the arms of Victory," Themistocles continued, "he must also be held accountable for defeat, especially one caused by his own recklessness or negligence. But Kimon is grievously mistaken about Tempe. It was no Paria. The excursion to the Vale was no victory, but it cannot be fairly described as a defeat—and certainly not a disaster. We fought no battle. We lost a total of two men, one to snakebite and another who fell over a cliff. Of the sixty-two hundred men who left Athens, ninety-nine-point-seven percent of them returned. Once we learned that the battleground would leave us vulnerable to encirclement by the Persians, we withdrew. No lives were squandered. The march there and back conditioned our men. So try me, if you will, on the charge of making our hoplites fitter."

This drew mild laughter. Themistocles continued: "There is another key difference between Themistocles at Tempe and Miltiades at Paria that Diodromes and Kimon have chosen to ignore. At Tempe, *I was not in overall command.* I would have advised against the march, despite the exercise it gave our troops, because I knew that there were too many ways into the Vale from all directions. As a subordinate officer, my advice was not sought. Even if it was, it still wouldn't have been my decision. So if you wish to try Euenetus the Spartan for wasting some of our money, good luck with that. I'm sure a lifetime ban from Athens will suit him just fine."

More light laughter. Themistocles thanked the Assembly for listening to him, as he always did, and went back to his seat.

He did not even mention another benefit of the Tempe expedition. The Spartans now owed him a huge favour. By taking the blame in front of Kadmos, Themistocles had allowed Euenetus to save face. When Spartans claim, as they often do, that this doesn't matter to them, they lie. Their reputations are the only treasures they have. The

Spartans gain no wealth from victory in battle, and rarely enlarge their territory. Honour, valour, and making heroic reputations for themselves are more important to them than their own lives. At Tempe, Euenetus was fully prepared to die against overwhelming odds because if he did, his people would remember him forever. To his credit, he ultimately saw the strategic purposelessness of getting slaughtered at Tempe, and by the end of the return journey, before the Spartans and Athenians went their separate ways again, he actually understood the value of Themistocles' military intelligence. The two of them embraced like brothers when they departed.

For the moment, I returned to my house. Themistocles had noticed that I'd been with him for months without a day's respite, so he gave me a few days' leave. I told him I was fine where I was, that I did not need time off.

"Then I must make it an order, Lexo," he said. "Every man needs some relaxation, even you. Even me."

"So you order yourself to relax too, sir?" I said.

"As a matter of fact, I do," he said. We were at the edge of the agora. He nodded towards a man a hundred yards away from us. It was Otreus, Themistocles' right hand man, with a tall striking woman who could only be Red Issa, the most expensive hetaera in Athens.

"I take my relaxation," he said, "in small amounts, but on a daily basis. And Issa is worth every blessed obol. In a few days, I'm going to need you with me for months. So take a short vacation. Rent a small boat and go fishing on the Eridanos for a couple of days. Take one of Phylo's horses out for an afternoon ride. Maybe visit a brothel or two."

I considered all of those options. A nice ride in the countryside sounded like a good idea.

On my way home, I ran into Phaedra and Audax. They'd just bought a large jar of Egyptian honey that they toted home in a hand-wagon.

Audax seemed a happy man now. Aristides' former slave tended Themistocles' pheasants and helped Phaedra haul and sell her soup every day. He was not only making some money with his two jobs but he'd now taken a wife—Phaedra, of course. They married while I was at Tempe. Between the two of them, they did well. They lived in her house and even had a slave to help them take care of it.

I asked Phaedra how in the names of all the gods she managed to get Phylo's wife impregnated.

"Well, I didn't do it myself," she said.

"But she consulted you," I said. "And she seemed much happier afterward. So did Phylo. What did you do?"

"Most of our talk must remain between her and me. But I can tell you that I instructed her in common sense and male anatomy."

"And that cured her?"

"No. As Phyloctetes suspected, Cythereia loves women. I did not cure her of that. No one can. She will never want to have sex with a man, no matter how well he treats her, but a woman of her social class has to do it anyway. So I taught her how to minimize the time it takes for a man to climax, and I advised her how to do so in a way that would most likely result in pregnancy. While it is not enjoyable for her, she now knows now that she won't have to do it more than a few times in her entire life. Basic anatomy, really, but nothing a Sapphic woman could be expected to know."

* * * * * * *

It was a hot day on land but the cruel sea wind in the straits of Artemisium whipped our faces like a winter god's revenge. I stood on the foredeck near Themistocles and was chilled bone deep as we rowed into view of the Persian ships, hundreds of them, monsters compared to our light triremes. Even from a distance, it looked like we were sending goats to fight elephants, and the elephants outnumbered the goats. If numbers and size were all that mattered, we were dead.

But we had Themistocles. The Persians did not. We would win for this reason alone.

On the foredeck of *Dimokratis*, the fleet's command ship, Eurybiades the Spartan bellowed, "We're too fast. Slow it down. One half measure." An experienced battlefield commander, his voice would have shattered bronze. I stood beside him. Timoleon stood on the other side. Eurybiades, in his first sea battle, gave the orders like he'd commanded ships all his life.

Or at least that's what men saw.

Eurybiades was magnificent, with his waist-length hair blowing in this wicked wind, his eyes fierce as a harpy's nightmare, but he only *relayed* the commands.

Two days earlier, he'd visited Themistocles in his tent. Themistocles had expected him. He offered Eurybiades wine. He sent away his servants and everyone else but Timoleon and me.

Eurybiades was legendarily fearless on a battlefield, his courage exceptional even by Spartan standards, but here in Themistocles' tent, he was nervous. He tried to mask it with a reproach.

"You take wine," he said to Themistocles, "while still on duty?"

Eurybiades looked disgusted—even by Spartan standards. Spartans always look like they find the rest of us somewhat repugnant. Frowns come easily to them. Even amongst themselves, they rarely smile. Some of us called them *synofryónomai*, 'the frowners.' We all admired their skill-at-arms and their courage, but almost nothing else about them.

Quick, Ephander, name a great Spartan poet or playwright. Tyrtaeus? Okay, that's one, but he's long dead, and all of his poems are about marching and fighting. Not exactly the type of poetry we recite to our lady friends. Name a living Spartan poet, or even one who died less than a hundred years ago. There aren't any. Creativity of any kind, whether in poetry, sculpture, plays, or even military tactics, is alien to their nature. Every now and then a Spartan says something clever, but it simply becomes yet another of their damned anonymous proverbs.

"Eurybiades," said Themistocles with a smile between sips of unwatered Chian, "I am *always* on duty. If I did not drink wine on duty, I would not drink wine at all. And we both know that ain't gonna happen." It was the sort of amiable joke that made most people laugh a little, but Spartans aren't most people. "Join me, my friend," he added, as he poured wine into a cup and held it up to Eurybiades.

"No," said Eurybiades, who remained standing and still looked at Themistocles like he was something he'd just scraped off the bottom of his sandal. "There is something I must discuss. Something extremely delicate, yet essential to victory."

His nervousness worried me. If something scared Eurybiades, what would it do to the rest of us? He was tall, over six feet, and had his scarlet cloak draped over his armour. He'd taken off his helmet, but only because the red horsehair crest would have gotten damaged against the top of the entranceway to the tent. Like all Spartan soldiers, he was fit as a god, even though he was well past forty. His beard was almost as long as his hair. His upper lip was clean-shaven, which the Spartans believe is a sign of humility before the gods. The only obvious signs of his age, if you weren't close enough to see the little creases at the sides of his eyes, were the grey streaks in his hair and beard. He'd stood in battle maybe two hundred times and looked like he had another two hundred in him. Now, he fidgeted. He picked imaginary lint off the edge of his cloak.

Eurybiades looked at Timoleon, then at me, then back at Themistocles. "As I said, Themistocles," he said, "a delicate matter. Confidentiality is crucial."

"These two are my best men," said Themistocles. "Not least because they can be trusted without reservation. They also know I'd kill them myself if they report this conversation to their own mothers. Then I'd kill their fucking mothers. If you're here to say what I think you're here to say, then these two men are essential to the plan. Here's a little test. Elektros—why is Eurybiades is here?"

The question caught me off guard, but I recovered quickly. "If I may speak frankly, sir," I said, "Lord Eurybiades is here for advice. He is a renowned infantry commander but has never commanded at sea. He will ask you to stand as his chief advisor and second-in-command."

Eurybiades' eyes widened. "How can you possibly know this?" he said to me. "I have not uttered a word to anyone."

"These two men," said Themistocles, waving a hand at Timoleon and me, "are unusually perceptive. They think along with me. And while I never expected it, because they don't know you, it looks like they think along with you too."

"Your man strikes at the crux of the matter," said Eurybiades, as he gave me a respectful nod, "but he's only partly right. I do not want you as my second-in-command. Officially, that's what you'll be. I want you to be the overall fleet commander."

Themistocles pretended to be surprised. "You know as well as I do," he said, "that Pausanias would never accept that."

"True," said Eurybiades. "I will take that wine now."

He sat down on the stool beside Themistocles. Typically Spartan, he did not know that Chian wine was to be savoured, not guzzled. He emptied his cup in one gulp, then held it out for a refill.

"Not only would my people not accept it," Eurybiades said, "I'd be tried for treason if I even suggested it. I'd probably be executed, and if I wasn't, I'd be called a trembler for the rest of my life. My wife and children would be outcasts. My parents would hang themselves in shame. So I cannot relinquish command.

"But consider this: I have only been to sea three times in my life. I spent most of the first time puking over the side. I didn't get seasick the next two times, but I'm not comfortable at sea. If asked to do so, I would stand alone against a million Persians—on land. At sea, I'd be lucky to stand up to one, because there you battle an enemy far greater—the sea itself."

This was the longest speech I'd ever heard from a Spartan. He sipped his wine again before he continued. "You know me, Themistocles. I am no fool. I am an excellent commander. I could learn to command at sea, and I would learn it more quickly than most men, but it would still require time that we do not have. I've never seen a sea battle. I do not even know what all the parts of a ship are called, or even where the commander stands during battle. So it would be foolhardy for me, and disastrous for all Hellenes, if I commanded the fleet."

"I have sailed all my life," said Themistocles. "I know our ships inside out. Some of our new triremes are faster than anything the Persians have. I know this because I made some design modifications myself. I have also studied the Persian ships, and even sailed on a few. I know their capabilities—and their limitations—better than the Persians do. But if I command at sea, even though I'm the best man for the job, the Hellenic League will collapse. Korinthos will leave immediately. So will Sparta. Others too."

"Precisely so," said Eurybiades. "And if I relinquish command, I will be sent home to stand trial. That's not the worst of it, though. I'm actually better suited than any other Spartan to command at sea simply because I recognize my own unsuitability. I have the greatest wisdom—the ability to recognize its absence in myself."

It was, at long last, a Spartan proverb that wasn't based on blank-eyed pigheadedness. It made so much sense to me that to this day, Ephander, I say it myself sometimes.

"Leotychidas and the ephors," Eurybiades continued, "would appoint my cousin Eurycleides in my place. He has even less sailing experience than me, but he's too proud to admit it. He would never seek the advice of a non-Spartan, especially you. He would appoint another Spartan as his second-in-command. That would lose us any sea battle before it even started."

It was agreed that Themistocles would make the actual battle decisions but that Eurybiades would give the commands. It would appear to all, except those immediately near him, that Eurybiades made all battle decisions.

Two days later, as we stood on the wind-whipped

foredeck of the *Dimokratis*, our fleet was in the straits of Artemisium, where its main task was to divert the Persians and prevent their ships from reinforcing their land army at Thermopylae. Themistocles sat in a chair near Eurybiades and quietly told him what commands to give. His chair had been nailed to the foredeck, out of most people's sight, and he stood up only when he needed to get a better look at what was happening. The less visible he was, the greater our chance of maintaining the façade. Timoleon and I stood beside Eurybiades and made sure no other crew members came anywhere near us.

The Persian ships approached. They were about a half mile away. We held our position. They held theirs.

"Be ready to order a rest," said Themistocles quietly.

"We don't attack?" Eurybiades asked, equally quietly. "I thought that's what we were here for."

"We will attack," said Themistocles. "But not just yet. If they choose to attack us now, with the winds and the currents in our favour, we'll cut them to pieces. They probably won't, but let's give them the chance to make that mistake. Order the oarsmen to rest and take some food."

Eurybiades bellowed the orders. By the gods, he was convincing. We would fight the Persian ships at some point, but if the Persians didn't move, we wouldn't either.

The two fleets basically just stared at each other. On land, the Spartan king Leonidas led three hundred Spartans—yes, Ephander, *those* three hundred Spartans—and several thousand more allied troops at the Hot Gates. Xerxes had ordered his entire land army to take the pass. From their starting point in Thessaly, it was the only land route to Attica. Xerxes had made a huge blunder. The Persians had elite forces, like Scythian cavalry and the Great King's legendary Immortals, and a hundred and fifty thousand fighting men. This was more than enough to eventually overrun the troops at Thermopylae, but Leonidas would fight, to the death if necessary, and hold the Gates for as long as possible. Even against such numbers, two or three days was not an unrealistic estimate of how long they could hold the pass, which narrowed to a few dozen yards at one point. Helot javelineers, slingers and stone-throwers could harass the Great King's armies from the high rocks above, while the Spartans and our other allies formed a wall of spears and shields that would be grim death to any enemy who tried to break it. The Persians, if they persisted, would win that battle, but the effort would seriously damage their army's morale which, with all its slave soldiers and conscripts, was never great to begin with.

"How many ships?" said Themistocles.

"Six hundred, sir," said Timoleon, known for his keen eyesight. "Give or take."

"Six hundred?" said Eurybiades. "I thought you said they had eight hundred."

"They do," said Themistocles. "The other two hundred are sailing southeast around Euboea to attack us from the rear."

A Spartan is more afraid of looking afraid than he is of any enemy. Eurybiades was no different. He was terrified of the sea, but he'd overcome it as much as anyone could in the short time he'd had to do so. But now, even though his body remained calm and his expression was stony, terror widened his eyes.

"It is insane for us to stay here," he said, "trapped and surrounded and outnumbered. I'll give the order to retreat."

"Eurybiades," said Themistocles, "be calm. It will take those two hundred ships another three days to get behind us. We will leave here before that happens. In the meantime, we are in a strong position. We will attack, but at the time that is best for us."

Eurybiades remained frozen. He wasn't convinced, but swallowed his fear and said no more.

So we remained where we were. Themistocles had an oversized round shield beside him. It was there to conceal his presence, to help maintain the illusion that Eurybiades was in command, but it had a second purpose. A small fishing boat rowed up from behind and slowed down beside us. A fully armoured man stood on one of its benches with a bow, an arrow nocked and ready.

Assassin! Without Themistocles, we were fucked.

Timoleon jumped in front of Themistocles with his shield up. I had my bow out of its gorytos and an arrow ready in less time than it takes to say it.

"Don't even *think* it, fucker!" I shouted at the archer.

"Stand down, lads," said Themistocles. "It's Otreus."

I looked more closely and recognized him. I'd never seen him in armour before. All his gear was too big for him. It probably belonged to Themistocles. Otreus looked like a little boy wearing his dad's clothing. Otreus was invaluable in peace and war. I just hoped he knew that if he fell into the water while wearing the armour, he was dead, even if he could swim, because the armour would drag him down to the bottom.

Themistocles stood up, and held up his oversized shield. Otreus shot an arrow into it. There was a small papyrus scroll attached to it. "Eurybiades," said Themistocles, "pull out the arrow, please, remove the message and read it, then hand it to me."

"Brilliant," said Eurybiades, almost with a smile. "I wondered how you'd get information."

Eurybiades read the message, unsure of its meaning, then handed it to Themistocles.

"This is good news," said Themistocles. "*Very* good news."

"How so?" said Eurybiades. Again, this was rare in a Spartan, the ability to admit to a non-Spartan that he didn't know something. When it comes to warfare, the Spartans tend to think that anything they don't already know is probably not worth knowing.

"Xerxes has set up a viewing platform for himself," Themistocles explained, "on the northern coast of the Gulf of Malia." He smiled broadly.

"He does not lead his men in battle," said Eurybiades.

"Exactly," said Themistocles. "He treats it like a day at the games. He does not take Leonidas' forces seriously."

Now Eurybiades smiled. "He'll regret that," he said.

Crewmen on nearby ships grumbled. They were restless. I understood. The worst part of any battle is waiting for it to start. The longer men wait, the more their minds play tricks on them. Worry will wear them down and, given time, can turn into fear, which is only a javelin-throw away from becoming panic. Eurybiades had to stop the grumbling. If allowed to continue, it could spread, like panic, like plague.

"Silence!" he roared. All heads, even those half a mile away, turned towards him.

A few men continued to complain. "Last warning!" Eurybiades thundered. "The next man who whines, I will personally throw into the sea with his hands tied behind his back and an anchor-stone around his neck!"

He looked like he meant it. The muttering stopped. Shortly afterwards, he advised the captains of the nearby ships to spread the word that our current inactivity served a strategic purpose. This satisfied the men for the moment and stopped the grumbling.

As late afternoon dragged into evening, we'd still done nothing. Neither had the Persians. Themistocles rose from his chair. "Watch this, Eurybiades," he said. "I'll bet you a silver talent that I can take down at least one Persian ship without a fight."

"Not possible," said Eurybiades. "And I never gamble, especially on a battlefield."

"Lexo," said Themistocles. "Fetch my ceremonial helm."

I went down to the hold and got the helm. He'd brought two along. The ceremonial one was oversized, gold-plated, and had a huge transverse crest. The red-dyed horsehair had three large purple heron feathers sticking out of it. The helmet was for parades and was wholly impractical in battle. It slipped off with any sudden movement and impaired the vision. The gold on its brim and earpieces sparkled in the sunlight. It could be seen from miles away. Herakles' arse, Ephander, it could probably be seen from Susa.

"Now every single fucking Persian," said Eurybiades, "will know you're on this ship."

"I want them to," said Themistocles. "Give the order to row a few hundred yards forward. Not the whole fleet. Just this ship."

"You would endanger us?" said Eurybiades, the terror flashing in his eyes again.

"Yes, there is great danger here," Themistocles said, "but not for us. Give the order and you'll see."

"I hope you know what you're doing."

"Always do."

Eurybiades gave the order. Then he saw me grinning. "You know something I don't, soldier?" he snapped.

"I'm from these parts, sir," I said. "You were wise not to take the bet."

The *Demikratis* took a position a couple hundred yards ahead of the rest of the fleet. Alone. Easy prey.

Too easy. Themistocles stood on the foredeck in his absurd helmet and pretended to scout the enemy. Ariabignes, the Persian fleet commander, wasn't fooled. He recognized Themistocles and, more importantly, knew his reputation well enough to suspect a trap. The Persians stayed put.

Then suddenly three Persian ships, the ones that had been closest to the north shore of the strait, broke from formation and came at us. They saw a chance for a major prize, Themistocles' ship, maybe Themistocles himself. They rushed at us, full speed, even as other ships' captains screamed at them to come back. In almost no time at all, they'd halved the distance between us.

"Give the 'panic protocol one' command," said Themistocles.

"You shitting me?" said Eurybiades.

"No," said Themistocles. "Gordias knows what to do. Say it!"

"Panic protocol one!" bellowed Eurybiades.

Gordias, the oar-master, echoed the command with a big grin on his face. He too was from this area and knew what was about to happen.

Our portside oars shipped while the starboard oars rowed a few strokes. Then the portside oars rowed while the starboard oars shipped. This practiced manoeuvre was repeated twice more. The bow of the *Demikratis* moved from side to side. From a distance it looked like we'd panicked. Then Eurybiades relayed Themistocles' command to turn hard about, portside.

Now it looked like we were fleeing. The three Persian ships, all large pentekonters, gained on us. They had momentum. We did not. Unless something happened, they'd be on us in less than a minute like angry barracudas.

Then a screaking *crrrrunch*! tore through the sea air. The pentekonter closest to shore just had a great part of its keel ripped out by the rocky underwater shoal it had just run into at top speed. The second ship did the same, but not before it tried, too late, to veer portside to avoid the shoal. It succeeded only in fouling the starboard oars of the third ship, whose portside oars rowed two more strokes. With the starboard oars inoperative, this turned the third ship to starboard, still at close to full speed, directly into the same deadly shoal. Now all three ships were badly holed, taking on water, and sinking. Their crews wailed.

"Hard about port," said Themistocles quietly. "We need prisoners."

Eurybiades gave the command. Some of the Persian sailors were already lost, they'd gone under and would not come back up. A few could swim, but both the shore and the other Persian ships were too far away. If they wanted to live, they had to surrender to us. Before we set out that day, Themistocles told me to fetch six extra coils of rope. Until that moment, I hadn't known why. Now we could throw ropes to the survivors and bring them in without having to come too close to the shoal ourselves.

This shoal, Ephander, is well-known to local sailors. It's called Achilles' Revenge. When brave Achilles died at Troy, killed by a mortal man, his mother, the sea nymph Thetis, wanted to kill all men in retribution. Zeus forbade this, but put this shoal in place for her, knowing that it would kill at least a few men every year, as it had just done now.

Eurybiades stood on the foredeck with a big grin.

"You never told me," he said to Themistocles, "that this was going to be fun."

19—ARTEMISIUM

The Persians made no attempt to come at us for the rest of that day, which was almost over anyway. Most of their ships beached. We turned around and headed to shallower waters for the night. We would spend the night at sea but did not fear an attack. The loss of the three ships had adequately spooked the Persians about trying these unknown waters in the dark.

Themistocles went down to the hold and slept. Timoleon did too. Eurybiades tried to sleep but could not. I stood watch on the foredeck. Around midnight, Eurybiades joined me.

"Is it true," he asked me, "that your father is Belkos the Olympian? You don't look like him."

"It's true, sir," I said. "My mother was Scythian."

"Is Belkos still with us?"

"No, sir. The plague took him a few years ago."

"Sorry to hear it. A fine man. I ran against him, you know."

"I'd heard that you were an elite athlete, sir."

"Not as elite as Belkos. I raced him seven times. Came second seven times. The last time, I thought I could beat him in the *dolichos* at the Korinthian Games because he had a minor injury. I led the race from the start, but at the very end he shot past me. Even with a sore hamstring he was unbeatable. Did you ever see him run?"

"No, sir. He retired before I was born."

"A pity. Smoothest runner I've ever seen. Some said he had a divine gift, but what I saw was perfect fluidity, a total absence of unnecessary movement in his stride and in his arms. This conserved energy, so he always had a big sprint at the end. You run too?"

"Yes, sir. Not as much as I'd like to, though."

"Same here. If I'm ever in Athens, or you're ever in Sparta, I'd like to run with the son of Belkos."

"I would be honoured, sir."

A sudden small movement in the water caught my eye. The sea, even on a peaceful night, is never completely still, but what I'd seen wasn't natural. Eurybiades hadn't seen it. I tapped him on the arm and pointed to the water.

A couple of minutes later, I saw it again. A hollow reed, the type that an underwater swimmer would use to get air, poked up six inches out of the water. Then it went under again. Eurybiades didn't see it that time either, but he did a minute later when it came up twenty feet closer.

"Sir, let me get in front of you," I whispered. I had my bow out, arrow nocked.

Eurybiades quietly went down to the hold, awakened Themistocles, and came back to the foredeck with Timoleon and some rope. Themistocles joined us a few seconds later.

"Next time you see the reed," said Eurybiades, "shoot!"

"Do not shoot," said Themistocles. "He's one of ours."

The reed came up again. So did a pale head and shoulders. Timoleon tossed the rope.

"Thank you!" came the voice from the sea. It was much higher than I expected.

The swimmer grabbed the rope. We pulled him in and up onto the deck.

It wasn't a him. A shivering naked girl stood in front of us. Themistocles had a blanket ready for her, and a dry tunic. Her dark hair was cut short, and she was broad in the shoulders and thighs, which made her look a little mannish, but she was clearly a woman.

"Welcome, Hydna," said Themistocles, as he wrapped the blanket around her and hugged her in a single motion. "I expected Scyllias. Is he okay?"

"He's right behind me," she said. "Or at least he was." She looked back towards the sea, suddenly concerned.

"Owwww! You fucking moron!" a voice cried angrily near the ship beside us. "I'm on your side. Where the fuck is Themistocles?"

"Here, Scyllias," shouted Themistocles. "You okay?"

"I would be," he said, "if one of your idiot sailor-boys didn't put an arrow into me."

Eurybiades ordered the other ship's crew to bring Scyllias aboard. When this was done, he asked about Scyllias' wound.

"He'll be okay, sir," came the reply from the other ship's captain. "Hit his shoulder, no vital organs. We're lucky Oliatos is such a crappy shot."

On *Dimokratis*, Hydna was visibly relieved. She and her father had been on a Persian ship, working as crew members, he as a rower, she as a food-server, and both of them had jumped into the water and swam here, a distance of at least five miles, in the dark.

Eurybiades, Timoleon and I were astonished.

Themistocles was not. "Scyllias is known for this," he told us. "I knew he'd been training his daughter, but I hadn't known she was ready yet."

Themistocles ordered food and warmed wine brought up for Hydna. She wanted to talk. "We can wait," said Themistocles. "We have all night. Let's get you warmed up."

"You have much more time than you think," said Hydna, unable to contain a broad smile. "Sorry, sir, but this news is too good to keep in. You know the two hundred ships sailing around Euboea?"

"I do," said Themistocles.

"They're at the bottom of the sea," she said. "The storm took every last one of them."

This took time to sink in. Themistocles knew about the storm, which didn't hit us here, but not about its severity. It was like all Hellas had just been granted a magic wish.

"How many survivors?" he asked.

"At last report," said Hydna, "zero."

This too took time to sink in. The Persians had just lost close to forty thousand men without inflicting a single casualty on us. Over the next few days, we would hear reports that thousands of bloated Persian corpses washed up on the shores of Euboea. At the port of Helleniko, on Euboea's northern coast, there had been so many bodies in the water that ships could not get in or out of the harbour.

Themistocles grabbed Hydna in a bear-hug, lifted her off the deck and kissed her on the mouth. She spilled her wine but still laughed. Then he hugged Timoleon and me at the same time, then clapped us both hard on the back.

"Good news, to be sure," said Eurybiades, whose dour face did not change. "Do not forget that the Persians still have twice as many ships as we do, and that huge land army."

"So true, my friend," said Themistocles, "but think what this will do for our morale. And theirs too. Do you honour the gods, Eurybiades?"

"Of course."

"Is this not the will of the gods? Perhaps they punish Xerxes for his earlier blasphemy. And if they punish him once, they might very well punish him again."

Themistocles was referring to Xerxes' attempt to build a bridge across the Hellespont. Hours after this huge undertaking was completed, the bridge was destroyed by an unusually severe storm. In his rage, the story goes, Xerxes ordered his men to give the sea three hundred lashes as punishment for its disobedience. He also ordered the decapitation of all the engineers who worked on the bridge.

I personally doubted this story, as did Themistocles. It would have been doubly foolhardy for Xerxes to blame his best engineers for the failure of a near-impossible task, and then by their executions create a shortage of engineers for himself. We did not yet know Xerxes as much as we'd known his father Darius, but we did know that he was no fool. Xerxes was a Zoroastrian, and while he encouraged conversion to the true faith, he did not compel it, and was known, like Darius, for religious tolerance. This was a stark necessity in his empire. He had a hundred and fifty thousand soldiers, and they had dozens of different religions, with hundreds of gods. A significant number of his men, especially the Hellenes, would be horrified if he deigned to punish the sea. They would fear Poseidon's wrath at such blasphemy. Xerxes was not stupid enough to punish the sea, but if our sailors and soldiers thought it really happened, and saw this wreckage of two hundred enemy ships as divine retribution, then they might indeed think the gods favoured our cause. There was a saying in Athens that in war, the first casualty was truth.

"I have always thought weather is just weather," said Eurybiades. "If we'd been on the eastern side of Euboea, where storms are frequent, then it would have been us instead of the Persians."

"I agree," said Themistocles. "Weather is just weather. But let's just keep that to ourselves, eh?"

Themistocles shouted the news of the Persian casualties to the ships on either side of us, who in turn passed it up and down the line. A cheer went up whenever another ship's crew heard the news. Eurybiades gave the order for each man to receive an extra half-ration of wine tonight.

"This is fortunate for us," said the Spartan, "but we must still caution against overconfidence."

Later that night, we learned that forty or fifty of the Persian ships that had faced us the previous day had also gotten caught in the tail-end of the storm as they headed to shore for the night. Again, all hands on all ships were lost, another seven thousand men.

Then even more good news, an indirect result of the storm. We were reinforced by another sixty ships. They'd originally been positioned to ambush the Persian ships who had been sent to attack our rear and had sat out the storm in a sheltered cove, but now, with no one to ambush, they joined us the next day. We had almost our whole fleet here now, and even though the Persians still had us outnumbered two to one, we were confident. The Persians were not. They'd lost a quarter of their fleet, and their huge land army still could not get past a few thousand men at Thermopylae. More than a few Persians already thought their own cause was doomed.

The next day, we approached the Persian fleet again. They approached us. But neither side engaged. Again, we sat half a mile away from each other.

"We still do not attack?" asked Eurybiades.

"We will pick our moment," said Themistocles. "As you said, we must guard against overconfidence."

We then received news of how badly the Persians struggled at the Hot Gates. Xerxes' elite regiment, his ten thousand Immortals, had been soundly defeated by the Spartans, who literally pushed a good number of them off the pass and into the sea. Spartan casualties were few. Themistocles estimated that it cost Xerxes fifty men to kill one Spartan. He had the numbers to succeed if he persisted, but if he lost thousands of men just trying to get into Attica, his remaining men would be demoralized, especially after they'd learned the news about the storm-wrecked ships—and Themistocles would make sure they knew about such things as soon as possible. If the battle at Thermopylae continued for much longer, Xerxes might even be forced to abandon the Hot Gates altogether.

Meanwhile, the fleet's primary goal was still to prevent the Persians from landing men behind our soldiers at Thermopylae. So far, we'd succeeded. The Persians did not attack us on the second day, even though we fully expected them to. All day long, we waited and waited, then waited some more. By evening, as the sun slogged across the sky, about half of the Persian ships had already turned away from us, headed for their Euboean beaches for the night. There was no more than maybe a half-hour of good sunlight left, not enough time for a battle.

Eurybiades was about to give the order to withdraw when Themistocles told him to order an attack.

"Insanity, Themistocles," said Eurybiades. "It will be dark soon."

"True," said Themistocles, "but look at them. They do not expect an attack. Their crews are already thinking about wine and meat and sleep on the beach. They have no formation. We have enough daylight left to strike quickly, sink a bunch of ships, then retreat immediately. In the dark, they will not follow. Order the attack."

Eurybiades gave the order, still uncertain what Themistocles had in mind. We rowed at the Persians full speed. As we got closer, we could see that many of them had thought this a bluff, like Themistocles' feint the day before. By the time they realized it was really happening, they rushed to turn their ships around, and came back at us in disarray. Themistocles then had Eurybiades give the *kyklos* order. Eurybiades bellowed the order so convincingly that you'd never have known that he had no idea what it meant.

Fifty of the Athenian ships, including *Demikratis*, rowed ahead of the rest, and with surprising grace formed up in a circle, sterns in the middle, bows pointing outward, so that if a god looked down from overhead he'd see a huge aster, with each ship as one of its petals. I'd seen the formation practiced more times than I could count.

What surprised me was that the Persians didn't seem to know about it. The kyklos had to be rehearsed for days, in open waters, in broad daylight. It could not be concealed. The Persians had spies in Athens. We didn't know how they would counter the formation. Right now, though, they were confused because we'd attacked, and even more confused by the sight of the kyklos.

Then they did the worst thing possible for themselves. They circled us, like sharks around a wounded dolphin.

They probably considered the kyklos a stunt, a flamboyant ploy intended to distract them, with no real strategic value. *Demikratis* was in the thick of it. I saw the faces of some of the Persian captains. They all seemed amused, like they would play along with our silly little game before they sank us. After all, they had us surrounded and outnumbered.

But they weren't sharks and we weren't dolphins. As the Persians circled, they presented their portsides to our bows. We held our formation until the Persians had sufficiently tired out their crews. Then Themistocles had Eurybiades give the order to ram.

All fifty of our ships suddenly shot straight ahead, and most of them pounded their iron rams into the sides of Persian ships on the first try. The Persians panicked, and instead of a counterattack, made a disorderly retreat.

We also retreated. This was the plan. Forty-seven of our fifty ships had each rammed and sunk one enemy vessel. Two of the others missed their marks, but still managed to disable their targets by smashing their oars, then they backed up and rammed their targets on the second attempt. The last ship missed its mark completely and was rammed broadside by a Persian quadrireme. It went down, but almost all of the men aboard survived because they swam back towards the rest of our fleet. Themistocles had a dozen ships ready in those waters for this very purpose.

I looked back. Themistocles had been right. The Persians did not pursue. One of our ships had gotten its ram stuck so deep into a huge Persian pentekonter that it could not withdraw, and went down with its target. Its crew also swam to safety. We lost two ships and fewer than ten men, but the Persians had forty-seven ships sunk and several more disabled. We learned later that we'd taken out the Persian fleet's entire Cilician contingent of about ten thousand seamen.

"A good days work, boys," said Eurybiades. "Slow it down, two measures. No one's following us." He was a fast learner. He gave this command, the right one, without prompting from Themistocles.

The next day, our third at Artemisium, we rowed out to face the Persians again. By this time, misfortunate weather and Themistoclean cunning had cost them three hundred ships. Two days earlier, few of us believed we could defeat the Persians at sea. Now few of us believed we could not.

The Persians came forward again but did not attack. The ocean currents and the morning winds were still in our favour. Even so, the enemy was here to fight today.

"They're getting desperate," said Themistocles. We'd learned that the Persians were still bogged down at the Hot Gates. They'd thrown everything they had at our allies, who numbered less than seven thousand, and so far all they'd done was lose a lot of men. Xerxes, who lacked his father's battle experience, sometimes made mistakes out of anger, which he'd just done now: he'd ordered five hundred of his infantry executed in front of the rest of the army for what he called *treasonously substandard battlefield zeal*. Our sources told us that he regretted this action, even before it had been completed, but went through with it anyway so he would not lose face or appear indecisive. It worsened rather than improved his army's morale. It also did not help that when Persian infantrymen advanced towards the Spartans' wall of shields and spears, they now had to climb over the rotting bodies of their own men. By the time they reached the Spartans, half their men were puking from the stench, which the Spartans and our other allies had gotten used to. "A dead enemy," Xenocrates once told me, "always smells good."

If truth was the first casualty in this war, Persian morale was the second. The Immortals were gone. Literally gone. If they could not prevail, what chance did Carian spearmen have, with their wicker shields and almost no armour? The Hellenes were worn down too. Their sword arms, as the saying goes, ached from overuse. They'd killed at least fourteen thousand of the enemy, while their own casualties had been a few hundred.

We suspected that the Persians wanted to force a battle at sea today, even against contrary winds, unfavourable currents, and a well-rested enemy, so they could finally get men behind the Spartans and put an end to the battle of Thermopylae. The longer that battle lasted, the better it would be for us.

Now our ships faced the Persians in three lines. The bows of the second line ships were ready to fill the gaps between the ships in the front line. The third line included our rescue ships.

The Persian fleet now came at us full speed. Even with

their losses, they still had over five hundred ships. We had half their number, and most of their ships were bigger and faster than ours. Eurybiades' eyes showed once again that he forced his terror down as hundreds of warships came at us like angry jackals. He thought we should be doing something instead of just waiting. The Persians were less than half a mile away now. Themistocles had been right about everything so far, so Eurybiades relayed his *stand by* order.

Themistocles smiled.

"What are you so fucking happy about, son of Neocles?" Eurybiades asked.

"They come too quickly," Themistocles replied. "They shifted into top speed too early and will tire too soon. Give the *panic protocol two* order."

"They won't fall for it a second time," said Eurybiades.

"Oh, they will," said Themistocles firmly. "Two nights ago, we did panic protocol one. They've never seen what we're about to do."

Eurybiades, now more curious than scared, roared the order with a smile. He'd learned not to doubt Themistocles.

Every Hellene ship turned a hundred and eighty degrees. Some turned to starboard, some to port, all meticulously prearranged and choreographed. Then every single ship rowed away from the oncoming Persians. The Persians saw us fleeing and sped up, hungry to attack foes who fled at the sight of the enemy. We'd rowed only a few strokes before Eurybiades relayed Themistocles' next command: "Panic protocol three!"

Every single Hellene ship, led by the two hundred Athenian triremes in the front, turned around and headed straight for the Persians.

"Now we go at 'em," said Themistocles quietly.

Eurybiades understood. "Attack!" he roared. "Pick a target, ram it, then back up and pick another!"

The Persians still came at us hard and fast, but just before we made contact, they'd visibly slowed down. Themistocles was right. They'd gone into top speed too soon and their crews were winded by the time they reached us, while our oarsmen, much fresher, went at them full speed. The Persians clearly did not expect us to attack their larger fleet. This was Themistocles' genius: he always did the one thing the Persians never expected. As we drew close enough to see the faces of some of the Persian oarsmen, I saw a lot of worried frowns. The battle hadn't even started but their faces were covered in doubt.

Eurybiades began to whoop like a schoolboy, very unSpartanlike, but it helped him contain his own fear and also inspired the men who heard it. Timoleon and I whooped too. It was soon picked up by our crew, and the others around us. So now the Persians were being attacked by a horde of whooping lunatics.

Few of the Persian ships had iron rams, but every single one of ours did. That first clash was terrifying, and we lost five ships, but the Persians lost thirty. *Demikratis* went nose-to-nose with a five-banked pentekonter twice its size, and I thought we were doomed as we advanced on this monster, until the last second when Themistocles ordered us to veer off slightly to starboard and then ship oars as we rammed the pentekonter near its bow. We'd punched a hole five feet wide, just ahead of its front-most oars. I hung on to the rail at the moment of collision, then got out my bow and started to shoot. My first arrow hit water as I adjusted to the bobbing deck, but my second shot went into the Persian captain's gut. If the wound didn't kill him, he would die as his ship went down. Themistocles had timed the ram-and-withdraw so expertly that we were well clear of the pentekonter as it sank, and we already had another Persian ship lined up.

"Do not shoot captains whose ships are going down," Eurybiades said to me. "They are already dead. Save your arrows for captains whose ships still present a danger to us. Helmsmen are even better targets."

Of course he was right, and I marveled again at how quickly he learned to command at sea. As we passed a Phoenician quadrireme that was too far away for us to ram, I shot an arrow into its helmsman's chest. The captain got someone else to take the man's place, but not quickly enough. The ship had a crucial few seconds when no one steered. The dying helmsman had fallen onto his steering oar and made the ship turn slightly to port. This enabled one of our ships to punch a hole into it almost full broadside. Doomed men screamed as the impact of the Hellenic trireme splintered the quadrireme's oars. Then our boys quickly backed away and looked for another target.

I surveyed the battle. Unlike a land battle, where you face an enemy who will kill you if you take your eyes off of him, at sea you can look around and get an idea of what's going on. While it wasn't as one-sided as the day before, we were still getting the better of the Persians. In less than half an hour, about sixty Persian ships were dead or dying, and a dozen more were disabled.

Here was another example of Themistocles' genius. By teaching every sailor to swim, he not only minimized casualties, which did wonders for morale, but also maintained our fighting strength. He had units of hoplites on some of our rescue ships. Some Persian ships had had their oars snapped by our ships but were otherwise still seaworthy. The hoplites boarded those ships, killed the remaining crew members, then helped transport our rescued oarsmen and captains onto the captured ships.

Our rescue ships also carried dozens of extra oars, so within minutes, some of the captured ships, which also carried spare oars, were re-crewed by our men. Their captains ordered the oarsmen to row the ships behind our line for a little practice, and once the crews felt comfortable with the bigger ships, they went right back into battle against the Persians. Almost all Persian sailors who went into the water died, but almost all of ours survived to rejoin the fight. And I could only imagine what the Persian sailors thought when they saw what appeared to be their own ships coming at them.

It was during this battle that Themistocles learned something first-hand about the Persian naval strategy. Basically, it didn't exist. The Persian fleet was not united. Its only tactic was to keep coming at us in wave after wave. Its Aigyptian ships fought as a separate contingent, as did its Lydian ships, its Phoenician ships, its Halicarnassian ships, its Lesbian ships, and all the other contingents from the many Persian provinces. The forty Rhodian ships, identifiable by their crimson and gold banners, took heavy losses in the first clash. When more than half of them had been sunk, the rest withdrew. If an order to stand and fight had been given them, they ignored it. Rhodes is an island and produces some of the best seamen in the world. The remaining Rhodians could still have done a lot of damage to us, but they'd had enough. They retreated, and we didn't see them again that day. In their rush to get out of there, they accidentally straked the oars of a Phoenician ship, disabling it before it had even begun to fight. The hoplites from one of our rescue ships quickly boarded it and ignored the pleas of its Hellene oarsmen, who they unhesitatingly slaughtered. The Phoenician ship was ours now.

The battle continued all day. By late afternoon, we'd

sunk almost three hundred enemy ships. We'd only lost seventy of our own. But still Themistocles was worried.

"Order the retreat," he said to Eurybiades.

"Retreat?" said Eurybiades. "We are winning."

"We are," said Themistocles, "but it is now becoming too costly. Do you see the Persian ships at the rear of their formation?"

Eurybiades looked. His eyes widened. "There are at least two hundred," he said.

"And they're fresh," said Themistocles. "Our men are tired."

"Withdraw!" Eurybiades bellowed. "Turn about, increase speed one measure. Set course for Salamis!"

A few Persian ships tried to chase us, but eventually they all turned back, and Eurybiades ordered a ten-minute rest for the oarsmen before we proceeded to Salamis.

The next thing we saw was Otreus in his comical armour, on his little fishing boat as it pulled up beside us. He stood on the rowing bench with his bow and arrow.

Themistocles held up his huge round shield. Otreus shot an arrow into it. He removed the message from the arrow and handed it to Eurybiades.

Eurybiades' mouth dropped open like he'd just been clubbed on the head. Themistocles took the message from his hand.

"Aw, fuck," he said.

The Persians had finally defeated the Spartans at Thermopylae. The three hundred Spartans had been defeated, fighting bravely to the end. In victory, Xerxes made another rage-induced error. He'd ordered Leonidas' body beheaded, then crucified. There were many Hellenes in his army, and they were horrified by this desecration. In their eyes, courageous enemies should be buried with honour. To abuse a corpse, even an enemy's, was to invite the eternal fury of its shade.

It was treachery that gave the Persians victory. A local shepherd named Ephialtes had shown the Persians a hidden goat-trail that crossed the top of the ridge at Thermopylae and came down behind the Spartans. Several thousand Persians took the trail during the night, then popped up behind the Spartans the next day. Leonidas had been tipped off about the treachery and could have escaped, but he refused. He ordered his allies to depart, rather than stay at the pass be killed. Most did, but the Thespians and the Thebans would not, even though they knew there was a zero percent chance of survival.

No, Ephander, I did not misspeak. Thebans fought alongside the Thespians and Spartans at Thermopylae. In Thebes, the decision to side with the Great King was never supported unanimously. Four hundred Theban hoplites, all of whom supported the coalition of Hellenic cities, died at Thermopylae. Sadly, the deaths of these men virtually guaranteed that the Thebans would fight against us for the rest of this war. That wine-soaked whopper-weaver Herodotus says they surrendered on the last day but he is, as usual, full of gryphon shit.

"When this war is over," Themistocles said to me, "you'll pay this Ephialtes a little visit."

Eurybiades stifled a sob.

"I'm sorry, Eurybiades," said Themistocles. "I know your brother was there, and some of your friends. Grieve if you must, but no one can see the Fleet Commander weep. My men will cover you." Themistocles then motioned to Timoleon and me to conceal Eurybiades with our shields.

Eurybiades said nothing, just nodded and then crouched down like he was adjusting a sandal strap. His tears flowed. A few minutes later, though, he was back on his feet looking stern and resolute.

"I do not much care," said Eurybiades, "for two

defeats in one day."

"These are far from defeats," said Themistocles. "We retreat to preserve our victory. And while the courage of the Three Hundred Spartans will inspire all Hellenes, their greater achievement is what they've done to Persian morale, which is now in shreds. We can beat them now. Three days ago, I wasn't so sure."

Less than an hour later, the beach at Salamis was in sight. Eurybiades stood at his command post on the foredeck. He wanted to be alone in his grief. He stood and stared ahead at dark nothing. He wore his armour, all of it, including his greaves and arm-guards, with his red cloak over his shoulders like a cape. I kept my distance, a good twenty feet behind him, but I still kept an eye on him.

Eurybiades had retreated into his own pain and grief, and did not pay attention to the sea. An amateur's mistake.

When the medium-sized wave came and rocked our ship, it was not serious, but it was still enough to knock Eurybiades off balance and into the sea. The weight of his armour would drag him down to the bottom.

I dove in right after him. And yes, I wore armour too.

20—INTELLIGENCE

Six days earlier, Ephander, I'd just finished another long afternoon at sea with Themistocles on the *Demikratis*. Our ships had been practicing fleet maneuvers, including the kyklos and the panic protocols. The maneuvers were better than they'd been a few days earlier but were still far from battle-ready. Our ships couldn't do the kyklos without fouling each other's oars, and the whole movement was slow and sloppy.

My day was done. Hot and ornery, I stood on a dock at the Phaleron, hungry as a caged hog. I was about to head over to a nearby tavern with passably edible food, which at that famished moment I defined as not having any live bugs in it. A pink, round, sweaty man ran towards the dock carrying a large sack. He laboured, clearly not an athlete, and I grinned as I recognized Phylo. He'd jogged part of the way, not much more than a few hundred yards, but the effort left him wheezing. He sweated like ten Gamelion donkeys. It would have been funny if it wasn't so sad.

In his hands he held a breastplate. It looked flimsy and cheap.

"Brother, I'm glad I caught you here," he said after he'd recovered his wind a little. "I need your help. Try this on."

"Who made this piece of crap?" I said.

"I did, but forget how it looks. It's a prototype. We'll fine-tune it later. It's a revolutionary concept that will change the face of modern warfare."

"You shitting me?"

"Just try it on."

I took off my heavy bronze and leather breastplate and

Phylo helped me put on his crappy one. It was poorly made, like it had been done in a hurry, with hand stitching that looked like a child's first attempt. The leather was stiff and uncomfortable. It itched. Underwires poked my skin in several places. Its only advantage was that it was light, maybe a quarter of the weight of my other breastplate. While it wasn't the worst armour I'd ever seen, it was pretty damned close.

"What's this made of?" I said. "It's too light to be bronze."

"Leather and wood."

"It won't stop a spear-thrust."

"No, but it will stop an arrow or a sword. I still need to test it for one thing."

"And what might that be?"

"Buoyancy." Then he pushed me off the dock and into the water.

"You crazy asshole!" I said after I'd splashed into the water and bobbed back up to the surface. "You trying to kill me?"

"Kill you?" he said, big smile now. "This will save thousands of lives."

"What the fuck are you talking about?"

"You're floating. I've just invented sea armour."

With the shock of getting knocked off the dock and hitting the cold water, it took me a few seconds to realize that I hadn't sunk, even though I'd made almost no effort to keep my head above the water. The armour, which contained no metal apart from the underwire and some nails, floated. All of our ship's crews and oarsmen could swim now, but most hoplites couldn't. In a sea battle, if a hoplite fell into the water, he almost always drowned when his armour dragged him down to the bottom. Phylo was right, this armour would save lives. And, almost as importantly, men who wore this armour would be less distracted by the prospect of drowning. In battle, one less worry is always an advantage.

"I want in," I said. "I want to invest in this."

"I figured I'd have to offer you that," he said, "so you wouldn't kill me for pushing you into the drink."

And so, as we headed into port after the third and final day of the Battle of Artemisium, I wore this crappy-looking armour on the deck of *Demikratis* when Eurybiades fell overboard.

"Man in the water!" I yelled as loudly as I could.

When I dove into the water, I couldn't see Eurybiades. I only guessed where he'd gone in and hoped I'd come close to the right spot. I struggled to get myself underwater—the sea armour was so buoyant that this was actually difficult—and I just waved my arms around down there. I felt nothing. I feared I was too late.

I swept my hand downward one last time. Something soft brushed my hand. I reached down a little further and grabbed at it.

It was Eurybiades' cloak. I pulled on it and prayed to every god that it was fastened securely. It actually came loose when I grabbed it, but the instant Eurybiades felt the tug, he grabbed onto it. I pulled him up to the surface, then held him above water while he recovered a little. He spat out some water but was still conscious.

"You were wrong about one thing," he said.

"What was that, sir?" I asked him.

"If ever I run with the son of Belkos," he said, "*I* will be the one honoured."

Timoleon and some of the crewmen were ready with rope and pulled us in. Here's the irony: when I first came onto the *Demikratis* with my sea armour, Eurybiades teased me about it. He said it couldn't stop a baby's fist. And even though this little incident became well-known, it proved beyond any doubt that this sea armour was effective, but the armour never caught on. A few men tried the sea armour and absolutely hated the way it felt. Phylo and I had had five hundred sets of the armour made up. We ended up with four-hundred and eighty-three of them in a pile in Phylo's warehouse. When Hellenes wear armour, they want bronze, not wood, even at sea, where a single misstep in heavy armour means sure death.

* * * * * * *

"You want me to cut off *what*?!?"

The next evening, I sat with Timoleon in front of the tent we shared on Salamis, where our fleet was stationed. Timoleon and I had just finished our evening meal when Sikinnis, the slave who tutored Themistocles' children, approached us. Something was on his mind.

"A private word, young sir," he said to me.

"Sure, old sir," I said. That was our little thing, he called me *young sir*, I called him *old sir*, even though as a slave he didn't expect such courtesy. "Speak."

He looked at Timoleon. "I just remembered," said Timoleon, "that I need to take a whiz."

Timoleon left. Then Sikinnis asked me to cut off his ears.

"You want me to cut off *what*?!?"

"You heard me right, young sir," said Sikinnis.

"Yes, I heard you, old sir," I said. "Have you lost your wits?"

"Never been saner," he said.

"But why would I do this to you?"
"I cannot say."
"Then I cannot do it."
"You must."
"I won't."

Sikinnis was a squat little man, with a long curly beard and a bald head. He was past sixty but didn't look forty. I looked for signs of derangement in his eyes, indications that despair or exhaustion or fear had broken him. I saw none, but I'm not an expert, and he'd just walked into my tent and asked me to slice off his ears like it was the most normal request in the world, like he wanted me to help him move a heavy piece of furniture. This is not something a rational man does. I also looked at his ears for signs of a consumptive disease that would kill him if the ears weren't removed, and saw nothing like that either. I couldn't mutilate a good man without a good reason.

"I want you to do it," he said, "because you're so good with the sword. You won't make a mess of it."

"I can't do it, Sikinnis. Sorry."

"Please speak to the Archon, young sir."

I went to the command tent of Themistocles, where he and Eurybiades leaned over a big table as they studied a map.

As soon as I entered, Themistocles barely looked up. "Just do it, Lexo," he said.

"Sir?" I said. "Are you punishing him?" I couldn't imagine that. Sikinnis was totally devoted to Themistocles, honest and hardworking.

"Of course not," said Themistocles. "I've never once had reason to punish him. But you must do as he asks."

"Why, sir?"

Themistocles hesitated. Eurybiades said, "I believe we can trust Elektros. If I was ever ordered to disfigure an innocent man, I too would need to know why."

Themistocles motioned for me to come closer to him so he wouldn't have to speak any louder than necessary. "Sikinnis must disinform the Persians about our plans," he whispered into my ear. "He must convince them that Eurybiades and I have become dysfunctional commanders. He will say that that Eurybiades sliced off his ears in a burst of rage when he learned that Leonidas was dead and his body dishonoured. Sikinnis will claim to defect to the Persians out of fear for his own life."

"They might kill him," I said. "Sikinnis is a valuable man."

"Lexo, they might kill all of us," said Themistocles. "In war, no worthwhile action is without risk. So we must take this chance."

"But how can you make him do this?" I said.

"I didn't," he replied. "Sikinnis volunteered for this."

"In fact," said Eurybiades, "he came up with the plan."

"You must reward him well," I said, and I knew the moment the words were out of my mouth that they were unnecessary.

"He will have enough silver," Themistocles said, "to live well as a free man for the rest of his days. Assuming we survive, of course."

I went back to my tent. Sikinnis waited for me there. I'd brought along Glaukopis, one of our battlefield surgeons, to treat the wounds Sikinnis was about to get. I told Glaukopis that he must tell no one about what we were about to do and must ask no questions. "I will explain it to you someday," I said. "Today, however, cannot be that day."

Glaukopis had been around Themistocles long enough to know not to press for details. I asked him if Sikinnis would be deaf. He said no, the visible part of the ear acts as an echo chamber, but the part that actually hears is inside the earhole. Sikinnis would hear less well but would not be deaf. Glaukopis gave him a cup of wine mixed with poppy seed, then had me clean my sword with vinegar to minimize the chances of infection,

"If you change your mind, old sir," I said to Sikinnis, "right up to the moment I'm about to do it, just say the word and I'll stop."

"I am certain of this, young sir," said Sikinnis. "Cut cleanly."

I took off my breastplate and put it on Sikinnis so my sword wouldn't cut his shoulder on my follow-through. I stood behind him, pulled his left ear outwards with my left hand and sliced off his ear in a single clean cut. He flinched a little, wobbled for a second, then steadied himself. Glaukopis held wine-soaked gauze to the wound, which bled much more than I would ever have expected, then daubed the wound with honey to stop the bleeding. Glaukopis wanted to bandage the wound but Sikinnis wouldn't let him. He wouldn't say why, but I guessed that if he'd had time to get his wounds bandaged, his claim of a hurried escape would be less credible to the Persians. We couldn't tell Glaukopis that, though.

"Let me know when you're ready for the next one," I said.

"Ready now," said Sikinnis. I switched hands, pulled out his right ear with my right hand. He closed his eyes and I clipped his other ear off cleanly. Glaukopis treated that wound too, and didn't bandage it.

"Thank you, young sir," he said. He hadn't uttered a sound and took the pain like the bravest man alive—which he was, even though he'd never once stood in battle. He would attach his severed ears to a leather cord that he would wear as a grim necklace. Then he would tell the Persians that Eurybiades forced him to do this as a further humiliation.

"Your courage, old sir," I said, "sets a fine example. Later, when it is safe to do so, I will make sure everyone knows of it."

"I don't care about that," he said. "I just want to win this war."

He took another sip of wine and poppy.

"Now," Sikinnis said, "do the nose."

* * * * * * *

The next day, standing in front of the command tent of Pausanias, fifty angry men, the generals from all member cities of the Hellenic League, had come to argue about what the Hellenic League's next actions would be.

Adeimanthos the Korinthian had the floor. "You may abandon your city, son of Neocles," he said, "but I will not abandon mine." He referred, of course, to Themistocles' plan to evacuate the entire city of Athens. The Persians, now that they'd gotten through the Hot Gates, had nothing to stop them from marching on Athens. They would burn every house and farm in their path, then demolish the entire city. But as hard as that was to accept, it wasn't Themistocles' biggest problem at the moment.

It had just been revealed that the Spartans and Korinthians and the leaders from the other Peloponnesian cities had started to build a wall across the isthmus, just north of Korinthos. It would be finished in a few days. They planned to make a stand here against the Persian army and use our ships to delay the Persian fleet. The endeavour, foolhardy to begin with, was doomed because they'd made some glaring miscalculations. The first was that they tried to keep the wall secret from Themistocles. He'd been at sea for the last three days, so they figured he would not be privy to happenings on land.

Were they still so clueless about how Themistocles operated? He knew about their wall before the first stone was laid.

Their second mistake was their belief, or more accurately their delusion, that the Persians would fight at the wall. This revealed a grievous misunderstanding of the enemy. If the Persian fleet was not eliminated, they'd use it to transport troops *around* the wall. Even if the fleet was eliminated, the Persians could winter in Attica, which they'd soon have all to themselves, and wait until more ships came from Xerxes' empire in the spring. The wall-building contingent failed to recognize that Xerxes still had warships—a separate Euxine fleet of at least three hundred—and the gold and shipyards to build hundreds more over the winter. This war would not end with a single victory. The isthmian wall was a fool's hope.

Their third big mistake was their plan to have the fleet fight the Persians on open ocean, where the Persians could use their superior numbers to swarm our ships in a battle we could not win.

Themistocles was frustrated by the obstinacy of these men, and by how little they'd learned in the last few days. It had taken him years to convince the people of Athens that the defense of Hellas would require both land and sea forces, but those were mostly civilians, not military strategists like these men were purported to be. He thought that strategoi, whose very title suggested an understanding of strategy, would grasp that Hellenes could no longer rely solely on land armies against the Persians. He privately cursed himself for not seeing this sooner.

"First, get one thing into your heads," Themistocles said. "Xerxes has made mistakes in this war, but he is not an idiot. He did, after all, find a way to win at Thermopylae. He learned a huge lesson there. He will not again commit all his troops to a battle where his numbers can't be used to surround us. Why would he? His ships give him the ability to transport his troops to the places where we're weakest. So if we don't win at sea, we cannot win on land because he'll just put his troops behind the wall."

"Why should anyone listen to you?" said Adeimanthos. "So far, your strategies have gotten the troops at Thermopylae slaughtered and the-gods-know-how-many of our ships sunk."

This last item was untrue, because we knew *exactly* how many ships we'd lost, seventy-four, and we'd also captured six good Persian warships that we could immediately use against them. Every man here was impressed with the fleet's performance so far, although Themistocles' bitterest enemies wouldn't openly admit it.

Adeimanthos continued his rant: "And since you no longer have a city, why the fuck are you even here? All of us represent our poleis. You represent what will soon be a pile of rubble. Show of hands: who here thinks that a pile of rubble is a polis? A man without a city has no legal right to be here."

A few hands went up here and there, but the total did not form anywhere close to a majority. The men who raised their hands were, notably, all from the Peloponnese, the ones who believed the Korinthian wall would benefit them. Not one of the generals from Plataea, Megara, or other cities north of the wall raised their hands. They still believed in the fleet, if only because a fight at the wall, even if successful, would not help their cities.

"Athens is not simply a polis," said Themistocles. "Athens is its people. If, ultimately, they cannot go back home, then I will use the Athenian fleet to transport them to a new location. We have allies in Thurii and Sybaris. If you choose not to fight properly at sea, then Themistocles will take his ships and his people elsewhere."

"You would abandon us when we need you most?" This came from the Spartan Pausanias, the overall commander of the armed forces. Even Eurybiades answered to him.

"Themistocles does not abandon his allies," said Themistocles. "Themistocles abandons stupidity. We can beat the Persians at sea. They have no strategy. We have Themistocles. But if our fleet makes a stand in open sea, as you propose, the Persians will not need strategy. They will simply keep coming at us from all directions until they finish us off. We now know that swarming us with superior numbers is their primary tactic. Your proposal favours them. If we fight them in a narrow channel, their numbers become a disadvantage. I plan to fight them in the straits between Salamis and the southern coast of Attica."

"Do you now?" snorted Adeimanthos. "Tell us how you got the Persians to agree to this?" A few men chuckled at this.

"While you sat here with your thumb up your purple whiny ass, Adeimanthos," said Themistocles, "I sent them a disinformant."

"A disinformant?" said Pausanias, who always looked slightly angry but now looked downright rabid. "On whose authority?"

"On my own authority," said Themistocles, "because I knew if I brought this to you beforehand, you would refuse to allow it."

"So your disinformant will persuade the Persians to

send their ships through the straits?" asked Pausanias.

"He will tell them that we cannot agree on strategy," said Themistocles, "and that the Hellenic League is on the verge of collapse. He will tell them that we plan a foolish defense off the coast of the Argolis."

This drew cries of alarm and curses. "Traitor!" more than one general said. "Medizer!" said others. If what Themistocles had just said was true, then his disinformant was about to tell the Persians exactly what the Hellenic high command planned to do.

Themistocles just rolled his eyes. "Relax, gentlemen," he said. "If that's the strategy you're seriously considering, it wouldn't be secret for long anyway, but if my man is believed, the Persians will split up their fleet. They'll send some of their ships through the straits to catch us off guard in the morning, and the rest of it to circle the southern coast of Salamis and attack us in the rear."

"And that's a good thing?" said Pausanias.

"Absolutely," said Themistocles. "They will be convinced that our fleet is headed south and west from the Bay of Eleusis towards the Argolis. But we won't be there. So the Persians will send several hundred ships on a harpy hunt. Then they'll tire out their main fleet as it rushes to catch us off guard in the morning. If we play it right, the Persian ships coming through the straits will think we're sailing calmly in the opposite direction. So we will have the advantage of surprise, rested crews, and a narrow battle site that will make their greater numbers a disadvantage."

"I don't like it," said Pausanias. "Your plan has a lot of *if* and *maybe* to it. *If* the Persians believe your disinformant, *maybe* they'll come through the straits. I don't see how this is better than a land battle."

"Pausanias, with all due respect," said Themistocles,

"if we take out their fleet, we'll weaken their land forces. We'll cut off their supplies and reinforcements, then we can fight their land army on our own terms."

Pausanias was still not convinced. He was an expert infantry commander, so another battle like Marathon was what he wanted. He failed to see, like so many others here, that the Persians would not commit to another winner-take-all land battle unless we'd first driven them to desperation, which we could only do if we defeated their fleet. Without naval support, the Persian army would winter in Attica, where they would be vulnerable to Themistocles' other advanced stratagems, such as getting dysentery or typhus into their camps, or finding ways to destroy their morale.

Then Eurybiades rose to speak. He was subordinate to Pausanias, but his word carried more weight than it did before because of the fleet's success at Artemisium, because remember, Ephander, everyone here still thought he was our primary naval strategist and that Themistocles was merely his advisor.

Pausanias smiled because he expected Eurybiades to echo his own opinion. He would not smile for long.

"Gentlemen," he began, "I cannot tell you how much I've learned about sea warfare in the last few days. I saw how our fleet could be used for delaying tactics, which was our purpose at Artemisium, but I would have sworn to all the gods that we stood no chance against the Persians in a real sea battle. The Persians have twice as many ships as us, and most are bigger and faster than ours. Their crews come from nations that have been plying the sea for centuries. The Athenians have been sailing warships for only a few years. We Spartans have been doing it for only a few months. So if experience and fleet size are your only considerations, it would be madness for us to even consider a sea battle.

"But we have Themistocles. I know some of you despise the man. How could you not? He is cunning. Deceitful. Treacherous, even. Not to mention pig-arse ugly." Everyone laughed at this, even Pausanias. Even Themistocles.

"As much as you hate him, you fear him even more. You fear his ambition, his ruthlessness, and—don't insult our intelligence by denying this, son of Neocles—his lust for power. He wants to rule us all. He is already the uncrowned king of Athens.

"But you don't really disapprove of that. In your hearts, you envy him. Every man here is cunning, ruthless, and deceitful when it serves his purposes. You hate to admit it, but you're all cut from the same stone as Themistocles. You all seek power. His primary crime, in your eyes, is that he's much better at it than you are.

"The plan Themistocles has just described is not without risk. If it succeeds, however, it will turn this entire war around. So put your petty jealousies aside and consider this: at the end of our first day at Artemisium, I saw Themistocles sink three Persian ships by luring them into shoals. Yes, I gave the orders, but Themistocles devised the plan. In only a few minutes, we killed six hundred Persian sailors. Our casualties were zero. At the end of the second day, Themistocles led his Athenian ships into a complicated maneuver that sunk forty-seven enemy ships and cost us only two—and all but a handful of the crewmen on our lost ships were rescued. Every single one of the men on the downed Persian ships, over ten thousand of them, died. On the third day, I saw Themistocles induce the Persians to tire out their crews to get at us, then he had us attack before they could get their wind back. We lost a few hundred men on that day, but the Persians lost thousands.

"We've lost seventy-four ships, it's true, but the Persians have lost over three hundred. So your envy of Themistocles clouds your judgement and does not permit you to see something crucial. *So far, we are actually winning the battle at sea*! Our fleet is better led than the enemy's. How can you not see that? The defensive strategy of a stand at Argolis is doomed. Themistocles' plan will neutralize the enemy's primary advantage, its superior numbers, and will in fact turn it into a disadvantage. I know genius when I see it, even if you don't. If they cram their ships into the straits of Salamis, they will run into each other and foul each other's oars. They will once again be tired when they reach us. So our wisest course of action is Themistocles' plan for a sea battle at Salamis."

"Advocate all you like, Eurybiades," Pausanias growled. "The decision is not yours to make."

"The problem, sir," said Themistocles quietly, "is that the Persians have probably already left."

"It's nighttime," said Pausanias. "Too dark to sail."

"If we thought a night attack would bring us victory, sir," said Eurybiades, "we would do it, despite the risk. So we have to assume the Persians would think likewise."

Pausanias glared at Eurybiades, whose failure to support the plan to fight at the Argolis would doom him. At the moment, Pausanias was even angrier at Themistocles, whose actions he deemed insubordinate and downright treasonous. "I'm very tempted, Athenian," he said, "to clamp you in irons and throw you into the sea."

"Put our strategy to a vote, sir," said Adeimanthos. This was greeted with nods and murmurs of agreement. Adeimanthos knew that if the generals voted, they might opt for the wall plan.

"This isn't Athens," said Pausanias, sneering the word *Athens* like it left a feculent taste on his tongue. "Military command isn't democratic. When you go to war, do your commanders normally put their orders to a vote? I will command. All of you will follow orders. Any man who has a problem with that, stand up and I'll fucking kill you right now, with my own hands. So, any takers?"

Pausanias was the biggest man here, six and a half feet tall, known to be ruthless, and everyone believed he meant what he said. He walked amongst the assembled generals, shoved a couple around, then walked back to his original position in front of his tent looking more disgusted than he had before, which I hadn't thought possible. Adeimanthos wouldn't look him in the eye.

"The naval action at Argolis," said Pausanias, "will be a delaying tactic, just as our fleet did at Artemisium for brave Leonidas."

"No," said Eurybiades.

"*What?*" Pausanias rounded on Eurybiades. As great a specimen as Eurybiades was, Pausanias was greater, stronger, more dangerous. The fire in his eye was that of a man of action, not a negotiator.

"I will take the fleet to the straits, sir," said Eurybiades. "We must fight the Persians where we can defeat them. Your Argolis strategy will get our entire fleet destroyed in a single day and serve no useful purpose."

"You command the fleet no longer, Eurybiades," said Pausanias. "I relieve you of it. You'll go back to Sparta in chains, then you'll be tried for treason. Or maybe I should just fucking execute you here and now."

"No, Pausanias," said Eurybiades. "I do not relinquish command of the fleet. If I order our captains to sail to the straits, that's what they will do. They will not listen to you."

Pausanias drew his sword. Themistocles and Eurybiades and I drew ours. After a few tense moments, Pausanias saw he was outnumbered and re-sheathed his sword. We did too. "You will die for this, Eurybiades," said Pausanias. "Maybe not today, maybe not here, but when you return to Sparta, you will die."

"A small price to pay," said Eurybiades, "especially since your idiotic plan would get *all of us* killed."

After the war, back in Sparta, Eurybiades would indeed pay for this, but that's a story for another day. As Pausanias and Eurybiades glared at each other, a messenger arrived on horseback with urgent news from the port. It was one of Pausanias' own men. Themistocles had worried that if the messenger was from Athens, the assembled generals might not believe him. This man was a helot who'd been promised his freedom by the Spartans if the war was won.

His news drew gasps when he announced it. The Persian fleet had already left its beaches and ports on Euboea, even though daylight was a few hours away. A third of the fleet had headed south to circle Salamis, exactly as Themistocles had predicted. Sikinnis had succeeded. The Persians, including Xerxes himself, had believed him. Sikinnis was still in extreme danger, though. Once the Persians learned of his deception, they would kill him, probably as slowly as possible. At this moment, Themistocles went to Adeimanthos and whispered something in his ear. Adeimanthos nodded. I found out later that Themistocles had just offered Adeimanthos two talents of silver to support his naval strategy, which Adeimanthos had accepted.

Most of the men here began to walk away. "Where do you fools think you're going?" barked Pausanias. "I haven't dismissed this meeting."

"We're going to our ships," said Adeimanthos. "We've got a sea battle to fight."

Pausanias was too enraged to speak. If looks could kill, there would have been a lot of dead men on that spot.

21—SALAMIS

The Phoenician ship captain's face froze. The sun had just risen, but a light fog reduced visibility to a few hundred yards. The bulk of the Persian fleet, some six hundred ships, rowed into the straits of Salamis—and they almost collided head-on with our entire fleet. We weren't supposed to be there. The Phoenicians had been told we were at the other end of the straits, on our way to open water off Argolis. Now they faced us here, where the strait was narrow. The lead ships had seen us and slowed down, but the rearmost ones did not. Their captains couldn't see us in the fog and hadn't received a change in orders. Worse, their oarsmen had already been rowing pretty hard for three hours.

Then to add to the Phoenician captain's confusion, his own ship suddenly turned to port. He'd given no such order. He glared at his helmsman, but he too was confused.

The Persians knew we'd used a few bowmen when we fought them at Artemisium, so they had a few of their own today, but the sea was rougher here than it had been at Artemisium. The swells were higher and the spray was greater, and a light rain fell off and on. This would not seriously impede navigation, but it made my bowstring wet—and useless. If I tried to use it, the bowstring would stretch, then propel the arrow only a few feet, and not even accurately. I left my bow in its gorytos. The Persians put theirs away too.

We, however, had Zosimos' and his slingers. Slingers become slightly less accurate in wet weather, mostly because they see their targets less well, but they still can do serious damage to an enemy. Zosimos had all his men coat their leather slings in beeswax, which made them waterproof. The Phoenician captain and helmsman didn't know that their ship turned to port, seemingly by its own will, because Zosimos and the other five slingers on the foredeck of *Dimokratis* had just taken out half of the ship's portside oarsmen. In less than a minute our slingers fired several volleys of sling-bolts at them. They only killed one oarsman, but the others who'd been hit were now wounded or distracted, and the ones who hadn't been hit were terrified and confused. Most of the portside oarsmen stopped rowing, while the starboard oarsmen were unaffected. This made the big ship turn, and its starboard side now faced us. As the Phoenician captain and oarmaster tried to figure out what was happening and get their ship moving again, they took their eyes off of us and didn't even see us ram them. We smashed their starboard oars and put a hole in the side that you could've pushed an elephant through. Eurybiades ordered the slingers to shoot at another ship's oarsmen, as we backed out of the sinking Phoenician.

"Give the order," Themistocles said to Eurybiades, "to stand."

"This looks like a good time to attack," said Eurybiades.

"It is," agreed Themistocles. "But a few minutes from now will be even better."

Eurybiades gave the order to stand. Themistocles had years earlier acquired the nickname *The Oracle*, a sly reference to rumours that he'd bribed Delphic priestesses to for favourable prophecies, but at Artemisium he'd truly earned the name because his battle predictions all came true. He'd insisted to Pausanias and the other coalition generals that the narrowness of these straits would cause the Persians to inadvertently take out some of their own ships. I didn't completely believe it at the time, but that's exactly what happened now. As the big Phoenician went down, the ship at its stern tried to row around it but didn't quite make it. It slowed as it caught some of the oars of the sinking ship, then a third Phoenician ship rammed into the second ship's stern. The damage limited both ships' mobility. A fourth ship veered to starboard to avoid the two ships in front of it but only put itself in the path of a fifth ship. Both of those ships now had damaged oars and were temporarily disabled. There was a chain reaction as ships veered into the paths of the ships behind them. While all of this was happening, the crewmen on the first Phoenician ship screamed in terror as their ship went down and the hungry sea swallowed them. It can't be a good feeling, Ephander, to head into battle behind the death screams of your countrymen.

Eurybiades knew little ways to inspire men. When the order was given for us to ram our next ship, another big Phoenician whose oarsmen had also been partially disabled by our slingers, Eurybiades stood on our bow as we made contact, shook his fist at the sinking ship and yelled, "Take that, you pants-wearing pansies!" Timoleon and I laughed out loud, mostly because it was so unSpartanlike. I glanced down at our oarsmen and most of them grinned too.

Timoleon and the slingers and I all wore war-paint. It was Eurybiades idea, and he had many of the other ships' on-deck personnel wear it too. Its purpose was to add to the Persians' discomfort level. While I can't say for sure that it actually unnerved them, I am certain that it helped us. When you wear war-paint, and the men around you do too, you look scarier to your enemies. And crazier. I looked at Timoleon, and he gave me his war glare. I gave him mine. In addition to the black and yellow grease-paint around his eyes and on his forehead, he'd added pig's blood, real pig's blood, to his cheeks. He looked like the nightmare that awaited you in the nether depths of Hades. We both laughed and looked back at the enemy.

The crews of the enemy ships looked panicked now. We were calm. We laughed and hooted and howled like sea wolves. I told our hostages to whoop and holler with the rest of the men, because it would make them feel better too.

Herakles' arse, Ephander, I just realized I never told you about the hostages.

Two boys stood on the foredeck just behind Themistocles. They wore brand new armour. It was stiff and unused because they were far too young to fight in the phalanx, one twelve years old, the other ten. Both were scared. Before the battle, Themistocles took me aside and quietly said, "If I order you to kill either of these boys, ask no questions. Just do it."

I agreed, even I wasn't sure I could kill children if I was commanded to do so. I did accept, however, that inhuman actions were sometimes part of the political world in which I now lived. I would not fret about that command until it was actually given me.

The boys were the firstborn sons of Kebalinos, who commanded the Aeginetes, and Adeimanthos. A few days before this battle, Adeimanthos wanted to abandon the coalition, take his ships back home and submit to the Persians. This was always a risk. Korinthos' lively sea trade would get even better if its merchant ships had access to Persian ports when other Hellene cities did not. We'd always known that Adeimanthos liked money more than most men did, so we weren't terribly surprised. In fact, Themistocles had brought along several talents of silver for the specific purpose of bribing coalition members. Themistocles paid Adeimanthos two talents to stay and fight. Adeimanthos had demanded the silver up front.

Themistocles agreed but also demanded Adeimanthos' son as a hostage. Adeimanthos hated this idea—we strongly suspected that once he had the money, he would abandon the coalition anyway—and he must have considered refusing to surrender his son, but he knew Themistocles too well. In the tiny cool hours of the morning, Timoleon and I brought the silver to Adeimanthos' tent, then led the boy back to Themistocles. Themistocles also made the Korinthian ships line up right next to the Athenians. If Adeimanthos abandoned us, he would be close enough for Zosimos to kill with a sling bullet.

The Aeginetes were also suspected of Persian sympathies. More than suspected—before Marathon, they'd openly medized, and even now they allowed the Persians to use one of their ports. So Themistocles made a deal with Kebalinos. I wasn't privy to the details, other than it involved significant silver and a firstborn son. I wondered why their ships weren't here beside us, where Themistocles could keep an eye on them. In fact, I couldn't see them anywhere.

"Wouldn't the lads be safer belowdecks, sir?" I asked as we approached the Persians.

"Maybe a little," said Themistocles. "But I want them to see—"

"—how well the fleet is commanded in battle!" piped in Eurybiades. He'd grasped Themistocles' political mind so well that he now sometimes finished Themistocles' sentences. While Themistocles normally hated that, he liked how well and how quickly Eurybiades had learned sea command. What a change from the pissing lubber he'd been before Artemisium, just a few days earlier.

The two boys were still years away from proper military training. Both had swords they were scared to touch. Both vomited over the side at least once. One horrible thought must have crossed the poor little bastards' minds: their fathers might sacrifice their lives, take the money and flee. I wouldn't put it past Adeimanthos, who had many sons and maybe wouldn't miss this one, but I didn't know Kebalinos well enough to speculate.

Themistocles had put the boys' lives in my hands. If *Dimokratis* went down, my job was to get them out of their armour. "Do you guys swim?" I asked.

Both shook their heads. Non-swimmers in armour are dead in the water. Even swimmers will die if they can't get their armour off quickly enough. I got some rope from the hold, looped a goodly length around each boy's waist, then tied the other end to the foredeck side-rail. "If we start to go down," I said, "the first thing you do, even before you untie yourselves, is take off each other's breastplates."

The boys' eyes widened in horror. "I'm just saying," I said. "Probably won't happen, but if it does, the gods forbid, I'll help you with it. I'll also keep your heads above water until we get rescued."

Their expressions were still frozen in fear. The younger one sobbed. My war paint spooked them and must have made them wonder what kind of lunatics ran this ship.

"Relax, boys," I said. "You haven't seen our fleet in action yet, so you don't know how good it is. We've won every engagement so far. I expect to survive this one. At the end of this battle, you boys will most likely be right where you are now. Get ready for the thrill ride of your life."

Both boys smiled a little. I quit while I was ahead and said no more.

In those first few minutes of battle, thousands of Persian seamen died. Almost all were killed by the sea itself after their ships went down. Only a handful died of wounds, which had all been afflicted by our slingers.

Zosimos was a wonder to watch. Rhodian slingmasters are magical. The best ones devote their lives to it. Zosimos had trained twenty-four Athenians, who were distributed on four ships. The Athenians were competent enough to either hit or come close to their targets, and they'd even practiced on rough seas in anticipation of this moment. Zosimos had trained them to shoot rapidly at the enemy, to make up in volume and frequency what they lacked in accuracy. On ship after ship, the Persians were hit with barrages of sling-stones. The slingers had been ordered to shoot at the rowing benches because the oarsmen were bunched together there, and any shot in their general direction had a chance of hitting someone. They'd also been ordered to shoot at the oarsmen on only one side of each ship, which would unbalance the ship's navigational abilities. To be steered properly, both sides of a ship had to have the same number of oarsmen. If you took a few out on one side, you weakened it and the ship would turn towards that side. By the time the oarmaster replaced disabled oarsmen from one side with healthy men from the other, it was usually too late. The damage our slingers did to the enemy is impossible to measure.

"Sir," Zosimos said to Eurybiades as he pointed to the Persian pentekonter directly ahead of us. "Ariabignes."

Eurybiades' eyes widened. Ariabignes was Xerxes' brother and commanded the Persian fleet. Eurybiades was surprised to see Ariabignes in the most dangerous area of the battle. He'd assumed that he'd follow his brother's royal example and watch the fight from a safe distance.

"We can take him out, sir," said Zosimos. "Unless you want him alive."

Eurybiades turned to Themistocles. "No," said Themistocles. "We already know everything Ariabignes knows."

"He has no value as a hostage?" said Eurybiades.

"No," said Themistocles. "He's Xerxes' brother, but Xerxes has a lot of brothers. Take him out."

"Fire at will," said Eurybiades to Zosimos.

Zosimos ordered his men to fire at Ariabignes, who was less than a hundred feet from us on the bow of his command ship. Ariabignes was stunned as sling-bolts punched into his arms and legs and clattered off his breastplate, *fwipp fwipp fwipp clang, fwipp fwipp fwipp clang clang clang*. I saw blood on one of his hands. Zosimos let his men shoot first, then took his first and only shot at Ariabignes. It struck the Persian in the forehead. Ariabignes' eyes rolled back into his head before he collapsed. By letting his men shoot first, each one could claim that his shot was the one that felled the admiral, even though they all must have known in their hearts, as I did, that only Zosimos had the skill to make such a precise shot. They'd all shot at Ariabignes, though, and they wounded him, so there was truth to their later claim that his death was a team effort. The slingers cheered, as did all of our hoplites and oarsmen, then Eurybiades ordered the slingers to take out some of the Persian command ship's oarsmen. As the pentekonter turned involuntarily, a Korinthian ship to our portside rammed it.

"Spread the word!" Eurybiades bellowed. "Admiral Ariabignes is dead! Let's make sure every single one of our enemies knows it! Elektros, yell it in Persian as loud as you can."

"*Ariabignes eínai nekrós!*" I cried out again and again, as the hoplites on our ship yelled it in Hellenic to the ships around us. Every time a new Hellene crew heard the news, the men cheered. The Persians now headed into battle knowing they had no leader, no plan, and a disturbingly cheerful enemy.

More Persian ships came forward but most hesitated to

attack. The ones in the front hung back, which prevented any of the ships behind them from advancing. The few that dared to attack were quickly rammed and sunk.

"See the captain?" Zosimos said, nodding towards the officer on the foredeck of the pentekonter just ahead of us. "I'll put one in his eye."

"I'd like to see that," I said. I didn't believe he could do it, with the wind and the rain and our ship bobbing on the swells. I thought it was a battle boast, but seconds later, the Persian captain screamed, put his hand to his eye, and fell over backwards, probably dead before he hit the deck as Zosimos' bolt went through his eye and out the back of his skull. Our men cheered, even the oarsmen who couldn't actually see what had happened but knew that the cheers of fellow crew members are always good to hear in battle.

"Bowman off the port bow," said Zosimos. "In his ear."

Again, that kind of accuracy seemed impossible. The bowman stood on the foredeck of a Lydian trireme, trying desperately to get a wet bowstring onto his bow, which would not work well even if he managed to get it on. Another Lydian said something to him, and as the bowman turned his head to answer, a sling-bolt burst into one side of his head and exploded out the other, taking chunks of skull and brain with it. We didn't see for sure that Zosimos had actually put it into the man's ear, but we didn't care as we cheered and hooted and howled again.

"Whaddya think, boys?" I said to our hostages. "Having fun?" Both boys nodded, big grins on their faces now.

Eurybiades, who normally would find such cockiness objectionable in battle, thoroughly enjoyed the little show Zosimos gave us. He even suggested Zosimos' next slinging feat.

"Six shots at six oarsmen," he said. "A shot to the right bicep of each man."

"As you command, sir," said Zosimos with a grin.

Zosimos then slung six bolts in less than twenty seconds and six Persian oarsmen screamed, dropped their oars and grabbed their right arms. The bolts were embedded in the bone. All six men were useless now.

"Better than kills," observed Eurybiades. "Their screams will demoralize every enemy who hears them." With the Persian fleet bunched up as it was, thousands of men heard those screams. We rammed the ship easily, then backed away and calmly looked for our next victim.

Another ship approached us overcautiously. This doomed it already. You can't be irresolute at sea against Themistocles. "Helmsman," said Zosimos. "In his open mouth."

"Impossible," I said. The helmsman was at his steering oar, at the stern, twice as far away as Zosimos' other targets had been. His mouth was also closed more than it was open. Every few seconds the man took a deep breath and opened his mouth, but only for a second or two. Even though Zosimos had just amazed me three times, I was tempted to wager on this one.

Timoleon was more than just tempted. "Twenty-five silver drachmae," he said, "says you can't."

"You're on, Timoleon," said Zosimos.

Unlike he'd done with his previous targets, Zosimos took his time on this one. He watched the helmsman for a minute, and once he'd detected a pattern in the way the man opened and closed his mouth, he fired. To be honest, we couldn't tell if he'd made the exact shot. The helmsman grabbed his own throat, stunned by whatever had just hit him. At first, the only blood we saw on him was on the back of his neck, which was consistent with a sling-bolt that went into his mouth and out the back of his skull. Seconds later, blood came out his mouth as he slumped forward.

"Didn't actually see it go into his mouth," said Timoleon, "but that was such a good shot that I'll pay up anyway. And I won't bet against you again, Rhodian, on anything!" That ship was no longer being steered and our other slingers had hit some of their starboard oarsmen, so the ship now turned its portside towards us. It was an easy, breezy ram-and-run.

I must speak, Ephander, of the valour of Evagoras, our blind slinger. When he was sent to Zosimos for training so many months ago, I thought it was a charitable gesture rather than anything that would pay off militarily. Zosimos thought so too, at least initially, although he immediately recognized that if a blind man could learn to be a slinger, it would shame any reluctant able-bodied man. Evagoras was not totally blind. He lost his visual acuity from a childhood illness, but he could make out shapes and some colours. Zosimos ordered him to shoot in the general direction of enemy ships, and while Evagoras lacked accuracy, he'd practiced and practiced and practiced until he shot harder than any of our slingers, including, amazingly, even Zosimos. Evagoras could sling a bolt so hard it could go through three men. During the battle, Zosimos had him shoot at the sides of the ships, low near the waterline, because he could shoot right through a wooden hull. While we couldn't confirm that he actually sunk any ships, we do know that the resulting holes were big enough to cause leakage that would not go unnoticed by a ship's oarsmen. If your ship is already under attack, the last thing you want to see is that you've sprung a leak or two or three.

The entire Persian fleet now attempted to flee. This only made things worse for them.

In the confined straits, it was impossible for any ship to turn around without fouling the oars of another. Dozens of ships now stood broadside to us, just waiting like Ceramicus whores for us to ram into them. Others foundered and floundered and flopped, as their captains cursed their men, the other ships' captains and the gods themselves. Their movements looked suspiciously like what we'd done at Artemisium, and I wondered if they were faking.

"That's real panic, boys," said Themistocles, guessing my thoughts.

Eurybiades gave the two word command we all wanted to hear. "Get 'em!" he roared.

Dimokratis rammed five ships in succession in a few minutes, with not even the slightest attempt at a counterattack from the Persians. We whooped and we hollered, but our voices were drowned out—no pun intended, Ephander—by the screams of doomed Persians. In fact, I looked back and forth across our front, which was maybe a quarter mile wide, and I did not see a single Persian ship attempting to attack. Every one of them was either sinking or fleeing. It was like we were lions and they were a herd of trapped gazelles. A few of our ships had gone down—though most of their crews were rescued—but that was bound to happen because this confined space could be as dangerous to us as it was to the Persians, especially if a ship charged too eagerly into the chaos and couldn't get clear of floundering enemy vessels.

And chaos it was, as Persian ships crossed into the paths of other Persian ships and disabled them. When a ship straked another ship's oars, the damage was greater than just the broken oars. The snapped oars now had sharp ends, the pressure on them often caused them to impale the oarsmen or pin them against the inside walls of the ship, crushing their rib cages.

We now heard uninterrupted screams from the enemy. It had become our battle song.

Eurybiades ordered all ships to advance slowly, not only to avoid getting caught up in the Persian panic but also not to overexert our crews. The Persians still had us outnumbered, and if they managed to turn around and get a few hundred ships out of the straits, they could be trouble if we exhausted ourselves and they counterattacked.

Then some Persian ships were rammed, clearly intentionally, by other ships from their own fleet.

Themistocles grinned. The Persian contingent from Lesbos, twenty-six triremes, had just changed sides. A man stood on the bow of their lead ship and waved a green banner, a prearranged signal. Themistocles stood and waved his wide shield back in acknowledgement. Eurybiades quickly ordered our other ships not to ram the Lesbians. I later learned that Themistocles had sent Simonides a few days earlier to persuade the Lesbians, with silver and threats, to change sides in the middle of the battle. They would be deep within the Persian formation, and unlike most of the enemy ships, the Lesbians had great bronze rams on every one of their triremes. We quickly saw how well they used them. Within minutes, every one of the Lesbian triremes had taken out at least two enemy vessels. There were maybe forty disabled but undamaged Persian ships between us and the Lesbians, and they wouldn't remain Persian for long. Their crews tried to surrender to us, but we had no place to put prisoners. Our hoplites would board the enemy ships, quickly defeat whatever infantry they had onboard, throw the on-deck crew into the sea, and then order the oarsmen to do as they were told or they would die too. Most of those oarsmen survived the battle, although they would now be slaves. We captured many ships this way, ships we could use in future battles.

If the remaining Persians weren't discombobulated enough, they'd now gone into full blown hysteria. As they tried so desperately to get away, with helmsmen no longer listening to captains and oarsmen no longer listening to oarmasters, they were sloppy and disordered, and ended up sinking some of their own ships. Few of their captains remained calm, and now every last one of them just wanted to get the hell out of there.

We saw another Persian ship intentionally ram one of its own, and I initially thought another contingent had changed sides. "Artemisia," said Themistocles, laughing.

I looked closely and indeed saw that the armoured figure on the foredeck of that ship was a woman, with long flowing black hair under a golden helm. I'd seen Artemisia before. She was the satrap of Halicarnassus when I lived there, with a reputation for both ruthlessness and fairness as a ruler. Her husband had been satrap of Halicarnassus. When he died of natural causes, she temporarily took over and did such a good job of it that the Great King officially made her the first, and only, woman satrap in the history of the Persian Empire. Unlike most of the other Persian commanders, she'd kept her head. Earlier, she'd had her crew pretend that the ship was disabled, and when a Korinthian trireme went to ram it, she had her ship turn suddenly and take out the Korinthian. When she now rammed one of her own ships, the captain of the Lesbian ship that was coming for her thought she'd changed sides and did not follow her. This enabled Artemisia to escape.

The story went around later that Xerxes, after seeing Artemisia's quick thinking, said, "Have my men become women and my women men?" It was that drunk moron Herodotus who told this story, so there's only a remote chance that it's actually true, but it was still probably a true reflection of Xerxes' esteem for Artemisia. The ship she'd sunk put it between us and her. Xerxes admired that too. It was typical of the Persian high command: high-ranking officers like Artemisia were to be protected at all costs, and it was perfectly acceptable to sacrifice several hundred common sailors in the process. If Themistocles ever did something like that, he'd be tried for multiple counts of murder in the Assembly and probably executed.

It looked like things could not possibly get any worse for the fleeing Persians.

Then they did.

Themistocles, through Eurybiades, ordered all ships to follow them at a steady pace but not to attack. We followed the Persians for close to an hour. They rowed hard and began to pull away from us.

"So what do you think is happening now, boys?" I said to the hostages. They were quite calm now, clearly thrilled to have witnessed a glorious victory. They would tell their friends about this for the rest of their lives.

"The Persians are not getting away, sir," said the older boy. "They only think they are."

"You're a fast learner," I said. The boy beamed at the compliment. "I do not know what our Fleet Commander intends to do," I added, "but I do know that we will like it and the Persians will not."

We followed the Persians for another hour. Even though we hadn't increased our speed, we started to gain on them as they couldn't maintain their frantic pace. They would soon be too tired to mount any kind of a defense.

Then we saw, in the distance ahead of the Persians, a small oncoming fleet of triremes. Persian reinforcements? They wouldn't help. The ships we followed would be in their way, although they might be able to escort some of the ships to safety.

Themistocles grinned.

As we cruised closer, the oncoming ships attacked the now-helpless Persians.

"The Aeginetes," said Eurybiades.

"Right on schedule," Themistocles added.

The Aeginetes had changed sides. Ariabignes had kept them in their own port as a reserve. They'd sunk the Persian ships in their harbour and now came after the rest of the Persian fleet. While their role was dangerous—if the Persians suspected treachery, their army would have occupied Aegina and slaughtered the population—their actual sea battle was quite easy, as they faced exhausted crews with little fight left in them.

I wasn't terribly close to this part of the battle, Ephander, so there's little I can tell you that you don't already know. A handful of Persian ships managed to escape, including Artemisia's, but most of the Persian ships were either sunk or boarded. From this point on, we lost not a single man. The surviving Persian oarsmen, thousands of them, were given to the Aeginetes to sell as slaves. It was a sweet deal for them, and while this caused resentment here and there, everyone acknowledged that Themistocles had finally formed a true alliance with the Aeginetes, a previously impossible task, and it made all of us stronger because of the skill and experience of the Aeginetan sailors and ships.

As we watched the Aeginetes vanquish our exhausted enemy, another battle took place on Psyttaleia, a small but strategically important isle east of Salamis and off the southwest coast of Attica. The Persians had left a garrison of four hundred men there. A portion of the Aeginetan fleet had been dispatched there with a thousand hoplites. When the Aeginetan ships approached, the garrison assumed they were bringing news of a great Persian victory. The Aeginetes were allies, so they sailed unimpeded into the port.

The garrison was in a camp that did not even have a stockade around its perimeter. The thousand hoplites, ably led by Aristides—yes, *that* Aristides, recently recalled from exile—massacred the garrison and looted the camp.

Xerxes, on the advice of Mardonius, left our lands. He still had a huge empire to run. While he was away, intrigues dominated his court, and some of the outlying provinces started to rebel. He would never return to our side of the Aegean.

Mardonius remained in Attica. The Persian fleet was no more, but he still had a hundred and fifty thousand soldiers. They would winter in our lands, and there was nothing we could do about that.

Well, not exactly nothing. We still had Themistocles. He had men inside the Persian camp. They would poison food and water supplies—without the Persian fleet, resupply was now difficult for them—and they had many months to do everything possible to erode the enemy army's morale. I myself would sneak into the Persian camp, and lead cavalry attacks on their supply convoys.

But those are stories, Ephander, for another day. I now had to get to Athens. We won this battle but still had to evacuate the city.

22—REGRET

"I *can't*," the woman pleaded. "Please don't make me."

The people of Athens who walked this road to the Phaleron looked like a parade of the damned. They were all women and children, along with boys too young to fight and men too old, and a few men who were physically unable to hold a spear or an oar or a sling. Almost everyone had their belongings in sacks. Few spoke. They trudged like a defeated people, even though we'd just won a great sea battle. Most stared at the ground. If they'd been marching to Hades, which some probably believed they were, they wouldn't have looked more dispirited.

The woman had stopped walking. She sat by the side of the road and cried. She clutched a stoppered bronze vase to her chest like it was life itself. She was no older than thirty, but the strain of her grief made her look much older.

"You have to," said her husband, who crouched beside her and put his arm around her.

"I can't," she said. "Please don't make me."

"You know the rules," said the husband. "We all have to make sacrifices. We can only bring a few things with us, money, food, medicine, a change of clothes, and a tent. You have to leave her."

"I *can't*."

Timoleon and I supervised the evacuees who passed on this stretch of road. As unhappy as all these people were, and as much as they hated this, they made little trouble. Themistocles ordered us to be gentle but firm. He'd insisted that no one be allowed to use carts or horses for transport. Exceptions were made only for invalids, like the two women who'd given birth the previous day, and the old or infirm who were unable to walk. Themistocles had made it clear that if a possession couldn't be carried, then it must be left behind. It seemed punitive, but he made the rule because there would not be space on the transport ships for much more than the people themselves. Two of our fellow guardsmen, who were assigned to the area just outside the city's Itonian Gate, told us that they had to make a few people leave chairs and tables and trunks behind. People actually thought they'd be able to carry heavy furniture five miles to the port.

"What's the trouble?" Timoleon asked the man and woman.

"It's her mother," the man said. "She doesn't want to leave her."

"Her mother?" I said. "Do we need to go back for her?"

"No, no," said the man, still crouched beside his wife. "It's her ashes. In the vase. She doesn't want to leave her to the Persians." I wondered why the man was here. He looked able-bodied. Even if he couldn't afford armour, we could always use oarsmen and peltasts. Was he a coward? Then he rose, which was difficult for him, and I saw his wooden leg. Most of his left hand was missing too.

"Marathon," he said, as if he'd read the thoughts I now felt ashamed for having.

"I was there too," I said. "Both of us," I added, indicating Timoleon.

"I remember you, Elektros," he said. "I was in the line when a Persian in front of me took a javelin through his chest. I heard you threw it."

"I don't know if I killed that particular Persian," I said. "I wasn't the only one throwing javelins. But yes, I did kill a few that way."

"It's really important to my wife," he said, "to keep her mom's ashes. Any chance you can make an exception for an old soldier?"

"Sorry, friend," said Timoleon. "Can't do it. If we made an exception for you, everyone else would want one. But I have an idea."

Timoleon crouched in front of the woman. "What's your name, ma'am?" he said.

"Amarhyllis," she said.

"My name is Timoleon," he said in barely a whisper. "I'm speaking quietly, Amarhyllis, because I don't want anyone else to hear this. You see the two boulders behind me?"

She looked over his shoulder at two enormous rocks, about thirty yards off the road. There was a space between them just big enough for a person to pass through. "Yes," said Amarhyllis.

"Let's take the vase there," said Timoleon, "and bury it. You can retrieve it when we return to the city."

No one would steal the ashes, but Timoleon was being secretive because the vase was finely hammered bronze that shone like gold. Some people could mistake it for gold.

"It's a good idea, dear," said the husband. "We'll come back for it when this is all over."

Timoleon showed her his wineskin. "After we bury it, I'll pour a libation to ask for the travelling god's protection."

The woman finally agreed. Timoleon told her to keep the vase covered inside her cloak and to hunch over like she was ill. Then Timoleon and her husband ushered her to the rocks.

"Nature calls," I said to the few people who looked up. Timoleon used his sword to break up the sandy ground behind the rocks, then he and the husband dug the hole with their bare hands. Amarhyllis placed the vase inside, they filled in the hole, then Timoleon poured a libation and spoke a quiet prayer to Hermes. Afterwards, Amarhyllis and her husband rejoined the sad parade.

It took a combination of threatening promises and promising threats to get Athenians to evacuate the city. When Themistocles told everyone, a mere three days earlier, that they'd have to leave their homes and their farms to live temporarily in tents on the isles of Salamis and Aegina, the response was something less than genteel.

It was almost a riot. I feared for Themistocles' life. It was the first time I ever thought the citizens of Athens would turn on him. A few days earlier, after the grand success of the Battle of Salamis, the Assembly had elected him War Archon, a fancy term for temporary king. He now had the authority to enact emergency measures without putting them to a vote. He was too smart to put the evacuation to a vote.

"You lying fuck!" one man screamed at Themistocles. "You want us to leave? You said we could fight the fucking Persians from behind our new walls!" Many other voices echoed the opinion.

"I said no such thing," said Themistocles. "The walls defend us from other Hellenes, from Thebans and Argives and Spartans. The fucking Persians are not like our fellow Hellenes. If the Thebans, for example, attacked us with a significant force, they would leave their own city undefended. They have enemies besides us, so they couldn't besiege us for long. We would simply outwait them. The Persians, unfortunately, can besiege us without leaving their own cities undefended. They have a hundred and fifty thousand men and can besiege us here for years if they have to. So against them, our walls trap us. We must evacuate the city. We have no choice."

He'd persuaded the men of Athens to put millions of drachmae into shipbuilding, but it took years. He only had two days to convince them to evacuate Athens. The Persians had passed through Thermopylae and were now only a few days march away from Athens. So he enacted the Decree of Themistocles. When he campaigned for warships, he remained popular even when his shipbuilding proposal was not. People saw it as a quirk, a lovable peccadillo they could live with. But his insistence on evacuating the city was seen as madness, perhaps temporary, but madness nonetheless.

Themistocles' first act as War Archon was to allow freedmen and metics into the Assembly. So I stood beside him when an angry man in one of the high seats threw an apple at him. Other things were thrown, fruit, stones, a sandal, but Themistocles focused on the apple-thrower. The apple had hit him on the shoulder before I could get my shield in front of him. Themistocles winced but wasn't seriously hurt.

Two of his men, Dymnos and Philokles, took a few steps into the crowd. Themistocles stopped them.

"Do that again, Antenor, son of Memnos," said Themistocles, "and I won't send my men after you. *I'll come up there and wring your fucking neck myself!* If you disagree with Themistocles, that it your right. We are men of Athens, entitled to our opinions and free to express them. If you have a better suggestion than mine, you may take the floor and state it. But you do *not* have the right to throw things at Themistocles. I like to think we are better than that. You, Antenor son of Memnos, clearly are not."

I was impressed that Themistocles could recognize the man from a few hundred feet away. Antenor thought the crowd made him anonymous. Themistocles had just proved him wrong. Antenor was a torrent of rage when he threw the apple, but now he meekly stepped forward.

"Forgive me, Archon," Antenor yelled, "but you must admit, evacuating the city is insane. Our shops and our homes will be looted! And that's before the Persians even get here."

Kimon jumped onstage and squalled about how ridiculous an evacuation would be. "Themistocles cannot make up his mind," he said. "First we build a fleet. Then we fight the Persians on land in the Vale of Tempe. Then we retreat from Tempe and look for another place to fight them. Then we cower behind our walls. And now we run away from Athens and hide! What will he want us to do tomorrow? Bring the Persians tussie-mussies and ask them all to marry us?"

"Sit the fuck down, Kimon," Themistocles growled, "and shut the fuck up. The matter is not up for debate. I announce the Decree of Themistocles in the Assembly as a courtesy to my fellow citizens. We can talk about it, and I will explain the rationale behind it, but we will not vote on it. It is already the law."

"You sound more and more like a king," shouted Kimon, "every time you open your mouth!"

"Kimon, Kimon, Kimon," said Themistocles, shaking his head and smiling indulgently like he was a tutor and Kimon was a schoolboy who couldn't grasp the concept of simple sums. "Must I explain to you, yet again, that a War Archon actually is, in effect, a king? He has the autocratic authority to lead Athens. The title is only granted in times of emergency, like right now, when decisive action is required. Now go back to your place, idiot, or I'll have you thrown in jail—which is also well within my authority as War Archon."

Kimon didn't sit down. He left the Assembly altogether. A few of his aristocratic cronies followed. Everyone else stayed.

"My fellow citizens," Themistocles said in the sweetish voice he used when he wanted to sound gentle but still needed to be heard. It was higher than his usual speaking voice and carried farther. It was hard to believe that this was the same man who growled at Kimon mere seconds earlier. "Disregard whatever you may have heard about the Vale of Tempe. I was not in command there. I went along with it even though I knew that we could never fight the Persians there. I wanted to get our troops some exercise and show our Spartan allies that I can cooperate with them. Those two goals were achieved. It was all part of a greater plan, which, unfortunately, I cannot reveal in its entirety to the Assembly. I trust ninety-nine-point-nine-nine percent of you, but if even one man has a loose tongue, our enemy will know our plan and thwart us at every turn. So the fewer who know the plan, the safer we'll all be. Even my most trusted advisors do not know much more than you do. Themistocles is the only one who knows all of it. So I must now ask you for a favour."

He paused for emphasis. As War Archon, he did not need to ask for favours. There was now total silence where a couple of minutes earlier there had been a storm of rage.

"Rest assured, friends, that we will fight the Persians on land. We will defeat them. But I must ask you,"—at this point his voice grew quieter, an orator's trick to make people listen more carefully, "I must ask you to trust Themistocles for a little while longer. Can you do that for me?"

I can guarantee you, Ephander, that this is not how the Great King issued decrees. Themistocles acknowledged that his power, though temporarily absolute, came from the Assembly.

"I ask you to accept that we must evacuate the city. I do not ask you to like it. I do not like it myself. My own house and its furnishings will be left behind, and I can assure you, the Persians will target my home. I expect to find rubble in its place when we return." Themistocles was actually wrong about this, but more about that later.

"So do this for me, and I promise you victory. We will not fail. If we do, you must have me executed. I will willingly submit. But please, trust me. Will you?"

Mild applause began here and there, then a little more, then even more until almost everyone was clapping. It was not the raucous, unrestrained ovation that would accompany a great victory or an announcement of more silver at Laurion. Instead, it was the resigned acceptance that evacuation was necessary, and even though nobody liked it, they accepted it because the smartest man in all Hellas advised it. Only minutes earlier, I feared for Themistocles' life, but now he shook hands with people as they filed past him to their homes to sleep well for one more night. The next morning, they would leave everything to our enemies.

On the road to the Phaleron, Timoleon and I had seen thousands of people in this grim procession, and so far all had been sad. Brave, but sad. Then we saw two women who laughed and joked as they walked. In fact, they were in unusually high spirits.

"Sweet Issa," I said to the red-haired one who looked ridiculously attractive even though she wore a long loose chiton that revealed no flesh, apart from her face. "No one could ever be happy to evacuate a house as fine as yours. What are you two up to?"

The other woman, a younger blue-eyed blonde, who was also dressed modestly, looked at me with her big blue eyes and would have been the soul of innocence if I hadn't known she was a whore. The two women had four slaves who carried their goods for them. The two women walked arm in arm like they were strolling by the river on a fine spring morning.

"We are up to nothing at all, Elektros," said Issa. "We are merely optimistic."

"We have faith," said the blonde woman, "that our soldiers and generals know exactly what they're doing and will bring us victory."

I laughed at their sarcasm. We all hoped for victory, but no one yet believed it would come. All Athenians were now refugees, which usually only happens when you *lose* a war. They would spend the next month, or longer, in camps on the isles of Aegina. They would not be maltreated but they would not be permitted to leave. If the Persians won, they'd be enslaved. They'd left their fine homes to live in tents, and even Themistocles, despite appearances, wasn't as confident of victory as these two women claimed to be.

"No, really," I said. "Why are you two so cheerful?"

"Can you not guess?" said Issa. "No? Well, just think of where we'll be. There will be no gymnasium, no theatre, no wine-shops or taverns. People will be bored. Men need distractions. Even old men."

I admired her resourcefulness. Men who were too old to fight would not necessarily be too old to use Red Issa's services. Fighting men would be permitted to visit their families on Aegina, and they too would be happy to see Red Issa and her companion. When the Persians were defeated and the Athenians went back to their city, Red Issa would probably be wealthy.

The invalid wagons came last, eighteen of them. My friend Simeon rode on one, and he hated it so much, being stuck with the old and the crippled, that he frequently got off the wagon and walked. He was young, but he would never completely recover from the head injury he'd suffered at Paria. He could only walk short distances. His legs were okay, but his balance was poor. He could go no more than a hundred yards without getting dizzy. He needed a walking stick. He could not run. He tried to not think of himself as crippled. He supervised his family's export business and did it so well that during peacetime he could deem himself an able-bodied man. Then the war was upon us and his disability stood out. He was no coward—I fought in the line beside him once and can vouch for that—but he still had to go with the women and children and old men. It constantly reminded him of the man he could no longer be.

When he saw me, though, he hobbled over as quickly as he could. "Good to see you, Lex," he said. "Kill a hundred trousies for me." *Trousies* was the current faddish term for the Persians, a reference to their ridiculous trousers. As we hugged each other, he said in a low voice, "Check the wagon behind mine. One of the 'invalids' isn't breathing."

Simeon climbed back onto his assigned wagon. Timoleon and I inspected the others. Each wagon had six or seven elderly people laid out on it. Some greeted us, while others had no idea where they were going or why. Some sat and stared blankly at the sky, or at the people around them. Some prayed. We found the one that Simeon said wasn't breathing.

An old couple sat beside the body, which appeared to be a woman.

"I am sorry for your loss," said Timoleon, "but we cannot take our dead with us."

"We can't do a proper funeral here," said the old woman, tears in her eyes.

"We'll have to do the best we can," I said. "Have you a coin for the ferryman?"

"Huh?" said the old woman. "No. We are poor folk,

young sir."

"Here, I've got one," I said as I pulled a drachma from my tunic pocket.

"No, really, it's okay," said the old man. "We'll manage."

"You can pay me back later," I said, "if that's what you're worried about."

"No, young sir, it's okay," he said. Now he looked worried.

"I insist," I said. I lifted the veil over the face of the deceased. The two blue eyes that stared at me were painted on. It was a mask. There was nothing behind it.

"What the fuck?" said Timoleon, as he pulled the robe off of the 'deceased,' only to find six burlap sacks, their contents shaped to look like a body.

Timoleon pulled open one of the sacks. There were dried green leaves inside it. "What is this stuff?" he asked.

I recognized the smell. "Cannabis," I said. "A lifetime supply. Longer than a lifetime, considering how old these two are."

"I take it for menstrual cramps," said the old lady.

I laughed out loud. "Menstrual cramps?" I said. "You must be seventy years old."

"Seventy-two," she said. "And I haven't had a menstrual cramp in over twenty-five years. It really does work."

"And you?" I said, still laughing, to the old man. "Do you take it for menstrual cramps too?"

"Don't be absurd, young sir," he said. "I use it because it makes me hungry. My old body doesn't do that on its own anymore. Plus I like the way it makes me feel."

I believed them. Timoleon didn't. He thought they were profiteers. We compromised. We let them keep two sacks and confiscated the other four.

When the wagon started moving again, Timoleon

asked me about cannabis. I told him that the Scythians burned it and inhaled the fumes. They called it dreamsmoke and used it in their rituals, and it sometimes induced visions as well as having other medicinal qualities. "Takes all kinds," he said.

He then handed out the confiscated bags to other people in the procession. "Good for what ails you, I hear," he said. "Scythian medicine. You burn it and inhale the fumes."

Some people knew what it was, some did not. Timoleon thought I didn't see him cram a fistful into his tunic pocket.

I was worried about Meli, because I hadn't seen her yet. She should have passed by here hours ago. I hoped she hadn't done anything foolish, like the few sad clowns who remained in their homes and prayed, or the forty others who'd barricaded themselves inside the Bluebeard Temple on the Acropolis, insisting that Athena would protect them from all harm. All of those people were killed when the Persians came.

The last wagon rolled towards us. And there was Meli, walking beside it. She'd made a new friend, who walked beside her.

"Ladies," I said. "I'm very glad, and very relieved, to see you."

"And we're very glad, and very relieved, to see you," said Siren. She and Meli were well rested. Siren had talked the guards all along the route into letting Meli and her ride in the wagons, even though they were in perfect health and the wagons were supposed to be for the infirm. They walked now only to stretch their legs a little.

I hugged and kissed Meli, but when I looked over her shoulder, Siren winked at me and slowly dragged her tongue across her upper lip, a devastatingly sexy gesture that had the desired effect. My eyes widened and my brain stopped working.

I was long done with Siren, I thought.

And I thought she was done with me, too.

I bore Siren no ill will. I'd assumed that was also mutual, but when when I saw her with Meli, I knew I would pay somehow. Siren did not normally associate with working women like Meli.

After Siren and I stopped seeing each other, she seemed to have lost all desire to be discreet. The marriage that Themistocles had tried to arrange for her did not happen because someone from the groom's family had seen her walk down the street hand in hand with Gral the Tall, a Scythian archer. There were other public incidents with other men, too. Siren had made herself so disrespectable that neither Themistocles nor Hyperion were able to arrange a marriage for her. She would arrange her own, or not marry at all.

I hadn't been with Siren for several years now, and her reputation wasn't my concern. I was probably the first man who ever voluntarily chose to stop enjoying her. If she'd needed to get over it, which I seriously doubted, it would have happened by now.

How little I knew.

"Hi Lex," said Siren, lovely as the sun itself, and a smile like a Nile crocodile.

"Parthenia," I said. "You look—uh, well." I thought it unwise to compliment her beauty too much in Meli's presence.

"You told Meli about you and me, right, Lex?" Siren said.

"I have," I said.

"We were lovers," said Siren, as she stepped forward and demurely kissed me on the cheek. "Lex has been to my house many times. Has he not told you that?"

"Not the specifics," said Meli. "It was years ago."

"Really?" said Siren, who paused just long enough to make Meli suspicious, delighted at my discomfiture. "Did he not tell you that we saw each other at Korinthos?"

Meli looked at me with some shock.

"We had dinner together," I said to Meli. "Hyperion was with us."

"That's not what I remember," said Siren.

Meli and I never pressed each other for details about past lovers. They were in the past and that made them no longer relevant. Meli was my present and my future, and the only woman who mattered to me.

"Meli has news," Siren said.

"I am with child," said Meli.

I was speechless because this was news I didn't expect. Before I recovered my senses enough to celebrate this news, Siren spoke up.

"You're some walkin', talkin, baby-makin' bacon god," she said, "because I too am with child. I got pregnant in Korinthos."

"Not by me!" I said.

"Don't worry," Siren said, "I don't expect you to marry me."

I was stunned into silence. I should have been telling Meli that this was great news, and how much I loved her and wanted a child with her. Instead, I had to persuade her that I hadn't lain with Siren in Korinthos. I looked at the two women, one as lovely as a crimson moon, the other a gentle rain that makes a rainbow. Siren had a soft life but a hard heart. Meli had a hard life but a soft heart.

"Asshole!" said Meli. "You said you were done with her years ago. I believed you!"

"Yet you won't believe me now," I said. "She toys with us. Tell her, Thena. Tell her the truth."

"I better not get involved," said Siren.

"So *now* you decide to not get involved," I said.

But the damage had been done. Siren laughed at me.

Meli stomped away, past the procession of evacuees, frustrated that they blocked the road. I ran after her and caught her after she'd gone fifty yards.

I grabbed her by the elbow. "Don't touch me, lying asshole!" she screamed.

"C'mon, leave the poor girl alone," yelled a woman with four children in tow and an infant in her arms.

"Meli," I said. "Please. Let's talk. Parthenia is old news. She just likes fucking with people's heads."

You've probably noticed, Ephander, that Siren did not actually say that I'd had sex with her in Korinthos. She'd merely inferred it. This was yet another way she could weaponize her beauty: if she claimed, or merely hinted, that a man had slept with her, the man's woman found it nigh impossible to believe otherwise.

Before Meli and I could work this out, I had another problem to deal with. A man on a horse charged towards us from the direction of the port. It was Hyperion. His angry eyes never once left mine.

"What the fuck?" said Timoleon. "Hey moron! Get off that horse!"

"No, Timoleon," I said. "Let him come. I have to deal with this myself."

Timoleon looked at me like I was nuts. Hyperion leapt off his horse before it had completely stopped, the best way I know to break your ankles, but he was unhurt and his momentum carried him until he was only a few feet in front of me.

"I defended you," he said. "When people called you a half-savage lowlife, I said you were a man of honour. Then you sleep with my sister!"

"It was years ago," I said.

"That's not what she says," said Hyperion, "and why would that even matter? I should kill you."

Did she lie outright to Hyperion or merely infer it again? It hardly mattered.

"If you fight every man she's slept with," I said, "then you'll be taking on a small army." It's the worst thing I could have said because it inferred that he, as her guardian, wasn't doing a good job of it.

"None of the other men in that small army," he said, "was a close friend of mine."

This I knew not to be true, but, again, it would only make him angrier if I corrected him.

He wanted to fight. Had to fight. He was of that class of Athenian who believed that women were incapable of reasoned judgement when they took lovers, so only the man was technically at fault. It did not matter that Siren was so jaw-droppingly, brain-foggingly, cock-hardeningly beautiful that the usual mores of Athenian society did not apply to her. He was unarmed, so I unbuckled my sword belt and gorytos and let them drop to the ground.

Hyperion punched me in the head. I saw it coming but didn't dodge it. He was entitled to his rage, and he could fight. When we were ephebes, he was our best boxer. I boxed with him once back then. He demolished me. I never learned how to win a boxing match, nor did I want to. Too many damned rules. My only rule in a fight was, and to this day still is, to end it as quickly as possible. Xenocrates taught nothing else. I would head-butt my opponent, maybe, or stomp his toes, take his legs out from under him, or use my elbows, but none of those things are allowed in boxing. To stand toe to toe trying to outpunch a man, and only hitting him above the belt, was as absurd to me as it was to Xenocrates. You can get badly hurt doing that, even if you win the fight. I'd rather just kick my opponent in the nuts to get him to stop punching me.

Hyperion's first shot made me see little lights flash, and his follow-up left jab into my ribs momentarily paralyzed my entire right side. By the gods, the man could punch. But his third shot, another hard right to the head that almost certainly would have knocked me down, didn't make clean contact because I ducked it. Ribs still aching, I grabbed his right wrist with my left hand, then twisted his arm behind him.

"Your anger with me is justifiable," I said, "but two shots are all you get." The blood on his fist was mine. I felt a small warm trickle down the left side of my face, and my eye began to swell shut.

I released him. "Hyperion, I am truly—"

"Do not try to apologize," he said. "You, Elektros of Skiathos, are dead to me."

This hurt me more than his fists ever could.

He led Siren away. Throughout this entire scene, she never stopped smiling. She blew me a kiss as she left.

"Such fun!" she said. "Let's all do this again some time."

I ran after Meli and caught up to her. She'd been crying but had stopped by now.

"If she is old news for you," said Meli, "then why was Hyperion here now?"

"She probably just told him about her and me," I said.

The last of the evacuees and the wagons had passed by now. Timoleon came over and reminded me that we had to leave. Themistocles was to meet with some of the other Hellenic League leaders again, and he wanted Timoleon and me with him.

"I have to leave," I said to Meli. "The Archon commands it."

"Maybe you should just fucking marry Themistocles," Meli spat at me. "You spend more time with him than you do with me."

"Come on, Meli," I said. "You know as well as I do that this is a duty I can't abandon. Go to the camp and get settled in, put up our tent. We'll talk later. Forget that troublemaking bitch. It's you I love."

I made a big mistake here. I should've stayed with Meli. I should have recognized that the defense of Hellas could continue without me for a few hours. I should have made a proper apology to Meli, reassured her that I was thrilled that she carried my child, and told her I'd marry her as soon as it could be arranged. I should've said that the child was the start of our future together. It was what I wanted and what I believed.

Instead, the moment was so unpleasant to me that I bungled it. I just wanted this conversation to end. I was actually relieved when Timoleon reminded me that we had to go. I also thought that I could go see Meli at Aegina later that night, or the next day, when she would be calmer and, gods-willing, in a more forgiving mood.

So I took the easy way out. "It won't always be like this," I told her. "I promise. Please, just go to Aegina and get settled in. I'll come to you as soon as I can."

As it turned out, it would be a two days before I would be free to visit her.

Way too late.

23—ANTIO

It took us two days to get everyone off the mainland and onto ships, and for two camps to get set up. There were too many people to put on Aegina, so a second camp had to be set up on Salamis, where Timoleon and I had been assigned to overlook the new arrivals. We had to break up a few fights—people were ill-tempered because they were stressed—but apart from that, we had few difficulties. On the second day, I'd been given leave to go visit Meli on Aegina. Salamis was seven miles away, so I paid a fisherman to paddle me there.

He got me there very late in the afternoon when the sun still shone proudly. When I reached the refugee camp, there was a ruckus ahead, just beyond the beach, with people shouting angrily and gathered around something or somebody.

A little boy, maybe six years old, ran screaming to me. "Help! Help!" he cried. "They're killing her! They're killing her!"

"Who?" I said. "Who's killing who?"

"My grammy," he said. "Those ladies are killing my grammy." He sobbed now.

"Okay, little buddy, don't cry," I said. "I'll see what I can do."

I ran to the throng of angry women and pushed myself into the middle of it. There were maybe forty or fifty women and a few old men. They had beaten a woman's face to bloody mush. I exaggerate not, Ephander.

Most people slipped away as soon as they saw me. This often happened. With my Scythian features, they mistook me for one of the Scythians who policed Athens, even though I wore a plain grey tunic instead of the bright orange patterned trousers the Scythians wore. Even when they recognized that I wasn't one of those Scythians, some saw me as one of Themistocles' men and assumed I could arrest people. Few realized that my authority in this camp was even less than their own, since they were Athenian citizens and I was not.

This also was not my fight. I had no idea who the old woman was. Even if I did, her face was such a mess now that she was unrecognizable. It had been pummeled flat. I once saw a man get his face sheared off by a sword in battle. This woman looked worse than he did. Her white hair had soaked up so much blood that it looked like a wet red wig. Her face was crushed into the ground. Her eyes were gone, either removed altogether or pounded into the mush that was once her face. Beside her was the blood-covered rock that had killed her. Whoever beat her had kept at it long after she was dead. That was some serious rage.

The boy approached. I quickly picked him up and turned him away from this. "Don't look back," I said. "She's gone." He tried to look back anyway, so I carried him towards the camp. As I did, my friend Simeon approached.

"Elektros!" he said. "Need any help?"

"I do," I said. "Can you take this little guy somewhere?"

"Yes, of course," he said. Simeon took the little boy, who had seen more than I'd wanted him to and now seemed too numb to cry, to a different part of the camp. Simeon rejoined me a few minutes later.

"Left him with Simonia," he said. That was his sister.

"So what happened here?" I asked.

"Orithyia went too far," he said. "She stole as much money and jewelry from people as she could get her hands

354

on."

"Really?" I said. "How could an old woman do that?"

"She had three big sons," he said. "One was a simple-minded deaf mute, one had a mangled arm, and the other had a bad knee. None could stand in the phalanx or take an oar, but here, where there are no able-bodied men, they could bully women, children, and old men. They made women hand over their valuables. The last straw was when they raped and killed a girl this morning."

"They did all that in two days?" I said. "Pure evil. What happened to the sons?"

"The women swarmed them with daggers, killed them, then threw their bodies into the sea. I warned Orithyia that something like this would happen, but she didn't listen."

Orithyia and her sons were fools. Did they not realize that this camp was temporary and that these women had husbands, fathers and brothers who would come back and avenge them? These evil oafs got what they deserved.

I went into the camp to search for Meli. I would marry her—this very day, if possible. I'd made an important decision: I would become an Athenian citizen immediately, so our child would be a citizen too. We would have more children. We'd be a real family.

I was ready to settle down. I had just turned twenty-eight. I had many years ahead of me and I now had the good sense to live them. I was at the Battle of Marathon, I fought a territorial war in Scythia, and I'd just taken part in two major sea battles. I wouldn't have traded those experiences for anything, but I'd had enough. The gods know how much death I'd seen, but I'd been lucky so far, and no man's luck is infinite.

I would do my part to eliminate the Persian horde that now held Attica, but thereafter I would take my place in the phalanx with my fellow citizens and defend my city when called upon to do so. Apart from that, I would kill no more. I would take no more missions from Themistocles, no matter how well they paid.

I would teach.

Themistocles had mentioned that his tribe, Leontis, needed a weapons instructor for its ephebes. I would ask for this job and probably get it. Every day I would teach young men how to fight, then every night I'd go home to my wife and family. I would also have time to take private students. I was reputed to be one of the best swordsmen in all Hellas, which would appeal to rich men who wanted their sons to have proper sword training.

I couldn't wait to tell Meli. I imagined her reaction. She would beam, she would glow, she would shed tears of joy. She would put all suspicion behind her. I would tell her how much I loved her and how much she meant to me. I'd easily convince her because all of it was true.

First, though, I had to find her. It should have been easy. This camp was well ordered. There were several large areas for communal cook-fires, and the tents were all in neat rows. It looked like a little town, with named streets, a designated place where a small market could be set up, and specific places where chamber pots were to be emptied so their contents would be washed out to sea. All of the dwellings had begun as tents, but some already had wooden roofs and little walls. Many had canopies at the front that allowed their occupants to sit outside on hot days and have shade.

But where was Meli? I stopped people and asked if they knew where she was. None did. I looked and looked. I walked up and down the little streets. How could she not be here? I approached a group of women who sat at a small fire in front of one of the tents. Suddenly I recognized one of them, Meli's friend Lyra. I was surprised not to see Meli here too.

Lyra's face froze in horror when she saw me.

"Where is she?" I said, too tired and frustrated to greet Lyra properly.

I knew by the way the women looked at each other, and away from me, that the news was not good.

"You must promise," Lyra finally said, "not to hurt me when I tell you."

"I'll fucking hurt you if you *don't* tell me right now!" I growled at her.

Lyra erupted into tears. I almost did too.

"Forgive me, Lyra," I said. "I've haven't slept in three days. I'm exhausted and I'm not myself. I swear to fair Athena that I won't hurt you or anyone else. Please tell me where Meli is."

"Follow me," Lyra said after she'd composed herself a little. She was a few years younger than Meli, with a round pretty face and a plump figure that wouldn't be plump for long in this camp.

I'd hoped Lyra would lead me to a makeshift hospital, where I would find Meli sick but still alive, where she would get better, but in my heart I knew if that was the case, the women would have just said so. Lyra and I were also headed in the wrong direction. Lyra led me a few hundred yards out of the camp to a small grove of trees. There was a small mound of sand. Upon the mound was a stone with the name Melita carved into it.

Melita. Her real name. I stood, stunned with grief, too numb to cry. Lyra began to leave. "Please stay," I said, "and tell me what happened."

"She was sad," Lyra said. "We all were, leaving our homes and coming to the-gods-know-what in a refugee camp, but Meli was saddest. She did not know if you wanted her or the child. None of us knew how long we'd be here—we still don't—and Meli decided that she did not want her baby born here. She told me that she finally saw it your way, that you should have a child under better circumstances. So she terminated her pregnancy."

"How?"

"Pennyroyal."

I knew of it. Pennyroyal was an herb that Kandra had carried with her at all times. It had many uses. Besides ending pregnancy, it could cure diarrhea, relieve cramps and fevers, and even keep insects away if rubbed on the skin. But it had to be used very sparingly. Despite its kindly-sounding name, pennyroyal was a deadly poison. Dosages had to be tiny. Even a miniscule overdose was fatal.

Lyra suddenly burst into tears. "I knew she had it," she said, "and I didn't take it away from her. I'm so sorry!"

"Not your fault," I said. "Did you actually administer it to her?"

"No, but I should have taken it from her!"

I took her in my arms until she stopped sobbing and was able to talk again.

"Not your fault, "I said. "Did she intend to end her life?"

"No. She only wanted to end her pregnancy."

"Where did she get the pennyroyal?"

"A healing woman sold it to her."

"Which healing woman?"

"I'd never seen her before. Her name was Lydiana."

Lydiana was Parthenia's slave-woman. I thought a dozen thoughts at once. Did Lydiana intentionally mislead Meli about the safe and proper dosage? Or did Meli make the mistake on her own, not knowing the potency of pennyroyal, with its innocent-sounding name? I couldn't answer these questions until I spoke to Lydiana herself.

"Where is Lydiana now?" I asked.

"I don't know," said Lyra. "When Meli took sick, we looked for Lydiana everywhere. She's not in this camp."

I thanked Lyra for the information and sat on the beach beside the little grave of Meli and Hermistocles—in my mind, I had already named the unborn child after my grandfather, if it was a boy, and after my mother Roxella if it was a girl. I spent the entire night at the grave, silent, unsleeping. My thoughts were black, evil, pained. Parthenia would die, Lydiana too, once I found them. They were murderers, even if all they did was fail to teach Meli the proper dosage of pennyroyal.

At sunrise, Zosimos appeared at my side. He'd spoken to Lyra and the others. "I'm so sorry," he said. He wept.

"Themistocles has given you permission," he said after a few minutes, "to take your vengeance on the one who tried to have you killed. I'll help you if you promise to help me with Simonides. If you feel up to it."

I did. I had to do something, had to move. I still hadn't slept, but now didn't want to. Zosimos said I should take my revenge immediately because time was a factor—my enemy was ill and would die soon.

Zosimos had a small boat waiting.

24—ANIMPOROS

"Marisa!" the gnarled old voice croaked. "Marisa! Get in here, stupid girl!"

"Marisa's gone," I said. "So is everyone else. Your slaves have fled the city and your own family has left you here to die."

We were in the old woman's family home on the Phaleron road, a few miles out of Athens, half a mile from the port. The Persians had already destroyed Athens. Our spies reported that the only buildings left intact were hovels and shacks in the poorer quarters that weren't worth the trouble to demolish, and one or two houses that their commanders used for headquarters. Now ten thousand of their troops were minutes away from us. We didn't believe they would destroy the port—they would need it for their own resupplies in the spring—but they were determined to knock down every building they didn't need, including this house. On our way here, Zosimos and I twice had to hide from their mounted scouts. Even from here, over four miles from the city walls, we could see the smoke of the city's doomed buildings.

"They left me here, idiot," the old woman said, "because I told them to. I will be dead in a day or two anyway. But Marisa is supposed to stay with me to the end. Marisa! Get in here, girl!"

"I just told you," I said. "Marisa's gone. We sent her away. Do you have any idea what the Persians would do if they found her?"

"Not my problem," said the old woman. "You don't live as long as I have if you worry too much about slaves." She laid flat on her back in her bed in her bedchamber on the second floor of the house. The room smelled of urine.

I wouldn't debate her. If the Persians took Marisa, they had a hundred and fifty thousand men who would want to rape her.

"I know you," she said. "The Scythian. One of Themistocles' bugger-boys."

She did not seem surprised to see me. Her withered mouth curved into a sneer. Her consumption was in its latter stages and would kill her very soon, so she knew there was little I could do to her. The curtains were drawn over the window in this room and the light was dim, but I could still see the greyness of her face, with skin so papery it looked like you could poke a finger through it.

She was already more dead than alive. She moaned. She reached for the bottle of poppy juice on the bedside table. It wasn't there.

"Looking for this, Euphrosyne?" I said, holding the bottle up.

"You give me that right now, mongrel," she said. "You've no right to keep it from me. Haven't you done enough to me already?"

"What is it you think I've done to you?"

"You killed my son."

"Proxenos?" I said. "I had, with great, great regrets, absolutely nothing to do with that. He was killed by the barbarian raiders he'd double-crossed."

"It happened because of you. You killed my nephew too."

"Who's your nephew?"

"Cnoethos. You cut off his hand. He died a few

days later."

I remembered. Euphrosyne's brother and two other men attacked me on a street in Athens on the night I was expelled from the ephebe barracks. One of the men tried to jump me from behind, but I spun around and hacked his hand off. I never knew his name until now.

"You think that's my fault, old wretch? The gutless fuck tried to attack me from behind. When a man does that, he has to expect that his intended victim will fight back, and that he has no one but himself to blame if he gets injured."

"I still blame you," she said. "And I curse you! I call on mighty Hades to curse you, mongrel bastard, and curse your bastard children! May none of them live to adulthood! A pox and a blight on your family for all time!"

I didn't believe in curses. Her words would go unheard by gods and men. If the gods wanted to curse me, it would be for their own reasons, not at a mortal's instigation. But I still had a dilemma here. According to Themistocles, Euphrosyne had hired two men to kill me at the funeral of young Neocles. Both men were dead, but they were mere hirelings. The focus of my vengeance was Euphrosyne. I'd come here, taking a huge risk of capture by the Persians, for no other reason than to kill her. I drew my sword and walked towards her bed.

Could I kill a helpless old woman?

Grandfather, though long gone, still influenced my thoughts and actions. When I had an ethical dilemma, I asked myself what he would have done. He believed in righteous revenge as much as anyone, but I could not imagine he'd approve of killing an old woman on her deathbed, no matter what she'd done in her life.

I put the point of my sword to her throat. She laughed. "I will die before the next sun rises," she said. "Go ahead and kill me, oaf."

I wanted to. I really, really, wanted to. She moaned in pain again. I'd already taken away her poppy juice, so she would suffer until she died.

Perhaps that would have to be my revenge.

I put my sword back in its scabbard.

Zosimos had been standing watch in front of the house. Now he came up the stairs and into the bedroom. "Persian horsemen," he said. "Less than a mile away. We must go!"

"Okay," I said. As much as I wanted Euphrosyne dead, I couldn't kill her, not least because it was what she now desired.

I would not have true revenge. Grandfather told me that some things went unavenged, and a wise man just accepted them and moved on.

Then I saw the coin on her bedside table.

"Do you believe in the immortal gods, Euphrosyne?" I asked.

"Only a barbarian dolt," she rasped weakly, "would even ask such a question."

She saw my eye on the coin and grabbed it. I pried it out of her cold hand.

"Thief!" she rasped. "You give me that back right now."

"I don't think so," I said. The coin was a silver dekadrachm, a heavy piece of silver. Most people were buried with a single drachma. Euphrosyne must have thought the ten-drachma piece would give her preferential treatment on Charon's boat across the Styx. Typical aristocrat.

Now she looked truly terrified. The sneer finally left her face. With no coin for the ferryman, she believed her shade would wander aimlessly for eternity.

So I had revenge after all. She would die, in agony, in dread of the afterlife. Zosimos and I left.

We both ran all the way to the port and got on the small boat. We'd had to pay the terrified boatman three times the usual rate, even though the Persians had no ships left in the area and were therefore no threat on the water.

Euphrosyne's screams and curses were much louder than you'd expect from a woman so close to her last breath, and as we climbed onto the boat, we could already hear the whickers and snorts of the Persian horses.

We pushed off.

GLOSSARY

An asterisk * indicates an actual historic figure.

Aberkios, Athenian cobbler.
***Adeimanthos**, Korinthian general.
Ahura Mazda, the principle Zoroastrian god to the Persians.
Aigyptos, Hellenic name for modern-day Egypt.
Aklepiades, father of Zosimos.
Alastor, man of Skiathos.
***Alexander I**, nominal king of Thessaly.
Amarhyllis, woman of Athens.
Anakletos, Athenian drunkard and famously incompetent slave tracker.
animporos, Hellenic for helpless.
antio, Hellenic for goodbye.
Arcas, Spartan delegate at Korinthos.
***Archippe**, wife of Themistocles.
***Ariabignes**, fleet commander at Artemisium & Salamis, brother of Xerxes.
***Arimnestos**, Plataean delegate at Korinthos.
***Aristides,** Athenian aristocrat. Nicknamed 'The Just' for his impeccable honesty. It is not always a compliment.
***Artemisia**, satrap of Halicarnassus.
Athanatos, 'deathless,' one of Elektros' fellow passengers on his return to Skiathos.
Audax, Athenian slave, later a freedman.
Balak, Scythian archer in Athens.
Basileides, Athenian shipbuilder.
bireme, a ship with two decks of oarsmen.
Blathyllos, Athenian guardsman.
Carneades, Athenian armed guard.

Carneia, an annual religious festival to Demeter, goddess of the harvest.
Chian, a person from Chios but also wine from that island, reputed to be the best in Hellas.
Chrysaphenios, 'the golden one,' Theban nickname for Elektros' half-brother Phyloctetes.
Cythereia, 'Cythi,' Athenian wife of Phyloctetes.
Cnoethos, nephew of Euphrosyne.
Delphi, sacred polis that was the location of the Delphic oracle. The priestess there, the Pythia, uttered the oracle that was famous for being cryptic and therefore subject to misinterpretation.
Dimokratis, Themistocles' command ship.
Diodoros, Athenian friend of Elektros.
Diodromes, an Athenian.
Diotrephes, Athenian accounts manager.
dolichos, the long-distance footrace. The distance was not standardized but was generally around three miles.
Dorak, Scythian archer in Athens.
Doros, father of Diotrephes.
Doryssos, Athenian guardsman.
Dymnos, Athenian guardsman.
ekphora, Hellenic funeral procession that normally went from the home of the deceased to the interment site.
Elektros, half Scythian, half Hellene swordsman.
ephebe, Athenian military trainee. Eighteen-year-old Athenians trained as hoplites for two years. Upon completion, they became full citizens.
*****Ephialtes,** Hellene who betrayed the Spartans at Thermopylae.
*****Epicydes**, Athenian aristocrat.
Eridanos, river that runs through Athens.
*****Euenetus**, Spartan commander at Tempe.
*****Euphrosyne**, legendary Athenian mother.

*Eurybiades, Spartan general.
Eurycleides, cousin of Eurybiades.
Exekias, Athenian slinger.
Faenus, Athenian freedman.
Ganymede, mythical young man whose beauty was so striking that Zeus himself found him attractive. Ganymede, who by some accounts already had divine blood, became Zeus' cup-bearer on Olympos.
Gauanes, Athenian merchant.
*Gelon, king of Syracuse.
Georgias, Skiathan farmhand.
gorytos, a leather case that holds a bow and up to seventy-five arrows.
Gerousia, the Spartan council of elders
Glaukopis, "bright-eyed," Athenian surgeon.
Gordias, oar-master on Themistocles' *Dimokratis*.
Gral, Scythian archer in Athens.
gynaikon, women's quarters in Hellene households, usually the top floor of the house.
hetaera, a prostitute, usually a higher class one who could charge high prices and therefore limit her number of clients. They were generally known for their intelligence as well as their attractiveness.
Hellas. What the ancient Greeks called their own lands. They called themselves Hellenes, and their language Hellenic. The words *Greece* and *Greek* didn't exist yet.
Helleniko, harbour on the northern coast of Euboea.
Hermanos, Athenian hoplite.
Hestios, would-be harbourmaster at Skiathos.
hoplite. 1, n., a heavily armoured infantryman. 2, adj., a style of combat in which heavy infantrymen presented a wall of spears and shields to their enemies. Hellenes excelled at it, especially the Spartans.
*Hydna, long-distance swimmer, daughter of Scyllias.
Hyperion, Athenian friend of Elektros.

Ilissos, river that flows outside of Athens.
Isidoros, Athenian guardsman.
Ismene, slave girl in the house of Themistocles.
Issa, aka **Red Issa**, Athenian hetaera.
Kadmos, Thessalian nobleman.
Kaletor, Athenian farmer.
Kalliaros, husband of Meli.
Karopophores, Korinthian innkeeper.
Kebalinos, commander of the Aeginetan fleet.
Kephalon, captain of a Hellenic merchant ship.
Khlöe, woman of Athens.
*****Kimon**, Athenian aristocrat, son of Miltiades
Kleitos, Athenian carter.
Korat, Elektros' cousin.
Krios, 'the ram,' Athenian friend of Elektros
ku, Scythian for 'boy,' often used as an insult.
kyklos, a circular naval formation in which the ships form a circle, with their sterns at the centre and their bows pointing outward.
Lampon, slave of Themistocles.
Lanike, sister of Themistocles.
Lectoros, chronic Scythian mispronunciation of Elektros. It means 'lecturer,' although this is unintended by the Scythians.
Leontis, Themistocles' tribe, one of the ten tribes of Athens.
*****Leotychidas**, king of Sparta.
Lycophon, Skiathan farmhand.
Lydiana, Parthenia's slave-woman.
Lyra, woman of Athens.
*****Lysimachus**, Athenian aristocrat, father of Aristides.
Marathon, site of Hellene land victory against the Persians in 490 B.C.E.
Marisa, Athenian slave.

Megakles, Athenian aristocrat, uncle of Aristides.
Melicheilia, 'honey lips,' usually called Meli, Athenian woman. See also **Melita.**
Melita, Melicheilia's real name.
*****Menestheus**, legendary king of Athens who fought in the Trojan War.
metic, non-Athenian resident of Athens
*****Miltiades**, Athenian general, hero of Marathon
*****Mnesiphilos,** tutor to Themistocles.
Nemerte, mother of Alexander of Thessaly.
*****Neocles the Elder**, father of Themistocles.
*****Neocles the Younger**, son of Themistocles.
Nomion, Athenian armed guard.
Oiorpata, Scythian for 'man slayer,' nickname of Elektros' mother Roxella.
Oliatos, Hellene soldier.
Orithyia, woman of Athens.
Otonia, household slave on Skiathos.
Otreus, secretary to Themistocles.
Pankratios, father-in-law to Phyloctetes, father of Cythereia.
Paria, island in the Aegean, site of unsuccessful Athenian invasion led my Miltiades
Parthenia, 'virgin,' sister of Hyperion, also called Siren.
*****Pausanias**, Spartan regent and overall commander of Hellenic League forces.
Phaedra, Elektros' housekeeper in Athens.
Phaleron, the port of Athens, five miles from the city.
Philostratos, Athenian friend of Elektros.
Phrynikos, Athenian soldier.
Phylia, Athenian slave.
polemarch, supreme military commander
polis, plural *poleis*. Hellenic city-state.
Polydora, woman of Athens. Professional mourner.
prothesis, the laying out of the body before a funeral.

Pygolampída, 'firefly,' an Athenian.
putuk, Scythian slang for female genitalia, used most often as an insult.
*****Scyllias**, noted long-distance swimmer, father of Hydna.
Sikelia, modern-day Sicily.
*****Sikinnis,** slave who tutored Themistocles' children.
Simeon, Athenian friend of Elektros.
Simmios, Skiathan healer.
Simonia, sister of Simeon.
Siren, nickname of Parthenia, sister of Hyperion. In Hellenic mythology, the Sirens were immortal creatures, half-bird, half-woman, whose irresistible song caused sailors to steer their ships into rocks that would sink them.
Sisyphean, adjective which compares any futile task to that of mythological **Sisyphus**, whose punishment in Hades was to roll a huge boulder up a side of a hill, only to have it roll back down. He was condemned to repeat this task for eternity.
*****Solon,** the Lawgiver of Athens.
Stavros, Athenian fish-vendor.
strategos, pl. *strategoi*, a Hellenic general or commander. In some cases it was an elected position.
synofryónomai, 'frowners.' Athenian nickname for Spartans.
Sword of Oiorpata, Elektros' legendary sword that originally belonged to his mother.
symposion, Athenian men-only dining and drinking session.
Syracuse, Hellenic city on the island of Sikelia.
Talamaenes, a Megaran olive farmer.
Tamara, wife of Talamaenes and former travelling companion of Elektros.
*****Themistocles**, Athenian politician & general
Thena, diminutive form of Parthenia

Thermopylae, 'the hot gates,' site of the famous stand of three hundred Spartans and several thousand allies who held off the 150,000-man Persian army for three days at a narrow pass that favoured the hoplite phalanx. The Persians prevailed only because a Malian shepherd, Ephialtes, showed them a hidden path that allowed them to get behind the Spartans and envelope them.
Thriasian Gate, northwest gate in and out of Athens.
Timoleon, Athenian guardsman.
trousies, slang term for Persians, from their fondness for wearing trousers, which Hellenes thought ridiculous and effeminate.
***Tyrtaeus,** 7th century Spartan poet.
Xandros, brother of Zosimos.
Xenocrates, legendary swordsman, trainer of Elektros and others.
***Xerxes,** Great King of Persia.
Zosimos, Rhodian nobleman.

Marcellus Durrell has done many horrible jobs. He is currently a librarian, a decidedly non-horrible job, in Hamilton, Ontario, Canada. His greatest fear is that he exists only as someone else's imaginary friend.

Await Not in Silence is his fifth novel and Book 4 of The Elektros Saga.

Made in the USA
Middletown, DE
13 October 2018